A TASTE OF HONEY

A DREAMSPINNER PRESS ANTHOLOGY

Dreamspinner Press

Published by
DREAMSPINNER PRESS

5032 Capital Circle SW, Suite 2, PMB# 279, Tallahassee, FL 32305-7886 USA
http://www.dreamspinnerpress.com/

This is a work of fiction. Names, characters, places, and incidents either are the product of author imagination or are used fictitiously, and any resemblance to actual persons, living or dead, business establishments, events, or locales is entirely coincidental.

A Taste of Honey
© 2014 Dreamspinner Press.
Edited by B.G. Thomas and Anne Regan

The Bear Fetish © 2014 John Amory.
The Bear Next Door © 2014 Jack Byrne.
The Bear at the Bar © 2014 J. Scott Coatsworth.
Barefoot © 2014 Lillian Francis.
Just Breathe © 2014 John Genest.
Bear Chasing © 2014 Renae Kaye.
Golden Bear © 2014 G.P. Keith.
Hunting Bear: A Fairy Tale with a Very Hairy Ending © 2014 Edmond Manning.
The Do-It-Yourself Guide to Getting Over Yourself © 2014 Robert B. McDiarmid.
Truck Stop © 2014 Christopher Hawthorne Moss.
Banyan Court © 2014 Samuel Scott Preston.
Amped © 2014 Zoe X. Rider.
The Bear King of Snowbird Mountain © 2014 Michael Rupured.
Life's Tiny Surprises © 2014 Tara Spears.

Cover Photo by Jamil Hellu.
Cover Design
© 2014 Paul Richmond.
http://www.paulrichmondstudio.com
Cover content is for illustrative purposes only and any person depicted on the cover is a model.

All rights reserved. This book is licensed to the original purchaser only. Duplication or distribution via any means is illegal and a violation of international copyright law, subject to criminal prosecution and upon conviction, fines, and/or imprisonment. Any eBook format cannot be legally loaned or given to others. No part of this book may be reproduced or transmitted in any form or by any means, electronic or mechanical, including photocopying, recording, or by any information storage and retrieval system, without the written permission of the Publisher, except where permitted by law. To request permission and all other inquiries, contact Dreamspinner Press, 5032 Capital Circle SW, Suite 2, PMB# 279, Tallahassee, FL 32305-7886, USA, or http://www.dreamspinnerpress.com/.

ISBN: 978-1-63216-355-4
Digital ISBN: 978-1-63216-356-1
Library of Congress Control Number: 2014943198
First Edition August 2014

Printed in the United States of America
(∞)
This paper meets the requirements of
ANSI/NISO Z39.48-1992 (Permanence of Paper).

Table of Contents

So Just What Is a Bear? by B.G. Thomas 5
Truck Stop by Christopher Hawthorne Moss 9
Bear Chasing by Renae Kaye 29
Life's Tiny Surprises by Tara Spears 59
The Bear King of Snowbird Mountain by Michael Rupured 71
Just Breathe by John Genest 90
Barefoot by Lillian Francis 113
Golden Bear by G.P. Keith 143
Banyan Court by Samuel Scott Preston 178
The Bear at the Bar by J. Scott Coatsworth 208
Amped by Zoe X. Rider 225
The Bear Next Door by Jack Byrne 238
The Bear Fetish by John Amory 260
The Do-It-Yourself Guide to Getting Over Yourself
by Robert B. McDiarmid 275
Hunting Bear: A Fairy Tale with a Very Hairy Ending
by Edmond Manning 290

So Just What is a Bear?

NOW THAT is a *big* question—no pun intended. I bet if you were to ask ten different bears that question, you would get ten different answers. In fact, when I started asking around, I found out that's true. "Bear" can take on a hell of a lot of definitions, depending on who you ask. And the bear community is a rich and varied culture that continues to grow and change.

I will say this, though. As I talked with these men—either in person or through e-mails and ads and Facebook—I found that I began to hear a common theme. There was a *theme* going on, baby.

However, all those different men? Those bears? They're not the ones writing this introduction. I am. And instead of trying to answer the above question with those many-splendored explanations, I'm going to tell you what being a bear means to me.

But first—first I want to step back a few decades and share something very personal about myself.

So there I was, in my early twenties, living with a (wonderful) woman and trying *not* to be gay—pretending I was straight.

I wasn't fooling anyone. Not me (not really). Not the mother of my daughter (we met while cruising the same man). Not friends. Everyone knew I was gay. People passing me on the street knew I was gay. To paraphrase Will Truman from *Will & Grace*, blind and deaf people knew I was gay.

Except all those people, including myself, were *wrong*.

I *wasn't* gay. I was homosexual.

What? What was that you asked? What's the difference?

Okay. I'll tell you. It was something I had to learn myself.

No one is born gay.

What they *are* is born homosexual.

They are born with the genetically unavoidable predisposition to be sexually attracted to members of their own sex. They can deny it all they want. Fight it like crazy. Fool themselves. But they can't change it any more than they can the color of their eyes or the color of their hair. Sure, they can wear colored contacts or bleach or dye their hair, but they're only covering up. Wearing a disguise. They can even avoid sexual contact with a member of their own sex—but they are still homosexual.

Being gay is something else completely.

Being gay was that day when I finally realized I didn't want to be anything else.

Invariably, many gay men will get asked a certain question: "But would you be straight if you could be? If you could take a pill and wake up heterosexual, would you?"

At first my answer was "Hell yes!" I used to cry myself to sleep many a night begging God to make me straight.

With time the answer, thankfully, evolved into, "Well, life would be *easier* if I were heterosexual, but I've made peace with what I am."

A step up—but I wasn't gay yet. I was still homosexual. I was still "making peace" with what I was. Like I had diabetes or something. Like it *was* something I had to learn to live with.

But then finally I got to the point in my life where I *knew* I would never *consider* taking that pill. I'd die first. That being homosexual was intrinsic to who I was. It wasn't even the eye and hair color thing. Because my hair and eye color did nothing to shape me into the man I am today. Everything that has been a part of my existence—the "good" and the "bad," the opportunities provided or denied, the aspects of human behavior experienced or witnessed—are things that happened to me because I am "not straight," things that would not have happened to me had I been "straight."

I came to feel as if I had been chosen!

Guess what?

I was gay.

When called to the colors, I'd gladly wave the rainbow flag. Had I never gotten to that point, I would never have been able to know myself.

Now what does this have to do with the question about bears?

Well, I'll tell you, but first there's going to be one more tangent.

For some reason I have worked almost exclusively with women all my life. I was either the only man on the job or one of the only men. And for some reason, since I'm a gay man, the women would soon seem to forget I *was* a man at all and talk about things I'm betting most men don't hear. Some of these subjects I am not mentioning. What I will say is I have heard the complaint about how unfair it is to be a woman in our culture. That a man can show up in jeans, a shirt, and bedraggled tennis shoes and forget to shave, and all it does is make him look manly. But a woman has to wear makeup and spend a lot of money on her hair, and they have to shave their legs and pits and wear uncomfortable shoes and hose and…

…if they don't, forget advancing in the workplace and forget attracting a good man. Women who don't do all these things are virtually invisible to men. At least that is what *those* women told me….

Well, let me tell you what happened to me when I finally came out and hit the bars. The men *ignored* me! I would ask a guy to dance and he would look right *through* me! He wouldn't even say, "Not now, I'm resting." He would flat-out ignore me. I found out I didn't wear the right clothes or have the right hair, that I was too heavy or that I should "manscape" or shave my chest altogether. At that time, even the five-o'clock shadow thing was frowned upon, let alone beards or facial hair. I couldn't believe the money gay men spent on a haircut!

I went through years of wearing clothes I didn't like (but pretended to) and putting up with hairstyles I couldn't stand, shaving my face (and I look like shit without facial hair!) and dieting yo-yo style—starving myself to be good enough to get a man, only to gain it all back when I couldn't find or keep one.

Then in 1997 I went to my first bear event.

OMG!

I was a hit! The men positively pawed me—pun intended. I could have had sex every hour on the hour if I'd wanted. And I was no boy either. I was a good fifty pounds "overweight," had facial hair, and was wearing shorts and a T-shirt. I was popular!

It was the most liberating experience of my sexual life. Men *liked* me! They "really, *really* liked me!" Because you know why? Some men like big butts. It's a song, even, and I tell no lie! Suddenly, if I was losing weight, it was because the doctor told me my knee replacements would last years longer if I took some weight off them. I lost weight because *I* wanted to. These were men who loved each other despite the "flaws" they supposedly had. Men who judged each other for what was in their hearts and not their guts. Lovely men. Amazing men. Beautiful men!

Bears. We come in all shapes and varieties. Besides your "typical" bear (a hairy, stocky to heavyset man), there are chubs (heavyset men who aren't necessarily hairy), cubs (young bears or bears who are very young at heart), daddy bears (older guys, sometimes looking for a "daddy/son" relationship with a younger guy or cub—definitely *not* talking pederasty here), leather bears (bears who like to wear leather), muscle bears (can be very muscular, but they tend not to worry about abs in favor of some nice padding), polar bears (bears whose hair has gone gray/white), panda bears (bears of Asian descent), black bears (bears of African descent), pocket bears (short bears), Ewoks (*very* short bears), ginger bears (redheaded bears), and grizzly bears (usually much shaggier and taller and sometimes dominant). And then there are otters (hairy guys who are slim)!

But the one thing we have in common is we aren't hung up on what most of gay culture, or the world for that matter, qualifies and quantifies as hot or sexy. We are beautiful and sexy in our own way. And we accept each other far more than the average community.

Because that's what being a bear is all about. It's more than size. It is accepting ourselves and each other for who and what we are. And refusing to define beauty by what *GQ* magazine, or Gold's Gym, or MTV, or shows like *True Blood, Hawaii Five-0,* and *Grey's Anatomy* say we should be.

In the following anthology you will see all kinds of bears and read all kinds of bear stories. Tales of men accepting themselves for who and what they are. Stories of men who realize they like bears (another word: those men are called "admirers"). You are going to cry. You are going to think. You are going to laugh your ass off. We've even thrown in a few tales of the extraordinary and fantastical. Almost half of the fourteen authors represented herein are new to Dreamspinner Press. At least one of those made his first sale ever (and a great story it is!) in this anthology.

So now I am finally going to stop talking and turn this over to you. I hope you love this book even half as much as I loved being involved. It was a dream come true (but then, that is what Dreamspinner Press is all about). I've fantasized since I was in fourth grade about helping put something like this together. We would get this little catalogue in English class filled with books. A lot of my selections were anthologies, and I would marvel at what it must be like to collect stories and put them all together in one book. And now I know! We received dozens and dozens of stories and whittling them down to the fourteen you are about to read was tough work. How do you choose out of so many amazing stories? Despite that, I would do it again in a heartbeat.

It was amazing working with Anne Regan, and I hope I wasn't too much of a pain in her butt! I have learned so much. Thank you, Anne!

Okay! I'm done! I've done my part; now it's time for you to do yours. Read! Have fun!

And finally, "Woof!"

(That means "I like you" in bear-talk.)

B.G. Thomas

Truck Stop
Christopher Hawthorne Moss

"Have You Ever Been Lonely" poured out of the jukebox at Cleve's Gas and Grub so loudly that Cleve didn't hear the tinkle of the bell on the diner door and was startled to turn around and find the postman standing at the counter with a silly grin on his face.

"Dell!" was all he could manage for the moment. He glanced at what Dell was holding. It was in a plain brown wrapper as the advertisement promised, but one end was torn. He blanched, defensively crossed his arms in front of him, and ran his palms over his hairy forearms, looking up again to see what Dell would say.

"This came for you, Cleve. I promise I didn't open it. It was torn and I sort of saw what's inside." He still had that grin.

Cleve's brow furrowed, and he said with unaccustomed severity, "Yeah, and…?" He could guess what the postman saw. He just hoped the man would take it at face value.

"Didn't know you went in for that he-man stuff." Dell handed him what Cleve knew was a copy of *Physique Culture*, a pictorial magazine that had only been out for a few years, purportedly about the health benefits of physical fitness and featuring page after page of good-looking, muscular young men in suggestive poses. Not nude… that was illegal.

Cleve made a vague gesture at his tubby body. "Gotta start somewhere, you know."

"Well, I'm not looking forward to delivering your barbells and that kind of stuff," Dell chuckled.

Cleve relaxed. "I promise if I get that far I'll go into Reno and buy them."

Dell extracted a few bills and advertisements for the new 1949 car models and dropped them on the lunch counter. "Good luck to you, that's all I gotta say. I get so damned tired crawling all over this godforsaken mail route I got no energy to do anything but try to watch what comes in on the TV." He looked over at Ginny, the teenager who sometimes worked at the diner. "Oh, sorry, Ginny. If I'd known you was there...."

Ginny shrugged, her lips red as blood and her top button undone on her waitress uniform. "Aw, Mr. Simons, you know my daddy swears worse than that." She gave both men the benefit of a provocative wiggle as she crossed to the jukebox. She scanned the selection and shook her head. "Still no Nat King Cole or nothing but these cowboys."

Cleve took the mail and turned to carry it to his little room behind the kitchen. "You know it's cowboys the customers want."

The postman shook his head, his eye on Cleve's limp, about as far from an athletic muscleman as a person could get. "Bye-bye, Ginny... Cleve. Gotta get on my way," he said.

The two called "See ya" and "Bye-bye" as they watched the postman go out to his truck through the falling snow.

"Snow's picking up out there, Ginny. Better go on home now." Cleve didn't expect a lot of diners once the snow got going, and besides, he was anxious to look over the magazine.

Ginny went to the counter, climbed on a stool, and tore two paper napkins from the dispenser. She scrubbed at her lipstick. "Don't want my daddy seeing me in this or he'd have my hide." She held up the napkin to show Cleve what looked like a bloody bandage.

Cleve smiled affectionately at the girl. "I don't know why you bother to put it on, Ginny. No one to see you here but me and a bunch of old dried-up truckers."

Ginny leaned over the counter to plant a kiss on his cheek. She winced as her lips met his stubble. "Ooh, you gotta shave more often. Besides, how do you know I don't wear it for you?"

"Aw, Gins, don't tease," Cleve answered, blushing.

Ginny gave him one of her sauciest looks and jumped down from the stool. "You never know. I don't think I know anyone nicer than you. You could tell my daddy on me, but you won't."

Cleve shook his head. "Not my business." He watched her sashay to the door, buttoning her top button and dragging her coat from the coat rack.

"See you tomorrow," she called to him.

"Not if the storm is still blowing. Too dangerous. I'll close the diner anyway. Now you wrap that scarf around your neck. You don't need a case of pneumonia."

Ginny grinned at him and headed out to where she had parked her little jalopy.

Cleve rubbed the stubble on his jaw. He shaved every morning, but his beard was always back by the end of the day. He sighed and turned to glance around the diner. Located out in the high desert of Nevada, it had been built in the twenties and it showed its age. He had been able to put in a new stove and beverage dispenser, the latter with the help of the Coca-Cola Company in exchange for letting them hang their red-and-white posters and signs all over, but the counter was covered with cigarette burns and the once dark red stool cushions had bits of stuffing coming out where there were splits. The floor tile was old but scrupulously clean. The windows were too. Cleve knew the new state road they were putting in would be his little diner-and-gas-station's doom, but that was how things were. He supposed he would struggle on or get out. He could go to Reno, maybe, or if he really followed his heart, he would head for California and the beaches. That reminded him of his magazine. He pulled off his stained apron and scrunched it into a ball, stuffing it into his pants pocket as he headed for his room.

If the diner was tawdry, his closet of a room was worse. It might have been an office once; he wasn't sure. The only things in it were a cot, a small table with a lamp, and a small chest of drawers. On the wall was one of those cutie calendars with pinups. The women on it, all women if truth be told, were of no interest to him, but he needed a calendar and this one was free from the oil company he got his gas from. The one tiny window was the one thing Cleve did not keep clean. It was as good as a set of blinds to leave it filthy. He didn't need a lot of privacy, but he needed some now and then. You had to go outside to go to the men's room, and he didn't want to have to go there every time he wanted relief of that kind. Now was one of those times.

He sat on his cot and picked up the torn package. He only had to rip it a little to pull out the magazine. He had first seen *Physique Culture* when he was in San Francisco on his way back from the war. He was surprised to find one of Bob Mizer's photos used in an ad for the magazine in a copy of *Esquire*. It was billed as a fitness magazine, but as small as it was, he could not take his eyes off the boy in the photo, probably no more than nineteen or twenty, posing artfully on a beach with only the barest of what he supposed was meant to be a swimsuit, his muscles bulging and a big white toothy grin on his face under sun-bleached hair. He had gone to one of those dirty magazine stores they had in cities like San Francisco and tried to dig up the courage to ask for the magazine, but fortunately his eyes had lit on a copy shoved in with other magazines of the same type. Not nudie magazines—those had mostly pictures of naked women. These magazines had nothing but young men. It didn't take a rocket scientist to guess what, or whom, the magazines were intended for. He bought one. It took him a couple years after that to get the nerve to order a subscription.

Cleve opened the magazine after shutting off the little light on the table and using only the light from the diner to look at the pictures. He knew someone still might come in, so he tried to keep his hands off his fly, knowing it was not going to be easy. One look at the young men on the page he opened to started to make him hard. There were two, a blond and a brunet, standing on the shore looking off-camera, one holding a bow and arrow and the other with his hand on his own hip. They wore the briefest of pouches over their cocks and balls. Cleve saw immediately why the publisher was having trouble with the postal censors. The pouches hardly hid the contours of their big, semihard cocks. He closed his eyes and sighed, imagining how they would feel on his palm if he cupped the bulge.

There was a tinge of regret in his sigh. Cleve remembered Luigi, the young stud he had met in Italy. The fellow was a prostitute, but he was so good-looking and so willing. Cleve did not have much cash, but he had little else to spend it on. He wasn't the only Yank who patronized the dark-haired, dark-eyed Adonis, and he was not just risking exposure, but also his heart. Luigi was so fun loving, so unexpectedly sweet, rubbing Cleve's hairy chest and calling him "my American grizzly bear." Cleve would have to leave sooner or later when his platoon moved up. The decision was made for him when he busted up his leg in an accident. They took him to the Army hospital, and he never saw Luigi again. He worried about the young man, how he would get along when the Yanks moved on, but he had no way to contact him. He was no more than a wistful memory now, as well as fuel for self-abuse.

Cleve heard a vehicle pull into the gas station. It sounded like a truck, a big one, and he dropped the magazine on his table. He willed his erection to subside as best he could, then remembered the apron in his pocket. He stood up and shoved the magazine in his top dresser drawer, shut it, and draped the apron so it would hide what was left of his arousal. Just in time, as the jingle of the bell on the diner door let him know he had a customer.

He peered around the edge of the door to his little room and saw one of his infrequent but regular customers, a truck driver whose route brought him by the Gas and Grub every couple of months. "Welcome," he called, trying to think if he had ever known his name.

The man stood just inside the door, looking about. He grunted a response to Cleve, dragged his cap off his head, and glowered at the jukebox. He was of more than medium height, a couple inches taller than Cleve, weathered and none too well dressed. He wore his company's gray jacket, nondescript pants, a cowboy-style shirt, and sturdy work boots on his feet instead of cowboy boots. Unlike Cleve, he seemed virtually hairless except for the wisps that topped his head. He pulled out a dirty red bandanna and wiped his eyes, which were starting to stream, irritated from the cold. "Gonna be a nasty blow."

Cleve remembered him now. He was the one who rarely spoke at all. He was used to taciturn truck drivers, but he realized suddenly that the five words the man had just uttered were the most he could remember issuing from his mouth. Usually it was "Coffee" or "Cherry" in response for what kind of pie he wanted, or more likely just a grunt of assent or a long-suffering glare in answer to a question. He remembered Ginny had tried her charms on him to get him to say more, but he was even less forthcoming with her.

"Coffee?" Cleve offered, stifling a chuckle at his own one-word question. He had to turn to the coffee urn to hide his smile when the other man grunted in reply.

Turning back with the hefty mug in his fist, he saw that the weathered trucker had seated himself on the far-end stool as was his custom. He brought the mug down and put it in front of him, then reached to shove the sugar dispenser closer. "You want cream?"

The fellow looked up from the mug and nodded. "Spoon be handy too," he said with a note of mockery in his voice.

Cleve fetched the canned milk that passed for cream thereabouts and a spoon, snagged a napkin from the holder and put them all in front of him. "Hope you aren't planning to drive in that," he observed.

The man looked up at him, over to the window, and back to his coffee, into which he was pouring quite a lot of sugar. He grunted noncommittally.

"You got a bunk in that rig? I mean, I don't think you're going anywhere tonight. It's almost fifty miles to the junction. The way it's blowing out there you wouldn't get fifty yards."

"You think so, huh?"

Cleve stepped back from the counter. "Suit yourself."

He watched the man as he drank his coffee, still trying to remember his name, if he'd ever known it. Not a remarkable man, really—gangly and angular, with a long neck and a protruding Adam's apple. Cleve wasn't sure how old he was. He could be his own age, twenty-six or thereabouts, or he could be as old as forty. He had a dried-out, discontented look. Cleve twisted his lips in disappointment. If he was going to be stuck in the diner overnight with some guy, unable to get back to his magazine, at least if he were friendly and garrulous he wouldn't be bored. But this guy was worse than being alone.

"That all you got on the jukebox?"

The words startled Cleve out of his contemplation. "What do you mean? Country and Western?"

"Naw, damned love songs."

"You don't like love songs?" Cleve asked. He registered that Jimmy Wakely was pouring out "I Love You So Much It Hurts" on the box.

"Just said so, didn't I?"

Cleve frowned. "Hey, it's your nickel. Play what you want." He turned and set to wiping his counter with a damp cloth.

He heard the stool creak and the slide of boots on his spotless tile floor. He glanced over his shoulder to see the fellow leaning over the panel on the colorfully lit-up jukebox that listed all the selections, his ass pointing straight at Cleve. Not bad for a skinny guy, he thought.

The man chuckled and rooted into his pocket for coins. He took out a nickel and put it into the coin slot. He pointed one gnarled finger at a button and pushed it. In no time the machine was whirring. Cleve heard the disk drop onto the spindle and the needle take its place in the groove. Eddy Arnold came on singing "Don't Rob Another Man's Castle," by Jenny Lou Carson. He came back to his stool, picked up his mug, and held it out for a refill.

They listened to the song. When the line "No matter how lonesome you feel" came on, Cleve was on the brink of asking if the trucker's wife had left him, but he thought better of it. It was not his business, and it might make the fellow even more morose. Instead he asked, "You in the war?" It was a pretty safe topic these days.

The man looked up from adding sugar to his coffee. "Pie?" he asked.

"Cherry, apple, and blueberry. Oh, and coconut cream."

"Cherry."

"You want ice cream on that?" Cleve waited for the shake of the man's head, turned, fetched a fork, and opened the glass pie case and brought out a slice of cherry pie on a plate. He set them down in front of him and stood with his hands on the counter waiting for him to speak.

"You want something?" the trucker asked.

"I asked you a question."

He gazed at Cleve for a moment and said, "Navy."

It was Cleve's turn to grunt. "I was in the Army."

"That where you got the gimpy leg?"

Cleve was surprised he had noticed. He hadn't been out from behind the counter except when the man came in. Maybe he had noticed some other time. "Yeah, but not a wound. Got hit by a motorcycle."

"Get you sent home?" he said around a mouthful of pie. At Cleve's nod he chuckled. "Worth it, then." When Cleve didn't reply he looked up at him. "No one to come home to?"

Cleve didn't answer. It was more than no one to come home to. It was having to leave someone behind in Italy. Then it was the fact that his limp and the pain in his leg had made him stop keeping fit. He got fat. Far from being one of those smooth, chiseled beach boys, now he was downright ugly. Any chance of finding someone to replace Luigi, even if only for sex, was gone.

Perhaps the thoughtlessness of his comment made its way into the man's consciousness, because he suddenly put out his hand to shake. "I suppose you're Cleve, of Cleve's Gas and Grub. My name's Sully."

Cleve wiped his palm on his apron, extended it, and shook Sully's hand. "Yeah, I'm Cleve. Pleased to meet you."

Sully nodded and went back to his pie.

Cleve was getting tired of standing, so he waited a minute, then went back to sit on his cot. He sat staring at nothing, listening to Sully eat and slurp coffee. He glanced at the closed top drawer of his dresser and his shoulders slumped. It was going to be a hell of a long night.

The Eddy Arnold song was long over, and the jukebox had finished the two other songs in its queue. When he heard Sully get up and go over to the jukebox, Cleve called out to him, "You know, two bits will get you six songs."

No answer came, and he couldn't tell from the sound whether Sully had put in a nickel or a quarter. The next disc fell into place, and he heard Hank Williams start up "I'm a Long Gone Daddy." He must have put in two bits because after that "Never Trust a Woman" came on, followed by "Bouquet of Roses." So much hurt in his selections. Cleve thought he had better use his operator choices on a few songs he liked or he would be stuck all night listening to edgy torch songs.

He came out of his room and leaned behind the jukebox to fiddle with the controls, and chose half a dozen songs more to his liking. He turned back to see Sully holding out his mug for more coffee. "Why don't you join me?"

Cleve looked at him and shrugged. "Don't mind if I do."

He fetched a second mug and the whole coffee pot and sat down next to Sully at the counter. "On me," he advised. "We're gonna be here all night."

Sully started shoveling sugar into his mug, so Cleve reached for another sugar dispenser and set it in front of Sully.

"You don't like sugar?"

Cleve grinned self-mockingly and replied, "Oh, I definitely like sugar. But…." He waved a hand at his belly as he had done with the postman. "Gotta take some of this off."

Sully gave him the up and down, which made Cleve's face redden. "You ain't so bad." The gaunt man looked away quickly.

After a few moments, Cleve said, "So you didn't say. You got a cot or bunk or something in your truck cab?"

Shaking his head, Sully said, "Sleeping bag. You got an extra cot?"

Cleve felt his face start to redden again. "Naw."

Sully looked around. "I can just stretch out on the floor, then. Done it plenty of times."

The two looked out the window toward the road. The storm had worsened, the visibility down to about five yards. The snow was beginning to accumulate in drifts. "Is there someplace I can pull my rig around to that's better sheltered from all that shit?"

Cleve nodded. "Pull it around back. It'll be out of the worst of it there."

He was surprised when he found Sully's short absence to move his truck made him feel suddenly bereft. He shook his head to clear it. This guy was not much company. Did his feelings mean he was even lonelier and more miserable than he realized? Must be time to get out. If he could, that is.

He heard Sully come in the back door of the diner, which would take him by Cleve's little room. He paled, but remembered he had stowed the magazine out of sight.

"I see what you mean."

"About what?"

Sully chuckled. "Your bed. It'll hardly sleep one, much less two." Sully quickly added, "Not that I sleep with other men, you know."

Cleve let a short laugh be his only answer.

"You got any beer?"

Cleve realized Sully's question was rhetorical, as neon and other signs advertising bottled beer were all over the place. "Yeah, cold ones too. I'll get 'em."

"First round's on me," the angular man offered.

Cleve waved dismissively. "At this point it don't matter. No one's coming in. I might as well lock up and we can just sit a spell and jaw or something."

One of Cleve's choices came onto the jukebox, a pretty little cowboy ballad sung by Roy Rogers. "You like that cowboy shit?" Sully asked with a derisive grin.

A few beers later Sully started to loosen up. "I'm from Tennessee. After I joined the Navy after Pearl, I met a girl in Annapolis and we got hitched. Kind of in a hurry 'cause I was shipping out." He frowned.

"Where do you two live now?" Cleve asked.

Sully's disgusted snort told half the story. "Nowhere. When I got out of the military she had flown the coop. No idea where she went."

"That's too bad."

Sully shook his head. "Not much of a loss," he said bitterly.

Cleve looked at him. "How come you say that?"

Sully shrugged. "We, uh, didn't have much of a spark... uh... you know. In bed."

Cleve saw a little color make it into the thin man's cheeks. He felt sorry for the guy. "Some women are like that."

"Naw, it wasn't her. She was plenty into it. I just wasn't so much. Dunno why. Maybe I was nervous about shipping out or something." He looked sorry he had brought it up. "You married?" he asked.

Cleve shook his head. "I had someone overseas... a... girlfriend, kind of. Still back there." His own face was warming now. He wished he hadn't mentioned it.

He looked up to find Sully's attention on him. It made his face go scarlet.

"So you don't aim to go back there? To get hitched or anything?" Sully asked him.

"Can't. No money."

Sully's familiar grunt was the only answer he got.

Cleve went back and forth to the jukebox over the next hour or more. The two got some comic relief over a song called "I'm My Own Grandpa" and actually sang along with "Cool Water." The final fractured chord out of their mouths at the end of the song had Cleve painfully aware of Sully's arm around his shoulder. Just companionship, just us guys, he assured himself... an assurance that made him sad. "You miss the Navy?" he asked to make conversation.

"Hell, no. Spent half the war in the brig."

Cleve grinned. "Real hell-raiser, eh?"

A sentimental waltz came on the jukebox. "Hey, when you were in the Army, did you guys ever put on a show?" Sully asked, slurring his words.

Cleve laughed. "Sure we did. Why?"

Sully jumped off his stool and extended his arms. "No women on a ship, so we had to dance with each other. Sometimes we draped towels around our waists and put mops on our heads so we'd look like dames." He made a shallow, awkward bow. "May I have the pleasure of this dance, miss?" he said to Cleve.

"Uh, no, really. I can't," Cleve refused nervously.

"Aw, c'mon. Doesn't mean nothing."

"My leg," Cleve hedged.

"It's a slow dance. C'mon. You chicken?"

Cleve reluctantly got off his stool. He let Sully take one hairy hand to place on his shoulder and lift the other in his own raised hand. Cleve tried to keep their bodies as far apart as he could, but after just a few turns Sully pulled Cleve against him. Sully laughed at Cleve's fierce blush. "Relax. Not like with all that fur I could mistake you for a dame."

When he felt Sully put his cheek against his as he twirled him clumsily around, Cleve broke away. "Now, let's not get carried away," he laughed, going back to the stool.

Sully muttered, "Spoilsport," and continued to dance with a phantom partner.

Cleve could tell that Sully had drunk enough to make him sentimental when a song called "Waltz of the Wind" came on the jukebox and Sully's face grew sad again.

"I had a buddy in the Navy. Brad. We got into lots of fistfights on shore leave. He was quite a guy. Uh, I mean a big guy, like you."

"What happened to him?" Cleve asked.

Sully's face went dark. Cleve thought he heard a catch in the grim man's voice. "Got himself killed. Robbed and knifed in an alley behind a bar."

"My God! That's terrible! Did they catch the guy?"

"Dunno. We left port right after. There was a war on, you know." Cleve thought he heard regret in Sully's voice.

The wind had picked up, and all of a sudden the electric lights went out and the jukebox whined to a stop. Sully gave Cleve a stunned look. "What...?" he asked.

"Don't worry. I have a generator. Gotta, with these refrigerators and the freezer."

Sully followed him out through the back door to where the generator sat in a wooden box next to the outer wall of the diner. "I wondered what that was when I drove my rig back here. Thought maybe it was just some sort of lockup."

He reached over to help Cleve lift the cover. "I can do it," Cleve objected. Sully stepped away without comment. When Cleve found pulling the starter cord was more difficult than he could handle, Sully stepped in and took over. Cleve was grateful the man didn't make anything of it.

"We should probably unplug the jukebox," he said as the two went back into the diner. "Reserve the generator for the freezer and fridge."

"I think it's time we bunked down anyway," Sully said. He had taken the time to retrieve his sleeping bag when they were out by his rig. "Where can I stretch out?"

Cleve looked around. With a short laugh, he answered, "Anywhere!" He watched as Sully looked for a good place to lay out the bag. "Well, g'night, I guess. Turn off whatever lights you want to."

He left Sully fiddling with his bag and turned to go into his little room. It had no door, just a doorway. He turned on the little table lamp, only long enough to pull back the blanket and sheet and sit down.

Cleve lay on the uncomfortable but familiar cot, unable to sleep, waiting for his guest to start snoring. All he could hear was the whoosh and whine of the storm. He kept thinking about the magazine and Luigi. He finally broke down and whacked himself off, praying the wind drowned out his heavy breathing. It was only after that he drifted off.

CLEVE WOKE to hear Sully, or so he presumed, fiddling with the big coffee urn. Sitting up, he slid out from under the covers. He made his way as quickly as he could to the outhouse to relieve his morning hard-on. It was no easy task in drifted snow and a freezing wind. Back in a jiffy, Cleve hoped he could get his underwear changed fast enough that Sully would not see him do it. Just in case, he turned his back so only his butt would be visible. He pulled open the dresser drawer and reached for a clean pair of boxers.

"How the hell do you..." came Sully's voice from behind him. "What the hell is that?"

Cleve spun to see his guest standing in the doorway with the empty coffee pot in his hand. He followed Sully's wide-eyed gaze and saw he had caught sight of the copy of *Physique Culture*.

"Uh, nothing.... Just a fitness magazine." Cleve held up his arm and made a gesture like a bodybuilder. "You know, gotta build these muscles."

Sully snorted dubiously. "Uh-huh." He raised his eyes to Cleve's. "You some kind of homo?"

Cleve shook his head vehemently. "Of course not."

The look on his face must have held no conviction.

"Aw, shit." Sully shoved the coffeepot at Cleve and spun. He went to his bedroll and started to gather it up.

Cleve put the pot on the table in his room and came out after him. "C'mon, Sully. You don't have to leave. I'm no homo."

Sully didn't pause in his effort to get out of the diner fast. "When I went through to the privy I saw the boner you had. I suppose you were having a wet dream." He shuddered and headed to the door, grabbing his jacket and cap from the hat stand. The door was still locked so he could only pull at the knob. "God damn it!"

"Here, let me do it." Cleve resignedly went to the door. He was appalled when Sully jumped back as if to avoid any contact with him. He turned the lock and stepped back, hanging his head.

As Sully snatched open the door, Cleve came to him. "Wait, Sully. The snow is still blowing about. Your truck won't—"

Sully wasn't listening. He strode purposefully to the corner of the diner and headed around back. A few moments later Cleve, standing helpless, his arms dangling at his sides, heard the rumble and choke of the big rig's motor. It didn't sound good. It died twice, but then Sully got the engine to turn. Cleve watched as the truck came out from behind the building with its tires spinning and slid in the snow and ice when it turned too sharply onto the road.

"Oh dear God," Cleve murmured as he watched. The truck skidded sideways, righted itself, then choked and died. It swerved drunkenly to the right, then went over the shoulder and slammed into the useless light pole.

Cleve did not hesitate. He ran across the gas station to where the truck was canted enough that one of its tires was spinning in the air. He pulled open the driver's door and found Sully leaning over at an odd angle toward the passenger seat. There was blood on his forehead. Cleve called his name and, getting no response, realized Sully was unconscious. "Oh God," he said again. He reached to feel what he could to check if Sully had broken any bones. Satisfied he had not, he started tugging at him to pull him out of the cab.

Cleve stopped when he realized he needed something for Sully to lie on to drag him into the diner. Remembering the sleeping bag, he located it wedged tightly behind the driver's seat. It tore when he pulled as hard as he could, but it finally loosened, and he stretched it on the ground. He realized the snow would actually help him, as it would make a slippery surface for the makeshift travois. Pulling on Sully, he got him out of the cab. He purposely let himself fall backward with Sully landing on him, to cushion the man's landing. Cleve grinned wryly, first because he knew his being fat was coming in handy, then realizing if Sully came around now he wouldn't care at all for their relative positions.

Sully didn't come to. Cleve managed to worm his way out from under him and had to sit for a minute to catch his breath. Then he struggled up and reached down to grasp the end of the sleeping bag. He felt something in his back and leg protest. He tried to remember what they had told him in the Army about using his knees for leverage. Unable to keep his eyes open in the frigid wind, he tried to gauge where the door of the diner was. It must have taken him ten minutes to get where he thought he wanted to be, but when he felt around for the door he found only empty air. He managed to open his eyes just enough to see he had gone too far to the right. Changing direction allowed him to gain the benefit of the windbreak the building afforded. Finding the door, he loosed his grip on the bag so he could go in and find something to prop it open while he dragged Sully over the low sill. He was grateful there was no step.

"YOU'RE AWAKE!" Cleve said hours later when Sully, lying on Cleve's cot, finally opened his eyes.

"Jesus H. Christ, my head hurts. What happened?"

Before Cleve could come over with a glass of water and respond to his question, Sully said, "Oh yeah, the crash. You dragged me all the way in here?" He quickly looked down as if to make sure he still had his clothes on. He did, though his shirt buttons were undone and his belt unbuckled.

Cleve said in a defeated voice, "Don't worry, your virtue is intact. I just had to loosen your clothes so you could rest easy. I promise I touched nothing under them." His voice and the look on his face spoke of embarrassment and humiliation. He turned and limped back into the diner.

Cleve glanced over at Sully and thought he saw a little color growing in his cheeks. So embarrassed. It was too much to hope that Sully felt bad about the way he was acting, when Cleve had only done what was right. More likely he was afraid Cleve had looked at his penis.

Sully cleared his throat. "My truck."

"It'll need a tow. Just to get it out of the ditch—it looks fine. None of your load was dumped."

Sully looked around. "I gotta get up." He cried out when he tried to pull himself up.

"No you don't, buddy," Cleve said sternly, coming to the doorway. "Head hurts bad, huh? You were out for a long time. If I could have, I would've gotten a sawbones out here to look at you. But we're still on generator. The phone lines are out too." He reached for a bowl on the table, took out a cloth and wrung the water out of it. He reached over to dab at the bump on the prone man's forehead. Sully winced. "Easy, easy," Cleve said. "I'm just putting a cloth on your head."

"I know that's all you're doing. It hurts. Wanna make something of it?" He grimaced, then went on, "You soaked that in ice water? Feels wonderful. You got a gentle touch."

Cleve raised his eyebrows but said nothing.

"Just let this lie on your head. Sip this," Cleve said when he had smoothed Sully's forehead. He held the glass to the injured man's lips. Sully drank gratefully.

Over the next many hours Sully dozed on and off. When he was awake he watched Cleve putter about the diner.

The storm was expected to continue sporadically over the next few days. Even after it died down, Cleve knew it would take time for road crews to clear up the deeper drifts. Then there were probably lots of wrecks for the tow trucks, and it would be days before anyone would be able to leave the diner. "Boy, am I glad all I had in this load was building materials," Sully told him. "No livestock or perishables. All I gotta do with the lumber is sweep the snow off or wait for it to melt."

With the generator running the Frigidaire and freezer, the heat was off in the diner. Cleve covered Sully with the sleeping bag, ignoring the man's protests that he needed to stay warm too. Cleve made a joke of having his own insulation. "Got a built-in fur coat," he quipped. But it was obvious that Cleve was uncomfortable and shivering.

There being even less to do now than when the two had spent the evening drinking beer and listening to the jukebox, they started to talk. Cleve sat on the nearest stool to the doorway of his room while Sully sat propped up on the cot. Cleve was leery of sharing much about his private life with Sully, but when the latter asked him if the person he left behind in Italy was a man, Cleve colored and shrugged. That was a clear enough yes.

Cleve talked about coming home from the war and discovering he could buy the little diner with a loan from the Veteran's Administration.

He shared his concern that the new state road would rob him of the little traffic he got and his thoughts about leaving.

"Where would you go?" Sully asked, sounding genuinely interested.

Cleve looked into some middle distance. "I dunno. City, I guess. Maybe LA."

Sully's response was a disgusted "Hmph!"

"I said I didn't know," Cleve said.

Sully nodded. "I bought my truck with what was left of the pay I had coming. I knew with my record I'd have trouble getting a trucking company to take me on. Figured I would just freelance."

"Your record?" Cleve quickly added, "If that's not too personal."

Sully chuckled. "Naw. I got into a lot of fights in the Navy. I was stir-crazy, you know. We were packed in four men to a bunk...." He trailed off, and Cleve saw a spot of color on his cheeks. "And I went AWOL last time we were in Pearl. After... after Brad."

They sat in silence for several minutes. Sully finally asked, "Do you think we can spare the electricity and turn on the juke for a while?"

Cleve got up and limped over to the garish box and leaned behind it to plug it into the socket. He made some selections. The music started on "Honky Tonkin'."

"Good old Hank. Got a sense of humor, he does," Sully muttered to himself.

After a couple of songs, Sully stretched himself and lifted the blanket. He threw his legs over the edge of the cot and sat with his hands on either side of his knees.

"You sure you're ready to do that?" Cleve asked.

"Stop nagging. You ain't my wife. I gotta pee. You can't do that for me, can you? I'll take it easy."

He got up but started to fall back on the cot. Cleve dashed over to Sully and stopped him. "C'mon, man, I'm just gonna help you out. I'm not gonna grope your sorry ass."

Sully grunted but let Cleve help him to the back door. He spat "Jesus H. Christ!" when the icy wind hit him. "I thought this was a desert." The two struggled to the men's room. Cleve stayed outside in the cold while Sully did his business. When the door opened again, Cleve was waiting for him, shivering.

Back in Cleve's little room, Sully sat with his head bowed and his gaze on the tiles. After some minutes he spoke hesitantly. "Hey, man, about what I said...."

"Forget it."

"Naw, I ain't gonna forget it. You've been real decent to me. I mean, you didn't have to do all this. You're a nice guy. That's all."

Cleve started to protest. Sully stopped him irritably. "Let me talk. This ain't easy for me. I mean, you just ain't what I thought a pansy was like. You're just, you know, a regular guy."

"No fairy wings, huh?" Cleve scoffed.

"No, no wings." Sully laughed uncomfortably. "Tell me," he went on after a pause. "About the boy in Italy."

Cleve stiffened. "First of all, he wasn't a boy. He was a man. And just what could you want to know? About what we did in bed or something?"

Sully colored deeply at Cleve's sharp tone. "Naw, nothing like that. Just, like, how you met. What happened to him?"

Cleve sighed. "You mean, how we knew we were both...."

Sully looked to the side, avoiding Cleve's eyes. "Yeah, I guess. I mean, can you?"

"Wasn't hard for me to know he was queer. He was a whore."

Sully looked surprised. "There are men whores?"

Cleve laughed aloud. "Oh, c'mon, don't tell me you didn't know that."

Sully shrugged.

"Well, there are, and they go with other men. They have them everywhere. It's not hard to find one in any city. They don't exactly hide."

"But don't they get arrested? Or beat up?"

"Yeah, so do women whores, but that doesn't stop them. What do they call them, 'the oldest profession'?"

Sully nodded, looking away again. "So you found him. Then what? I mean, did you keep… seeing him? What happened to him?"

Cleve stood up. "Let me get some coffee. You stay here."

Sully followed him unsteadily out to the diner and took a stool. Cleve was startled when he turned after he picked up the coffee pot. He brought it over, put two mugs on the counter, and poured, grabbed spoons and the can of milk. Cleve sat on a stool two away from Sully.

"Yeah, I kept seeing him. For the sex, yeah, but also because I kind of liked him. He was such a joker. I worried about him. He trusted everyone. If I told him he could get hurt, he just made fun of me."

"So what happened? Did your platoon move up?"

"No, I was on my way to see him one evening and I got run over by a motorbike. The bike took off. I lay in an alley all night. I guess my leg was busted up real bad, because the Army docs couldn't set it properly. Had to be shipped home. I couldn't figure out a way to get word to Luigi. That was my… friend's name. I guess he must have thought I lost interest. I feel real bad about that, because I had promised to help him. He must have thought I was lying."

Sully had been gazing at Cleve's face for some time. "What happened to him?"

"I dunno."

Sully continued to gaze. "You know, you're a nice guy. I don't think I've ever met a nice guy like you. All my life I been treated badly. But mean as I was to you, you helped me out. Saved me from freezing to death, probably."

Shaking his head, Cleve responded, "I couldn't just leave you out there, now could I?"

Sully shook his head. "No, but you didn't have to be so nice about it all. You treated me real good."

At a sound, Cleve looked up. "The power's back on. I gotta go turn off the generator." He got up and went out the back.

When he came back, he found Sully feeding a quarter into the jukebox. A sweet song came on, "Waltz of the Wind," the same Hank Williams song that had made Sully tear up the other night. He turned back and said, "Dance with me."

Cleve stared at him dubiously. "Do what?"

"You heard me," Sully said and held out his arms.

On an impulse Cleve stepped forward and let Sully take the lead as he had done when they were drunk. Sully pulled him into an embrace and put his cheek against Cleve's. He started to dance with Cleve, speaking low in his ear. "Lord knows I'm no prize."

"I never asked…. You don't have to…," Cleve protested, embarrassed. "You don't owe me."

"I didn't mean—" Sully cut himself short. "Okay, maybe I did. Look, I can't promise much will come of it. We may not even… you know, after we dance. It's just that I been lonely all my life, and I think maybe I kinda guessed, if you get my drift. I mean… why I was… you know… feeling…." He trailed off.

Cleve let the song and movement dull his anxiety. "Yeah. No promises… no pressure. You call the shots." He relaxed and let Sully lead him in the waltz.

Sully started to hum as the harmonica took the melody. Then he sang along to Fred Rose's immortal words:

"It was there I knew I would love you forever,
As we danced to the waltz of the wind…."

Sully smiled, put his lips to Cleve's, and began to swing him in time to the dance.

CHRISTOPHER HAWTHORNE MOSS wrote his first short story when he was seven and has spent some of the happiest hours of his life fully involved with his colorful, passionate, and often humorous, characters. Moss spent some time away from fiction, writing content for websites before his first book came out under the name Nan Hawthorne in 1991. He has since become a novelist and is a prolific and popular blogger; he is the historical fiction editor for the GLBT Bookshelf, where you can find his short stories and thoughtful and expert book reviews. Moss is transgender, having been born with a female body but a male heart and mind. He lives full time as a gay man in the Pacific Northwest with his partner of over thirty years and their doted upon cats. He owns Shield-wall Productions at http://www.shield-wall.com. He welcomes comment from readers sent to christopherhmoss@gmail.com and can be found on Facebook and Twitter.

Bear Chasing
Renae Kaye

I.

HE WAS a bear.

There was no doubt about it. He had that grizzly, strong, acorn-fed, oh-my look about him. And believe me, I had looked.

He'd moved into the house across the street all of three weeks ago—and bless me, I'd spent a lot of time gazing out my window since then. And it wasn't the beautiful Perth sunshine that had me entranced. Jeannie hadn't been impressed—three big guys with V-8 engines moving in? Then, on the second day, when they backed a trailer up to their new house with a shiny, professional dragster perched on top, Jeannie's eyes had widened and she began talking about noise barriers and planting trees out front.

I didn't want trees. I wanted my view. Of the house across the street. And my bear.

After they moved in, there was the required house party that first weekend where the street was lined with gorgeous machines that told me his friends were all car-mad too. Jeannie had muttered and cussed, but truthfully, the baby had slept right through the noise. Since then, the three men had been model neighbors.

There were three of them. One was Gavin—I knew this because Bear had hollered his name while they were moving their furniture inside and he'd come running. Gavin was a stout redhead with a big, full red beard and a stomach that pushed out against his shirts. He had a loud, jovial laugh and could usually be seen with a beer bottle in his hand after hours. Frank, on the other hand, was dark and of some eastern European descent. His face sported designer stubble, and he seemed to enjoy the look of flannel. He was muscled, but lacked the bulk of Gavin and Bear, looking downright puny next to them. He had bedroom eyes. But neither Gavin nor Frank could hold my interest. There was only one big man who could.

And he was big—not only tall, but with wide shoulders and tree trunks for arms and legs. He had working-man muscles, but wasn't super thin like he only ate egg whites and veal for a meal like some men thought was attractive. He was a man, the way men were created and meant to be. Manly, muscly, and a body that had never seen a strip of wax. He had a trimmed beard that covered his broad jaw, but I'd seen his wide smile. I wanted that smile turned my way. But men like him would never look at geeky, skinny men like me, even if they were gay.

My dick was a little sore from me imagining him gay—with his two housemates, of course. In my fantasies I dressed him up in a leather harness and not much else, and had him participate in orgies with Gavin and Frank. Somehow, halfway through, it would end up as me on the floor with Bear freakin' the hell out of me. Luckily I washed my own sheets, or else my sister would be horrified at the amount of semen a man could produce.

So on the Saturday morning that the three guys across the street decided not to be model neighbors, my sister sent me over to have a word with them. Yes, my sister, who has known me for all twenty-three years of our lives, sent me, the man who weighs 160 pounds only when he is wet and carrying a twenty-pound sack of flour, across the gray expanse of the street to have a word with three big men who were revving the engine of their dragster at 7:15 in the morning.

I didn't know my sister hated me so much.

I ran my clammy hands down my dark blue T-shirt and adjusted my glasses on my nose as I approached the three men. They had their green machine out on the front lawn with the hood popped and their heads in the engine. It gave me a nice view of some chunky arses, but I really needed to speak to someone face-to-face.

"Umm, excuse me?" I tried to call over the engine noise. They didn't hear me. I tried again without luck. Finally I tapped Bear (he was the closest) on his spine and jumped back as he jerked inside the engine.

"Shit! Ow!" He emerged rubbing his head and frowned ferociously at me. "Don't do that!"

"Sorry," I said. "I just needed to—"

He interrupted my sentence by turning and roaring loudly, "Shut her off, Frank!" The engine cut, and we all blinked in the abrupt silence.

Bear turned back to me with a friendly smile and began wiping his hands on an old rag. "Sorry. I can't hear over her singing. Can I help you?"

Now that I had his attention, I wanted to scuttle away. Frank and Gavin had stood up too, looking at me curiously. I took a deep breath and promised myself I had enough money to move to a foreign country if I needed to. "I… umm… it's seven in the morning," I stumbled out. "Can you wait another hour?"

Although I was staring at Bear, it was Frank who answered. "We have a competition tonight. We need to do the work."

I nodded understandingly, because I did understand. It was just that Jeannie didn't. "Yes. Sorry. We just don't want you to wake the baby." I gestured toward my sister's house, and three pairs of eyes followed my direction. I knew what they would see. A single-story, brick-and-tile home with two windows facing the road. One window was my bedroom, and all you could see there was the white backing of the curtains behind the white lace. The other bedroom window was covered in large, colorful decorations showing the Disney princesses Cinderella, Ariel, Belle, Rapunzel, and Snow White. It was obviously a child's room. "Could you please give us another thirty or forty minutes before you start the car again?"

Would they understand? Ari had been a right pain last night. I really needed her to sleep in this morning. Bear answered me, "Sure. Shit, we didn't think about that. We can keep it down until eight."

I sighed my thanks and waved good-bye, crossing back over the street and going inside. True to their word, they didn't start the car up again until after eight o'clock, by which time Ari was awake. I managed to get a bit of work done on my computer before then—in between sessions of staring at Bear's arse through the lace curtaining.

Then Lachie came to fetch me. "Uncle Neil! We need you. Mummy can't remember how to make pancakes." So I left my view and went to save breakfast.

II.

MONDAY MORNING was my usual chaos. The twins were trying to brush their own teeth, and I just knew that one of them was going to spill toothpaste all the way down their school uniform; Ari was only halfway through her bottle and had lost interest, which meant that she was going to be hungry and grumpy again in thirty minutes; the breakfast dishes were still waiting to be put in the dishwasher; the dog was waiting rather impatiently for her breakfast; and the cat had decided there weren't enough biscuits in his bowl, so he clawed me each time I walked past him. I couldn't find my shoes, my hair wasn't combed, and we had ten minutes until we all (humans minus animals) needed to be in the car.

As I said, my usual morning chaos.

The knock at the door startled me, but I was even more startled when I saw Bear on the other side.

"Umm, hi," I said.

I had to tilt my head back to see all of him. He seemed taller this morning. I ran my eyes down his navy blue overalls, appreciating the stretch of material across his chest, but even more so across his crotch. Finally my eyes landed on his boots, and I had my reason as to why he seemed taller than two days ago. He was wearing steel-caps with a two-inch thick sole, giving him extra height.

Suddenly I realized I had been checking out the guy and blushed a furious red as I took a step backward. He looked at me with quizzical eyes, as if he was saying, "Did I just see what I thought I saw?" I cleared my throat.

"Is there a problem?" If a man didn't want to be checked out, he shouldn't be so damn sexy.

He held up his hand, from which a mangled metal scooter hung. "Does this belong to one of your kids? It was left on the road, and I accidently backed over it this morning."

With mortification, I looked at the contraption. "Oh crap. Does it have Spider-Man or Ben 10 on it?"

We both peered at the twisted piece and I saw with a sinking heart it was Ben 10. My chaotic morning was just about to hit detonation levels. Bear raised both eyebrows. "Ben 10 is bad, I take it?"

"Catastrophic. Excuse me a moment." I took another step back inside the house and yelled, "Sammy!"

Lachie came running and I saw that yes, indeed, he had got toothpaste on his uniform. That showed Uncle Neil not to let four-year-olds try to brush their teeth by themselves. It didn't save time after all. "Lachie, where's Sammy? You've got toothpaste on you, buddy. Go and get another shirt and I'll have to wash that one today."

Lachie saw the scooter and screwed up his face as if he was about to cry. "Oh no!"

"It's alright. It isn't yours. It's Sammy's one."

"Sorry!"

I sighed. Lachie had a habit of apologizing for everything, even when it wasn't his fault.

Bear look apologetic too. "I didn't see it on the road, mate. Your brother must've left it there. I'm really sorry I ran over it."

"Sorry," Lachie said again.

I patted him on the head before whipping his shirt up and off. "I think it was Sammy, not you. Now go and put this in the hamper and find another shirt." Lachie ran off obediently, and I turned back to Bear just as Ari gave a screech, upset at being ignored for so long. I raced for her before she could work herself into a tantrum. She was already showing signs of being a little miss. "Sorry," I called to Bear. "Come on in, but mind the cat. He thinks he's starving to death."

Bear stepped inside and looked around nervously. With all its baby paraphernalia, scattered preschool toys, and 659 crayon drawings proudly displayed, I'm sure the inside of our house looked a lot different from the inside of his. Sammy appeared, her short dark hair slicked back and her socks pulled up to her knees under her shorts. I loved my tomboy of a niece. "Sammy, did you leave your scooter on the road? Look! Our neighbor ran over it."

"My scooter!" she cried. I knew she would—that thing was her prized possession.

"You shouldn't have left it on the road," I scolded her. "What were you doing out there, anyway? You know you're not allowed to ride your scooter on the road. See what happens? Now you don't have a scooter."

Tears began rolling down her face. "I didn't! It must've rolled there."

I sighed at that blatant lie. "How could it do that? It only has two wheels."

I could see her think about that one, trying to work out a scenario that would place her scooter on the other side of the road but not get her into trouble. "Maybe Lachie put it there?"

I shook my head as I swapped Ari onto my other shoulder so I could put lunchboxes into their insulated bags. "No. You did it. Don't lie to me. Now, tell me why you were out on the road?"

Her little bottom lip curled under and she sobbed, "I was looking at the race car! I didn't touch it, I promise. I just wanted to see. It has roll bars and shiny rims and everything. I just wanted to see if it was real."

And that explained it all. My four-year-old niece, who was obsessed with cars and especially race cars, just wanted to see Bear's dragster up close. And as a cherry on top? It was green—the color of Ben 10.

I rubbed my tired eyes. On the one hand I needed to punish her for breaking the rules, but on the other hand I knew how much she loved cars and loved her scooter.

To my surprise, Bear squatted down in front of her. "Do you like my car? You do? How about this, then—if you can come over and help me wash my car, perhaps you can earn some pocket money and buy a new scooter. Do you think your daddy will let you do that?"

I knew immediately that he'd made assumptions, so I corrected him. "Uncle Neil."

He looked up, startled. "*Uncle* Neil?"

"Yes. And I think it's a great idea for Sammy to help you wash your car. You just tell me when, and I'll send her over."

"Her?"

Again his assumptions were wrong, and while I didn't mind being mistaken for their father, I did get kind of uppity about his assumption of Sammy's gender. If he was thinking that girls couldn't be into race cars, then he had another thing coming. My own upbringing had been one where I'd been constantly berated for not being "manly" enough. I was determined to shelter my niece from comments that suggested she was not "girly" enough.

But again Bear amazed me. He stood and ruffled Sammy's short locks and smiled. "No problem, kiddo. I have a race meet on Friday, so you can come over Saturday and make her all pretty again, alright?"

Sammy raced off happy while I finished putting the lunches away into the appropriate school bags. "I'm really sorry," I apologized, "about the scooter in the street. She knows not to do it. She's just so car-mad at the moment I guess she couldn't resist. I'm sorry for delaying your morning, you must need to get to work." I stepped toward the man, the baby still on my shoulder, intending on showing him out the door and not delaying him any longer, but he stood his ground. I stopped, unsure of what to do, of what he wanted and of what to do next. Out of every single idea that flowed through my mind, what he *did* do surprised the shit out of me.

He took a fat finger, ran it down the width of my smooth cheek and said, "Woof."

Then he turned and left, leaving me stunned and half-aroused. *Woof?* What the hell was that supposed to mean?

Unfortunately I didn't get a chance to ponder it, because we were late. I hustled the kids into the car and drove them to school. Being only four, they had Kindy two and a half days a week. So on Mondays and Tuesdays I dropped them off with pleasure, letting the Education Department babysit them for six hours. On Wednesday my mother would be by to take all three children from me, dealing with the half day at school and babysitting them until nearly seven, when Jeannie would pick them up after work and bring them home. Thursdays were day-care days: as soon as I could get them ready, I took them to the center and almost ran back to my car to escape.

So that day I only had Ari to look after. I tossed a load of washing on, did the dishes, quickly picked up the toys, and then settled down in front of my computer to get some work accomplished. Ari had figured out the routine by now. She played on the mat with her toys and only interrupted Uncle Neil if it was an emergency. Hungry bellies and wet bums counted as emergencies. She was even so good as to sometimes put herself to sleep, simply flopping down tiredly wherever she was and closing those pretty blue eyes.

That gave me plenty of time to finish all the programming I needed to get done, before my mind began to wander again.

Woof?

I googled the word and found you could create a Facebook-type profile for your dog and that the stock market actually had stocks called WOOF, but it didn't explain why one man would say it to another. That gave me a clue. I typed in "gay woof" to Google and it sent me a link that had my stomach dropping to the floor.

If you see a hot guy, you say: "Woof."

Did that mean…? The man, for whom I would gladly miss the next episode of *Game of Thrones*, thought I was hot?

The link also pointed me in the direction of the subculture of bears. I started reading, and my eyes got wider and wider. There was so much in there that I never realized. It's fine to be a twenty-three-year-old gay person in Australia, but apparently I had been missing out. Apparently you needed to label yourself and join a club. Perhaps my club was he-who-stays-home-to-help-his-sister-and-spends-too-much-time-on-the-computer. Perhaps I could start an online club.

Bears. Cubs. Polar bears. Panda bears. Koala bears. Otters. The list went on—and I had no idea what any of the terms meant.

Then I followed a link about a chaser.

Someone who likes bears. A bear chaser.

I looked at the pictures of bears on the site and nodded sadly. It seemed I had a label already. Unfortunately, I sounded like an alcoholic drink instead of someone cool. I sighed and went back to my programming.

III.

SATURDAY SWUNG around, and Bear was knocking on our door. Awkwardly, it was before I was dressed, and Jeannie opened the security screen and let the man in anyway. I was sitting at the breakfast table reading the newspaper while eating my oh-so-sophisticated Cheerios, unshowered, unshaved, and still in my cotton boxers and sleep T-shirt.

Jeannie's voice was the first clue I was about to be embarrassed. "Oh, hi there! Come on in. Sammy hasn't stopped talking about you and your car. Are you sure you're okay with her helping you wash it? I'm Jeannie, by the way. Neil didn't catch your name."

"Brett."

"Pleased to meet you. I haven't got the twins dressed yet, so if you could just hang out with Neil for two minutes, I'll put Sammy in some clothes." She rushed off and left us together.

I tried to make it seem like I entertained strangers in my pajamas every day. I smoothed down my hair and quickly patted my crotch to make sure nothing untoward was showing. Brett caught the movement and grinned as he sat down at one of the chairs at the table.

"Sorry," he apologized. "I thought you'd be up by eight. You were the other week."

I blushed red and casually placed the newspaper over my lap. Just in case. "Ari had a bad night last night," I explained. "She was awake and wanting to play between two and five. So I had a bit of a sleep in this morning."

"Her mother didn't sit with her?"

"No. Apparently Uncle Neil has the special touch at night. Most nights, anyway. Jeannie works twelve-hour days, four days a week, so I usually get up with the kids when they wake at night. Jeannie pulls day shift with the three of them when she's not at work, so I get to have a nap then, if I need it."

"So can Uncle Neil come out and play with Sammy? I was hoping that I could get some extra help with washing the car."

It would be best if someone did supervise Sammy. Sending a four-year-old girl across to a stranger's house without supervision was asking for trouble. I hesitated. "You want me to help?"

He grinned at me from behind his beard. "Yes."

"Oh. I'll need to get changed."

"That's a pity. Make sure you don't put too much on. I'm liking what I see."

Even someone as socially awkward as me could tell that was a come-on. I blushed bright red and tried to think of something intelligent to say. "The woof thing? I had to google it," I told him truthfully. That made him chuckle, and he scooted his chair closer to me.

"That's alright. I don't mind. Did you find out what a good response to that was?"

My face and mind blanked. A response? I was supposed to say something back?

But Brett didn't mind. He picked up my hand and brought it over to his body, smoothing it down his curved stomach. The blush on my face moved rapidly south. Under my hand, the heat from his body radiated outward. He was wearing a cotton T-shirt, and I suddenly wished he was wearing a shirt with buttons so I could slip my fingers between them and feel that hairy skin underneath. And it was hairy. I could feel it through the material. *Thank goodness for newspapers on laps*, was all I could think of.

Brett growled deep in his throat, its vibration going through his chest until I could feel it on my palm. "Lesson one," he said. "When someone says 'woof' to you? The correct response is either to say 'woof' back to them or give them a belly pat. I'll accept an arse pat from you too."

Thankfully Sammy came tearing into the room just then, interrupting something I didn't know how to handle. "Hi, Car-man! Are we going to wash your car now?" Lachie was on her heels.

Brett sat back to put a decent distance between us and smiled at the twins. "Hey, guys. Are you both coming to help me?" When two heads nodded so hard they nearly fell off, he smiled and said, "No problem. Uncle Neil's just going to get changed, and then he's coming over to help too."

My sister's sarcastic comment came from behind me. "Oh, so is he now?"

Brett just smiled. "Yes, he is."

I panicked. "But I haven't had a shower or shaved or anything!"

Ignoring the presence of my family in the room, Brett leaned in close and whispered, "Good. I like you just like that."

Sammy and Lachie almost dragged me to my bedroom so I could change. I had no idea what to wear. What does one wear to wash a car with a guy he is trying to impress? Now imagine the wardrobe of a geeky computer nerd who wouldn't know how to dress to impress someone he liked even if you gave him a thousand bucks. Sad.

I grabbed some jeans and a white T-shirt. My sister always said that if in doubt, go for a classic look. Socks and sneakers, and I was ready. Brett had already returned home, and I saw as I crossed the street that he had lined up all four cars on the front lawn. It appeared I actually did have to work after all. Brett was ready for the twins—two identical red buckets were standing by, overflowing with bubbles, and two large yellow sponges were placed out for their use. He started them on his black V-8 Ford ute, with Sammy given the responsibility of washing the door, while Lachie was told to do the wheels. Then Brett turned to me and chucked a spare sponge in my direction. Unfortunately it was wet and full of water. Even more unfortunate, I have the hand-eye coordination of a slug when it comes to catching objects. Give me a keyboard and I have no equals. Give me a game controller and prepare to be soundly beaten. Throw a wet sponge in my direction, I completely miss and it splatters wetly on my white shirt.

Brett laughed as I picked up the dropped object. "Sorry, mate. You okay?" I straightened my glasses as he approached and was shocked to receive my own belly pat—directly on the wet patch of my shirt. "I take it back. I don't think I'm sorry after all."

I looked down at my now transparent shirt with dawning humiliation. So much for trying to impress the guy.

I helped the kids wash the ute, reaching the places they couldn't, then rinsing the bubbles off with the hose. Brett moved in to wash an imagined speck of dirt away just as I directed the hose at the car. The water splashed and managed to hit him on the chest, dead center as if someone had painted a target on him. He roared in surprise, and so I jerked the hose up, hitting him in the face and completely soaking him before I could get the hose pointed away.

"Argh! You did that on purpose!" he shouted.

"I… I didn't!" I stuttered as he looked down at his soaked self. Water dripped from his beard and hair. My heart stopped. He was such a big guy. What would he do to me in retaliation? If he hit me, I would be dead.

Brett shook his head, flicking water droplets everywhere while he pulled at his wet shirt. "I didn't need another shower," he groused.

I stood there with my knees trembling, wondering what his reaction would be. But instead of charging at me as I expected, he began to laugh.

Big, deep belly laughs. Then he grabbed the hem of his shirt and stripped it off his torso, revealing his large, hairy body beneath.

He was gorgeous. And rounded.

His pecs were rounded. His biceps were rounded. And yes, his gut was rounded too. And it was all covered with a healthy amount of manly hair that proclaimed his masculinity. The saliva pooled in my mouth.

The hose was still running as he scowled in my direction. "I'm s-s-sorry," I stuttered.

Gavin and Frank appeared from inside the house. Gavin's shirt wasn't buttoned up, and his torso was on full display. I looked and appreciated, but he couldn't hold a candle to Brett.

"What's going on?" Gavin demanded, looking between us.

Brett swiped at the droplets on his face with his wet T-shirt. "Neil got me with the hose," he explained.

"Is that all?" Gavin asked, perplexed. "I thought someone had left a window on the car down or something." Frank was grinning from behind Gavin, and it was only because I was looking in his direction and desperately trying not to look at Brett that I caught the movement of his hand. It snuck around the front of Gavin and patted him on the roundest bit of his stomach.

"C'mon, Gav. Leave 'em to sort it out." Frank spoke and then turned back to the house. My brain spun. Were they all gay? Did they *really* have orgies complete with leather chaps and handcuffs, like in my dreams?

Gavin smiled at Brett. "You always find an excuse to pull your clothes off in front of the cute ones. Bring him to the party tonight. I have a feeling he'll enjoy it." Then Gavin was gone.

I held the hose limply, staring after him. *Cute one? Party? Clothes off? And exactly what will I enjoy?*

I gathered my wits enough to help Brett finish off the cars. Lachie lasted ten minutes more before he lost interest and returned home. Sammy lasted three cars. She helped Brett dry the dragster while I started washing the final car before she said, "Uncle Neil? Can I go home now?"

My clothes were damp and my hands completely soapy, so I smiled my permission. "Sure, sweetie. I'll just help Brett finish off and I'll be home. Now, look for cars before you cross the road. That's it. Good girl." I watched until she was safely across and the front door banged behind her before I turned back to soaping the car's roof. Brett had grabbed the bucket and was applying the sponge to the hood.

I tried not to look at his bare chest as he worked in the morning sunshine.

I *did* try. I swear.

Brett made casual conversation as we worked. "Uncle Neil, huh? So how does Uncle Neil end up living with his nieces and nephew?"

I soaped the door. "Being stupidly gullible and completely unable to resist my sister's pleading puppy-dog eyes," I told him. Brett snorted. "My sister's ex-husband left her when the twins were only a couple of weeks old," I explained further. "Apparently blonde strippers were more his scene than fatherhood with two crying babies. I was studying at university, so I moved in to help out. Rent-free accommodation in exchange for babysitting duties. Then the ex came back. They tried for a reconciliation, but according to that selfish bastard, it was never going to work because I'd turned his children against him." I grabbed the hose and began to rinse the bubbles from the section I'd just washed. "His idea of fatherhood was having a child who fetched items for him, but was otherwise not seen or heard. The reconciliation lasted four weeks. Just long enough for another pregnancy before he ran."

"Damn."

Yes. I'd used that word when I'd found out, along with a couple of other choices. "So I'll stick around until Jeannie's got it together enough to cope."

Brett stepped back and indicated I should hose down the whole car. I made sure I didn't hit him this time. "But why her brother?" he asked. "That seems like an odd choice."

"We're twins," I said. "I guess we're closer than normal siblings."

"Another set of twins?" he gaped in astonishment.

"Of course," I laughed gaily. "Twins run in my family. You can *not* know the relief I felt when Ari wasn't a twin too. Our grandmother had three sets of twins."

Brett laughed as he turned off the hose for me and grabbed the drying cloth. "That's not the only thing that runs in your family."

"Huh?" Brett had learned his lesson and didn't try to throw a cloth to me this time. He came over and placed it in my hand before whispering in my ear. "Cuteness. I think cuteness runs in your family too. Woof."

IV.

THE INSIDE of Brett's house was wonderful and manly—big screen TV; huge, comfy lounges that were dark brown so the dirt wouldn't show as easily; chunky, solid furniture that would take the weight of a chunky, solid guy; pictures of drag cars on the walls; and as a crowning touch, a screwdriver and can of degreaser left on the end of the kitchen bench.

I wasn't sure how I came to be inside Brett's house. Frank and Gavin had appeared just as we finished drying the last car. The two men jumped in Gavin's blue beast and drove away, muttering something about beer and hot dogs. I was roped into helping Brett put the dragster away in the back shed and picking up the buckets and all. Once everything was set away, Brett hauled me into the house and opened the fridge. "Is it too early for you to have a beer? I can offer you Coke, water, orange juice, or milk."

I nervously fingered the hem of my white T-shirt and leaned against the kitchen cabinets. "I'm alright, thanks. I should get out of your hair now." I was muttering my sentences to the floor, unable to make eye contact, since Brett hadn't seen the need to put another shirt back on. Looking at his face meant I was constantly distracted by his chest.

"You're sure?" he persisted. "Is there *anything* I can do for you?"

My eyes goggled and flew up to his face. *He didn't mean...?*

"Besides," he told me, "I need to convince you to come to the party with me tonight. A bunch of us are getting together. Can you come? It's just a casual thing, so there'll be plenty of beer and the barbecue will make its usual appearance. Costas has a pool, so there may be some swimming if you're into that."

My jaw worked as I tried to formulate an answer that didn't sound too dorky. "I don't do well in social situations," I finally managed, flushing bright red in embarrassment.

He closed the fridge and took a step closer. "You'll be fine. You'll be with me." My heart started pounding in my ears at that statement. I was going to have a heart attack if he kept saying things like that. His hand reached out, and suddenly he had one meaty paw on my hip. "Can you come, Neil? I'd like you to come with me. There'll be plenty of bears to perv on, if that does it for you." He stepped in closer so that his bare stomach was brushing my damp shirt, and I could smell the manly essence of his musk. "Personally, I like the little guys, but I love hanging out with other bears. Will you come?"

I was getting aroused—quickly! I tried to draw in a deeper breath because my lungs felt like they were being squeezed, but that didn't work because all I could smell was Brett.

He took my hand and placed it on his stomach—the stomach I'd been trying to avoid staring at. "Neil?" he whispered, moving in closer.

"Ahh…." Yes, even my school reports had all said *Does not do well in social situations*.

Brett fixed that for me by moving the situation from *social* to *sexual*. He pushed me against the cabinet using his body, and with two large palms cupping my jaw, brought my mouth up to his. I closed my eyes and melted. He was in charge, and that was more than fine with me.

His beard was soft, enclosing my mouth and giving me tingles from the top of my skull to the tips of my toes. He kissed me roughly and thoroughly. He wrapped his large arms around me and crushed me to his solid body. My fingers had a mind of their own and explored in the fur of his chest until I found his nipples. We kissed for endless minutes, his beard scratching on my chin in a way I knew I wouldn't be able to hide.

Brett nibbled his way across my cheek and found my earlobe. I shuddered violently. "Do you like that?" he asked. I couldn't answer as I was concentrating on the feel of the rough skin on his hands delving under my T-shirt. "Are you going to come to the party with me?" he insisted.

"Social. Don't. Well. Do." I would work out how to speak in full sentences later.

Brett's hand reached for my denim-covered butt and pulled me against him. "What can I do to persuade you?" He was sucking at my neck, then wetly licking the skin before gently biting down. "What can I do so you'll come, Neil?"

"Come?" I finally managed to ask.

"Okay," Brett answered and dropped to his knees in front of me.

Wait—what? I blinked rapidly and went over the last thirty seconds of conversation. He'd asked… then I'd said… so he said okay and….

Oh Seven Hells!

I looked down to where Brett had already unzipped my pants and was drawing me out of my underwear and concluded to myself that exclamations from *Game of Thrones* were just not going to cut it in this situation. I was going to have to do better and find a more suitable iconic show.

"Oh Vaping Moffs!" Yep, that sounded better. *Star Wars* always managed to fill the void for me. Speaking of filling voids....

I grunted as Brett took me inside his mouth. My eyes completed an entire revolution in my head as the sensation of warmth, wetness, and suction registered. Brett grabbed two fistfuls of the material bagging around my upper thighs and pulled me in. I thrust in several times, not believing my good fortune to have a man as gorgeous as Brett allowing me to fuck his face. If this continued much longer, I was going to have to find some swear words in Wookieespeak in order to express myself completely.

Critical mass was approaching rapidly. "Brett... I'm going to come!" He grunted and pulled me in tighter, so I let go, exploding my nuts—and what felt like my brain matter—into his mouth. Not even Wookieespeak could describe that sensation.

I breathed rapidly for long minutes before I remembered where I was. I blinked as Brett grinned and zipped me up. "You okay there, mate? Because I just heard Frank and Gavin drive up, so you may want to try to wipe that look off your face." Sure enough, there was the sound of a key in the door, and I quickly grabbed a clean glass from the shelf and filled it with water so that my back was to the men coming inside.

"Brett? Did you manage to convince your...." Gavin's voice trailed off as he entered the room and realized I was still in the house. Brett was leaning casually against the bench but was still wiping at his beard. I'm sure I turned tomato red, because both Gavin and Frank got sly grins on their faces as they looked between the two of us. "Ahh—do you need us to head down to the shop again?" Gavin offered.

I didn't think I could get any redder, but Brett proved me wrong. He laughed. "Nah, mate. I think I've managed to convince Neil to join the party tonight. Neil? You coming?"

I managed to nod my agreement as Frank grabbed a fistful of Gavin's shirt and dragged him away in the direction of the bedrooms. "C'mon, Gav. Leave Brett alone. We'll be in our room with the music on loud, 'kay?" Frank waved, but Gavin had the last word as they disappeared.

"Woof, brother!"

Brett shook his head and grinned at me while he rolled his eyes. "Sorry. Next time I'll make sure there's a door between us and them."

Next time?

DESPITE PROTESTING that I didn't want to go, somehow I was showering and getting ready at six that night. Brett had spoken to Jeannie, whose smile was so broad when she heard about our "date" that you would've thought that Brett had offered her a million dollars. Jeannie assured Brett I would be over at their house at the designated time, then nagged me until I agreed that I was going.

Button-up shirts looked dreadful on me, as they hung loosely around my skinny frame, so I donned a black T-shirt and slipped on a black shirt over the top, leaving it unbuttoned. My hair had a kink to it and did its own thing, so I threw some of Jeannie's gel in it and vowed that if it embarrassed me I would shave it off. It thankfully behaved.

Finally I was ready, and with Jeannie's blessing I crossed the street just as the three men were coming out. Gavin noticed me first. "Woof, brother!" he cried jovially.

I remembered what Brett had said, so nervously replied, "W-woof."

They all laughed at me, so I don't think I quite got the inflection right. Brett slung his arm around my shoulder and dragged me over to his car. "They're taking Frank's car," he told me and opened the door for me. The engine of a vehicle fired behind me as I slipped into the passenger seat. Gavin hung out the window as the car reversed and yelled something about us not being allowed to take the detour. I banged my door closed as Brett chuckled and started the engine.

We were soon on our way, and I took a look at Brett. He was dressed casually, which made me calm down a bit about what I was wearing. He just had on regular blue jeans and a regular cotton shirt. The short sleeves were stretched tight over his biceps, which made me shiver with excitement, and the top button was undone showing me a tuft of chest hair that had my mouth drying in anticipation. He caught me looking.

"Woof," he told me quietly.

This time I was a bit more enthusiastic. "Woof!" We grinned at each other.

The party was being held at Costas's house, and it appeared that Costas had plenty of friends. His front lawn was covered with cars, so Brett found a spot a little farther up the street, and we walked back to where we could hear the music coming from. Brett grabbed my hand and I startled, unused to public displays of gay affection. "Relax," Brett told me. "Most of the guys inside are either gay or bi. There are a couple of straight guys, but you won't be able to pick 'em. We're all just blokes, and that's the way we like it."

What I walked into was something that blew my mind. Men who were men and not ashamed to flaunt it were stacked wall-to-wall. There were at least thirty guys inside the house and spilling out onto the back patio, and not one of them would fit in at a gay nightclub. For a start, they were mostly older—and it seemed that facial hair was the way to go. There were trimmed beards, long beards, and plenty of in-betweens. My hair was probably the only one in the room sporting gel. Casual wear appeared to be the dress code—anything from shorts worn with open shoes to jeans with steel-cap boots. And not a single one of the guys was primped or plucked to within an inch of his life.

Men were standing around with beers or soft drinks in their hands, smiling and laughing and having good ol' chats with their mates. Several large bowls of chips were scattered throughout the room, and I could see the smoke rising from the barbecue out back.

The first guy to spot us was around Brett's age—early to mid thirties. He was dressed in jeans and a loud Hawaiian print shirt, and of course he sported a beard, a beer, and a belly that pushed out at his shirt. His face lit up and he turned to Brett with a "Woof, brother!" The men embraced, with a couple of hearty slaps on each other's backs as their idea of a greeting. The stranger looked over at me. "Hey! I'm Scotty." My arm was pumped vigorously, and I wondered if you could dislocate your shoulder from shaking someone's hand.

"Scott, this is Neil," Brett told him proudly. "He's our neighbor."

"How convenient," Scotty said with a wink. "Chubby chaser?" he asked me eagerly.

I blinked at the unfamiliar term, but Brett growled low in his throat and slung an arm around my waist. "Mine," he told the man. Scotty smiled affably and took a step back, allowing us farther into the room.

Brett took me around and introduced me to the others. Their names whirled through my head—Joey, Stack, Barney, Pops, Bluey, Greg, Steve, Rick, Dez, Don, Dave, and Dim. I gave up trying to remember after that. A beer was thrust into my hand and, plastered to Brett's side, I found I was relaxed enough in the easy atmosphere to chat with the nearest person. The partygoers came from all walks of life. I asked about professions and found brickies, lawyers, truck drivers, teachers, accountants, salesmen, engineers, welders, and even a fireman. There were plenty of *woofs* bandied around, but the men seemed very laid-back and jovial in the testosterone-fueled environment.

Despite moving in with my sister when I was only nineteen to help her with the kids, and despite the fact I worked from home on my computer, I did actually have friends in the real world—and we did occasionally go out to pubs and clubs. I usually found the gay clubs were full of preeners and jocks who were saying, "Look at me! Look at me!" Most of them were only interested in hooking up for the night, and it seemed like one big cattle sale, where the best buyers would take home the prime beef and the others had to do with whatever they could find.

There was none of that at this party. Guys were relaxed and mellow. I noticed a couple of arse pats, a few tummy rubs, and several spontaneous kisses, but all in all there wasn't that desperate feel to the crowd, as though they were competing for the prize.

Costas hijacked Brett to come and help him with the barbecue, so Brett left me with a circle of guys, and soon I was deep in conversation with an older guy they called Petey. He was about fifty, with a graying beard and thinning hair.

"So, how'd you meet Brett?" he asked.

"He moved in across the street a couple of weeks back," I replied.

"So are you a chubby chaser?"

There was that term again. *Chubby chaser.* I hated to look stupid in front of people and desperately wished I could pull my phone out and google the term before replying, but Petey was looking at me expectantly. The guys had all been so welcoming and relaxed that I felt comfortable in saying to Petey, "I'm actually not sure what that means."

Petey smiled and helped me out. "A chubby chaser is a guy who likes big men. Specifically men who are overweight."

My mind struggled to understand. I was of a generation where the David Beckhams and Brad Pitts of the world were seen as gods. "You mean there are guys who prefer overweight men?"

"Sure," Petey told me happily. "They don't stand up and proclaim it loudly because of reactions like yours. So instead you'll find them lurking around websites, drooling over the 'before' pictures of the weight-loss sites and attending parties like this one. That's what we're about here. No judgment. We take you as you are. No frowns, no displeasure. Just a welcome, and tell us what you like."

"Oh." This gathering was like being whirled into the Land of Oz.

"Personally, I like a guy with a decent gut on him," Petey continued on. "You skinny guys don't have anything to cuddle. So I'm always on the lookout for a chubby cubby."

I blinked again. "A chubby cubby?" I was a guy who was fluent in both Dothraki and Wookieespeak, but I couldn't understand this person.

Petey laughed again and slung a large arm over my shoulders. "Okay. I'll teach you. You ready for your lesson, boy?" I nodded, and he pointed over to Scotty where he was happily chomping down on the end of a sausage in a bun that had just come off the barbecue. "Scotty's a chubby," Petey said. "He's a larger guy with a beauty of a gut on him. Brett, however, is a bear, although he doesn't have much gut on him yet. He's a big guy, with a beard and plenty of body hair. Scotty's also a bear, but we would more likely define him as a chubby."

Right. I nodded my understanding, so Petey pointed to Dim. I'd spoken to the guy earlier, and we'd had a great chat since he was my age and into electronic games like me. He preferred *Grand Theft Auto*, whereas I was more into strategy games, but at least we knew what the other was talking about. "Dim's a young bear—not as big and bulky as Brett, but he's getting there. Since he's young, he's known as a cub."

If I'd been in a cartoon, the lightbulb would've dinged above my head. "So a chubby cubby is a chubby younger guy?"

Petey agreed. "Yes. Now, have a look over at Frank and Gavin." I searched the crowd for them and found them near the pool. Frank had stripped down to his shorts and was preparing to dive into the water. His chest was covered in black fur that I really enjoyed, but his physique was in no way beefy or flabby. Gavin laughed outrageously as Frank splashed into the pool and wet the nearby spectators. As I watched, Gavin flung off his shirt and once again revealed his rounded belly. I smiled at the sight of his gingery-colored chest hair.

"So is Gavin a chubby or a bear?" I asked.

"Gavin?" Petey shrugged. "Both. He's not quite as big as some of the chubbies around, but he holds his own. But Gavin is our ginger bear." Once again I was clueless. "He's a redhead." Petey explained.

"Ah! Gotcha."

"But what I was pointing out to you was Frank. He isn't a bear, because he's too slim. So he's what we call an otter."

I chuckled and got the reference immediately. Frank was hairy, but without the bulk needed to be a bear.

"Exactly," Petey said. "Then you have your panda bears, which are guys of Asian descent. Likewise you have your black bears. And when I go overseas, I'm known as a koala bear, because I'm from Australia."

"But koalas aren't actually bears," I felt the need to point out. "They're marsupials."

Petey gave me a wink. "Don't tell the Yanks that. Some guys go crazy for the koala bear."

I chuckled like he meant me to. "Are there more?"

"Of course. Your leather bears are those into domination, a pocket bear is the name given to short guys, and your grizzly bears are usually taller and shaggier than the rest. And last of all you have me."

"You?"

"I'm a polar bear."

"Because you're Caucasian?"

"No, because I'm going gray."

I laughed, delighted at the knowledge and the new terms I'd found. "So what am I?" I asked.

"You, my friend, I believe are a chaser. My only question is, are you a chubby chaser or a bear chaser?"

I looked at Scotty, and then I looked at Frank where he was floating in the pool. Then, like my eyes were magnetized in his direction, I found Brett where he was loading up a platter of buns with sausages in them to offer around the room. "Petey," I said, "I believe I'm a bear chaser."

V.

THE NIGHT was still rocking when Brett tugged me away from the crowd and out the front door. Music still played and the guys were getting more than a bit tipsy. The food had been passed around, and around, and around. Solid decent food like party pies, sausages, and chips, not the pretend food like the hors d'oeuvres you got at some parties. A slice of raw salmon on a cracker is not filling and wouldn't be acceptable at Costas's party. Despite the food to soak up the alcohol, at least half of the attendees were drunk. The pool had become a playground for those who were feeling adventurous—and clothing was not a requirement. Big guys snuggled and cuddled with their buddies on large sofas in the lounge, others still laughed and chatted in their groups. As the night wore on, I glimpsed a whole lot of chest hair and more nipple rings than I could've imagined as shirts were undone, bellies shown off, and clothing not replaced.

Brett grabbed my hand and pulled me through the crush until we were out in the cool night air. In the shadows, we leaned against a white 4WD and breathed in the crisp air. "Have you been having fun?" he asked.

I nodded. "Yes. I've had great fun."

"Did you want to go home?"

I frowned in disappointment. I'd been enjoying myself, but maybe Brett hadn't? Maybe he wanted to take me home and return to the party without me? It was still quite early by party standards. I swallowed my regret and tried to sound upbeat. "Sure. If you want to. I'm cool whatever you need to do."

Brett turned to me. "No, I meant do you want to come back to my house. Now. Frank and Gavin will probably be at least another hour at the party, and I want to find out if you're a screamer."

Oh.

"Are you sure?" I whispered in the darkness. I wasn't used to being pursued. Brett grabbed me with both hands and hauled me into his body. In the next heartbeat he was forcefully kissing me, holding my head with one large hand so I couldn't resist. Not that I wanted to.

Once my lips were numb from the pressure, he drew back. "Never surer of anything in my life."

The ride home seemed three times as long as the initial journey. I changed my mind eight times—flipping from "Look man, I think I'll just go home instead" to "Get your pants off now!" to "I'm not sure if this is a good idea" to "Oh God yes! Take me however you want!" and then back again. I was considering the line "Look, I know I owe you a blow job, so how about we just do that and I'll go home?" when we pulled into the driveway. I glanced over at my house, relieved to see Ari's light off, which hopefully meant my sister had her asleep.

"You okay?" Brett asked.

"What? Yes. Fine. Just checking to see if Ari's asleep." I sounded nervous even to myself, and I saw Brett hesitate. Suddenly my thoughts crystallized, and I knew I wanted whatever Brett had in store for me. "I haven't changed my mind. It's true I'm a little unsure of myself, but that's just because I can't believe that someone as nice as you wants to be with me. I've been checking you out since you moved in. I've wanted you for weeks, but now I've met you, I want you even more."

We were still sitting in the car, and Brett fingered the key ring still in the ignition. "I don't want to rush you into a relationship, Neil, if you don't have feelings for me other than wanting to fuck. I have a bad habit of that, they tell me, running in and committing my heart before the other guy is ready. When I see something I like, I go for it with all my soul. The first day I saw you, I liked what I saw. But the first day you spoke to me? I just wanted to take you inside and keep you there, and at that stage I didn't even know if you were gay. Sexually you turn me on something fierce, but there's more to it than that. I don't know how to say it properly, but I'd love to see your face every morning over cornflakes."

My tongue felt all swollen with the words I wanted to blurt out, but before I had a chance, Brett was opening the door and getting out. I scrambled after him. "Am I still invited inside?" I said rather breathlessly.

He had a wide smile for me. "I think that's a standing invitation for you, Neil." He unlocked his front door and pulled me through the dark house to his bedroom. My nerves had completely disappeared by this time. The cornflakes comment had taken them away.

Brett's room was masculine, with dark blues and blacks, the large bed dominating the floor space. He flicked on the lamp beside the pillows as I sank down on the edge of the mattress.

There was just one thing I needed to check. "Umm, Brett? Top or bottom?"

His grin was definitely saucy as he began to undo the buttons on his shirt. "Do you have preconceived ideas about big guys? Do you think that just because we're big, we're always dominant?" I was getting distracted from the tufts of hair he was uncovering. "Do you think that bears are always the top?"

My heart sank. "So you prefer the bottom, do you?" I asked timidly. I wasn't sure if I could do that. I wasn't exactly a virgin, but I could definitely count on one hand the number of times I had topped. The surest way to drive the man of your dreams away? Top him badly.

Brett's shirt was gracing the floor, and he was working his button and zipper by the time he replied, "Neil? How about you get undressed? Because I'm going down on you and sucking until you have just about lost your mind. But I'm not going to allow you to come this time, because you're going to wait for me. Then, when you're all worked up and wanting it badly, you're going to open that lovely mouth of yours and you're going to swallow my meat whole. Then, when I'm about to blow, I'm going to throw you down on that bed, I'm going to shove your legs over my shoulders, and I'm going to work my cock into that tight hole of yours and not come out for hours."

I had a fleeting moment to appreciate that I'd made the right move to miss the live stream of *Game of Thrones* from the US for this date. But then all thoughts of electronic devices and TV shows completely left my mind as Brett's pants dropped to the floor and I was staring at the most delicious-looking thing I had seen in a long while.

His cock was hard and sticking straight out from a dense bush of hair, curving slightly. I'd once read that guys with a curve to their erection could tickle special places inside your body. I hoped I was paying enough attention when the time came, because I was in need of some very special tickling.

Brett's voice startled me out of the staring trance I had fallen into. "Are you just going to sit there all night?"

Hell, no! Usually I felt shy and awkward about my body when it came to the serious part of sex. I was skinny, and Jeannie always teased me about my muscles—saying that stuffed toys have more muscle than me. But the party had mellowed me out. The guys at the gathering had been accepting of everyone in whatever body shape they came in. There was no pointing out of flaws or subtly suggesting that a bit more attention to grooming would be appreciated. Men were welcomed for being men—large, small, hairy, hairless, old, young, black, gray, red, or whatever you came as.

I scrambled out of my clothes as Brett growled in approval. Then he enveloped me in a big bear hug and bore me down on the bed, our nakedness rubbing together as our lips met in a hot kiss. My glasses were chucked aside, and our hands explored with abandon. The fuzz on Brett's chest felt delicious, and I plunged my fingers into the dense hair and found his nipples.

"Oh yeah, Neil. Pinch me there hard," Brett panted as he pulled my knee up over his hip so he could rub against me faster. I did as he asked and was rewarded with a rumble from deep in his chest that vibrated down my spine. His large hands were exploring my skin, running over my ribs and hipbones before clutching at my butt to pull me firmly into his embrace.

He kissed and licked at my neck before pushing my arms over my head and holding my wrists in place with a single hand. I was helpless and loving it as he kissed his way over my chest, paying particular attention to my nubs before heading farther south.

As he promised, he took me into his mouth, slurping and licking my dick with obvious enjoyment. He squeezed the head hard to push my precome out for his tasting. I was not going to last, so I gritted my teeth to stop my orgasm until I could no longer stand it. Finally I scurried from under his mass and pushed him back on the bed. He gave me a lustful grin and sank backward on the bed so that his frame was on display for my pleasure. I didn't know where to start.

I ran my hand up his hairy thigh until I was nudging his balls with my fingers. He responded by spreading his legs further for my investigation. I cupped his balls which, to my delight, were large and loose in his sack. With my other hand I gripped his shaft tight and ran my thumb over the moisture on the tip.

"C'mon, Neil. Suck me," Brett pleaded.

I took him in my mouth and worked up some saliva around his flesh. He tasted great, and I eagerly swallowed his flavor as I stimulated him. He was all wet and juicy when I stretched my neck and tried to clamp down my gag reflex. I could do it, but sometimes it took me a little practicing.

"Oh fuck. Yeah, baby. Work me in." Brett was encouraging and excited as I pushed him into my throat. I pushed down and he slipped in, but immediately I had to pull off as I was choking. I sucked in a breath and swallowed. Brett gave me a minute, then said, "C'mon, baby. You can do it." I gave him a brief smile and pushed down again. This time he helped, with a large hand providing extra pressure at the crown of my head. It worked. I fought the gag and he slipped in easily. I bobbed and a shout erupted from my lover.

"Hell, yeah. That's it."

He allowed me up for another breath, but then pushed me down with force until he was in my throat. It was easier now, and I held my breath as he thrust into me with powerful jerks. I was getting ready to go down for my sixth or seventh time when, with a dominant roar, Brett suddenly grabbed me and thrust me to my back on the bed. I saw him shove his thick middle finger into his mouth to get it wet and knew immediately where that broad digit was headed.

"Brett," I gasped in anticipation. He pushed my legs back and folded me in half before exploring my pucker and pushing that finger into me. I sighed in relief as he did. I couldn't believe that he was *finally* penetrating me. It seemed I had been waiting and wanting it for weeks.

He was thrusting two broad fingers in and out of me before he stopped for some protection and lube. I was thankful for both. Spit is all well and good, unless you want to walk properly the day after. Appropriately covered and slicked up, Brett paused so that the head of his cock was resting against my hole. "Neil? I wanna hear you moan, baby. I want to hear you scream my name so I know that you're loving this."

It was more of a yell than a moan as he pushed inside of my body. He gave me plenty of time to adjust to his size as he slowly moved in. There was the anticipatory pressure, the initial burn, and then the pinch as my body tried to reject this intruder. But I knew the heaven that awaited. I pushed back, willing my body to accept, when suddenly he slid all the way in.

I sighed as the angels began to sing hallelujah choruses around me, telling me I'd reached heaven. I groaned my relief and pleasure. Brett pulled back and gently pushed in again until his hips rested against my buttocks. I screamed as that wicked curve to his cock did its job.

Despite Brett's promise to throw my legs over his shoulders, he didn't. Instead I wrapped my legs around his waist and my arms around his neck, bringing his entire weight down on my body. We kissed furiously while he thrust powerfully inside me, working his hips frantically and bringing us both closer to orgasm. I arched my back and urged him on with groans and muttered exhortations. I delighted in his strength and stamina, grinding my hips into his so that he touched every single place inside me.

Finally his pace picked up, and I knew he was close.

Usually at about that stage, I would take matters into my own hand, jerking myself off so that I could come just before my lover, since there was nothing worse than being left wanting.

But with Brett I didn't need to. My erection was squashed between us, sliding over his hair-roughened stomach and providing me with plenty of stimulation.

"Neil!"

I recognized his shout for what it was—a warning of impending explosion—and gave myself permission to come. I could feel his cock brush over my prostate again and again in that final frenzy, and that did me in. My orgasm rushed in on me, shooting up between us in creamy jets and covering us with come. Brett hugged me tighter and came with a roar that was muted against my shoulder, jerking his hips uncontrollably and taking his pleasure in my body without shame.

Then 270 pounds of pure bear flesh collapsed on top of me.

I could feel my big man shaking with the force of his release, so I hugged him as tight as I could until he recovered enough to disengage. He flopped onto his back and I immediately followed him, cuddling up to that hairy chest and rubbing my face in his musk.

When I could catch my breath, I caressed his stomach in apology and said, "I have to get home, Brett. Jeannie's expecting me."

His arm tightened around me. "I know. I just wish it wasn't so. I want you here in my bed, not fifty steps away in the house across the street."

I didn't know what to say. I'd made a commitment to my sister and she was relying on me. No matter how sexy Brett was, and how well he blew my mind (and other things), I couldn't just drop the ball while Jeannie was depending on my support. I sighed softly and kissed Brett's hairy skin as it lay under my chest.

"Neil?" His voice was hushed in the half-light.

"Hmm?"

"Will you consider being my boyfriend?"

My eyes flew open in shock. That was *not* what I was expecting. "Ahh…." My vocal chords strangled and I couldn't get anything out.

Brett jumped in and started talking rapidly, coaxing me and trying to get me to agree. Unnecessarily. He didn't know it yet, but he'd had me at "hello."

"I mean, just to see how we go? I like you more than just a friend or a fuck buddy, and I'd really like to have a go at a relationship with you. I know you have your sister and the baby and the twins and all, and that's fine with me. I can tell you love them, and you can't just dump them, and I'm not asking you to. I'm just asking for dinner a couple of times a week, and perhaps a few sleepovers? Please, Neil?"

My vocal chords didn't work, but my hands and lips still did. I climbed on top of him and pressed a passionate kiss to his fuzzy face. Finally I was able to say to him, "Brett? Before getting ready to come out with you tonight, I googled to see what was the acceptable number of dates before you could ask someone to be your boyfriend. It seemed to vary between four dates and one month. So I decided to work on the one-month scenario. As of six o'clock tonight, one month was 720 hours away. It's now five hours later, so we must be down to about 715 hours."

"Do you mean I have to wait another 715 hours until I can ask you to be my boyfriend?" he asked in confusion.

I grinned. "No. It means that *I* was going to wait another 715 hours until I asked *you*. But it appears you've beaten me to the punch."

The information sank in, and the next thing I knew Brett was laughing uproariously, squeezing me tightly to his chest. "So is that your way of saying yes?"

"Oh God, yes!" We kissed for another minute before I pulled away with regret. "But I meant what I said. I need to get home."

I dressed quickly while he watched despondently. "Neil? You didn't promise to live with your sister until the baby is eighteen, did you?"

I snorted. "I'm not that dumb. No—I promised I'd help her until she found her feet. The twins will be starting full-time school in five months. By that time Ari will be eight months old, and with any luck, sleeping through the night. I reckon Jeannie will be on her feet by then. She will still need a babysitter, and plenty of support, but I'm hoping that I can move out about then."

"Five months?" Brett asked.

"Yes."

He picked up his phone and began tapping at the icons. I pulled on my shoes and frowned over at him. "What is it?"

He smiled and tapped a bit more. "3672 hours."

"Until what?" I queried, perplexed.

"Until I can ask you to move in."

I stood and wrapped my arm around his waist. He was still shirtless, so I snuggled into his warmth and masculine scent. It was scary how natural it felt for his massive arm to wrap around my waist and draw me close. "Brett? I'll be counting."

I kissed him firmly and left, briskly walking across the street to my sister's house with the scent of his musk still clinging to my skin and his promise ringing in my ears.

RENAE KAYE is a lover and hoarder of books who thinks libraries are devilish places because they make you give the books back. She consumed her first adult romance book at the tender age of thirteen and hasn't stopped since. After years—and thousands of stories!—of not having book characters do what she wants, she decided she would write her own novel and found the characters still didn't do what she wanted. It hasn't stopped her, though. She believes that maybe one day the world will create a perfect couple—and it will be the most boring story ever. So until then she is stuck with quirky, snarky, and imperfect characters who just want their story told.

Renae lives in Perth, Western Australia, and writes in five-minute snatches between the demands of two kids, a forbearing husband, too many pets, too much housework, and her beloved veggie garden. She is a survivor of being the youngest in a large family and believes that laughter (and a good book) can cure anything.

You can contact her at renaekaye@iinet.net.au.

Life's Tiny Surprises
Tara Spears

Mac sat in the restaurant being his own piteous birthday party of one. Earlier at work there had been a cake—which he never even saw a piece of—and some of the other teachers had signed a card and left it near the coffee maker in the lounge, but it had been a rather mundane effort compared to other faculty birthday celebrations.

He'd been teaching at Griffin High School for four years now, and his fellow teachers were still nervous around Mac due to his large size and overly quiet nature. Of course his booming voice, which could be heard throughout the school when he was stopping a bullying incident, might have something to do with that. Yet, having been teased through school himself, he had zero tolerance for that sort of thing. People just assumed he had a mean streak, but he was actually pretty shy, an introvert, and always had been. He supposed he could make more of an effort, but it wasn't as if any of them had tried to get to know Mac either.

Then Tim had canceled on him, making up some excuse about work, like his brother always did. It was Mac's thirtieth birthday, for God's sake, and he couldn't find an hour for his only brother. Mac released a melancholy sigh.

However, rather than feeling sorry for himself in his apartment, he had opted to use the reservation and stew at Giordo's instead.

Maybe if Mac hadn't picked Giordo's his brother wouldn't have canceled. But the Italian restaurant was a place of comfort, somewhere he didn't have to keep his personality—hell, his sexuality—subdued. The owners, and Mac guessed most of the waiters, were gay, and the place was known for its diversity and welcoming nature.

"Are you ready to order, sir?"

Mac looked up at the waiter. God, Mac could fit him in his paw, he was so tiny.

He didn't need the menu, and he'd rather look at the cute waiter, anyway. "Um, oh what the hell, it's my birthday. Lobster ravioli."

"Excuse me, sir, I didn't hear you." The waiter leaned down, edging his ear toward Mac. The guy had three vacant holes dancing up the edge of his ear. Piercings must not be allowed while working. He wondered where else the little guy was pierced. Mac felt the flame travel up his neck. *And that is none of your business.* The kid couldn't be more than twenty, probably a student at University of Washington working his way through college.

"Sir?"

"Sorry. Lobster ravioli," he returned.

"Excellent choice. Would you care for a glass of wine with your meal?"

Did he just lean in closer? Mac swore he had. He could smell his aftershave—something musky and really... nice on him. Mac wasn't one for cologne, but it really *was* nice. It added just a hint of sensuality to the young man.

"Sir? The wine?" the waiter asked, and Mac was sure he heard amusement in his voice.

"Right. What do you recommend?"

"May I bring you a glass of our Albariño?" Now Mac was positive he leaned closer. "It's an unconventional choice, but it's surprisingly amazing with seafood," he said, his voice a titillating stroke along Mac's neck. His toes curled, and his face grew warmer. Definitely closer.

"That would be—" He cleared his throat, reaching for his water. "—fine." Mac's thick fingers closed over the goblet. Then he watched in horror as it slipped and tumbled onto the burgundy linen tablecloth. "Oh God, I'm sorry. They shouldn't allow people like me in nice restaurants. I can be such a klutz." Mac blotted at the spreading water with his napkin, completely abashed.

One cute young guy flirts with me and I fall apart. The worst part of this fiasco being that he knew the waiter probably worked everyone for a better tip. The kid would undoubtedly end the night laughing with the other waiters about how pathetic and easily played the big guy had been.

Mac jumped, upending the water carafe, when the waiter's hands closed over his. *Could he be any more destructive?* Mac decided not to answer that, since he knew the answer was a resounding *yes*. He'd always been too big for this world.

"Please, I'll take care of this." Mac heard the pity in his voice as the waiter expertly folded the tablecloth over, as if this sort of thing happened all the time. But Mac knew at a place like Giordo's, it didn't.

He kept his head down, feeling shamed. "I'm sorry, I think I've done enough damage. Can you please bring my bill?"

"Sir.... *Dammit.*"

Mac glanced up, eyebrows raised. The kids eyes were closed, his hands wedged in his black mop of hair.

"You don't recognize me." He let out a stiff laugh. "Of course you wouldn't." He opened his eyes and blinked. Mac couldn't help noticing they were an anguished deep blue. The kid was right, he didn't recognize him. "You rocked my world for five weeks. And I've never forgotten you."

Mac had never rocked anyone's world for even five days. He shook his head, completely confused. "I'm sorry?"

The kid's chin fell to his chest. "This was stupid of me. You subbed my senior English lit class while our teacher was out having her baby. I developed such a crush on you.... Damn." He met Mac's eyes. "When I saw you come in, I traded tables so I could serve you. Mr. Halloran, that crush, it never went away."

What high school kid crushes on a behemoth? Mac had only worked as a substitute his first year, which meant the *kid* was around twenty-five, and Jesus, he still remembered Mac's name. The kid, waiter—Mac zeroed in on his nametag—Jerrod, hands behind his back, chewed on his lip as he gazed consideringly at Mac.

Then he smiled, more of a smirk, actually. "I'd really appreciate the chance to make your birthday special."

Mac's jaw dropped. Kid—Jerrod was hitting on him and seemed to have heard him just fine earlier, which meant he really had been flirting with Mac.

Jerrod leaned toward him. "*Really* special...."

Mac snapped his mouth shut and cleared his throat. Jerrod wasn't being cocky. There was a sweet sincerity in his voice that had Mac taking notice. He'd been Jerrod's age, for God's sake, the last time he'd had sex with anyone other than himself. Honestly? He wasn't above a one-night stand, but Jerrod was so tiny, he wasn't sure it would prove to be very satisfactory. Even so, he found himself smiling through a raging blush, and nodding.

Jerrod's eyes widened as he asked apprehensively, "Really?"

"Against my better judgment."

"Oh my. I'm going to have sex with my teacher." Although the phrasing had Mac squirming, the breathless way Jerrod said it made even Mac's jaded cock take notice.

Jerrod glanced at a clock near the door. "I'm off in ten. I'll grab some food and, ah, yeah. Oh, here," he grabbed Mac's hands and dragged him from the booth. *Whoa*, tiny was stronger than he looked. He moved Mac to a clean booth, sighing when his hands gently pushed on Mac's chest. "Sit."

Jerrod was breathing excitedly, which set Mac's own inhalations into overdrive. He couldn't believe he could have this type of effect on such a petite, and yes, pretty—very pretty—man. Mac never looked at guys like Jerrod. He knew he wasn't in their league. Hell, Mac's league was a very small one. Mac wasn't exactly fat, more brutish than anything. Rather Neanderthalian actually, except he did walk upright. He had a lot of hair, everywhere, and he'd given up trimming long ago. He stroked his chin absently, feeling the 10 grit there. He should probably shave, or he might tear that perfect sun-kissed skin to pieces.

With another rather dreamy sigh, Jerrod walked off, and Mac watched his pert little ass until it disappeared behind a set of swinging doors. Glancing out the rain-spattered window at bustling Pioneer Square, he wondered what the hell he thought he was doing. Sex would be nice, but it wasn't what he really wanted. Well, right now, actually, it was. However, he knew in the morning he would be left feeling empty and lonely. Guys never stayed with him, never called him, never returned his calls. He was pretty sure most of the guys he had slept with—he snorted, because they never slept, they never even stayed to cuddle, and Mac loved to cuddle—only did so out of curiosity. They wanted to conquer the big bear. Disgusted as much with himself as anything, he had quit trying years ago, quit looking altogether. But Jerrod… this was different.

His hands slapped over his face. Who was he kidding? This wouldn't be any different. Once Jerrod saw all the hair, the gut, the man-boobs with the monstrous nipples, he'd stay long enough to get off, then he'd leave.

"Please, don't be having second thoughts."

Dropping his hands, Mac barely missed knocking over the glass of white wine Jerrod had set in front of him. "I'm way past second thoughts," Mac admitted.

"Mr. Halloran—"

"Mac."

He smiled. "Mac, I've been waiting seven years for this. I know it sounds ridiculous, but I've been hoping I'd find you again, just a chance encounter. I even tried to find you online...." Jerrod fingered the edge of the tablecloth, a frown marring that pretty face of his.

"I don't like the Internet," Mac said, trying to act nonchalant, but actually blown away by what he was hearing.

He nodded. "I figured. That or you were a really private person. The Seattle school district website doesn't even have an e-mail address for you." He gave Mac an adorably imploring look. "Please don't run."

Mac blinked at him, surprised the kid—Jerrod—had read him so well. He hated feeling hope eating away his insides. Why did he always have to make these simple things so complicated by allowing his emotions to rule rather than good old-fashioned lust?

He gave Jerrod a tentative smile. "I promise I won't run."

In the five minutes it took Jerrod to return, Mac had emptied the wineglass. Upon seeing him still waiting, a relieved smile crossed Jerrod's face, bringing up a dimple on his left cheek. Mac loved dimples, no matter where they were. Maybe it was an omen... probably not.

"I have roommates... but, um...."

Mac chuckled at his obvious fishing. "I'm a two-minute ride on number 74."

"I'm not touching that one."

Mac gave him a quizzical glance.

Jerrod bit his lip. "Two-minute ride?"

Mac blushed. It had been a long time, but he was sure he had longer than two minutes in him... at least the second time around, anyway.

BEING AS it was Friday night, the bus was crowded with bar hoppers— some drunk, some past drunk, and some still trying to get there. Jerrod pressed himself against Mac as people jostled against him, and Mac found himself wanting to pick Jerrod up and tuck him under his coat for safekeeping. The little guy barely came up to Mac's chest, and the girl next to them kept stepping on him and giggling her apology. He was tough, though, and each time someone knocked against him, he glared and shoved back.

AS MAC unlocked the door, he glanced at Jerrod and apologized. "It's not much, teacher's salary and all."

"I share a two-bedroom loft with four guys and a girl, and I sleep on the couch. At least you have privacy."

"And I do have my own bed." *If that isn't shameless flirting.*

Jerrod's tongue made an appearance—Mac hadn't noticed the tongue stud before. "That's... definitely a plus," Jerrod said, his hand traveling down Mac's back.

He followed Mac in without hesitation and headed straight for the open kitchen with the bag of food. Locking the door, Mac set the chain. Then turning, he squeaked—honest-to-God squeaked—like a stepped-on mouse when he saw Jerrod pull his cock free of his black slacks. Mac's ass clenched, and he couldn't stop staring. For such a tiny thing, Jerrod was long. Mac watched a little porn—okay, at times a lot of porn—and most of the guys hung like that had a hard time getting it up. Jerrod, however, didn't seem to have that problem.

Jerrod gave himself a stroke. "God, that's better. I've been hard since you walked into Giordo's." Letting his coat slide to the floor, he set his eyes on Mac. *Oh shit*. He'd let some sexual predator in, he just knew it. Jerrod stalked toward him, unbuttoning his white shirt as he advanced. Predator or no, it was a thing of beauty, the way he moved with such confidence, one foot stepping lightly in front of the other, narrowed sapphire eyes never straying from Mac's face.

The keys *clunked* onto the tile. Mac left them where they fell.

Jerrod stepped in front of him, and Mac noticed he wasn't quite as in control as he appeared. His hands trembled as they reached for the buttons on Mac's lavender shirt.

"I thought we were going to eat?" *What a stupid question.*

"Later...." Jerrod met his eyes just as his hands met Mac's furry chest. Jerrod's eyelids fluttered as a moan escaped. Mac's dick strained against his wool slacks at the erotic sound. He couldn't remember anyone ever moaning just from touching him. Jerrod's fingers traveled through Mac's thick blond mat, then a gasp escaped as Jerrod rutted his cock against Mac's thigh. Mac hadn't even touched him, and Jerrod was going to get off from fondling his chest and humping his leg.

Oh God, that was sexy. Food could definitely wait. Maybe until tomorrow, even.

Mac's tie was jerked, then really yanked, pulling his head down. He opened his eyes, wondering when he had closed them, just as Jerrod's mouth crashed into his. The kiss was sloppy, and wild, and so wonderful. After a moment Mac realized Jerrod was still tugging on his tie, so Mac slid his hands under the waistband of Jerrod's black slacks and hoisted him up by that beautiful, pert ass of his.

Jerrod's arms immediately slithered around his neck, while his legs wound around Mac's waist. God, he was petite. Mac's arms engulfed him, and oddly that did something for Mac. Hell, it did a *lot* for him. And suddenly he wanted nothing more than to be naked and let this tiny man climb all over him. Much like he was doing now, only without all this clothing in the way. Mac headed for the bedroom.

The movement drew Jerrod's attention, and he pulled away, glancing around.

"Bedroom, bed," Mac informed him.

"Oh," Jerrod said, a little dazed. Then he grinned at Mac in a way that sent Mac's heart into overdrive. "Sorry, I guess I got excited."

Mac didn't like the thoughts shoving for attention in his mind. He'd rather take this for what it was. Even so, he found himself asking, "What's a guy like you doing with a guy like me?" He almost groaned at how cliché that sounded.

Jerrod looked down at Mac's chest, then wiggled down and gently laid his lips there before settling his eyes back on Mac. Yeah, Mac was a softy, and that was incredibly touching. Mac stopped inside his room and waited, really wanting to know Jerrod's answer.

Jerrod smiled shyly. "Ever since I was little, I slept with pillows all around me. When I realized I was gay—you know, no interest in girls—the guys I dated didn't do much for me either. They were cute, and muscly, but something was missing. Then you walked into class that day, and I got the biggest boner." Mac tried not to laugh at that, but failed. Jerrod grinned back. "Yeah, you can imagine the embarrassment. Anyway, I knew. From then on I only saw myself with someone like you." He cuddled into Mac's chest and let out a sigh. "But you know… you're hard to find."

Mac didn't know what to say to that. No one had ever made him feel so special, so wanted. Mac nestled him deeper against his chest and held on to him, wondering if he could keep him, just for a little while.

MAC JERKED when Jerrod's mouth went where no man's had gone before. He was making all Mac's fantasies come true in one amazing and exhausting evening. First an overly exuberant blow job and now.... Mac scrabbled for purchase as Jerrod's tongue lashed over Mac's hole. *Tongue stud... uhhnnnmmm.* Biting the pillow, Mac groaned as Jerrod spread his ass cheeks wider, his mouth humming against him. God, Jerrod had no idea what he was doing to Mac. Hell, he had no clue this was one of Mac's most private fantasies. Most of his porn collection contained some pretty rough rimming scenes, and Mac could shoot just watching them. Not in his wildest dreams had he imagined it ever happening to him, though.

"Lube?"

"Mmm?"

Jerrod chuckled. "I may be drooling, but I think lube would be better."

"Oh, right... um," Mac yanked open his nightstand drawer, pulling it right off the stays and causing it to crash to the floor. He looked at the mess, then slumped over the edge of the bed. "Damn it. I don't have any condoms." Once he quit going to bars, Mac hadn't seen the point of wasting money on them.

"I have a few." Jerrod scrabbled off the bed, retrieving his pants off the dresser mirror where they had landed during their frenzied undressing.

Even though Mac used to carry them around too, he still felt a pinch of remorse over the fact Jerrod had them in his wallet.

"I see that look, and I'm not *that* active." He shrugged. "What else can I say, other than I'm a guy." He grabbed the bottle of lube Mac was reaching for and straddled his back.

"Yeah, I was a guy once too," Mac said, enjoying the heat against his skin, the weight of Jerrod on top of him.

Jerrod kissed the small of Mac's back. "Okay, *old man*, let's see if you still remember what it's all about." Jerrod's thumb caressed, and then he pushed in without hesitation.

Mac's back arched. "*God,* that feels good."
Jerrod chuckled. "He remembers...."

JERROD'S SEX drive eclipsed Mac's a hundred times over at least. Either that, or Jerrod really couldn't get enough of Mac's body. *God, what a lovely thought.* And, man oh man, he fucked like the Energizer Bunny. Once he got going, Mac didn't even have time to think before he was caught up in a blinding orgasm. He was thinking now, though, and wow—orgasms like that didn't happen often in Mac's world. Mac had an ample ass, and most guys had a hard time staying inside him, which made sex... unsatisfying. But Jerrod didn't appear to have any trouble working his cock, and oh man, it was welcome back anytime... as long as Jerrod was operating it, of course.

Mere moments after Jerrod's last forceful thrust, he had tossed the condom, and still trembling, crawled beneath Mac's arm. With a few tugs on Mac's limbs, he completely enclosed himself within the circle of Mac's body. This was as close to bliss as Mac had ever been.

Mac was afraid if he spoke, if he moved, this perfect moment would evaporate before his very eyes. But he couldn't resist touching him. Dipping his head, he pressed his lips against the back of Jerrod's neck. He smelled so good. Like life, and youth, and desire, a smidge of garlic, probably from the restaurant, and a hint of the same soap Mac used. Jerrod wriggled, and somehow managed to tuck himself in even tighter against Mac's chest.

"Do I need to go?" Jerrod asked quietly.

"You want to stay?" Mac asked, unable to keep the surprise out of his voice.

"Very much."

Mac tried not to squeeze him to death. "I'd love that."

"Me too. Happy Birthday, Mac."

"Thank you for making it special."

Jerrod lifted Mac's hand, placing his lips against his palm. "Such a wonderful dream... I can't believe part of it came true."

Mac wasn't sure what Jerrod had meant by that, and didn't have a chance to ask. Jerrod began softly snoring.

TWO WEEKS later Mac was still waking every morning with Jerrod encased in his arms. He'd never been so satisfied or more scared in his life.

TWO MONTHS later Jerrod told Mac he loved him. He never imagined how good hearing that could feel. But he was still afraid he would wake to find Jerrod gone. Leaving him with just a glimpse of what he would never truly have.

TWO YEARS later Jerrod asked Mac to be his husband.

"I've always felt we belonged together. Mac, make my dream come true…. Marry me."

It was the first time Mac had ever cried, and he cried for days.

NOW TWENTY years later he'd managed to make Mac cry again.

"Hey—" Jerrod pulled Mac's hands from his face. "—this is supposed to be a happy day, celebrating when you came back to me."

Sniffling, Mac managed a nod as he took in the candlelit apartment strewn with white rose petals and overflowing with daylilies. The smells from the kitchen were luscious—olive oil, oregano, basil, cilantro….

Mac looked down into Jerrod's bright eyes. "You cooked?"

He smiled at Mac's teasing. "Yes, I actually cooked."

Despite being a chef, Jerrod rarely cooked at home, preferring to bring something back from the restaurant, usually prepared by his sous chef. But when Jerrod did cook, it was always something special just for them.

Mac's hands slid around and gently squeezed Jerrod's bare ass. "Like this?"

"I'm wearing an apron," he shot back.

Mac grinned as he pulled the tails of the perfect bow resting against the small of Jerrod's back. "Not anymore…." The frilly thing fell, catching on Jerrod's hard cock. Tugging the apron off, Mac ran a hand along Jerrod's length, watching as his husband's eyes warmed and his cheeks flushed. "I never would have imagined you'd still find me sexy after all these years." Mac's voice shook, tumbling over so many emotions.

Jerrod reached up and wiped Mac's cheeks. "Oh, hon, you've always been the sexiest man in the world to me. And that will never change."

Mac scooped Jerrod up and kissed him as he carried him to their bedroom. God, he hoped he was still able to do this in another twenty years.

Laughing, Jerrod pulled his lips free. "I thought we'd eat—"

"Later," Mac growled.

TARA SPEARS is rooted in the damp PNW, calling slugs her friends, and letting moss take over her yard. She began writing two years ago due to circumstances beyond her control, and when not running around a barrel pattern at thirty-five M.P.H on one of her horses (something that even the above circumstance couldn't take from her), she can be found staring at her computer and occasionally typing a word or two.

She had a rather wild youth and she has quieted considerably. However, you wouldn't know this by some of her books.

She spends a lot of time in her mind, and even her husband has to find her at times and draw her back to the real world with the promise of new books, or coffee—coffee always works.

Visit Tara's blog at http://www.taraspearswrites.blogspot.com

E-mail her at taraspearswrites@gmail.com

Or you can follow her on Facebook: Tara Spears

The Bear King of Snowbird Mountain

Michael Rupured

Flying high above the clouds fit my mood. Free at last. "If I'd known how good dumping the two-timing bastard would feel, I'd have kicked his sorry ass out a long time ago."

"You did the right thing." She patted my arm. "He had his chance—one more than I would have given him."

The landing gear whirred into place as we broke through the clouds. Upon boarding, the attractive young woman beside me had introduced herself and struck up a conversation. The book I'd brought with me, *A Bear Growls in Brooklyn*, remained in my backpack, untouched. "I'm sorry. I hope I haven't bored you."

"Not at all, Jeremy." She smiled. "I feel like I've known you forever."

"I feel the same way about you." I couldn't remember her name. No doubt I'd have paid more attention had I known we'd spend the next two hours discussing the rise and fall of my seven-year relationship with Mark Alonzo.

"Don't sit in your hotel room all weekend working on landscape plans. DuPont Circle is a great area for walking around." She pulled a business card from her purse and handed it to me. "If you get lonely before your conference starts on Monday, call me."

I glanced at the card. The savings from staying over Saturday night more than covered the extra night of lodging. I'd brought along several designs to work on and hoped to spend a few hours around the hotel swimming pool this afternoon and most of Sunday. "Thanks, Elizabeth. I just might do that."

She extended her hand. "Please do. I'm working on year-end reports all weekend and would welcome the break." She pointed down the corridor. "Luggage carousels are that way. Are you sure you don't want to ride the Metro? I don't mind waiting for you."

The e-mail message I'd printed out and brought with me included directions for taking the Metro to the conference hotel. But my fear of getting lost, wandering into a crime-ridden area of town, and washing up a few days later on the shore of a nearby river suggested the door-to-door services of a cab—something else I'd never done before. "No, really. I'll be fine. Thanks again." I shook her hand and then waved as she rolled her bag toward the Metro stop.

Mark's voice in my head ordered me to stop slouching. I took a deep breath, straightened my neck, and drew back my shoulders. Elizabeth had pointed out how Mark's criticism had escalated in direct proportion to my success. She was right. I'd outgrown him, but had been distracted from the truth by his constant harping about my weight, my attitude, the way I dressed, my stupid landscaping business, my friends, my family, and how snobby I'd become since finishing college.

I'd gone to the beach a few times with my family growing up. Otherwise, before the business took off, travel hadn't been in the budget. Being on my own for the first time in a city like Washington, DC was exhilarating, intoxicating, and absolutely terrifying. All around me, people carried on conversations in unfamiliar languages wearing clothes I'd only seen on the covers of the *National Geographic* magazines at the barbershop back home in Del Rio. I gawked at the monuments I'd seen on television and prayed the driver wouldn't wreck.

In no time, the cab pulled up in front of the hotel and stopped. I gave him the fare plus a tip and wracked my brain to come up with a little extra something more valuable than money, like Momma taught me to do. "Planting marigolds around your tomatoes keeps the bugs away."

"You don't say." He snorted, shook his head, and then pulled into traffic. The reaction surprised me. Perhaps he didn't garden. Next time, I'd try to come up with something more generic. I picked up my suitcase, walked up the steps through the revolving door, and made my way to the front desk.

"Checking in?"

I nodded and stepped toward the smiling young woman in the hotel blazer with *Monique* stamped in black letters on her gold name badge. "Jeremy Jenkins. I have a reservation."

She ran her finger down a list. "Yes, Mr. Jenkins." She snickered. "You're here with A-N-A-L?"

"Yes, ma'am." I nodded again. "It's A-N-U-A-L—like the flowers. The Association of Non-Urban American Landscapers."

She smiled. "Sorry. They left the U out for your group code. I just need to see your credit card and a picture ID."

I handed her my Tennessee driver's license and my only credit card. "Where's the pool?"

"I'm sorry, Mr. Jenkins. The pool is closed for renovations." She handed me a little envelope. "Your room number is written inside. The elevators are just around the corner to your left. Enjoy your stay!"

"Rinsing with white vinegar will really make your hair shine."

Concern washed over her face and she ran her fingers through her hair. "Uh, okay. Thanks for the tip."

At least she hadn't snorted or shaken her head. I pushed the button for the ninth floor, and my stomach dropped as the elevator lurched into motion. My room was at the end of the hall, across from the ice and vending machines. The fourth time I inserted and removed the key card, the little light turned green and I opened the door.

Stuffy. I cranked the air conditioning as low as it would go, unpacked, and stashed my suitcase in the closet. No pool access changed everything. The room was nice, with a king-sized bed and a view of the busy street below, but staying in all weekend and working on the plans I'd brought along didn't appeal to me. Inspired by the sight of so many people walking around, I changed into shorts, a T-shirt, and comfortable shoes to explore and maybe look for something to eat.

Opting to keep the sun on my back rather than in my eyes, I joined the stream of people heading east. An international parade passed by me as a smorgasbord of aromas ranging from the awful to the sublime escaped from restaurants and alleys. A cacophony of blaring horns, jackhammers, sirens, and roaring engines went unnoticed by the men and women hurrying along the sidewalk. After so long under Mark's ever-watchful and distrusting eye, I savored my invisibility.

I came to the kind of intersection that kept me from trying to drive in places like DC. Half a dozen roads came together in concentric circles around a little park. I crossed over four lanes of traffic to take a closer look at the statuary comprising an ornate fountain in the center.

The big man by the fountain would stand out in any crowd. He looked like the actor who played Hercules on television—I never can remember his name. Tall, tan, and the most muscular man I'd ever seen in the flesh, he had a buzz cut and wore mirrored shades, a plaid shirt with the sleeves ripped out, tiny cutoff blue jeans, and construction boots. Mark would have called him a San Francisco clone—the gay equivalent of a hoochy momma. I'd seen the same look in porn, but never in person, and I tried not to stare.

I wasn't the only one. Several guys approached him, all rebuffed with a shake of his head and words I couldn't hear. He turned toward me with his furry legs slightly apart and his hands on his hips. Were the eyes behind those mirrored lenses watching me?

Like every gay man who ever lived, I'd fantasized about random encounters—with guys who didn't come close to being as hot as this one. Nobody like the men in my fantasies lived in Del Rio. Until now, they'd been just figments of my imagination. He smiled and nodded in my direction. I darted a quick glance behind me but saw no one looking his way. He waved. I stopped and pointed to myself. "Me?"

He nodded again and flashed pearly white teeth. "Yeah, you, hot stuff. I've been waiting for you." He pushed his shades up over his eyebrows and offered me his hand. "Donald Matthews. Thrilled to finally meet you."

His words made no sense. Waiting for me? Thrilled to finally meet me? Having seen him fend off the advances of everyone who'd approached him, his affable demeanor surprised me almost as much as what he'd said. I shook his hand, the jolt from his firm grasp exploding somewhere in my gonads. "Jeremy Jenkins." He kept squeezing my hand, caressing my palm with his thumb. Then he let go and draped his muscular arm across my shoulder. I thought I'd swoon. My fantasies had never moved this fast.

"Damn. Love those big bedroom eyes. Staying around here?"

I nodded, too shocked for words. Even ugly guys with gym bods like his didn't pay much attention to the likes of me. Warning bells went off in the back of my mind. If it sounds too good to be true....

He squeezed my shoulder. "Good. Want to show me your room?"

I looked at him, wondering if this was some kind of scam. At six foot two, I'm a big guy. Donald was at least six foot five and built like a brick shithouse. Rape was more wishful thinking than a serious concern, but I did worry he might beat me up and steal my wallet. "Are you serious?"

"Never been more serious in my life." Turning me toward him, he leaned down, pulled me close, and rammed his tongue into my mouth with a force I felt all the way down to my toes. I pushed him away with both hands, looking around to see if anyone had seen us. He smiled. "You're the only reason I came to DC this weekend."

"You're full of shit." He fucked me with his eyes. I'm not kidding! With just a look, the man ripped off my clothes, threw me down, and fucked me. My knees trembled, and though never a smoker, I had a sudden, strong desire for a cigarette.

"I'm kind of spoiled," he said, dazzling me with his electric smile. "You might as well give me what I want before I throw a big tantrum right here in DuPont Circle."

Who could resist Hercules? I didn't care if he did rob me. "Well, if you insist...."

"I do," he said, fucking me with his eyes again.

Ten minutes later, having fended off his advances in the elevator and down the long hall to my room, I closed the door to my still stuffy room behind us and turned around. Donald ripped off his shirt and motioned me toward him. I knew women back in Del Rio who'd kill to have boobs the size of his pecs. He wrapped his arms around my waist, pulled me up against him, and kissed me again.

This time I didn't hold back, returning his kisses with an unfamiliar fervor, savoring his earthy scent—like moss on a forest floor. He broke off, gasping. "Damn, where have you been all my life?"

"Del Rio, Tennessee."

He laughed and resumed his assault, moving his lips to each of my eyebrows and down my cheeks. He tickled my lips with the tip of his tongue, his firm grasp on my ass cheeks forcing me onto my tiptoes. I looped my arms around his neck, pinching the back of my hand hard to make sure I was awake. This was no dream. The men in my dreams didn't hold a candle to the tall, dark, handsome hunk who couldn't keep his hands off me.

We kissed with our eyes open—gauging reactions more than giving loving gazes. I slid a hand over his rock hard shoulder and across his matted chest. He gasped when I pinched his nipple, so I lowered my other hand, rolling nipples the size of pencil erasers between my thumb and forefinger as he moaned. I pinched again, hard. He growled and clenched my bottom lip between his teeth. I pinched harder and he let go of my lip with a gasp.

"Let's see what you're hiding under those clothes." He pulled my T-shirt over my head, stopping to tease my nipples with his teeth, then licking and sniffing his way up my chest and neck to claim my mouth again. He wrestled with my belt buckle and then the clasp and zipper until my shorts fell to the floor, sliding my boxer shorts down my hips as he dropped to his knees before me.

I gasped and grabbed his head to keep from falling as my cock disappeared into his mouth. The real thing topped my random hookup fantasies. Watching Donald suck me was better than any porn I'd ever seen. I slid my hands over his shoulders and he lifted his arms, flexing his biceps beneath my grasp. I grabbed his head again, pulling free of his hungry mouth to keep from coming. He stood up and kissed me again—urgent, demanding kisses telegraphing his need as he pushed me down onto the bed, yanking my shorts and underwear off over my tennis shoes.

"Damn." He ran his hands over my thighs, along my hips, and up to my chest. "You're even hotter than I'd imagined." He tossed a shoe over each shoulder.

I looked over my belly and studied the handsome face between my knees for some sign he was joking. His attention was focused on the head of my rigid cock as his hand massaged the shaft. The intensity of his gaze and the way he kept sniffing me turned me on. Shit. Everything about Donald turned me on. I tried to sit up, but he pushed me back down on the bed.

"Relax." He lowered his head and kissed my balls, milking my cock with one hand, twisting my nipple with the other. He inhaled deeply, then groaned and flattened his tongue against my scrotum. "Hmmm. Sweeter than honey."

I moaned and clutched his ears to pull his head away, but he was too strong. He tightened his grip around the base of my cock and moved his hand up the shaft, stopping now and then to lick a drop of precum from the head.

"That's so fucking hot." He milked out another drop onto his tongue and groaned.

"Yeah, hot," I said, panting. The man played me like a fiddle, taking me right up to the edge again and again and then stopping. Leaving no moan, gasp, or groan unturned, his oral and olfactory exploration produced a map of receptive areas he returned to with increasing precision and effect. My squirming and writhing to escape the exquisite torture fueled his passion, but I couldn't stop.

I gasped as my cock disappeared into his mouth again. My hands flew to his head, but he grabbed my wrists, pinning my arms to the bed, rendering me helpless. I'd never been so turned on in my life. Hell, back in Del Rio, a picture of a shirtless Donald would have been enough to get me off for weeks. In my fantasies, our places would be reversed, but I wasn't going to argue. Having him worship my cock for however long it had been was much hotter than anything I'd ever imagined.

His grip tightened on my wrists. I squirmed and tried to push him away with my legs, but he shifted position, pinning my thighs against the mattress with his upper arms. Other than rolling my head back and forth, I couldn't move. He tightened his grip on my wrists and intensified his oral assault on my cock.

Too helpless to do anything to stop him, I submitted. The tension of resistance drained from my body, and I relaxed. Donald licked the head of my cock, watching my face as the shaft slid past his lips until his nose was buried in my pubic hair. With no outward indication he was doing anything, an undulating pressure massaged the length of my cock. He held my gaze. My world narrowed to his brown eyes and the relentless, exquisite pressure moving up and down my cock.

"I'm going to cum." This announcement had always before been an unnecessary statement of the obvious. But then, sex with Mark had never lasted more than three or four minutes—tops. For him, taking condoms and lube out of the drawer was foreplay. The tingling in my balls intensified. I threw back my head and closed my eyes, breathing hard, my attention riveted to the mounting pressure and pending explosion of release.

I cried out, and my body jerked several times. Donald moaned, low rumbles in his throat that I felt in my cock. He let go of my wrists, milking my cock to make sure he got every drop. I grabbed under his arms and pulled. He stood up and I reached over to unfasten his shorts, skimpy enough we had no trouble slipping them off over his boots. He pushed me back onto the mattress and started to climb in beside me.

"Stop!"

He looked at me, confused.

"I just want to look at you a minute." He could have been Michelangelo's model, only hairier—a lot hairier. Rather than tightly curled, the hair all over his body was straight and didn't appear to have ever been trimmed. The bearish man flexed his muscles, showing off every angle with a number of different poses. An ornate tattoo on his left shoulder of a bear paw under a pair of crossed eagle feathers drew my eye. His goofy expressions with each shift in position made me laugh. Despite his size and obvious power, his affable and amiable demeanor kept him from coming across as menacing or threatening.

I'd never been so attracted to anyone in my life. The whole experience was surreal, and way hotter than anything I'd ever imagined. Every detail of his ursine form fanned the flames of lust he'd ignited in me. From head to toe, he was a gorgeous specimen. In a picture with no obvious reference to his height, his cock would appear to be about average. Up close and personal, the thickly veined, fully erect appendage was more than a little intimidating.

Donald smiled. "Why just look when you can touch?"

Seeing no reason to argue, I wiggled my finger. "Come here."

He slid in beside me, boots and all. Had we been in my bed back in Del Rio, I might have made him take them off. As these weren't my sheets, I didn't care. We snuggled up nose to nose and held each other tight. I brushed my fingers through his short hair, and his cock bounced against my thigh.

He rolled onto his back, pulling me down on top of him for more kisses. The fur on his chest glistened with sweat. I straddled him and held his wrists over his head on the pillow, knowing he could break free whenever he wanted, and smiled. "My turn."

"Take what you want," he said. "I'm all yours."

Faced with an appetizing buffet of all my favorite dishes, I didn't know where to start. His kisses curled my toes. I wanted to lick him all over, bury my face in his hairy chest, feel his hips pounding against me and know how that big cock felt inside me. Too bad I hadn't brought any lube or condoms with me. Hooking up had been the farthest thing from my mind when I'd packed. I flicked his swollen lips with my tongue, licking my way down the hollow of his neck and back up to his ear. Releasing his wrists, I slid my hands down his forearms to melon-sized biceps too big for me to wrap my hands around, sliding my balls up and down the twin mounds of his muscled chest and teasing his cock with my butt cheeks.

Time ceased to register, not stopping, but no longer mattering as we explored each other's bodies with hungry mouths and curious hands.

Everything about him pleased me—generous, considerate, and smoking hot. I wanted to please him too. "What do you want?"

"You," he replied. "Until the end of time." He pulled me down on top of him and kissed me again, shifting position, raising his knees and squeezing me between his thighs as he explored my mouth with his tongue. My fully restored erection pressed against the tight ring blocking access to unimagined pleasure. He grabbed my cock and squeezed, rubbing the head against his hole. "Fuck." He groaned. "Your cock is oozing buckets of precum."

No surprise there. My cup runneth over. Prior to meeting Donald, I hadn't gotten off in weeks—months, if jacking off didn't count. With enough time, a little lotion, and even mediocre porn, I could get off three times—on my worst day. With a man like Donald and enough bottled water to keep me from getting dehydrated, I was ready to shoot for a world record. I latched onto his nipple, sucking for a moment and then alternating between bites and flicks of my tongue. He palmed the back of my head and held my mouth against his chest. "Fuck yeah, bite it."

I complied and he jerked, forcing the head of my dick into his ass. We both gasped and I froze, fearful my lube-free penetration had hurt him. He grabbed my hips and pulled, lifting his legs until his knees were on my shoulders, sending my cock deeper. I rose up on my knees, pulled back, and then plunged my cock as hard as I could into his luscious ass.

Nothing I'd seen in person, in magazines, or in the hundreds of hours of porn I'd watched prepared me for his orgasm. Before I could pull back for another thrust, he tensed, grunted, and shot the mother lode across his chest, neck, and left ear. I came again before his second gush hit the headboard and was too shocked by the third geyser to say for sure whether he stopped at four or five.

"Sorry about that," he said, embarrassed. "Look at the mess I've made."

I couldn't look away. I'd never seen so much jizz in one place. "Do you always cum like that?"

He nodded. "Most of the time. Sometimes more." He sat up. "Shower?"

"Yeah, and then we've got to get some food. I'm starving."

SHOWERING TOGETHER hadn't saved us any time, and used far more water. Soaping each other up hadn't saved any time either, though I don't think I'd ever been so clean. One thing for sure—I'd never walk the same way again. Whoever said size doesn't matter hadn't met Donald.

By the time we left the hotel, the sun had set. If anything, there were more people out than I'd seen earlier when I'd first run into Donald. "What are you in the mood for?"

He draped his arm over my shoulder and pulled me close. "More of your ass."

I poked him in the ribs. "To eat, silly."

"Same answer." He kissed the top of my head.

Public displays of affection really weren't my thing. Hell, back in Del Rio, the way Donald was making over me might have gotten us killed. But I didn't mind one little bit here in what Donald said was the gay part of DC. Given all the attention he'd received at the fountain, he shouldn't have had to tell me, but until he'd said something, I hadn't noticed the rainbow flags on every building and the absence of all but a handful of women. Call me oblivious.

Aside from wanting to rip off his clothes, walking along Seventeenth Street with Donald was nice. I couldn't get over all the good-looking men around us. Wherever we went, all eyes were on him—and would have been, even if he hadn't still been wearing his Daisy Dukes, cutoff shirt, and construction boots—but he only had eyes for me.

Setting aside the ridiculous notion of love at first sight, I was head over heels in lust. The four guys I'd slept with before Donald had each only seen one side of me. Two had brought out my inner top. In between my bottom boyfriends, I'd spent a few months with a total top. And Mark had claimed to be versatile but was really more of a do-me queen.

Donald tapped into my inner nymphomaniac. Whatever he did to me, I wanted to do to him. Hard, easy, slow, fast. I didn't care. The man was a god, and I'd be only too happy to spend the rest of my life worshipping at his altar. No surprise there. The guys who saw us together must have thought I'd out-punted my coverage. I couldn't disagree. Donald's obvious interest in me was the shock that kept on shocking.

"How about here?" He'd stopped to read a menu, stapled to a board with today's specials printed below in colored chalk. "Looks like they've got something for everyone."

"Sure. Looks good to me," I said, not bothering to look. Unlike Mark, I wasn't afraid to try something new. A pretty young man in a green T-shirt with "I <3 Dicks" emblazoned across the front guided us to a table for two next to the sidewalk. "Enjoy," he said, slapping two menus on the table, staring at Donald the entire time like I didn't even exist.

Donald ignored him, flashing me his dazzling smile as he pulled my chair out from the table. "Thank you," I said, taking my seat.

He studied his menu. "Every guy in the place is checking you out," he said, without looking up.

I glanced around the room. "They can't take their eyes off you." I looked back at him and smiled. "Me either."

He closed his menu and shrugged. "I could be a serial killer for all they know. Other than my appearance—something I don't have much control over—the shallow bitches don't know shit about me." He reached across the table and took my hands in his. "Once they decide they want me, they turn their attention to you, ripping you apart as they try to figure out what I see in you."

Being a shallow bitch, I fell into his big brown eyes and didn't care if I drowned. But I was more than a little curious, and since he'd brought it up, I had to ask. "What *do* you see in me?"

I shook free of his grasp and moved my hands to my lap after a gap-toothed waiter with a ring in his lip stopped to take our order. I hadn't even looked at the menu. "Go ahead, Donald. I haven't quite made up my mind yet."

Donald took the menu from me, adding it to his and handing them to the waiter. "We'll have steaks. Rib eyes." He turned to me. "Medium rare?"

I nodded.

"Baked potatoes with everything," he continued, "and tossed salad." He turned to me again. "Honey mustard dressing?"

I nodded again, happy to have the difficult decisions behind me. More than two or three options and my selection process shut down.

"And a bottle of Beaujolais Villages—any even-numbered year will do."

"Yes sir," the waiter said. Then he turned to me. "Shall I bring a glass for you, sir?"

"Uh, yeah. Whatever he's having is fine with me."

The waiter disappeared and Donald smiled. "He'll be rewarded with a big tip for asking you about that glass. I hope you didn't mind me ordering for you."

"Not at all, especially considering that's exactly what I probably would have ordered anyway, less the bowjiewhatsitsname."

"Red wine." He unwrapped his silverware and placed the napkin in his lap.

I did the same thing, with far less grace. My knife fell with a loud clank, and when I bent down to pick it up, my napkin fell to the floor.

"Don't worry about it, sir." The waiter had returned with two glasses in hand and a bottle of wine under his arm. "I'll bring you another."

Donald ordering the wine spared me the humiliation of failing to carry out properly a long, drawn-out ritual I'd never seen before. The waiter—a napkin draped over his arm—presented the bottle to Donald, and after obtaining his approval, removed the cork with a few deft motions, placing it on the table. Donald picked up the cork, sniffed, and nodded again. The waiter poured a little wine into the bottom of his glass. Donald twirled the liquid around a few times, sniffed like the glass contained good coffee, and took a sip. "Perfect."

After filling my glass, the waiter left—returning with a napkin and a knife before I'd even had a chance to sample the wine. "I'll be right back with your salads."

"This could get expensive," Donald smiled. "He's already up to a twenty-five percent tip, and we don't even have any food yet." He raised his glass. "To us."

I touched his glass with mine. "To us." I wanted to look at my watch to see how many hours I'd known Donald. Not long enough to be toasting our future together. Not that I minded. To tell you the truth, I couldn't think of anything I'd rather do than spend the rest of my days gazing into his eyes.

Complete and sudden devotion wasn't really my style. Mark had pursued me for months before I'd agreed to a date for dinner. The idea of a random hookup appealed to me, but I'd never had the nerve. And yet, here I was, totally smitten with a guy I hadn't even known this morning.

He took a sip of his wine and looked over the glass at me. "As to what I see in you...."

I shook my head. "You don't owe me any explanation." He met my gaze. "I mean, we've only known each other such a short time."

"Time's a funny thing, don't you think?" He took another sip of wine, gesturing with his glass as he talked. "This moment passed hours ago on the other side of the world, and won't come for another hour or two, west of here." He lifted the bottle. "More wine?"

I nodded and he filled my glass and then his.

"And yet, now is now, no matter where you happen to be in the universe. We might call it two o'clock one place and five thirty somewhere else, but it's still now." He paused, studying my face for a long moment. "I see the beautiful man you are, that you have always been, and always will be—now—right this very moment."

The waiter materialized with our salads. "Fresh ground pepper?" I nodded, and an electric motor whirred until I waved my hand. He positioned the fancy grinder over Donald's plate. "And you, sir?" Donald nodded, the grinder whirred again, and the waiter disappeared.

I decided to change the subject and let the whole "what do you see in me" thing go. He'd only talked in riddles anyway, confusing me with nonanswers and tangents. "What do you do for work?"

He frowned. "My MBA is currently going to waste. I'm unemployed at the moment. Does it matter?"

I shrugged. "Not really. Just curious." Of course it didn't matter. We'd only just met. It wasn't like I was going to drag him back to Del Rio with me. What would the neighbors think? They'd be climbing over the fence and peeking through the windows to form an opinion. I decided to change the subject again. "I'm so glad I ran into you."

Donald shook his head. "You didn't run into me. I was waiting for you."

I looked at him. "But we've never met before."

He didn't say anything for a moment as he thought about his answer. "I've known we'd meet today by the fountain for some time now."

"Oh yeah?" Surely he was pulling my leg. "Since when?"

"Hmm, let me think." He scratched his head. "Seven years and nine months."

I gasped. "Impossible! I didn't even know about this conference until a few months ago."

Donald shrugged. "Yet here we are."

He reached for my hands, but I pulled away. "There's no way you could have known."

"Do you want me to leave?"

I couldn't read his face.

"I'd planned to stay with you until your conference starts Monday, but if—"

"How did you know?"

He rubbed his forehead and sighed. "You won't believe me."

"Try me."

He reached across the table and held my chin and my gaze. "You were promised to me."

"Promised?" Who besides me had the right to make such a big decision on my behalf? Part of me was annoyed, but the part that felt like I'd just won the lottery beat it back into the dark recesses of my mind. He nodded, his expression unchanged. What else did he know? Was he sincere or was this whole setup some kind of elaborate joke? "By whom?"

"More like by what."

"Okay then, by what?"

He gave me a sheepish grin. "Ouija board."

I laughed. "You're lying."

He shrugged. "Busted. But the truth isn't any easier to believe."

"I'm all ears." I picked up a fork—there were two, one a tad smaller than the longer-tined fork I decided to save for my steak—and speared a dressing-soaked lettuce leaf and crouton. "Are you an alien or something?"

He squirmed in his chair. "That would depend on exactly what you mean by 'alien.'"

My fork fell to the floor, and I thought I'd toss my salad. "You're from another planet?"

He shook his head. "No, I've always lived here on Earth." He paused for a minute. "My mother was human."

I grabbed my glass of wine and gulped the contents. "And what was your father?"

He blushed. "My great-great-grandmother, a full-blooded Cherokee, was a great shaman in the cult of the bear."

"The cult of the bear?" I was starting to have my doubts about Donald. Was he crazy? On drugs? Pulling my leg? I didn't know, and frankly, as I was unlikely to ever see him again, didn't much care. One look at his handsome face vaporized my concerns.

He nodded. "When the moon is full, the head of the cult turns into a bear and seeks a bride. If he finds a bride and mates with her, the tribe will see good hunting in the coming year. If not, many people will starve."

The waiter whisked away our empty salad plates, replacing them with our steaks and monstrous baked potatoes piled high with sour cream, cheese, bacon, and chives on big oval plates.

"Fearing they'd be raped by the man-bear, the women stayed inside whenever the moon was full. Month after month for several years, the night passed without the bear king taking a bride. The people stored whatever berries, nuts, and roots they could for the long cold winters, but many died of starvation every year.

"Every full moon, my grandmother urged the women to leave the village at night. But nobody listened, and again many people died over an especially long and hard winter. She tried again the following year, and after the women ignored her, roamed the forest herself when the moon was full. But the bear king wanted a young woman, strong enough to bear his child, and again the people suffered through a difficult winter.

"The next year, she sent her only daughter into the woods when the moon was full, only to have her return home the next morning, untouched save by mosquitos. But after the September full moon, she vanished. My great-great-grandmother searched the woods in vain until the morning after the first full moon of spring more than a year later, when she returned with a baby boy in her arms."

I gasped, unsure if I was hearing a legend, a fable, or the meanderings of a crazed man. "His father was the bear king?"

He nodded. "And on the last full moon before the winter of his eighteenth year, he was crowned the next bear king, to live out the rest of his days scavenging deep in the woods in his bear form whenever the moon is full."

"You're descended from bear kings?"

He nodded. "Yes, I am."

I didn't know what to think, but decided to humor him. "Did you become the bear king in the winter of your eighteenth year?"

He shook his head. "If I had, I wouldn't be here now." He smiled.

"Wait a minute. How old are you?"

"I'll be twenty-six in September."

I counted on my fingers for a minute. "So seven years and nine months ago, you should have turned into a bear when the moon was full."

He nodded. "The day of the full moon, I asked my mother—a powerful seer—what would become of me if I refused the crown. She cast her stones in the reflecting pool and showed me a long, happy life… with you." He shrugged. "Aside from being gay, I've never really wanted kids anyway. With people relying more on grocery stores than hunting or fishing, nobody went hungry when I turned down the job. Two years later, my little brother happily accepted the chief's bear-claw necklace, continuing the tradition and prowling the woods when the moon is full in search of a bride."

I sat quiet for a long moment, chewing my steak, trying to process what I'd just heard. "So, you're like… a werebear?"

He laughed. "I've never heard it put that way, but if you mean like a werewolf, then I guess the answer is yes."

"When the moon is full, you turn into a bear?"

He nodded. "I hope that's not a deal breaker."

"Shit! If we're sleeping together and the moon is full, will you maul me after you turn into a bear?" I couldn't believe my own words. I'd swallowed his story hook, line, and sinker. Now all he had to do was reel me in.

"I don't think so." He shrugged. "It's just one night a month. If I have to sleep in a cage or something, so be it." He smiled. "Beats living out my days in a zoo like poor Uncle Bruno."

The rest of my time in DC passed in a blur. I wanted to skip the conference to spend every possible second with him, but Donald insisted I make the most of the opportunity and never tired of hearing about the sessions I'd attended. By the end of the week, he was more involved in my business than Mark had ever been.

All the way back to Del Rio, I regretted telling Donald he couldn't come with me. But we'd only just met. Besides, he was crazy. Though it hadn't come up again, the bear thing was the elephant in the room. The way he sniffed things, the tattoo on his shoulder, and his habit of adding honey to practically everything he ate were subtle but ever-present reminders. I'd even caught myself wondering if maybe he was telling the truth.

Impossible. Werewolves and the like were fictional characters, like Sherlock Holmes, Rhett Butler, and Tarzan. The bearish man had merely invented a mystique to fit his size and hirsute appearance. A tall tale designed as a come-on he probably used with every man he met.

At first I ignored the e-mails from him that showed up in my inbox every morning. I was in Del Rio and he was someplace else, too far to make dating a viable option. Getting away for a business trip had been hard enough. Spending time and money for trips to visit Donald wasn't practical.

But I craved him like some kind of drug. My reliable old porn collection no longer did the trick. His presence loomed large in my imagination, and I couldn't close my eyes without seeing him. He would forever be the gold standard—the man to whom I would compare all others for the rest of my life. And I knew no one could ever measure up.

More than the sex, I missed talking to him. If I really didn't want to read them, I would have just deleted the unopened messages he'd sent. Maybe I was waiting to see how long he'd ignore my silence, thinking if I waited long enough, he'd stop. Or maybe I waited to see if my feelings for him would fade. Whatever my reasons, after two weeks I relented.

The messages he'd sent were chatty, undemanding, and sweet. A few contained ideas he'd come up with for my business—including many I could implement right away. I threw myself into work. Knowing he'd be here by my side if I just said the word made me miss him that much more.

Instead of taking to the woods in search of the bear king like Donald's ancestors, I paced the deck on the back of my house as the full moon rose over the trees, half expecting to see Donald come out of the mist in his bear form. I waited until the sun came up, and when he didn't show up, I knew what I had to do.

A MONTH later, we locked Donald in my garage. I waited outside, talking to him through the window as the sky turned from lavender to gray. I didn't know what to expect, but seeing was believing. By the time the full moon had risen over the trees, his transformation was complete.

His muzzle came through the open window, and his nostrils flared as he sniffed the night air. He looked at me with familiar eyes, and I knew he wasn't going to hurt me. I reached my hand through the window and rubbed his head. In the middle of town—even this late—letting him out was too risky. Bear sightings in town were rare enough to make the front page of our weekly paper.

We sold my house, bought some land down around Snowbird Mountain on Big Creek, and built a cabin. With Donald's extensive knowledge of management and marketing, my business took off. Him running things allowed me to focus more on designing residential and commercial landscapes. We built a couple of greenhouses, hired an expert in native plants, and opened a garden center for customers from as far as Knoxville, Asheville, and Chattanooga.

The people in town tell stories now about the Bear King of Snowbird Mountain. From time to time, a hiker, hunter, or camper will say they've seen him walking along a distant ridge with a bear by his side. Some say he's a Cherokee shaman, complete with feathered headdress and bear-claw necklace. They say the bear is his spirit animal. I laugh and say they must have imbibed a few of the many hallucinogenic mushrooms indigenous to the mountain woods. At no time have I ever donned a headdress for our moonlit adventures.

For as long as he can remember, MICHAEL RUPURED has loved to write. Before he learned the alphabet, he filled page after page with rows of tiny little circles he now believes were his first novels and has been writing ever since. He grew up in Lexington, Kentucky, where he came out as a gay man at the age of twenty-one in the late 1970s. He considers it a miracle that he survived his wild and reckless twenties.

By day, Michael is an academic. He develops and evaluates financial literacy programs for youth and adult audiences at the University of Georgia and is Assistant to the Dean for Family and Consumer Sciences Education. He's received numerous awards and honors over the years and is a Distinguished Fellow of the Association for Financial Counseling and Planning Education. Michael is also an avid gardener, a runner, and because he loves it and rarely misses a class, is known locally as the Zumba King.

In 2010, he joined the Athens Writers Workshop, which he credits for helping him transition from writing nonfiction to writing fiction. Michael writes gay romance thrillers that, in addition to entertaining the reader, highlight how far the gay rights movement has come in the last fifty years. A serial monogamist who is currently between relationships, Michael writes with his longhaired Chihuahua, Toodles, in his lap from his home in Athens, Georgia.

To find out what Michael's up to now, visit his blog: http://rupured.com, follow him on Twitter: @crotchetyman, or send an e-mail to mrupured@gmail.com.

Just Breathe
John Genest

Sitting at a table in the Atlas Diner, Will took another deep, cleansing breath and tried to calm his nerves. He had been told not to drink any alcohol or caffeine before the study, and he looked with envy at the other customers finishing their meals with a cup of coffee. He drank water rather than his usual diet Coke with his burger and fries, and it just wasn't the same.

What a shitty way to spend a Friday night, and Valentine's Day, no less, he thought. *Strapped to a bunch of electrodes reading my vitals just to find out what I already know. And how the hell am I supposed to sleep with all that stuff on? I'm gonna have to at least lie on my side. I just hope I don't wake up choking like I did Tuesday.*

His waitress, Melinda from her nametag, was a squat woman with a warm smile and a Bettie Page hairdo. She came by and asked if he wanted more water or maybe some dessert, and he returned her smile and just asked for the check. He got a sense she might have been flirting with him. She was a Big Beautiful Woman, but he was a dyed-in-the-woof Bear, though with all the weight he'd gained over the last seven months he'd been seen as more chub than cub in the eyes of those who pursued him online these days.

Looking at the hearts and chubby winged archers that hung from the ceiling of the diner, Will remembered Cupid's Greek counterpart was Eros, which meant Love was literally in the air tonight in this diner. *Yeah, just not for me. Not this year. Not without Boss Daddy.*

When Melinda returned with the check, he left her a healthy tip, grabbed his overnight bag, and paid at the front counter. Stepping out into the bitter cold of the February evening, he again regretted not being able to comfortably button up his wool coat and walked as quickly as his big legs would carry him across the intersection and up the steps to the entrance of the medical center. He walked down one long corridor and turned left into a bank of elevators. Taking one to the third floor, he made a quick right and entered the clinic.

The clock on the wall said it was a few minutes to seven, and the reception area was empty, so he hung up his coat, took a seat, and waited, hearing his pulse beat in his ears. As it began to fade, he heard a door open somewhere in back and a woman's voice. Most of the conversation was muffled, but he did manage to catch a couple of louder phrases: "Yeah, well, it's not a football, so…" and "Yes, please do take a shower, and not just because you need one." A few more murmurs, and the receiver slammed against its cradle.

The voice emerged as a slim bespectacled woman with spiky brown hair and chunky jewelry, and the scowl on her face morphed instantly into affable surprise as she said, "Mr. Bancroft?"

"Yes," he said, standing to shake her hand.

"Hi, I'm Marcy. How are you doing this evening?"

"Fine, thanks."

"Cold enough out there for ya?"

"A little too cold, yeah."

"Well, it's plenty warm in here, so why doncha come on back and I'll show you where you'll be sleeping tonight, okay?"

"Sure," Will said, shouldering his bag and following her down the hall into room 1. Before him, a widescreen TV was bolted to the ceiling above a queen-size bed with a cream and purple comforter and matching pillows, and a nightstand and digital clock beside it spoke of the comforts of home. A wheelable monitor stood in the corner of the far wall, where a countertop with white cabinets above and below it ran between two doors, and there was a desk and office chair to his immediate right.

"Please have a seat," she said, and he perched on the edge of the firm mattress as she settled into the desk chair. "So, you should have received a letter in the mail in preparation for your polysomnogram this evening. Have you had any caffeine or alcohol today?"

"No."

"Good. And no naps?"

"Not voluntarily, no. I was nodding off and on for about a half hour around two o'clock today. It might have been from lunch."

"Okay, well, that's what you're here for, right?" she said with a smile.

"Yep."

"And you brought some comfortable clothing to sleep in?"

"Yes."

"Great. Bathroom's to the left there, and I'll leave you to get changed and make yourself at home. Your sleep technician's stuck in traffic so he's running a little late, but he should be here momentarily. If you'd like to watch some TV while you're waiting, the remote's in the top drawer of the nightstand. Any other questions?"

"How long will it take to receive the results?"

"Well, they'll need to be reviewed by a doctor, so in anywhere from two to four weeks you'll be receiving another letter to make an appointment to discuss the results and treatment options."

"Okay." *Dammit, I'm gonna have shitty sleep for another two to four weeks 'til I get a CPAP.*

"Anything else I can clarify for you?"

"No, I don't think so."

"Okay. I'll be heading out once he gets here, so you have a nice weekend and we'll see you again soon."

"Thank you, Marcy. You have a great weekend too."

Smiling, she closed the door behind her.

Kicking off his shoes beside the nightstand and grabbing his bag, Will went into the small bathroom and relieved his bladder. He brushed his teeth, washed and dried his hands and face, and stripped down to his plaid boxers to put on a blue T-shirt and a pair of knee-length gray shorts. He hastily folded his work clothes onto his bag under the sink and stepped back into the room in his socked feet.

Grabbing the remote and propping himself up near the headboard, he remembered Friday was a shitty night for TV. *That's because people with lives and loves are out doing something fun to celebrate tonight. Jeez, even my mom's going to Bingo after she feeds my cat.* He flipped through the channels on the cable guide and was wondering if they had more than basic when there was a knock at the door.

Turning it off, he said, "Yep, come in."

The door opened and admitted one tall, deeply tan, and very handsome Daddybear wearing blue scrubs and holding a manila file folder. He immediately hit Will's top three criteria for ursine hotness: bald, glasses, and facial hair, a full auburn beard with just a few strands of gray at the chin. The fur coating his muscled forearms and pouring from the V-cut of his shirt was extra icing on his beefcake.

Looking at the top of his file, he said in a deep baritone, "William Bancroft?"

"Yep, Will's fine."

"Any relation to Anne?"

"No, but I get that a lot."

"Just thought I'd ask," he said, giving Will eye contact and a strong handshake before they both sat down. "My name's Les, and I'll be your sleep technician this evening. I see you've already made yourself comfortable and found the remote, so we'll get you all hooked up and ready for bed, okay?"

"Sure," Will said, trying to retain eye contact with those deep blue eyes but occasionally having to look away. *God, he's handsome.*

"So Marcy told me you haven't had any caffeine or alcohol today and were nodding off involuntarily this afternoon?" Les asked as he opened the folder.

"Right."

"Feeling tired now?"

"Not really."

"Well, I'm sure you'll get there eventually," he said, flashing a smile of straight but slightly yellowed teeth. "It says here we'll be doing an EEG to monitor brainwaves, the usual airway and heart hookups, and an NPT test, right?"

"Right. Wait, what does NPT stand for?"

"That would be a Nocturnal Penile Tumescence test."

Will felt the panic rush to his face. *Oh shit! Dr. Clarke mentioned that on my last visit when I asked if I could up my Viagra dosage. Now this hot bear knows I'm having trouble getting it up. This is so embarrassing. Is he gonna be hooking my dick up too?*

"Did your physician explain the test to you?"

Struggling to look at him again, Will said, "No, not really."

"Then I'll be happy to. As men sleep, we get about three to five erections a night, each lasting about ten to fifteen minutes. This test will monitor girth and rigidity while you sleep to rule out a possible physiological issue. So what we'll do is hook up your unit, I mean, your monitoring unit," he said with a deep-throated laugh that made his Adam's apple rise and fall, "to your thigh, and then you'll head into the bathroom and roll the two bands attached over the base of your shaft and beneath the head of your penis, okay?"

"Okay," Will said, relieved he would be applying the bands himself. He was a grower, not a shower, and not only didn't he want Les to see how little he had while soft, he wasn't quite sure, despite recent difficulties, that he'd have a problem getting a waking erection if Les applied the bands for him.

"Good. So the sooner we get you set up here, the sooner you can lie down and try to get some sleep. Any questions?"

"What if I need to use the bathroom in the middle of the night?"

"All the leads will be hooked up to that rollable monitor so you can take it with you. I'll be alerted if any of them happen to come loose, and if you have any issues, just give me a holler. There's an infrared camera in that corner," Les said, pointing over the door to the office, "and a two-way speaker near the nightstand."

"Good. Will I be able to sleep on my side?"

"Do you usually sleep that way at home?"

"Yeah, and sometimes on my stomach."

"You can sleep on either side as long as you roll the monitor over to that side of the bed, but with the feeds you'll have on your nose and mouth, on your stomach won't work tonight."

"Okay."

"Good. You ready?"

"Yep."

"Then have a seat in this chair and we'll get started," Les said. As they both stood, Will noticed Les had about half a foot on him in height and imagined how it would feel to hug him, his head on that chest, that furry chin on his head. Boss Daddy used to hug him like that.

As Les walked over to the cabinets, Will watched his broad shoulders expand, muscles straining, and saw the outline of Les's briefs hugging the firm mounds of his ass beneath his scrubs as he reached and bent to gather the leads, electrodes and other supplies he needed.

Well, at least he'll have to touch me to get the electrodes on. Even if he happens to be gay, which I kinda doubt, a bear with a face and a body like that can take his pick. He wouldn't want a chub like me, and he already knows I'm damaged goods with the NPT. What does it stand for? NPoTent, and that's the problem—it doesn't stand. I'm a chub who can't get a chubby.

"Okay, Will, the first thing we're gonna do is put some cleaning paste on certain areas of your scalp, face, and chest to apply the electrodes. It's a little abrasive, but we have to clean away any natural oils to put on the adhesive. Your buzz cut helps, almost as much as my chrome dome here," he said, patting the top of his head.

"I washed my face before too."

"Great. I'll be coming in to wake you and fit you with a CPAP mask to get some readings about halfway through the night, so that'll help give the mask a good seal over your nose and mouth, even with your beard. Do you know what CPAP stands for?"

"Continuous positive airway pressure?"

"You got it. So after I get the readings we need, you can use the CPAP machine, which will open up your soft palate with forced air and hopefully give you some of the best sleep you've had in a while. This might be a little bit cold—I apologize."

Applying the cleaning paste to Will's scalp and face with a Q-tip, Les wiped it off with some moist towelettes. As they were very close to one another, Will tried to look straight ahead while Les applied the electrodes.

"Okay, my friend, those are set. Now we're gonna need to put some on your chest too, and put some cloth belts around your chest and stomach to measure your breathing while you're sleeping. Could you take your shirt off, please?"

"Yep," Will said, but meant quite the opposite. *Great—now he's gonna see all the weight I gained. The loose skin under my arms, my big nipples, the shelf where my moobs hang over my stomach. Let's just get it over with.*

Pulling one arm into his shirt, he did the same with the other, then reached down and pulled it over his head. Tossing it onto the bed, he straightened his spine to create as little sagging as possible and waited for Les to continue.

"The adhesive will wash out of your chest hair later—it just might take a little longer," Les said as he cleansed a couple of areas and applied said adhesive and electrodes. "There we go. Now I'm gonna put these bands on. I apologize in advance if I happen to snag any body hair, but the snaps'll need to go in front for the leads to work, okay?"

"Yep."

"Good. So I'm gonna need you to stand up and raise your arms, okay? Thanks. All right, let's do this chest band first," Les said, raising it over Will's arms and bringing it down behind his shoulders. As he did so, Will bent his head down and saw Les's shirt lift at the bottom to reveal a small slice of hairy torso and a treasure trail leading down into the ample package in his pants. He was very tempted to untie the knotted string holding them up with his teeth and see what color briefs Les was wearing.

"Great," Les said, closing the band's snap and resting it on Will's sternum a couple inches above his nipples. "Okay, now for the stomach band," he said, lowering it down Will's torso and then kneeling on the floor.

You're killing me, man! Will thought as he stood very still and cherished the sight of Les's bald and bearded head before his crotch. He wanted to kiss, hell, lick that tanned skin where it creased in the back, and fought the urge to pull his head forward. He was thankful he wasn't pitching a tent right now, but he'd be wiping some stickiness away when he put the NPT bands on later.

Sitting back on his calves and snapping the band shut over the small cavern of Will's belly button, Les looked up at him and asked, "How does that feel?"

"A little snug, but comfortable."

"Good. While I'm down here, could you pull the right leg of your shorts all the way up to the top of your thigh, please?"

Will did as he asked. With Les at crotch level, Will thought he would do just about anything Les asked.

"There's an elastic sleeve attached to this NPT unit, but it needs to be secured properly to get a good reading, so I'm just gonna tape it directly to your thigh, okay?"

"Sure," Will said, and held it in place as Les wrapped the tape twice around his thigh and over the top and bottom of the unit.

"All right, Will, you can head into the bathroom and put these bands on."

"Sure," Will said, and Les reached up a hand for Will to help pull him off the floor.

Will entered the bathroom, pulled down his shorts and boxers, and reached beneath his belly. He noted he *was* a bit sticky from Les being so close to him as he slid the NPT bands on, which reminded him of rolling on a condom as he slid one around the base and the other around his frenulum. He never forgot the name for that ridge beneath the head, because Boss Daddy had told him what it was called one night in bed, then said, "Any frenulum is a friend of mine."

Saddened by this memory, he pushed it away, pulled up his shorts, washed his hands and splashed some water on his face to cool down, dried himself off, and returned to the office.

"Have a seat," Les said, grabbing two plastic pouches and wheeling the monitor over to Will.

"Okay, let's get you hooked up to the old polysomnograph here."

As Les methodically attached each electrode to a wire and plugged it into the monitor, Will remembered that Somnus was the god of sleep. He was the Roman counterpart to the Greek god Hypnos, father of the dream god Morpheus, and brother to Thanatos, also known as Death.

A classical mythology buff since junior high, this reminded him of a poem he'd written about the underworld that he shared with his tenth grade English teacher when they were reading *The Odyssey*. She liked it so much that she had the class read it as a supplement, then asked them to guess the author. When she revealed who it was, a few fellow students had congratulated him while the jocks in the back crumbled up their copies for spite or spitballs.

One stanza from the poem came rushing back to him now:

Beneath the horn and ivory vents
Stood Death and Sleep, the two,
And watched as Dream, their brethren, sent
Forth visions, false and true.

Will pondered what kind of dream Morpheus might send him tonight if he got some decent REM sleep for a change, then realized Les was humming a tune under his breath. It wasn't until Les was fastening a wire to his chest band that he realized it was "Whistle While You Work" from *Snow White,* and he stifled a smile.

"Almost there, Will. All I've gotta do now is tape this cannula under your nose, this little metal twig near your mouth, and this clamp around your pinkie, and you'll be jacked into the Matrix." Will laughed at this, and Les smiled as he finished, deftly tearing off the last pieces of tape and applying them.

"Okay, Will, why don't you climb into bed and get comfortable?"

Will carefully wheeled the monitor beside the nightstand, sat down on the bed—he noticed Les had pulled down the covers for him—and proceeded to lie down on his left side and pull the sheet up to his chest.

Les flipped a few switches, turned a dial to eliminate a buzzing sound, and turned the illuminated face of the monitor away from him.

"You're good to go, Will. If you need another pillow or anything, there's some in the closet over there. Try to get some sleep, and once you give me three hours' worth of readings you can take the CPAP for a test drive. Feel free to watch some TV if it helps you sleep, and if you need anything just talk into the speaker. There was supposed to be another guy testing here tonight but he had to cancel, so you've got my undivided attention. You need anything else?"

"Nope. Thanks for setting all this up."

"You're welcome," Les said, backing up and grabbing his folder on the way out the door. "Sleep well," he said, switching off the overhead lighting and closing the door behind him.

WALKING DOWN the hall to the control booth, Les switched on the monitoring equipment and took a moment to make sure all the proper readings were being received. When he was satisfied everything was working well, he tossed the remainder of his cold cup of coffee into the trash and unwrapped his footlong. Taking a healthy bite of meatball marinara with provolone, he chewed and swallowed, switched on the camera monitor, and saw Will in infrared green, lying in the same position as he'd left him.

He's cute, Les thought as he continued eating and took a pull off his bottled water. Once in a blue moon, he was pleasantly surprised to come to work and find a chubby little furball like Will waiting for him. When he didn't have to split focus with another test subject, all the better.

The last time this had happened was about a month ago, when he had monitored an adorable chubby daddy who bore more than a passing resemblance to actor Richard Riehle. When the woofy polar bear with the walrus 'stache said he usually slept in nothing but his jockey shorts, Les assured him that was fine—"it's just us guys."

During the first part of that study, Les had watched him toss and turn and eventually muted the speaker as he snored like a buzzsaw and farted several times. But when Les fitted him with the CPAP halfway through, he slept quiet and supine for the rest of the night and, though he wasn't being tested for it, demonstrated some impressive NPT three times before Les woke him in the morning. When his wife came to pick up the polar bear, he had wanted to congratulate her but just shook hands instead.

Digging into the other half of his sub and downing the rest of his water, Les hit the speaker button to listen and left his mic on mute. Will remained in the same position but Les didn't hear any snoring or obstructed breathing, and since the readouts showed signs of life, he was still awake. It had been about fifteen minutes—he'd give him a half hour before he recommended TV, or maybe playing some cards, until he got sleepy.

Balling up the soggy paper that had housed his sub, he tossed it in the trash, then visited the facilities and the water cooler to refill his bottle. He played a hand of solitaire, and once he finished he gathered the deck, turned off the mute on his mic, and said, "Hey Will, you still awake in there?"

"Yeah."

"Thought so. I didn't hear anything in here, and there's usually some snoring or struggle for air."

"Yeah, I guess I'm not that tired yet."

"Any shows you usually watch on Friday night?"

"Not really. I usually surf the net or watch streaming video on my computer."

"Uh-huh. You play cards?"

"Not really."

"Not even blackjack?"

"Yeah, I've played that."

"You wanna?"

He was silent for about five seconds. "Sure."

"Are you hungry? Thirsty?"

"Yeah, a little of both."

"Okay, why don't you get yourself settled at the desk, and I'll get us some snacks from the vending machine and another chair."

"Sounds good. Thank you."

"No problem. I'll see you in a sec," he said, hitting the mute again.

Giving the monitors one last look and watching as Will carefully climbed out of bed, Les grabbed his deck of cards and went to the vending machine on the fifth floor, locking the office as he left.

BY THE time Les returned, Will was seated at the desk with his monitor beside him. He remained shirtless, had adjusted the seatback so it and he stayed upright and rigid, and had bent the little metal twig in front of his mouth away from his lips and adjusted the tape so it hung down from his cheek.

Les rolled a similar desk chair into the room, its seat bearing a bottle of water and several snacks like a small cornucopia. "I wasn't sure whether you'd want salty or sweet, so I got a few choices to pick from. I'm afraid water was the only decaffeinated drink there was."

"Thank you very much," Will said as Les put the snacks on the desk along with his own water and the deck.

"Take your pick and I'll shuffle."

Will was going to take the granola bar, healthy snack and all, but he really wanted the Twinkies, especially since they'd been off the market for a while. He had his eye on the sour cream and onion chips too, but he was craving sweet and grabbed the Twinkies. Unwrapping the phallic sponge cakes with creamy filling, he took a bite.

"You ready?" Les asked, and Will nodded as he chewed. They played a few hands, Les winning more than he lost, and he took a moment to open some Swiss rolls and popped one whole into his mouth. He dealt a few more hands and when Will got blackjack, they high-fived with Will's free hand and shared a smile.

"So, you work on campus, Will?" Les asked, continuing to deal.

"Yep, just a few blocks from here. Hit."

"That's convenient, huh?"

"Yeah, I left my car in my usual garage and just walked over here from the office. Hit. Damn."

Les scooped the hand into the discard pile and dealt again. "So how long did it take you to get an appointment?"

"About a month and a half after my GP ordered it. Stay. You guys must be real busy around here."

"Yep, and weekends are prime time. People don't want to have to sleep here during the week, then head home to shower and come right back to work. Good one!"

"Thanks," Will said, starting on the second Twinkie.

"The other guy who was supposed to be here tonight forgot what day it is."

"Hit. Really?"

"Yeah, Marcy told me. He said he'd have a lot more health problems than apnea if he let his girlfriend know he'd forgotten it was Valentine's Day. You want another card?"

"Yep. Oh well. When did he cancel?"

"Monday, apparently, and it's gonna take him awhile before he gets another appointment," Les said, shuffling the deck. "So how about you, Will? No valentine this year, or did you just postpone until tomorrow night?"

"No valentine this year," Will said, clearing his throat and reaching for his water. "How about you?"

"Nope, not seeing anyone," Les answered, taking a swig of his own.

"Me neither."

"Well, Happy Valentine's Day, Mr. Bancroft," he said, proffering his hand.

Giving him a hearty shake, Will said, "Happy Valentine's Day to you too, Mr...."

"Moore."

"Mr. Moore." Pulling his hand away, Will thought for a second and, smile brimming on his face, said, "Wait a minute. Your name is Les Moore?"

Les stopped shuffling for a second as he rolled his eyes. "Yeah. Les is short for Lester, but yeah."

"Holy shit, man. What were your parents *thinking*?"

"They weren't, apparently, and it got even worse freshman year of high school."

"Why?"

"Well, I was kind of a shy kid, you know—chubby, acne—and I started sprouting body hair way before the other kids. So I'm sitting in homeroom and the teacher's doing roll call, and when she comes to my name she says, "Moore, Lester," and I said, "Here." And that's when it started.

"This asshole jock named Jeff McCafferty heard it and called me "Mo'Lester" for the next two years. He accused me of checking him out in the locker room, stealing his jock to sniff, following him in the halls, sitting outside his window with binoculars... all this bullshit he kept spouting to his friends, and they ran with it too. Of course none of it was true, but trying to ignore or defend myself against that crap for so long was really starting to mess with my self-esteem.

"Anyway, I couldn't imagine another year of that and knew I had to figure something out before I went back. So, in keeping with the old adage 'If you can't beat 'em, join 'em,' by the time I came back in the fall I'd grown a couple inches, packed on some muscle and more fur, and tried out for the wrestling team."

Les leaned back in his chair a bit and put his hands behind his head to stretch for a moment, and Will caught a glimpse of the muscle and fur Les was talking about. The loose sleeves on his scrubs fell to reveal bulging triceps and dark tufts of armpit hair. *Lickable*, Will thought, and looked away as Les continued.

"When Jeff saw me he started in immediately, saying I'd probably grown some hair on my palms over the summer too. I was pissed, and I used my anger, my weight, and my strength against him, his friends, and our competitors. It felt awesome to finally overpower that douche bag, to slam him on the mat, pin him under me, and force him to tap out. I had finally won, you know, and I kept winning over the next two years. His friends became mine after a while, and I went from being called Mo'Lester to 'Squatch because, you know. I was glad to be rid of Jeff at graduation, and I was much happier by the time I left for college," he said, chomping on a Dorito.

"Good for you! So did you ever see Jeff again after that?"

"As a matter of fact, I did. He came to the ten-year reunion. He was working as a used car salesman by then, and he really looked the part too. Cheap suit, big potbelly, mustache, male pattern baldness, and he visibly cringed when he saw me walking toward him. So imagine how shocked he was when I shook his hand and offered to buy him a beer, and we talked about recent developments. Our old teammates came by to chat as we talked, introduced their wives, and showed us pictures of their kids. We were the only two not married with children or divorced by then, but I saw everyone giving him sidelong glances, like 'Oh, how the mighty have fallen.'

"Later on, when things quieted down and we'd had a few more beers, he finally apologized for being such a dick to me in high school. I said it was fine, water under the bridge, and it was by that time, but I asked him what that 'Mo'Lester' shit had been all about. He said he was just looking for a scapegoat, someone he could push around to make himself look good. He hadn't thought about what I would eventually do to make him stop, and he admitted I was the better man, then and now.

"I told him I thought he was a vast improvement from the jock asshole he had been freshman year, and he thanked me. But when I said he was looking good, he thought I was trying to get even, giving him shit about going to pot since then."

"Were you?" Will asked.

"No, I was being serious. I didn't like him at all in high school. I preferred wrestling some of the bigger guys on our team and the teams we competed with, and that got even better in college."

"Things got easier for me in college too," Will said, and took a shot. "That's where I found out about bears."

"Amen, brother!" Les said with a huge grin, and they bumped fists. "I *knew* I had you pegged as a fellow furball!"

"Me too, when you walked in before."

"Good call! But yeah, I assured Jeff I was serious, that he looked a helluva lot better to me now, bulked up and rocking that 'stache, than he ever did as that lean, hairless jock I used to make my bitch on the mat."

Taking another sip of water, Will asked, "And what did he say?"

"He didn't say much after that, back in my hotel room. For old times' sake, I made him my bitch there, too, and it's not polite to talk with your mouth full."

Will grinned and raised his water bottle to Les, and they bumped those as well.

"So how about you, Will? Would you have gone for Jeff before, or after?"

"Definitely after."

"Just checking. You went for the Twinkies before, so I wasn't sure if that meant something."

Will laughed and said, "Hey, you scarfed down those Swiss rolls! Does that mean you're only into black guys?"

"No, I have no preference for dark over white meat. I just prefer an extra helping of meat on the bones, that's all."

"Gotcha. And if we're keeping with your meat analogy, I don't like lean meat either. I prefer aged beef."

"Touché! Good to know," Les shouted, shooting him another smile. When he looked over at the nightstand, his smile faded a bit. "So, Will, I've really enjoyed talking with you and getting to know you better, but we've gotta get you back into bed and see if you can get some sleep. It's almost ten, and we've gotta get some good readings on you, okay?"

"Sure," Will said, a little disappointed their conversation had to end. He felt more comfortable with Les now, especially with his unexpected preference for chubby cubs like himself. He grabbed the stand to his monitor and stood as Les did the same.

"I'll leave the snacks here in case you get hungry later. Let me know if you need more water, and I'll be back around two to fit you with the CPAP, okay?"

"Okay," he said, pulling the metal twig back toward his mouth.

"Let me get that for you," Les said, reaching out to readjust the twig and tape on his cheek. "There you go. Need anything else?"

"Nope, I'm all set. Thanks for the snacks, Les, and I enjoyed playing cards and talking with you too. Your story was more entertaining than anything on TV."

"My pleasure, Will," Les said, putting a hand on his shoulder. "I hope you'll be able to get some rest now, and I'm sure once you've got the machine working for you later you're gonna have the best sleep you've had in a while."

"Looking forward to it."

Giving Will's shoulder a squeeze, Les let go and said, "Good. Give a holler if you need anything, and I'll see you in a few hours."

"Okay," Will said, and watched Les's broad back as he switched off the light and left the room.

Climbing carefully back into bed, Will thought about how kind and sexy Les was, and wondered if he would see him again when he came back for his machine. Was he in charge of those things too, or did he just work nights here doing these studies?

Will had gotten wood listening to Les's story. Maybe there wasn't anything physically wrong that had caused him to go soft during his last couple of casual encounters. Maybe he just hadn't been that attracted to them; they said you needed that for Viagra to work, and when somebody gets pissed at you because you can't get or keep it up, it doesn't give you a hell of a lot of incentive to try again.

It had been a literal wake-up call after spending the night at that guy Chris's house about three months before that brought him here. He had rolled over to kiss Chris good morning and felt instant dread when he said, "Don't. Did you have a good night's sleep, Will? 'Cause that makes one of us! First you couldn't get it up last night, and then you kept me up all night snoring, and you stopped breathing and kept snorting yourself awake."

Hurling himself out of bed and moving quickly toward his bedroom door, Chris had pointed at him and shouted, "You need to get a fucking sleep test so you don't pull this shit on anybody else, and I want you gone when I get out of the shower!"

After Chris slammed the door, Will had pulled his tired self out of bed, gotten dressed, and left. Three weeks later, he mentioned his sleeping and erectile difficulties to his general practitioner during his appointment—and now here he was, electrodes attached to his head, heart, and hog, trying to fall asleep. Why was he having so much trouble? It came so easily to him at home, at work, and sometimes even while he was driving.

A spasm of emotional pain shot through him with this thought, but he quickly pushed it away. *I don't want to think about that right now, okay? I just want to get some sleep.*

Letting his thoughts drift back to Les, he focused on how good he had looked in his scrubs and tried to burn the sight of him into his memory for tomorrow, when he could go home and relieve his frustrations. His right hand never disappointed; it always knew exactly what he needed to get hard and get off. But he wasn't ready to stop having sex with other guys, and if his NPT test results were good, that meant he was doing a number on himself when he was awake. His big head was messing with the little one, and he'd have to figure out why.

Just not tonight, dammit.

Throwing off the sheet, Will took some deep breaths to calm himself, and after watching the back of his eyelids for a few minutes to clear his mind, he finally slipped off to sleep.

"HEY, WILL? I'm gonna need you to wake up for just a few minutes, buddy."

Will followed the voice into consciousness, and by the glow of the monitor he found Les sitting beside him in the dark. His mouth was so dry he had to work his tongue around for a moment to get a little moisture going before he could respond.

"What time is it?"

"About two thirty. How are you feeling?

"My mouth's dry, and I've gotta take a leak."

"Okay. You head into the bathroom, I'll get you a refill, and then we'll get the CPAP going. You need me to turn the overhead lights on for ya?"

"No, the monitor's enough light, thanks."

"Okay, see you in a sec."

Will pulled himself out of the comfortable bed, wheeled the monitor into the bathroom, and winced as he turned on the light. Pulling down his shorts, he reached beneath his belly, fished his penis out through the fly of his boxers, and held it between the NPT bands with his thumb and pointer finger, extending his pinkie outward to keep the clamp dry and using his other hand to hold the electrode wires up and out of the way. He let loose, quickly redirecting into the bowl after hitting the bottom of the lifted toilet seat, and chuckled to himself about what a production taking a leak had become.

When he was through, he shook himself off, tucked himself in, used some toilet paper to wipe up his mess, flushed, washed and dried his hands, and pulled up his shorts. He opened the door to find Les reaching into the bottom drawer of the nightstand and pulling out a plastic mask with a long hose and straps attached.

Will turned off the bathroom light and walked the monitor around Les to the other side of the bed. He got back into bed and chugged the water Les had brought him.

"You won't need this one anymore," Les said, removing the metal twig and tape from his cheek. "So, these straps here go around the back of your head, the mask goes over your nose and mouth, and when I turn the machine on it'll blow some cool air to keep your soft palate open and should give you a few hours of uninterrupted sleep, okay?"

"Yep, sounds great."

"If you feel the air pressure's too high or you're having any trouble breathing, just take the mask off, 'cause it'll be hard for you to talk through the airflow, and talk into the speaker. Let's try this on and see how it fits."

Will did so, and after Les turned on the machine he checked for any escaping air and adjusted the mask and Velcro straps until it was tight.

"How's that?"

Will nodded his head and gave a thumbs-up.

"Okay, bud, you sleep well and I'll wake you about six thirty. If all goes well, you're gonna wish I let you sleep longer," he said with a smile.

"Thanks," he muffled.

"Shh. Go back to sleep."

After Les closed the door, Will rolled over onto his right side, flipped the air hose over his shoulder, and after a minute or so he did just that.

WHEN WILL awoke later, something was wrong. He was lying on the bed in complete darkness and dead quiet. There was no glow from the monitor, no white noise from the machine, no whooshing sound in his mask as he exhaled, and no air pressure on his face.

Did the power go out?

But Will couldn't feel the mask or the straps on the back of his head, either. As he moved his hand up to look for it, he realized the clamp on his pinkie was gone. He met no resistance from the electrode wires, and when he searched his chest hair, the electrodes were gone too.

I guess Les must've unhooked me while I was sleeping. With this thought, he suddenly sensed someone was lying in bed beside him. He swallowed once, mouth no longer dry, and said, "Les, is that you?"

"No," a voice answered. "It's me, Bear Cub."

Will recognized the voice, and that pet name, immediately.

"Boss Daddy?"

"Yep, it's me. You're dreaming, Bear Cub. No need to panic. Everything's okay."

And in the darkness of his dream, Will felt his Boss Daddy's warm, strong arms wrap around him and hold him close, as he had so many nights before his untimely death. "It's okay, Bear Cub," Boss Daddy said as Will grasped those furry forearms tightly and shook with sobs. "I'm sorry it took me awhile to get here, but you needed to get a good night's sleep so you could dream. And you're dreaming now, so I'm here. I'm here for you, Bear Cub, so just let it all out, and listen to your Boss Daddy."

Either out of respect for his memory, or as an echo of the kind of relationship they'd once shared, Will sobered a bit and did what he was told.

"I love you, Bear Cub," Boss Daddy said, eliciting fresh tears from Will. "Those two years we shared together, you were my one and only, and I was so proud of you. Still am, watching you come here tonight, taking care of yourself. I might still be there with you now if I'd done the same, but I didn't, and that's all my fault."

As Will continued keening for his loss, his Boss Daddy held him tighter. He cried for all the painful memories, that late night call from the police seven months before, the closed casket funeral, the three fucking days of bereavement that weren't nearly enough. How was he supposed to show his face at work on Thursday and get through the rest of the week, or the month for that matter, when the love of his life had fallen asleep at the wheel on his way home and wrapped his truck around a telephone pole? Will had even been discouraged from identifying what was left of the body later.

"I know, Bear Cub, I know. I'm sorry for causing you so much pain, but just let it out, okay? Just let it go. It's okay, I've got ya. That's my buddy."

When Will finally regained some composure, Boss Daddy continued. "I wish there was more time for us, Bear Cub, but there's not. I'm here now, but I have to move on, and so do you. I know you've been doing your best to cope, to keep moving forward without me, and I'm so glad I could finally be here with you tonight, to help you let go."

"You're gonna be fine, Bear Cub, and so am I, but I want you to do me a favor. I want you to keep feeling how you're feeling about my passing until it gets easier, but I also want you to remember what we had before then. Remember how much we loved each other, how good it felt, and how happy we were, then get out there and find someone who makes you feel the same way. It might be that sleep tech guy, he really seems to like you, or it might be someone else. Remember what we had, and when you start to feel that way again, you found the right guy. But please keep looking until you find him, because you deserve nothing less. Okay?"

Will nodded.

"Good Bear Cub. Now roll over and give your Boss Daddy a big bear hug."

As Will did so, he suddenly felt the wires tethering him to the sleep monitor snap loose and woke up, cool air blowing in his face.

"WILL, BUDDY, you okay?" Les asked as he opened the door. "You rolled over and pulled out your leads!"

"Sorry," he said, voice muffled by the mask.

Les reached into the drawer and turned off the CPAP. "No problem, I was getting ready to wake you in a few minutes anyway. Why don't you give me that mask and I'll put it in here for ya."

Will pulled it off and handed it to him, noticing it was a little cooler in the room now.

"Was I talking in my sleep?" Will asked. *Or crying?*

"You said something about fifteen minutes ago but I couldn't make it out. So how do you feel? How'd you sleep?"

He felt better than he had when Les had woken him before to put on the mask. He didn't have dry mouth, and he was surprised not to feel any tears on his cheeks when he rubbed his eyes. Giving Les a warm smile, he said, "I actually feel really good right now."

"Good, glad to hear it," Les said. "So let's get you unwrapped and unstuck here, and you can head into the bathroom and wash off the adhesive."

"Okay," Will said and realized as he threw his legs over the side of the bed that he had morning wood. As Les removed everything except the NPT unit to free him up, Will decided his dream had freed him up too, and that it had been true. He felt no need to second guess it.

"I'll let you take care of that one yourself," Les said with a smile, nodding at either his unit or the unit attached to it.

Will smiled and blushed but made no effort to hide the tent in his shorts as he walked toward the bathroom.

"By the way, that's your fourth this evening, Will."

"Really?"

"Yep."

"Does that include the one I got last night when you told me that story?"

"No," Les said, laughing.

Will smiled back and said, "Hey, Les?"

"Yeah?"

"I wanna pay you back for the snacks last night. Can I buy you breakfast?"

"Sure, I'd like that. Just let me go finalize your study report and we'll go to the diner across the street, okay?"

"Sounds great. See you in a bit."

SEATED NEAR the same table at which he'd eaten dinner the night before, Will perused the menu and watched as Les, now wearing a leather jacket, did the same. Half expecting Melinda to walk over and wait on them, he was surprised when a waiter who looked like the human incarnation of Aladdin, but whose name tag read Alexio, walked over to their table and asked Les for his order.

"I'll have the spinach and feta cheese omelet, a side order of sausage, and a cup of coffee, please." Judging by the megawatt smile and prolonged eye contact the waiter was trying to give Les, Al was definitely cruising him. Poor guy.

When he finally tore his eyes away and acknowledged Will, his demeanor quickly changed to sullen.

"Hi, I'll have the Atlantean special, a cup of coffee, and a diet Coke, please." Will noticed Al's snort of derision when he asked for a special that was just about two of everything on the breakfast menu, and his smirk when he asked for a diet Coke.

"Anything else?" Al snarked, looking up from his pad.

"Yes, Al. You can give me a little less attitude, or you can go get me your manager."

Silenced, Al took their menus and walked away.

"Nice, Will," Les said. "Just hope he doesn't spit in your eggs."

"Even if he doesn't, he's not getting a tip. Or your attention."

"You got that right. So what are your plans for today?"

"Nothing, really. I'll probably just head home and try to get some more sleep, though I'm sure it won't be as good without the CPAP. I wish I didn't have to wait weeks for a doctor to check the results before I can get one."

"Well, your results have been sent for review, but it's out of my hands from now on, I'm afraid."

"Really?" Will asked as a waitress—Linda—brought his diet Coke and poured them both some coffee.

"Yep. I just handle the sleep studies at night, so you'll be hearing from Marcy to get your CPAP."

"Oh," Will said, crestfallen. *Shit, I'm not going to see him again at the clinic.*

Will added cream and sweetener to his coffee and watched Les sip his without. "You take yours black?"

"Yep. Swiss rolls, remember?"

"Oh yeah. Hey, where's that twink waiter with our food? He's kinda cute."

"No, he's not. Now you, on the other hand…," Les said, smiling as he brought the cup back to his lips.

"Why, thank you, kind sir. I'll see that, and raise you a woof."

When Linda brought their meals as well, Les and Will shared a laugh as Will poked through his eggs and checked between his flapjacks for any sign of spit, then said, "Coast is clear."

"Good," Les said, cutting a piece of omelet loose with his fork. "So if you're not doing anything after breakfast, Will, you're welcome to take a shower at my place, and a nap too. You know. After."

Watching Les stare as he slowly chewed his bite of omelet, Will asked, "After?"

Les's Adam's apple bobbed up and down as he swallowed, and he nodded slowly. "Yes, after."

There was no misconstruing the subtext here. Will smiled and repeated, "After."

"And I've got my own machine, so at least my snoring won't keep you awake."

"So you're not just a sleep technician, you're also a client?"

"Exactly."

"Excellent."

As they dug into their breakfasts and continued to get to know one another, Will thought about his Boss Daddy and his approval of Les in the dream. He wondered if his day with Les might turn into something more and decided, as he took a deep breath and let it go, that he would sleep on it.

After.

JOHN GENEST is a Connecticut native and avid reader from the age of three. When puberty led to nine years in the closet, fantasy fiction, classical mythology, and stories about magic provided an escape until he emerged at nineteen as a self-dedicated Wiccan and then came out to family and friends two years later.

Graduating with a BA in English the following year, John began a series of temporary positions and, during a couple of weeks off, let his beard grow. He has worn one ever since and self-identifies as a Big Bear or Ursus Major (as tattooed on his right calf).

Now a full-time Senior Administrative Assistant, John has begun writing about what he knows best: Bears and Witches. Foregoing pyrotechnic displays of magic and porn-perfect depictions of Über-Bears, he prefers to write realistic portrayals of modern-day Wiccans and hairy men who love men who are men. He is currently single and lives with his feline familiar, Fluffy.

Please contact him at (where else?) bearwytchproject@yahoo.com.

BAREFOOT
LILLIAN FRANCIS

"Clive?" I had no idea if that was the old man's real name, but I'd heard other guys at the shelter call him that. "Clive. Wait up."

I jogged to catch up with him, wanting to conduct this conversation on the main street, where he wouldn't feel trapped by my height and the enclosed walls of the narrow alleyway he was heading for. I probably could have walked and still caught up with him before he rounded the corner of the building, each of my long strides covering more ground than his hobbling gait could hope to navigate.

I fell into step beside him. A tactile person by nature, I had to fight my instinct to stop him with a placating hand to the shoulder. I'd learned the hard way that most of the guys who attended the shelter, and even more so those who didn't, hated to be touched. Maybe *hated* was overstating the issue. Or oversimplifying it. Many had reason to fear the touch of a stranger.

"Clive." I said his name once more, making sure he would be able to see me clearly, if he would only raise his gaze from the pavement. "It's Finn. From the shelter."

I kept my voice low. If there was one thing these guys hated as much as unsolicited contact, it was everybody knowing their business. Not that the streets were busy at this time in the evening. Most people were bundled up in front of their tellys, watching the daily tribulations of strangers in ongoing soaps or the latest reality show.

"What happened to your shoes?" I asked gently. We'd had a donation of several dozen pairs of shoes the previous week, and Clive had been at the top of the list for a replacement pair. His old pair had been held together by spit and hope—and an exceptionally strong elastic band—and let in so much water that he was in real danger of contracting trench foot. Many of the men had to be cajoled into throwing anything away, but I'd been privy to watching Clive willingly dump the old pair in the rubbish bin. He'd kept the elastic band, though.

Rheumy eyes regarded me suspiciously.

"I was there when they were handed out, remember?"

"Yeah. I remember." Clive's voice sounded scratchy, and I wondered if I was the first person he'd spoken to all day. He all but rolled his eyes, his expression conveying his contempt without the need to resort to such obvious displays to express his opinion of my idiocy.

Mentally I kicked myself. Clive was homeless, not stupid. I'd heard talk of him having been a bank manager or some type of financial advisor before whatever it was that had sent him plummeting into the despair that was his current existence. Who knew what the trigger had been. Despite his appearance to the contrary, I doubted he had reached retirement age.

I waited to see if Clive intended to answer my question. It didn't do to press for information.

Clive's gaze got shifty, skittering away from me toward the traffic in the high street, and I could see in his expression the exact moment he decided I wasn't worthy of the truth. I didn't take it personally—very few of us were.

"Didn't like 'em. They pinched." He shrugged, the movement enough to dislodge the cumbersome scarf that swathed his head, revealing a nasty bruise to the side of his face. I knew better than to mention it, but I'd bet a week's pay that Clive hadn't given up his shoes willingly.

I wiggled my toes. My old trainers were worn in and comfy, a favorite pair in a closet full of newer, barely worn pairs of shoes. To a casual observer, the ones I wore day in, day out were probably considered fit for nowhere but the bin.

Not the sort of shoes anyone, even another homeless person, would want to steal.

Not that too many would consider trying to steal anything from me. Six four, with broad shoulders and a solid torso that swore testament to Saturday mornings spent torturing myself with my old rugby mates. A couple of hours a week, mainly cardio workouts, just enough to keep me fit.

Thanks to a manic week with work, my facial scruff lingered in that no-man's-land between unkempt and a full beard. And with Jenna out with the flu I'd been covering all of her shifts at the shelter, leaving me with little time for more than the most basic of grooming habits. I couldn't even remember if I'd showered today. Thank God I worked from home most of the time.

I caught a glimpse of myself in the shop window to my right. The unintentional, and all too brief, nap I'd woken from earlier had left me with a terminal case of bedhead. My wavy mop of strawberry blond hair.... Okay, I'm ginger, but a working holiday to a sports camp in Thailand last month had bleached my hair, leaving me with a weird golden hue. I thought I liked it, certainly enough to take a couple of selfies on my phone to show my barber next time I bothered to go for a visit. Anyway, my wavy mop, which normally hung level with my jaw, currently resembled the nest of a manic magpie. In all honesty, I looked like a Yeti.

Beyond my reflection, from somewhere in the storefront, I could make out a suited figure staring back at me. It seemed my appearance, or perhaps my choice of companion, offended him. Anyone would think he'd never seen a homeless person before. Despite only being thirty miles or so from the capital, there wasn't the endemic issue that they suffered in London, where bundles of rags in shop doorways morphed into bedraggled ghosts before your very eyes. But having a castle within spitting distance—and a royal one at that—didn't make Berkshire immune to the problem.

Anyway, we were getting the evil eye from the store manager. He probably thought we were putting off the paying customers.

I felt a yawn coming on, the remnants of my earlier nap, and went with it. Mouth a cavernous yaw, I even went as far as to push my hand up under my shirt to scratch at the hair on my belly as though I was in the safety of my bedroom. The suited store clerk visibly recoiled at the display of my flesh. Not that I was hideous or anything. Maybe my rock-hard abs had softened to something less resembling a six-pack, but it was hard to maintain that sort of body without the daily training regime. Anyway, these days my chest hair spread far and wide, softening the appearance of my abdomen even more. Yet another excuse not to go to the gym. I felt self-conscious around all the smooth, waxed flesh on display—that was just the guys—and there was no way I was shaving.

Clive had managed several shuffling steps while I'd been distracted. His hobbling looked painful.

"Clive." He stopped, barely glancing back over his shoulder. I hopped on one foot to remove my trainers while moving closer to him.

The chill of the pavement bled through my sock when I swapped feet to remove the other shoe. Once both feet were back on the ground I held the trainers out to him. "Here, take these. I've got a new pair in here."

I waved my carrier bag at him, hoping he didn't realize it contained nothing but leaflets for the shelter.

Clive frowned, hesitating for a fraction of a second before grabbing the shoes from my hand. He grunted something that could have been thanks, but could just have likely been him clearing his throat. My shoes disappeared into a bag that magically appeared from beneath his capacious coat, and then he scurried away. Far faster than a man in his socks should be capable of.

I shifted from foot to foot, trying to stop the cold from creeping up into my calves. At the shelter I had a spare pair of shoes in my desk drawer, but first I had some shopping to do. Not at this store, though.

Through the window the manager toggled a button on his walky-talky and gave me another of those stares obviously designed to have me quaking in my shoes. Or socks.

I think he must have practiced on nine-year-old girls, because my ten-year-old niece wouldn't have been impressed. He raised the walky-talky to his mouth. I'd done nothing wrong and at any other time would have been happy to make my point, but I didn't have the time to deal with security guards and possibly the police today.

I eyeballed the manager back and considered sticking out my tongue. I wouldn't use his shop, despite its reputation as one of the cheaper stores.

The supermarket farther down the high street held much more inviting treats. Even if all I ever did was look, never touched. Hell, I'd not even summoned up the courage to say as much as hello, and I'd been looking for well over six months now. The object of my affections, CuteGuy^{TM}, worked on the cigarette kiosk—and I didn't smoke.

Not that it mattered. He probably already had a boyfriend. My type often did.

I channeled my niece, poked out my tongue at the still-glaring store manager, and watched for a moment as the man's mouth moved at speed, a rallying cry to the troops. Not wasting a moment more on the jumped-up little twat, I tested out my ability to run in socks and took off for the supermarket and my eye candy.

MY CONVERSATION with Clive had thrown my schedule all out of whack, and I was already running late when I headed into the supermarket, sparing little more than a flick of my eyes in the direction of the cigarette kiosk. No spiky-haired blond at the counter that I could see. CuteGuy™ liked to dye the very tips of his hair different colors— I'd seen it amethyst, emerald green, bright blue, even a rainbow of colors all at once—so believe me when I say I would have noticed. Maybe he was crouched on the floor while he restocked the shelves and would pop up in a moment. But I didn't have the time to stop and stare tonight. I was late, and it always made me feel like a bit of a creeper, browsing the papers and magazines on the off chance of catching a glimpse of him.

Armed with my basket, I headed straight to the cheapie shelf—a chiller cabinet where they stored the food that would be going out of date by the end of the day. We'd tried asking for the items to be donated to the shelter, rather than dumped in the filthy dumpster out back where perfectly edible food mingled with general waste, spilled beauty products, and any number of rats. The management of the store had made all kinds of sympathetic noises, but the words "company policy" came up more than once. Bottom line—the food was out of date and they couldn't risk a possible lawsuit if one of the homeless people became ill. Because that was going to happen. Maybe, in another, alternate reality where these men weren't starving. Where the more agile of the men didn't clamber into the bin to pick the items out of the rubbish, risking Weil's disease and serious strains of poisoning. There was even an urban legend about a homeless man who hadn't been able to get out of the oversized industrial bin, fell asleep in amongst the rubbish, and ended up in the back of the refuse truck that collected the bins in the early hours of the morning.

I shuddered at the thought of how that tale ended and scooped up six packets of scandalously cheap but high quality sausages, dropping them into my basket. There was pasta and crates of cheap tinned tomatoes in the store cupboard back at the shelter. I could rustle up a pretty decent pasta dish for tonight's special. The early evening volunteers would have been serving cooked food for a couple of hours now, but I tried to keep cooking as late as possible because some of the men wouldn't come into the shelter until it started to get dark. I added half a dozen packets of diced vegetables that claimed to be a soup mix, but that I would blend and use to bulk out the tomato-based sauce.

I eyed several packets of cream cakes and a trifle, but the arguments they would cause weren't worth the pleasure of providing dessert. There was a whole tray of crème fraîche, though, and if I could pick up some reduced-price scones in the bakery department, I could provide a tasty treat for more of our guests.

At the bread aisle my luck continued—six packs of scones and four mixed loaves of quality bread had my basket overflowing. Time to head for the checkout. On a whim I added a packet of crumpets. For my breakfast tomorrow. I was going to toast them, so did I care the sell by date was today's? Not for fifteen pence, I didn't.

Even though most of the cashiers weren't busy, I headed for the self-service tills. I preferred to ring up my own purchases rather than listen to the mindless chatter of the cashiers. It always seemed quicker. And anyway, the self-service tills had a direct line of sight to the cigarette kiosk.

See, there was method in my madness. I could stare to my heart's content—well, send sneaky glances his way—without getting stink eye from the security guard who stood by the door.

Of course, that plan only worked when CuteGuy™ was actually working. It appeared this was where my luck ran out. Today two middle-aged ladies were laughing behind the counter. I'd seen them both before, but always working with CuteGuy™, never together.

What if he had moved on? Another store, another job, another town? All before I'd summoned up the courage to talk to him?

So caught up in the sheer panic of my thoughts, I failed to notice the lack of a beep and barely even heard the woman's robotic voice from out of the machine.

"Unexpected item in bagging area...."

"Unexpected item in bagging area...."

Shhiit!

Grabbing the diced veggies that I had dropped into the bag without thinking, I tried to scan them for a second time. Still there was no comforting *blip* of acknowledgement.

"Having trouble there?"

I glanced over my shoulder, holding up the misbehaving vegetables to explain my problem, and damn near swallowed my tongue. CuteGuy™. There was no mistaking him, even with his hair flat and darkened to a burnt umber by some type of product, making even the colorful tips almost impossible to distinguish. And with him being a good five or six inches shorter than me, I had the perfect view as he took the item from my hands and leaned across me to the scanner. I should have moved away, given him room to work, but my feet were working about as well as my tongue.

"Nope," CuteGuy™ said, putting so much inflection into the word that the *p* popped audibly. "Not going to scan. I've told them about this in the produce department. The labels get damp in the chiller cabinet and, with all the handling, the lines of the bar code start to wear off."

As he spoke, CuteGuy™ edged his way in between me and the till, peering at the label. I shuffled back a few steps, both to give him room to work and to admire the view. His voice was deeper than I would have expected based on the high pitch of his laughter, which I'd heard on previous occasions drifting over from the kiosk.

CuteGuy™ keyed each number of the bar code individually, and the machine beeped its appreciation of a job well done.

"Thanks." Six months ogling the guy, and that was the best I could come up with.

"It's my job, but you're—" CuteGuy™ glanced up at me and, in the space of a heartbeat, his voice seemed to drop another octave. "—more than welcome."

Honeyed amber eyes darted restlessly, taking in every part of me. I started to feel warm just from the heat of them.

"Maybe I should stay here until you're done. Just to be sure the rest of your purchases go through okay."

"Sure." I needed to say something that amounted to more than one-word grunts. Had to, if I ever wanted to ask him out. Which I did. Now more than ever. "You're normally on the cigarette kiosk."

"Yeah." A pleased smile curled CuteGuy™'s lips, and I caught a flash of teeth. "I've been picked for management training."

Had the smile been because I noticed him on the kiosk before? Far more likely his happiness was due to the thought of his promotion. However, I could still feel his heated gaze as I stepped forward to swipe the remainder of my items.

The reflection I had seen in the window of the rival supermarket no longer amused me, and I fought the desire to finger comb my rat's nest of hair, knowing it would only draw further attention to my bedraggled appearance. Be confident, I chided, glancing to my left where CuteGuy™ was standing. He shifted his gaze with an embarrassed smile when I caught his eye, but before that, I swear he had been staring at me quite blatantly. Hungrily, even. Now would be the perfect time to give him my number, all casual-like. Except I didn't do casual—I exuded awkward. Besides, I didn't know my mobile number off the top of my head and, in my hurry tonight, I'd forgotten to grab it on my way out.

I could remember my name, though. Only just, in these circumstances, but....

"Finn."

"Sorry. What?"

"My name," I finished lamely, wishing I'd kept my mouth shut. Who introduces themselves to the checkout guy at the supermarket? No matter how you think he's been looking at you. Idiot!

"Finn," CuteGuy^{TM} repeated. He tapped the name badge pinned to his shirt, which I'd completely failed to notice. In my defense, the rest of him was far too distracting. "I'm Sam."

Grinning, CuteGuy^{TM}—Sam—looked like he was going to say something cheeky or flirtatious, and I knew I'd be expected to respond in kind. Panic swept over me and I fumbled the sausages, feeling them slip from my fingers. The milliseconds stretched out as though they were passing through black treacle, until the splat of uncooked meat hitting the linoleum jerked us back into real time.

"I'll get them," Sam offered with a wide smile, and as he squatted in front of me I could have sworn he tossed me a quick wink before dropping his gaze to search out the fallen sausages.

I could honestly say I don't think I had ever been so blatantly flirted with in such mundane, ordinary circumstances before. My face burned, not just because I felt extraordinarily self-conscious from the attention, but because my dick was showing an interest in the pretty boy all but kneeling at my feet. And even in my loose fitting cargo pants a chubby would be noticeable.

What can I say? My dick is in direct proportion to the rest of me. Have I mentioned I'm a bottom? Not through choice, mind, but when I see the look of fear on my partner's face, I voluntarily face plant myself on the bed, arse up. Not that I'm complaining, especially if they open me up with their tongue first, but for once I'd like to have someone look at my dick without trying to hide a wince.

None of these thoughts were doing anything to discourage my misbehaving member.

I glanced down, bypassing the distinct bulge in my trousers, to Sam's bowed head. He'd found the fallen package, his fingers squeezing my sausages. And that was a euphemism I could get behind. For a moment I thought he'd noticed my ever-growing arousal, but no, even more embarrassing, his line of sight continued to my sock-covered feet.

I wiggled my toes in their cotton-wool blend, my mind struggling for an explanation, because the truth—"I took my shoes off to give them to a homeless man"—well, that just made me sound like a nutter.

The movement of my toes seemed to galvanize him into motion. He stood abruptly, his gaze dropping to the sausages in his hand. He turned them until he could see the "reduced" label, and his eyes flickered to my bags, filled with the rest of my discounted produce.

"I've squashed your sausages." The flirtation of a moment ago had gone, even though the words were ripe for it. "I'll get you another pack."

"Those were the last ones," I said, but Sam was already headed to the meat aisle at a run.

He returned in less than a minute, a full-priced package of sausages in his hand.

"I can't afford—"

"It's fine." He scanned the reduced package but put the full-price sausages in my bag.

"Will you get in trouble?" I asked, not even bothering to hide my concern. I could do without a packet of sausages if that was the case.

"Nah." A small, worried frown replaced Sam's previous cheerful disposition. "Don't you get cold? It's not very warm, for April."

I glanced down at my feet, wiggling my toes again to get some life into them and wishing I'd worn thicker socks. "It's a bit nippy. Not to worry, I'll soon be in the warm."

"Oh. Good. You have a place...." He paused, teeth tugging on his lower lip as he searched for the right words. "To be?" he finished awkwardly, his lip shiny and reddened where he'd been biting it.

Shit. I had a place to be, all right. I glanced at my wrist, but it appeared I'd forgotten my watch too.

Sam glanced over my shoulder, his frown deepening. "It's eight twenty-five. You've got somewhere to go?" He seemed almost insistent about getting an answer.

"Yeah. The shelter on Chester Street." I still had to cook the bloody pasta dish or the sausages would be wasted. "It'll be getting busy."

"Good." Sam blew out a relieved sigh. "That's good. That you go there."

Any other time, I would have taken the opening, however hesitant, and chatted about my volunteering and the work we did at the shelter. We could always use more helpers, especially personable people, and Sam was easy to talk to. Maybe he could be convinced to help out once in a while, but today wasn't the day. I just didn't have the time. I *did* have a bag full of leaflets, though.

"Here." I tugged one from the bag at my feet and pressed it into Sam's hands, not realizing until he had taken it from me how dirty and dog-eared it looked. I should have taken one of the pristine leaflets from further down the pile.

Informing the till I had finished scanning, I was pleased to find I had a couple of bags of quality food for little more than a tenner, and the pocketful of loose change I'd grabbed from the dish by my front door should just about cover it. I pulled most of the change from my pocket, feeding the smaller coins into the machine first to reduce the amount of shrapnel in my pockets.

You know that feeling you get when you think you're being watched? I had that in spades. And couldn't hide my joy that possibly Sam was bestowing me with that hungry look again. Quickly, I glanced over in his direction, hoping to catch his eye, maybe share a smile, but Sam's intent focus was aimed at the leaflet I'd given him.

I waited for the machine to spit out my receipt—not that there was any chance to get the money back through petty cash—I just didn't want to get stopped at the door without it. I had a habit of setting off the beeper machines as I left stores. And at airports. Probably something to do with the parts they'd used to repair my shoulder.

Gathering my bags, I waited, hoping Sam would raise his gaze. When he didn't, I muttered a disconsolate, "See you around, maybe."

He finally looked up and graced me with a weak smile. "Yeah. Sure," he said, distractedly.

Biting back a disappointed sigh, I headed for the exit, but I couldn't help glancing over my shoulder one last time.

Sam hadn't moved but, as I watched, he carefully folded my leaflet and slipped it into his breast pocket.

THINGS HAD been remarkably quiet when I arrived at the shelter. So much so that within an hour of stepping through the door, I had whipped up a batch of sausage and tomato pasta, grated several blocks of cheese, and taken the huge cauldron-style pan through to the servers.

I'd even had time to beat myself up over my inability to talk normally when faced with a hot guy that I really liked and who had been totally flirting with me. Well, until he'd seen my socked feet and decided I was a madman, at least.

Of course, silence was golden, especially here, where an argument could start up over the number of peas on another person's plate. And the peace that I'd been enjoying shattered around me at the sound of raised voices.

One voice, above all others.

Freddie.

"No! I saw you! You're trying to kill me!"

Not again.

I raced from the kitchen, desperate to save Oliver from the onslaught of Freddie's paranoid ramblings. Oliver hadn't been with us long and had yet to work out exactly how to deal with some of our more difficult guests. I didn't want Freddie's meltdown to send my latest volunteer running screaming for the hills. Never to return.

It had happened before.

I slowed as I approached the doors—bursting into the room with all guns blazing wouldn't help anyone—and entered the main hall as casually as possible, taking in the scene with a sweeping glance.

A small cluster of men were gathered against the far wall. They had no food and were watching the proceedings with a myriad of expressions—fear, caution, and for some, outright glee. Behind the low serving table, slack-jawed and pale, Oliver gripped his serving spoon with rapidly whitening knuckles. A bowl had been abandoned on the table, most of its contents splashed across the beige Formica top. At least my pasta dish hadn't been launched at the wall. This time.

"Everything all right out here?" I asked, directing my question to Freddie and drawing his attention away from Oliver. Freddie wasn't really that dangerous—unless he caught you with flying crockery—but Oliver looked ready to piss his pants. I decided to play the situation down until I knew what I was dealing with. "Did you drop your food? Not a problem. Oliver can clear this up, and I'll get you a new portion."

Freddie reared back, the flaps of his layered coats and jackets flaring out around him, giving him the look of a frilled dragon lizard under attack.

"No! He tried to *kill* me." Freddie's words rose to a crescendo, and he stabbed a finger in Oliver's direction.

"I didn't," Oliver stuttered. "I just put cheese on his pasta. He asked for it."

"Poison!" Freddie roared, and with his heavy, unruly ginger beard and wild eyes, he sounded as scary as he looked. It was only training and years of experience that stopped me from running away like a frightened kitten. "He sprinkled poison all over my food. Brazenly, right in front of my eyes."

"Cheese," Oliver protested weakly.

"Oliver, clear up the mess, and then serve the rest of the gentlemen waiting. I'll serve Freddie myself."

Trusting Oliver to follow my instructions, I turned to Freddie, focusing only on him.

"I made this pasta myself, Freddie. It's fresh from the stove. You like my cooking, don't you?"

"Yes, Mr. Finn, but he"—Freddie gestured to Oliver with a dirt-encrusted finger—"put the poison on after."

There was little point arguing with Freddie once he had an idea in his head. The only way to sway him was to lead by example.

"How about I dish some up for the both of us? I'm starving." It wasn't until I uttered the words that I realized the truth behind them. I hadn't eaten since rolling out of bed after my impromptu nap earlier in the evening, which meant my last meal had been a sandwich at lunch. "And this does smell good."

As I spoke, I filled two bowls with pasta, placing them on the table in front of us. Carefully watching Freddie's reaction with every movement, I picked up the bowl of cheese.

"I'm having cheese on mine," I said as I sprinkled some over my pasta. Not much. Something in cheese had a tendency to bring me up in itchy red blotches. "Do you want some?"

He didn't protest about poison, which I took as an improvement, but he didn't actively ask for any either.

"It's good," I reassured him, taking a small amount between my fingers and popping it into my mouth. I prayed to a god I didn't really believe in that this cheese wasn't strong enough to give me an instantaneous reaction. The last thing I needed was for Freddie to see me break out in hives in front of him. "See. Tasty."

"Okay." Freddie's voice lost the aggressive edge that had made grown men quake just moments ago, sounding more like the Freddie we were used to when his paranoid delusions didn't get in the way. "Cheese is good on pasta."

"Yeah. It is." I sprinkled some on his bowl of pasta.

"Can I have more?" Freddie asked, a childlike quality to his question. "I like cheese."

"Sure. Just a little bit." I fought the temptation to let out a sigh of relief. Crisis averted. I wondered what had set Freddie off today. Maybe he would talk to me. He sometimes did after one of these episodes. "Want me to eat with you?"

"Please."

I dragged us off to a table in the far corner to give us some privacy. Not that it mattered. The others tended to keep their distance after one of Freddie's episodes.

We ate while Freddie rambled on about nothing of any consequence, and after a few attempts to lead the conversation back to his actions that evening were ignored, I knew I would get nothing out of him tonight. When he began to tell the same story for the third time, my thoughts started to wander.

I couldn't get the way Sam had looked at me out of my mind. I still wasn't used to men looking at me in that way, as though they wanted to climb me like a tree. I'd known envy as a sportsman, could recognize it easily—teammates jealous of my height and the breadth of my shoulders, or of my innate sense of balance. But having a man look at me as if he wanted to lick whipped cream from my abs was quite a different story.

I was the wrong side of twenty-five, and I could count the number of male partners I'd had on one hand. I blamed my late-blossoming attraction to guys on the fact that I'd been destined to be a professional sportsman, and we all know how well those two suspects go together. Twenty-one years old with my name being bandied about as a possible for the next England tour, my world and the plans I'd made had dissolved into pain, anguish, and thankfully, unconsciousness, after a bone-shattering tackle.

By the time the surgeons had rebuilt my shoulder, I'd all but got a grip on the fact that my rugby career was over before it had truly started. I guess it would have been easy to wallow in self-pity and alcohol, maybe even end up like some of the guys here at the shelter. I wish I could proclaim an iron will that kept me on the straight and narrow but, to be honest, I was on some pretty strong pain meds for the first few months, and by the time I could consider drinking without putting my life at risk, I had all but sorted myself out. Even to the point of acknowledging the truth behind my lack of girlfriends, and the reason why I had always showered with my back to my teammates.

By then I was already volunteering at the shelter and thinking about what to do with the rest of my life. My club helped pull a few strings, and I had gotten into a course studying sports science. I was putting that to use helping an architect friend I'd met at uni to design specialist playgrounds. We called them playgrounds, but they were mainly for adults, normally with a specialist theme in mind, or for sports schools where the school wanted the kids to think they were having fun while they were honing the skills for their particular discipline.

At university the feelings that I'd denied for so long had been given the space to emerge and grow, but being several years older than most of the others on my course and with my belief in my body shot to shit, I did little in the way of serious experimentation.

I had tried visiting several gay clubs but, not a clubbing type in general, I lacked the self-confidence to draw attention to myself by throwing some shapes on the dance floor, and there was no way I could make the first move. I worried my towering bulk would come across as threatening, especially with the type of guys I appeared to be attracted to. Those who saw me nursing a drink while trying to meld into the wall probably thought I was club security. Occasionally guys would approach me, but they only confirmed that I was woefully ill-prepared for my first forays into the gay scene.

During one such interaction, the guy—who was older than me and almost as big—had palmed my stomach. I'd been in physiotherapy at the time and still had a certain amount of definition on my abs. He'd leaned in closer, his breath heavy with whisky and tobacco as it fanned the side of my face, and told me I could be his perfect bear cub if I'd only stop exercising. I'd laughed along with him but had excused myself soon after, fleeing the club in fear that he'd wanted me for something kinky and unimaginable.

Later, in my room, after Google had enlightened me, I felt embarrassed for running away like that. By the time I'd logged off, my head was full of images of not just bears, but otters, wolves, and pups. Lots and lots of pups. Although I still had trouble differentiating between them and twinks. Not that it mattered, since apparently both types turned me on. With no desire to be a cub to somebody's bear, and lacking the faith in myself to go after what I really wanted, I didn't return to that club again.

My confidence had been all about my rugby, and it had more or less died out there on the pitch with the shoulder of my throwing arm. Most of that joint was plastic and metal now, and sometimes my self-belief seemed as brittle as the materials inside me.

University had provided me with a degree, several bed partners, and my longest relationship to date, and had slowly started to repair my spirit. And surrounded by spectacle-wearing hipsters in skinny jeans that had my dick perking up whether they showed any interest in me or not, I established my *type*.

Which led me neatly back to what to do about Sam. Did the fact that I had finally spoken to him hinder or help my case? It had certainly done nothing to quell my desire for him.

A clang echoed around the cavernous main hall, indicating the front door had been opened and allowed to slam shut. I glanced over to where someone would enter the hall if they had come in for anything other than to use the basic toilets but, when nobody appeared, I returned my attention to my food and Freddie's waning monologue. A movement in my peripheral vision had me turning toward the entrance once more, just in time to catch a glimpse of a jacket far too stylish to belong to one of our regular clientele, and the back of somebody's head. Somebody much shorter than me and with dark blond hair. Maybe even burnt umber.

The visitor could have been a thousand and one people. The chances of it being the one I wanted it to be were unlikely. Any resemblance must be simply because Sam was on my mind.

Chances were I'd never find out. He was gone before I could so much as push back my chair.

A COUPLE of loaves of bread and two packets of bacon. Hardly the haul of the century. As the supermarket's sliding doors opened in front of me, I trudged out into the chilled evening air and sighed heavily. My despondency had little to do with the lack of interesting pickings on the cheapie shelf, though. There'd been no sign of Sam today, not at the kiosk or the self-service tills. I'd even scanned the rest of the tills, but he'd been nowhere to be found.

I'd probably scared him off. Introducing myself, because I thought he'd been flirting, when in reality he was probably only being nice.

Trying to push Sam out of my mind, I forcibly turned my thoughts to what I could make with the bacon. Before I could come up with any ideas, though, I heard the slap of running footsteps hitting the pavement behind me. I moved to the side to allow the runner to pass while I carried on walking.

"Finn!"

I frowned but continued on my way, certain that I'd misheard my name in the howling of the wind.

"Finn! Slow up, mate."

The wind rarely managed to compose full sentences, so I did as instructed. A hand landed on my shoulder, then fell away as I turned around.

"I almost missed you," Sam said, words forced out between each inhale as he attempted to get his breath back. "I finished my shift and was waiting in the CCTV room for you to appear on the screen. Okay, that just sounds creepy. I'm not stalking you or anything. I just…. I hoped you'd be in today."

He hoped I'd be in! My heart skipped a beat, and I felt giddy with excitement. I had to remind myself I was twenty-seven and not a teenager with his first crush. Sam held up two sturdy carrier bags—the type you have to pay for—bulging at the seams, then proceeded to throw metaphorical cold water all over my brief flare of joy.

"I have no idea what I would have done with all this stuff if you hadn't shown up," Sam said, opening one of the bags to reveal it stuffed full of discounted food. "Everything was going so fast, and I didn't want you to miss out. So I bought some bits for you. I hope the stuff I picked up is suitable. I didn't know how much of it you could use."

"That's…"—not at all what I'd been expecting or hoping for, but I took the bags from him anyway—"very kind of you."

Luckily, Sam was rummaging around in the messenger bag slung over his shoulder, so any disappointment that I wasn't adept enough to hide went unnoticed.

"Here. I got you some shoes too." He pulled the trainers from his bag, his gaze dropping to my feet as he held them out to me. "Oh well. I—"

"They'll be greatly appreciated," I assured him as I reached for the shoes. My cold fingers brushed against his warmer ones, and I couldn't stop the shiver that ran through my body at the contact.

"Mate, you're cold," he said. "You totally need a hat."

For the first time since he stopped me I noticed the hat he was wearing. Although how I was only seeing it now was a testament to how surprised I'd been to have him chase me. A bright purple beanie with the face of a monster sewn into the front, it had ears, horns, and long plaited tassels that hung on either side of his face.

"I've been keeping an eye on the weather, and they reckon it's gonna be unseasonably cold over the next few nights," Sam continued. "There's talk of frosts and all sorts. Maybe even snow."

I took a breath for him—it seemed like an appropriate point for nonverbal punctuation—but he didn't stop or even slow down, just ploughed on.

"Even with that glorious mane of yours—has anyone mentioned you look like a lion?—but even that thick hair and facial fuzz won't keep you warm. You have to have a hat. Here—" He tugged at the hat and pulled it from his head, static dragging his hair in all directions. "—have mine."

"I couldn't—" I got no further, distracted by the flash of lime green fleece that lined the purple, and he took the opportunity to talk straight over me.

"'Course you can. I've got loads of them." He stretched up, leaning in close, and forced the hat over my hair. It was a tight fit. With the bags in one hand and Sam's shoes in the other, I couldn't have stopped him even if I wanted to. Which I didn't. Not when he was standing so close, all warm and sweet smelling. He sniffed, and I wondered if maybe he needed the hat to stave off a cold. "My mum gets them for me. The more unusual the better. Honestly, I think this one's a child's hat. Look, if you squeeze the bulbs on the ends that hang down, the monster's horns wiggle."

He gave me a demonstration but since I was wearing the hat, I could only visualize the effect. It made Sam grin, though. In that moment I was thankful I had my hands full, because the desire to cradle his face in my palms and kiss him until his smooth cheeks were red raw from my *lion's* fuzz overwhelmed me.

"Ridiculous hats to cover ridiculous hair. That's what my mum always says. And I think she goes out of her way to prove a point. At least no one would dare take the piss out of you for wearing it." Sam gestured in my direction, his eyes following the path of his hand. "You know, what with you being a mountain of a man."

I wanted to ask if anyone took the piss out of him, but what I actually said was, "I like your hair. It's not ridiculous."

"You do?"

"Yeah." I waved a hand above my head, knocking against what I could only assume were my newly acquired horns. "Especially when it was spiky and colorful."

"Yeah?" Sam looked pleased, and I allowed myself a smile. "Me too. Ah well, I only have to keep it like this when I'm working. Could be worse, right? I can have it as spiky and bright as I like when I hit the town."

Sam colored and glanced away, the bus trundling past us seeming to capture his attention. "Sorry, that was insensitive. Since you can't...." Finally lost for words, Sam gestured at the bags in my hand.

"Because I spend every evening at the shelter?" I asked, hoping that was what he meant. I chose to volunteer. And it wasn't always this manic. I did get more than the occasional night off, when we were fully staffed. "It does put the kibosh on any sort of social life or relationship, I guess."

"Why should it, though?" Sam protested, his tone turning serious. "Just because...." He made that flailing motion in my direction again. "Fuck it. If we were in a club, I'd be all up in your personal space by now."

I didn't point out that he had been up in my personal space already. "If we were in a club I guarantee you wouldn't even notice me. Apparently, I have the ability to make this bulk of mine completely invisible."

"The plight of—" Sam broke off from what he had been about to say and blurted out, "Come for a coffee with me?"

"Now?"

"Yeah."

God, how I would have loved to just drop everything to go and listen to Sam talking nineteen to the dozen with me inserting appropriate words in the spaces he left when he finally paused to breathe.

"I'd love to," I began. Sam's face lit up, his smile broadening into a grin. "But I can't."

His smile faded away. I knew people were relying on me, but that didn't make me feel any better for wiping the smile from his face, or about the way his eyes lost a little of their spark. I felt terrible for crushing the joy that he exuded, but I held up the bags he had given me, hoping they would be explanation enough. "Sorry, but I've got places to be."

"The shelter," Sam said in a tone far more understanding than I thought I was entitled to. Or that I felt toward the shelter in that moment.

"Maybe we could do it another time?" I ventured with a flare of uncharacteristic bravery. "Or, you could come with me."

"To the shelter?" A trail of faint lines furrowed the skin around Sam's eyes and between his eyebrows, the only indication of his discomfort and uncertainty. "I don't think.... It's just that—"

"No problem." I cut him off before he had to tarnish our conversation with a lie. I knew not everyone was cut out for volunteering. Didn't stop me wanting to get to know him. "If you still want to catch a coffee another time, I can always find time during the day. It's one of the perks—"

"Perks?" Sam spluttered, then seemed to recover. "I've got the early shift for the next few days, but I could meet you Friday at, say, ten. We could have breakfast."

"That sounds great." It sounded like a date, but I didn't want to jinx matters, so I kept that thought to myself.

"That's two days from now. We could meet here." He gestured back toward the entrance to the store. "There's a clock, and it's warm in the lobby area so you won't have to wait in the cold. I'm notorious for being late. *Please* don't think I've stood you up. Maybe I'll bring you some gloves? I have loads."

"Why? You don't have ridiculous fingers," I teased, glancing down at his hands. His fingers were long but slim, the nails bitten, and there was no way any gloves of Sam's would fit my huge paws.

Sam laughed softly, slipping his hands into the pocket of his dark puffa jacket. "I think they come in sets with the hats. Or the scarves she buys me. Mums, eh? She's given up trying to get meat on my bones, so she tries to keep me warm in other ways."

"Your jacket would do that. It looks like a quilt."

"I picked it because it gives me some bulk, but I guess it's like a girl wearing a padded bra. Take it off and the guys are disappointed."

Guys? Was he trying to confirm he was gay? I didn't claim to have fully functioning gaydar, but I'd already picked up enough vibes to be pretty sure he played for my team.

The hat must have been cutting off the blood supply to my brain, because I couldn't do flirting, didn't know how, but I decided to give it a go anyway. "I wouldn't be disappointed."

And failed.

"In a flat-chested woman?"

I sucked at flirting. Didn't stop me giving it another go, though. Guess I'd have to be more obvious and hope I didn't scare him away. "In what's under your coat."

Sam's smile was blinding, and I guess I had my answer.

"You should go." Sam said with a sigh and cocked his head in the direction I'd been heading before he'd stopped me. "You'll be late."

I glanced at the clock, housed in a tower above the store and testament to the fact it had once been a more prestigious building than a supermarket. Now only the facade of the listed building remained.

"You're right," I said, trying to keep the disappointment from my voice, then gestured toward the storefront. "I'll see you on Friday at ten."

"Yeah." Sam nodded. "I'll see you then."

"Thanks for the hat," I called after him as he turned and headed in the opposite direction. He raised a hand in acknowledgement, glancing back over his shoulder before he jogged away.

This time, I openly watched him until he was out of sight.

BLOODY FILING cabinet. I slammed the bottom drawer shut with my foot, simultaneously yanking on the handle of the top drawer. Even more annoyed at my loss of temper than the misbehaving metal drawers, I rested my elbows on the top of the filing cabinet and took a couple of calming breaths.

At the shelter, where sometimes it only took one wrong look to set someone off, a short fuse could blow up in your face. I'd be better off not being here than hanging around with the raving hump. Except that I had to stay, because I had an interview to conduct. Jenna had phoned me earlier and said she had been contacted by a guy who was interested in volunteering. And, as the longest-serving volunteer, the job of checking out new starters fell to me.

Hence the reason I was at the shelter several hours earlier than normal and in an epically bad mood, for me, which was probably mildly irritated for other people. I knew it had nothing to do with coming in early and everything to do with missing my trip to the supermarket. A ridiculous thing to get wound up about—Sam had all but told me he wouldn't be around because he was working the early shift, and we were meeting for coffee tomorrow. But this was the second day in a row I hadn't seen his smiling face, and I missed it. Missed him. Ludicrous feelings to have when this time last week we hadn't exchanged a single word, I know, but he was so easy to talk to, and I felt comfortable in his presence. I honestly couldn't say that for most of the people I met.

Normally, the thought of a date would have me wound tighter than a knotted rope, but even if this wasn't really a date, I couldn't wait for tomorrow.

Calmer now, I gave the drawer another try. It slid out easily, allowing me access to the forms and starter pack I would need for the new volunteer, if I found him suitable.

"Finn? Should you be in here?"

The soft, questioning tone, devoid of any accusation, surprised me almost as much as the question. And the fact that the person asking knew my name.

I pivoted on the balls of my feet, turning toward the open door of my office where an unexpectedly familiar figure stood.

"*Sam*? Wha—?"

"It's okay." Sam took two steps into the office, his hands held out at his sides, flat and open, palms facing me. I'd used that very same nonthreatening body language myself on many an occasion. I was impressed, but I did wonder why Sam felt he had to use it on me. "I won't tell anyone you were in here, but you probably shouldn't be looking through that filing cabinet."

As he spoke, his voice never deviating from that gentle but firm tone, he moved toward me. When he got close enough, he placed a hand on my arm, just above the elbow, as if to guide me from the room.

"Sam, it's *my* office."

"Of course, but maybe it would be better if we go and find one of your staff. I'm sure they could do with your help out front," Sam murmured patiently as he encouraged me toward the door.

I dug my heels in. "It *really* is my office." I gestured to a framed photo on the wall of me receiving a donation from a local Z list celebrity in the name of publicity, sorry, charity. I much preferred the shot of me with Austin Healy at a charity event run by my former rugby club, but that was on the opposite wall and vanity was hardly my number-one priority.

"*Your* office?" Already close, Sam swayed closer and appeared to sniff me. I could have sworn he muttered *Homme* under his breath. I was impressed he could identify my shower gel/body wash combo, if a little perturbed by the whole smelling-me thing. "Shit." Sam's hand fell away from my arm and he took a step back. I missed the warmth of his touch immediately. "Shit!"

"What are you doing here?" I managed to ask, just as Jenna bustled in through the door, frowning.

"Finn, have you seen our—" Her gaze settled on Sam and her face relaxed. I wouldn't say she smiled, because that wasn't her way. "Sam, there you are! Sorry to have left you on your own, but Bernie was acting up again. I see you two have met." She glanced between us and her heavily kohled eyes narrowed. "Do you two know each other?"

With Sam still looking at me as if I had two heads, and uncharacteristically struck dumb, I answered. "Sort of. Sam works in the store where I pick up the extra food for the evening shift. I gave him a leaflet a couple of days ago. The two bags of food from the other day were from him."

And the shoes. And the hat. I glanced toward my jacket, hanging from the old-fashioned coat stand in the corner, a flash of purple visible from the pocket. The hat that he had given to me, still warm from his body heat, with concerns about the overnight drop in temperature.

"Oh well, if that's the case there's hardly a need for an interview, then." She rounded on Sam, pinning him with her gaze. Vivid purple contacts today to match the streaks in her jet-black hair. "Why didn't you tell me the boss sent you? I'd have put you to work straight away and got him to complete the paperwork later. I'll grab you two a couple of coffees, then get back out there. Don't like to leave Oliver on his own too long."

"The boss," Sam muttered, then cursed under his breath.

I ignored it in favor of an awkward silence, lost as I was in my own epiphany.

"Well, this is embarrassing," Sam muttered, but for once I spoke over him.

"You thought I was homeless?" I blurted out.

Taking another step back, Sam shrugged and stuffed his hands into the pockets of his jeans. Tight, skinny jeans. Despite the abject horror that had swept over me at my realization, I couldn't help but admire his legs in those trousers.

He glanced down at my feet. "In fairness, the first time we met you weren't wearing any shoes. And you looked like Grizzly Adams."

I must have been gaping openmouthed, because he pulled a hand from his pocket and gestured to me. "You know? Tough-looking mountain man?"

I knew who Grizzly Adams was. That wasn't the part I had a problem with. "And I smelled offensive." At least now I understood the sniffing.

"Not offensive, no, Finn. Never. Just…. Aww, crap! This wasn't how this was supposed to go."

"And how was that?" There was more of an edge to my tone than I liked to admit. For some reason I felt as if I'd been played.

"I just wanted to learn a bit more about what life was like for you. I came down the other day, but you were there eating right near the door and I didn't want you to associate me with charity before I'd had a chance to ask—"

"Coffee, boys. Hope that's not too much milk for you, Sam. Didn't know if you'd want sugar." Jenna placed the mugs on my desk, ignoring the coasters and using my blotter instead. She tossed a couple of sugar sachets next to the mugs, the good ones left over from when we'd last had take-out coffee. The click of her tongue piercing against her teeth alerted me to her concerted appraisal. Even without her degree in psychology, the defensive nature of our body language was far too easy to read. Aware my arms were folded tightly across my chest, I dropped them to my sides.

"Is there a problem?" Jenna asked, making no attempt to hide her concern. Ignoring Sam, she graced me with an intense stare, her eyes zeroing in on my shoulder and lingering there a moment too long. When I didn't answer straight away, she raised one dark and perfectly sculpted eyebrow. She looked just like Mum, apart from the piercing. Sounded like her too. "Finn? Oh my God, he's not an ex-boy—"

"No! Jenna, it's fine." I hurried to placate her before she ripped Sam a new one for something he hadn't yet had the opportunity to do. "Just a slight misunderstanding. Go tend to the customers. Oliver must be run off his feet out there."

She gave Sam one of her patented glares, guaranteed to quieten even the most temperamental of our visitors, then left without another word. I knew the thought of Oliver out on his own would send her running. She had a soft spot for him a mile wide, not that she'd ever let that show to the outside world. Me, I'd known her before the tattoos and piercings—she couldn't hide from me.

"Customers?" Sam asked once she had gone.

"What would you call them?" I asked, snappier than I had any right to be with a prospective volunteer. "Homeless people? Down and outs? Tramps? Hobos?"

"Nah." Sam shook his head. "Hobo's an American word. It refers to migrant workers and originated in the late nineteenth century. Men who rode the railways searching for work at the end of the line, working on the railway or in the latest frontier town. Many were ex-servicemen who had trouble settling in one place for one reason or another." He paused, then muttered, "Don't look so surprised."

I wasn't aware of what I looked like. Sam's rambling had caught me unaware, but I was pleased he appeared to know the distinction in the various terms people bandied about.

"I do read, you know," Sam said, his tone more defensive than I'd ever heard him. "I have an A-level in English. Being a trainee supermarket manager isn't exactly my goal in life. And I'm talking too much again."

I dragged a hand through my hair, not thinking about how it would make me look until after the hand had fallen back to my side. "I like listening to you talk, Sam. It means I don't have to worry about filling the silences. Sometimes it's kinda overwhelming, though. Anyway, where was I?"

"Customers," Sam offered.

"I guess I don't have to tell you after that brief lesson on hobos, but don't ever let them hear you use any of those expressions. Pride is a big thing for the people who use the shelter, and we try to let them retain as much of it as possible. We refer to them as customers or guests. Remember that and you'll do fine." I picked up the Welcome pack from the top of the filing cabinet and dropped it on my desk, way too close to the discarded coffees. "You'll need to fill these in, and I'll have to run some background checks."

"That's fine, but you haven't even interviewed me."

"Much of this job is about empathy and common sense. You seem to have plenty of both. And I don't really get enough people through the door looking to help to turn someone away just because of a misunderstanding. You refused payment for a bag of food that I know cost more than twenty quid and handed in an almost new pair of trainers."

"I was giving that stuff to you, not the shelter. I thought—"

"Same thing," I interrupted before we could revisit old ground, and embarrassing old ground at that.

"Not really," Sam protested, although I couldn't see the distinction.

"You gave me your hat. Offered to buy me a coffee. Oh God!" I sighed heavily and buried my face in my hands. "You thought I was a homeless person and you still offered to buy me a coffee."

"You don't sound too happy about it."

"I thought—" *You were interested in me, when all you wanted to do was keep me warm.* I couldn't follow that line of thinking out loud, but Sam had no such compunction.

"I was asking you out on a date."

"Yeah," I agreed, more than a little mortified by this point.

"Yes, you'll go on a date? Because you don't sound too enamored with the idea anymore."

"What? Wait. Back up." Maybe I'd been a little too forceful, because Sam actually took a step back, banging his thigh against the corner of my desk. "You *were* asking me out on a date?"

"I thought we'd established that several days ago."

"Even though you thought I was homeless?" Despite his reassurance I obviously couldn't let this go.

"It was only coffee. I wasn't planning on taking you home." Sam grinned, a sight I realized I'd been missing for the last few minutes. He gestured in my direction, hand wafting in a zigzag across my torso before coming back up to make a circle in the general area of my head. "Okay, so looking like that, I probably would have taken you home. I'm shallow and you're gorgeous."

I had been an unholy mess who smelled a bit, with no shoes, and he'd thought I was gorgeous. He'd thought I lived on the streets and still wanted to take me out. I couldn't let him get away through my inability to articulate my feelings.

"Yes."

"What?" Sam frowned, and I realized I hadn't expressed myself particularly eloquently.

"You're not shallow. You wouldn't be here if you were, and you certainly wouldn't have asked out a homeless man. Yes, I'll go out for coffee with you."

"Even though you're my boss?"

"Nobody's the boss here." I gestured toward the rooms beyond the closed door of the office. "We all work together. I just get to do the paperwork because I'm here most often."

Sam looked thoughtful as he ran a finger along the edge of the desk. "I haven't filled in the paperwork yet."

Disappointment flooded through me. Sam had tracked me down, and now he wasn't interested in working here. Maybe he was as shallow as he claimed. "You don't want to volunteer?"

"Of course I do. I wouldn't have come here just to chase some tail. Equally, I don't want the other staff to think I'm dating the boss to get preferential treatment."

"Oh—" I didn't get any further with that sentence because Sam's hand snaked around the back of my neck, dragged me down, and crushed our mouths together. I took his open mouth as an invitation to capture what I'd desperately wanted for months. He tasted faintly of mint and something spicy, curry or chili, maybe? The hand at my neck relaxed into my hair, teasing at my wavy tresses, and his other hand rested at my hip, bunching the fabric of my shirt and T-shirt in his tight grasp.

Eventually, he pulled back, leaving me too breathless to speak.

"Now you can tell them that your boyfriend didn't want you to give up your charity work to spend more time with him, so he decided to volunteer too." He grinned.

"Boyfriend?"

"Moving too fast?"

"Maybe a little, but I'm fine with that."

"Fast for me too. I tend to check that we'd be compatible physically before I agree to date someone. I'm a tart, so sue me. And honestly, most of the guys that pick me up are only after one thing."

He rolled his hips in a lazy circle, brushing his groin against my thigh and leaving me in no doubt what he was talking about. His hard-on pressed against the zipper of his sinfully tight jeans. He hadn't been sporting that when he'd appeared in my office earlier—I'd have noticed.

The thought that just kissing me had him springing a boner sent a wave of lust coursing through me, coalescing at my cock. Thank God for my wardrobe full of baggy cargo pants.

"Does your door lock?" Sam's fingers had slipped beneath my shirt and brushed against the skin just below my ribs, making me shiver.

"What? We can't. Not here." He straddled my leg and pressed against me, the slow rocking of his hips driving me wild. I wanted to rip those skinny jeans down, just to the top of his thighs, and throw him over my desk, but.... "My sister's out there."

That stopped him in his tracks, unfortunately. "Jenna?"

I nodded, not wanting to talk about my sibling right at that moment. The rubbing against my thigh ceased, and I couldn't stifle my groan of disappointment.

"No wonder she looked like she wanted to skin me alive earlier," Sam said with a smile, but apprehension lingered around the edge of his voice. "You're right, we can't do this here."

"Scared?" I teased, leaning in for a quick kiss. Craving more contact, even though my hands still gripped the protruding bones of his pelvis.

"A little." His fingers danced lightly over the flesh of my stomach. "You're buff."

"A little." Nails scratched a path over the wide V of my treasure trail. "More hearth rug than six-pack these days."

"I like it." Sam snorted a laugh, and the puff of air brushed my cheekbone. "Maybe I can forego my normal rule of checking out the merchandise. For you."

"That's the sweetest thing anyone has said to me," I murmured into the skin of his jaw, and got another of those huffed sounds of amusement. Unfortunately, I wasn't joking. "Seriously. And I'll forego my rule of not putting out on the first date. Does that make me a sure thing?"

This time he pulled away and laughed outright, his head thrown back, all teeth and warm breath. "It makes you like every other guy I've ever met."

"That doesn't sound good." Even as I spoke, I ducked my head to place a kiss at the base of his exposed throat.

"But you're breaking your dating rules for me, just as I am for you." I nibbled at the bone revealed by his open-neck shirt and felt more than heard the strangled noise he let forth. "I do have one question, though."

"Yeah?"

"Do you top or bottom?"

"What?" I jerked my head up, narrowly avoiding a collision with his chin.

"I'm curious. You don't have to answer right now." Sam's grin was filthy now. "Just at any point before we get somewhere more private."

My facial hair normally hid my propensity to blush when I didn't know how to react, but I could feel the heat creeping out from under my scruff and heading over my cheekbones. I suspected if he pushed up the hem of my T-shirt, he'd find it spreading across my chest too. In fact, I'm surprised my chest hair hadn't burst into flames, such was the heat that accompanied the thought of topping Sam. My traitorous dick, already invested in the game, had picked up the ball and run with it.

"Hey, forget it." Sam's voice was back to that calming tone of earlier. The one that suggested I might be about to take flight. "Not important."

"Bottom," I blurted out, then figured I should provide some more information. Shame my tongue didn't agree, as I fell over it several times trying to clarify my response. "Well, that is. I mean, I haven't…."

At Sam's surprised expression, I managed to stammer out, "I'm not a virgin or anything. It's just… not with that many guys—" At some point in my ramblings, my hands had fallen away from Sam's hips and I'd taken a step backward. I shoved my hands in my pockets and shrugged. "And I've always…. But, well, it always seemed for the best."

Sam reached out, snagging two fingers in my belt loops and tugging me back against him. "You don't sound so sure."

"It's just, I'm…."—I hated to boast—"in proportion."

Sam rolled his hips into me and, with our height difference and the way he lounged against the desk, my dick rubbed against his abdomen, just above the waistband of his jeans.

"I figured as much, but I'm exceptionally pleased to have it confirmed." His voice dropped to a seductive growl. And I thought *I* was the bear cub. "I'd have been a little disappointed if you weren't. But only a little."

A palm closed over the prominent bulge in my pants, slumped to the left but rising all the while, and fingers searched out the solid line of my dick, defining its shape and length. Sam's hand was tiny compared to my own. It hardened my resolve, amongst other things.

"Bottom," I said, more forcefully than before.

"Shame."

"Shame?" I could do little more than croak the word out.

"Hmm. Such a waste." Sam punctuated the sentiment with a squeeze, and my dick throbbed an encouraging answer.

"You want me to top?"

I caught a flash of a wicked smile as Sam leaned close enough to whisper in my ear, "Size is everything."

I groaned. "You're going to kill me before the end of this shift."

"Can't have that." Sam slipped out from between me and the desk. "Let's go and help people less fortunate than ourselves. Maybe I can fill out the forms later."

"Sure." Despite being the one to put a stop to our shenanigans, I confess I hated that Sam had been the one to move away. "Take them home. I can pick them up tomorrow when we meet for coffee."

"About that." Sam bit his bottom lip in a most endearing manner, and then a cheeky grin bloomed on his face. "My flatmate has her boyfriend over tonight. They are *very* loud during sex."

"So you're temporarily homeless?" Sam had made all the running so far, so it was time for me to catch up. "Shall we change that coffee to breakfast? At mine."

"Hell, yeah. I'd happily follow you back to your cave." Sam let out a sexy chuckle. "I'd even do it in my socks."

LILLIAN FRANCIS is an English writer who likes to dabble in many genres.

Always determined she wanted to write, a "proper" job and raising a family distracted Lillian for over a decade. Over the years and, thanks to the charms of the Internet, Lillian realized she'd been writing at least one of her characters in the wrong gender. Ever since, she's been happily letting her "boys" run her writing life.

Lillian now divides her time between family, a job and the numerous men in her head all clamoring for "their" story to be told.

Lillian lives in an imposing castle on a wind-swept desolate moor or in an elaborate "shack" on the edge of a beach somewhere depending on her mood, with the heroes of her stories either chained up in the dungeon or wandering the shack serving drinks in nothing but skimpy barista aprons.

In reality, she would love to own a camper van and to live by the sea.

You can contact Lillian on her blog at http://lillianfrancis.blogspot.co.uk, on Twitter (@LillianFrancis_), or on Goodreads https://www.goodreads.com/Lillian_Francis.

Golden Bear
G.P. Keith

I.

IT WAS a dark and stormy night, but Norm still worked at his computer, ignoring the moaning wind and rattling windows. Every now and then an especially strong gust would come, almost shifting the house—and then he would find himself breaking off to stare balefully out at the darkness beyond the window.

Being alone in the house didn't help. Chris had left that morning, despite the weather, to spend the holidays with his parents. When Norm had pointed out that icy road conditions and strong winds would make the six-hour drive to Ottawa treacherous, his friend merely shrugged.

"Oh, they'll have salted the highways. I'll be fine."

Norm didn't mention his concern that maybe *he* wouldn't be.

Chris's parting remark, "Don't wreck the house while I'm gone," hadn't helped either, especially when weather conditions worsened—more freezing rain that, with plunging temperatures, put a fresh coat of ice on the already overburdened power lines and tree branches throughout the city. And now Chris's house was Norm's responsibility.

By evening the weather network said the massive storm system affecting most of southern Ontario and parts of the New England states had caused power outages for over 100,000 residents in Toronto, where Norm lived. Downed tree branches caused traffic mayhem throughout the city. One news item showed an image of a car flattened by a fallen tree, and several of roofs damaged by tree limbs as well. Asking himself what *he* would do if something crashed through *his* roof, Norm had only a vague idea of calling 911—and screaming a lot.

Work, therefore, was a welcome distraction, even though the larger gusts did challenge his concentration. When that happened, he found it helpful to remind himself of the ways in which he was fortunate in his present circumstance. For example, working at home he didn't have to brave the storm.

The prospect of a separate room for a home office had been one of the reasons he'd moved in with Chris in the first place—that and the reasonable rent his friend had offered for use of his two back bedrooms (having just broken up with his long-term partner, Chris hadn't wanted to live alone). Last summer the offer had been too good to turn down, but now, alone in the middle of this winter storm, Norm wished he was back in his tiny one-bedroom apartment in the steel-and-concrete tower that no storm could ever menace.

The wind was getting worse, and now a gust came that definitely shook the house. Norm closed his eyes, gritted his teeth, and returned to listing things he was thankful for, like the fact that the house still had power.

Just then there came a crash in the backyard and Norm leaped to his feet, his heart pounding.

For a full minute he listened, but there was nothing more, only the wind and the rattling windows. But when he turned back to his computer, he saw that the screen had gone entirely blue, with a single message: *Loss of Internet Connection. Contact Service Provider.*

"Oh hell!"

Norm went downstairs, turned on the porch light, and looked out into the backyard. A large tree branch had fallen onto the shed. It pinned down several wires that now stretched tautly up to the house. Another wire draped down from the front of the shed and lay like a dead snake on the snow.

Feeling aggrieved, Norm went into the living room and turned on the TV—but of course the cable was out too.

Muttering to himself he went to bed. What else was there to do?

Under his blankets, he found the noise of the wind and the windows less bothersome. Eventually they even lulled him to sleep.

Later that night Norm was shot out of his slumber by something that sounded like a scream. He sat up in bed, hair standing on end, nerves tingling. Had he dreamed that sound? Going to the window, he looked out, but could see only dark silhouettes of houses against the dull glow of the city. A few seconds later, the light next door came on. Norm stared, openmouthed, for there was an enormous tree limb, hanging horizontally just above the level of the fence, across the two backyards. It was suspended at one end by a splinter of wood connecting it to the parent tree in the neighbor's yard, and at the other by a frozen tangle of branches interlaced with those of other trees.

Norm stared until the neighbor's light went out. Then he went to the medicine cabinet for something to help him get back to sleep.

II.

HE WAS awakened the following morning by the *peep-peep-peep* of a truck backing up outside. He groaned and looked at his clock radio: 10:22 a.m. He rolled onto his other side—and saw glints of sunshine peering through the curtains.

He had survived the storm!

Feeling better, he got up and began stretching, when he heard men's voices outside. Going to the front window, he saw two Hydro utility workers standing in front of the house in heavy orange jumpsuits with bright yellow strips. Frost came from their mouths as they spoke, and the colors of their clothes fairly blazed in the morning sunlight. Set amid the brilliance of the ice-coated snow, the men acquired a heroic quality. Then Norm realized that they must be there to fix the cable behind the house.

Thinking that a hot drink on this cold day would provide a good opening for inquiring about this, Norm hurried downstairs to make hot chocolate. With the milk heating on the stove, he went to the living room window—and saw that one of the men had gone. He rushed back to the kitchen to turn up the heat and mix in the cocoa. In less than two minutes he was making his way down the front walk of the house with a mug of hot chocolate toward the man who was writing on a clipboard balanced on the hood of a Hydro truck.

"Hello!" Norm called as he approached. The man turned, and Norm held out the mug. "Nice day!" he said. "I made some cocoa for you. It's kinda cold."

The man looked surprised. Then he smiled—and with that smile his entire face lit up, and Norm felt his world change. The man's pearly teeth, set between red lips surrounded by a golden beard, plus the rosy complexion and sparkling eyes—the guy looked—*beautiful*!

"Gee, thanks," he said, taking the mug with his ungloved hand. He sipped, swallowed, and took a second sip. Then, looking at Norm, he grinned. "That's really good stuff. Thanks. Hits the spot."

Norm nodded, entranced. The guy took a larger sip, which left chocolate foam on his upper lip. When the pink tongue appeared and licked the foam off, Norm felt a wash of erotic heat go right through him.

As he stood there, a gust of wind played about Norm's ankles. It was very cold in his bathrobe, but he ignored that. "So," he said, "I guess you're here to fix the cable in my backyard."

The man looked at him, surprised. "What, you without power?"

"Oh, no. But I've lost Internet and cable."

"Too bad. But you're lucky to have power at all. Your side of the street is the end of the city grid. The other side"—he pointed to the houses opposite—"they're part of the East York dead zone that goes on for six blocks."

Norm whistled. "I guess I am lucky."

There was the sound of a chainsaw down the street, where several men were cutting up an enormous tree limb that had fallen across the road. After watching this for several seconds, Norm turned back to the Hydro worker and sighed. He raised his voice above the sound. "When I saw you here, I just thought—"

The man nodded. "You need to contact the Bell people. Have you called them?"

Oh! Norm hadn't even thought of doing that. He did own a cell phone. "Not yet."

"Well, you probably should do it as soon as you can. There'll be a lot of people calling."

Norm nodded. He was really freezing now, shivering all over, but still he couldn't turn away from the Hydro worker.

The guy took another swig of the hot chocolate and scanned Norm's face. "So, how'd it happen—losing the phone line, I mean?"

"In back," Norm said, nodding toward the house. "Part of a tree came down on top of the line."

The man shook his head. "Bad luck."

"Yeah, and a larger limb came down in the night—it's just hanging there."

But now the wind was picking up, and Norm was in real pain from the cold. "Well," he gasped, "I guess I'd better get inside and make that call." He turned and fled back to the house.

Inside, Norm had to stand in a hot shower for five minutes before the shivering stopped. Then he called the Bell hotline. He was still in the queue when the doorbell rang. Carrying the phone with him back downstairs, he peered through the window in the front door. It was the blond Hydro guy.

"Here's your mug," the man said when Norm opened the door.

"Oh, thanks." The guy was smiling, and Norm was again assaulted by the man's radiant beauty. Taking the proffered mug, he said, "Oh, but it's just a travel mug. You could have kept it."

The man shook his head. "Not allowed. Taking things from homeowners might be construed as accepting bribes."

"Oh."

"To get special treatment."

"Ah."

Was the guy joking? Norm's dazed state made it hard for him to decide.

After a short pause, the guy said, "You know, if you like, I could take a look at the situation in your backyard."

"Oh! Sure! Be my guest!" Norm stepped aside to let the guy inside.

The Hydro worker shook his head. "I'll go around the house. I got my boots on." Then he paused, tilted his head slightly, and smiled. Sticking out his hand, he said, "My name's Winston, by the way."

"Mine's Norman—Norm." They shook. Norm experienced a pleasant shock when the solid warmth of Winston's flesh closed on his own.

Norm ran to the back door, threw on a coat and boots, and met Winston as he was struggling with the latch on the back gate.

"It sticks," Norm said. He reached up and for an instant their fingers touched again, and Norm felt another tingle at the contact.

Their boots crunched through the ice that covered the snow as they headed down the yard. When they came to the hanging limb, Winston reached up and slapped it. Then he went to the fence and peered into the neighboring yard. He looked at Norm.

"It's just holding on. Amazing!"

"Yeah. When I heard it split last night, it scared me out of my wits."

Winston laughed. "I'll bet." He looked up at the limb from several angles. "It might take down more wires if it comes down, and some of those are power," he said. "I should report this."

"Oh." Norm felt strangely elated. "You're coming back, then—I mean, to clear this away?"

Winston looked at him for a second. "We're supposed to do only the current damage. There's just too much work for the people we have."

Norm nodded, disappointed. They crunched back up to the gate, where there was an awkward pause.

"Did you get through to Bell?" Winston asked casually, as if making conversation.

"Not yet. But no problem." Norm smiled wryly. "I know things have to follow procedure. Anyway, I've got power, and that tree limb will probably hold on long enough for me to get it taken care of."

Winston looked impressed. He smiled. "Say, that's a great attitude! You have no idea how many angry Torontonians I've had to deal with these past two days. People are just taking out their frustration on us workers. I mean, I understand and all that, but"—he shook his head—"after a while it's kind of hard to take." He thumped Norm lightly on the shoulder and grinned. "You're one of the good ones."

Norm, made a little silly at the direct compliment, laughed. "I like to think so."

After the guy left, and for the remainder of the day, Norm felt a bit moony. Without access to the Internet he couldn't do his work. There was paperwork he could do, but somehow he just didn't feel like it.

That afternoon the sky clouded over, reflecting Norm's mood. He stood at the window and admitted to himself that he would probably never see Winston again, while he absentmindedly rubbed his shoulder where the guy had tapped him.

III.

JUST BEFORE dinnertime, Chris called. "My house still standing?"

Norm frowned. "Yes, it is. And I'm fine too—thanks for asking."

Chris laughed.

"We've lost Internet connection, though," Norm continued, "and there are limbs down in the backyard."

"No shit! Anything hit?"

"Just the shed, but no damage—just the line for the Internet."

"Well, that's a relief."

"Yeah, except I can't get work done."

"Oh, right. Yeah, I guess that's not good."

After they rang off, Norm felt isolated and lonely. On impulse he decided to make a special meal for dinner—cabbage rolls, one of his specialties though a lot of work.

Having boiled the rice, sautéed the beef, onion and garlic, softened the cabbage leaves and finally assembled the rolls, he put the casserole dish in the oven to bake and drew a long sigh. It had improved his mood. He decided that wine would make the meal even more special, so he opened a bottle of red.

The sun had set by this time, and Norm went to close the curtains. He was in the living room when he heard something—a noise—outside the front door.

Peering through the glass he saw a dark shape bending toward one side of the porch. As he was trying to make out what it was, he heard a low growl. Instantly it occurred to him that a large wild animal, driven into the city by the weather, was prowling on his front porch. Then the shape shifted, turning toward the door, and Norm let out a stifled scream.

In response, the figure rose up, and it was immediately obvious from the shape that this was a man in a heavy winter coat. Embarrassed, Norm flipped the switch for the porch light. This revealed the smiling countenance of Winston. Filled with a mixture of relief, delight, and mortification, Norm hastened to open the door.

"Sorry," he said. "I—you looked—well, I thought you, maybe, were a bear."

Winston glanced down at his dark, shaggy coat and grinned. There was a pause, and he looked a little awkward. "I was thinking about that fallen tree limb. I thought I'd take it down for you—if you don't mind."

"I thought you said it was pretty secure," Norm said automatically—then wished he hadn't said the words.

Sure thing, genius, send him away! Bright move!

"Well, you probably heard, the second part of the storm system is supposed to move in tonight."

"What? Oh, no I didn't." Then he took hold of himself. "But—uh—thanks. It's very kind of you. I'd appreciate it very much."

Winston smiled, then reached down and lifted a chainsaw in one hand, some rope in the other. "Maybe you could help me?"

"Oh yes, sure!"

Winston stepped inside while Norm dressed.

"You're not wearing your uniform."

"Oh, I'm doing this on the side."

Norm looked up in surprise. "On the side—"

"Oh, don't worry about paying me," Winston said hastily. "I—well—I was just concerned." He shrugged.

Norm felt a tingle go down his spine.

The man cleared his throat and said, "I'm just a citizen at the moment, helping out other citizens in this time of natural disaster."

"Oh, well, that's very nice of you," Norm said. "Listen! I was just preparing dinner. You know what? I'd really appreciate it if you would at least accept a meal—to say thanks."

The man sniffed, then grinned. "Sure!" he said. "Smells wonderful."

Winston went around back, where Norm met him.

Winston held up the end of an orange power line. "You got an outside outlet?"

Norm nodded, took the end, and went up the porch steps. When he plugged it in, the yard was filled with a blaze of light. He turned to see a hazard light dangling from the fence near the hanging limb.

When Norm returned, Winston said, "I'll climb up, if you can hand stuff up to me."

"Sure."

Winston climbed onto the hanging limb after running a safety line to a branch of another tree higher up.

"Hand me up the chainsaw?"

Norm did this. Winston positioned himself and fired up the chainsaw. The noise was deafening at first, and Norm put his gloved hands over his ears. After several seconds there was a loud crash. The branched end of the limb swung down and hit the shed, while the other part fell heavily onto the top of the fence. The sound of the chainsaw died away, and there was a ringing silence. Winston kept his footing, holding on to his safety rope. When things had settled, he walked to the sawed end and started the chainsaw again.

Seconds later a foot-long piece of the limb fell heavily and hit the icy surface of the snow with a loud smack, burying itself beneath. As Winston started on another cut, Norm dug out the fallen piece and took it over to the shed.

Winston worked his way back to the fence calmly and methodically, cutting piece after piece. Norm watched him work with admiration. By the time Winston reached the fence, Norm had a pile of logs stacked against the shed. Winston handed down the chainsaw. Then, stepping from the limb, he shifted it with a foot, so that the end fell into the neighbor's yard with a crash.

Grinning down at Norm, Winston undid the safety rope that was holding him in place. Then he slipped on the icy fence and fell directly onto Norm.

It wasn't a long fall, but the man's weight was enough to bury Norm completely in the snow. As he lay there, encased in snow with Winston's full weight on top of him, Norm was surprised at how pleasant the experience was. He felt cocooned, protected even. Besides, he told himself—it had been a long time since he'd had a man lying on top of him. Too long.

Of course, this predicament lasted only seconds. Then Winston was up and lifting Norm to his feet.

"Hey," Winston said, brushing the snow that clung to Norm's coat and toque. "You okay, man? I'm really sorry about that!"

Norm, still a little in shock, looked at the expression on his companion's face and burst out laughing. "No problem," he said when he had recovered. Then he moved his arms and legs experimentally. "No damage."

Winston stared at him, then looked briefly down at himself and shook his head. "No damage here either, I guess," he said. Then he looked at Norm and added, remorsefully, "But I *landed on you*, man! You sure you're okay? I'm *really* sorry!"

Norm reached out and grasped Winston's arm. "Look," he said seriously. "There's no problem, okay? I just—well, thank you for doing all this work."

"Oh…," Winston waved this away.

They both looked around them at the freed yard. Then Norm looked at the neighbor's yard. "You're not going to cut up his wood, I guess," Norm said.

Winston was picking up his equipment. "It didn't hit any wires, and anyway"—he grinned at Norm—"*he* didn't bring me hot chocolate this morning."

IV.

THEY CARRIED the equipment back to the house and left it in the mudroom. When they entered the kitchen, Norm felt relieved by the warmth. And there was the smell of the cabbage rolls. He realized that despite their physical activity, he was chilled to the bone—it was that cold outside.

Winston, however, was rosy-cheeked and looked content—until Norm offered to hang up his coat. Then, for some reason, his face fell. He reluctantly removed the garment, and when he had, Norm realized that much of what he had assumed to be the coat's bulk in fact turned out to be Winston himself.

Norm put Winston's coat away and came back to see Winston standing on the mat by the door, looking around uneasily. The change in the man surprised him. The sunshine he had seemed to carry around with him was gone, and Norm realized with some disappointment that he didn't find Winston nearly as attractive.

Looking around for a distraction, Norm noticed that the left sleeve of Winston's shirt was bloody.

"Hey!" he said. "You're hurt!"

Winston looked down at his arm. He looked almost relieved to have something to focus on. "Huh. I must have scraped it in the fall."

Norm maternal instincts rose. "Okay," he said. "We have a first-aid kit in both the upstairs and downstairs bathrooms. Uh, why don't you use the one downstairs?"

"Oh, I don't think it's much," Winston said, rolling up his sleeve and revealing a long scrape.

Norm took hold of the man's wrist and examined the scrape. He shook his head. "You need to treat that. At least wash it off and put some antiseptic on it. I can help if you want a gauze wrapping."

"Oh no. Washing it will be enough."

"You sure? See how much it bleeds after you put on the ointment." Norm frowned. "You won't appreciate my food if you're bleeding to death."

Winston laughed and there, momentarily, was the sunlight again. Norm felt a small thrill. He went to the back door to lock it and then pushed Winston gently toward the basement stairs.

"Hey!" he said. "The back of your shirt is all wet. With that and the blood—look, why don't you have a shower and dress your wound while I wash your clothes?"

"Oh—"

"It's no trouble. In fact, I insist. There's a bathrobe on the back of the door, and the washer and dryer are right there. Just throw the stuff out the door, and I'll pop them in for you.

"You're wet too."

"Yeah. I'll shower upstairs."

Winston disappeared with a show of reluctance, and Norm headed upstairs for a shower. Afterward he picked up Winston's clothes and put them into the wash. Then he went to check on dinner.

The sound of the downstairs shower ended, and several minutes later the washer dinged. Norm went down and put the clothes in the dryer. He knocked on the bathroom door.

"You need any help dressing your arm?"

"No—it's not that bad."

"Okay. I've just put your clothes in the dryer. I had it on quick-wash cycle, but drying will take awhile, maybe twenty-five minutes. And dinner is ready now. Just come up as you are—casual dress code. I'm in my bathrobe too."

Norm set the table in the dining room, complete with candles. He had decided to make things really nice, just for the heck of it. As he worked, his thoughts kept coming back to the fact that the guy he'd thought so beautiful had turned out to be what was euphemistically termed "heavy."

Norm had never thought about that kind of body before. Before moving in with Chris, he'd been a typical downtown gay man—going regularly to the gym and lusting after the guys with the most chiseled bodies. He'd pursued them, too, with limited success.

Having just celebrated his thirtieth birthday, he'd ruminated unhappily on the fact that he hadn't had a single satisfying long-term relationship, though he'd come close a couple of times. Now he admitted that he didn't really know what to think—about anything.

By the time he'd everything set in the dining room, he had come to the conclusion that he didn't have anything *against* heavy guys, though he'd never had any experience with them either. Then he reminded himself that Winston was probably straight anyway.

Norm sighed. Both that morning, and this evening too, Winston had been so vital, so alive—capable and affable—and that *smile*! The mental image of it caused Norm to feel again the excitement, the excited tingling that passed through his entire body. It was so confusing!

So what's your problem? He asked himself. *You prejudiced about his imperfect body?*

There was a quiet cough. Norm started and saw Winston standing awkwardly in the doorway. He was wearing Chris's bathrobe, which hardly met over his torso. What struck Norm was how uncomfortable the man looked. The fact that he was trying to hide this just made it worse.

Norm went into host mode.

"Great!" he cried, clapping his hands together. "We are ready to feast!" He pointed to a chair. "Please be seated, sir."

Winston sat down, and Norm went over and held the wine bottle poised over Winston's glass.

"Would monsieur care for some wine with his dinner?"

Winston smiled slightly, and nodded.

The wine poured, both men picked up their glasses. "A toast," Norm said. "What to?"

There was silence. "What about," Norm said at last, "to neighbors helping neighbors?"

Winston smiled a slow smile and said, "Or—to citizens helping citizens in times of natural disaster."

Norm laughed, and they clinked glasses.

"Well, dig in," Norm said after taking a big swig of wine. He lifted the lid of the casserole dish, and the aroma of cabbage rolls filled the room.

"Smells good." Winston spooned out several cabbage rolls onto his plate. Norm proffered some sour cream and then served himself.

They ate for several minutes in silence, other than Winston remarking, "Is good!" The fact that he said it with his mouth full gratified Norm's sensibility as a cook—the guy was obviously enjoying the food.

As the silence continued, however, Norm began to feel constrained by his guest's obviously being ill at ease. Several times Winston pulled his bathrobe closed tighter and shifted awkwardly in his seat, and Norm concluded that the guy was self-conscious about his body. Even while he tried to dismiss this idea, Norm had to admit that he didn't find Winston at all attractive now. And this made him a little angry with himself.

You found him hot enough outside.

Look, I'm not responsible for who I find attractive.

But you're not giving him a chance. After this there was a mental pause.

That's true.

Okay.

And so he decided, however presumptuously, that he would give Winston "a chance." He looked at his guest, and realized that what he *really* wanted was to see that smile again.

But, before he had come up with a conversational opening, there was a ding from downstairs. "That'll be the dryer."

"If you don't mind," Winston said, "I'll get dressed."

Norm shrugged. Winston got up and headed downstairs. Norm shook his head. He thought he could hear the relief in the sound of that rapid descent.

Winston's relief was obvious when he returned fully clothed. Norm suddenly felt a bit foolish wearing a bathrobe himself. After casting about for a topic of conversation, he decided that another drink was indicated. He picked up his wine glass and said, "Another toast! What to this time?"

Winston lifted his own glass and then grinned for the briefest of seconds. "What else?" he said. "To the Great Ice Storm of 2013!"

Norm laughed, and they clinked glasses and drank. With that all-too-brief appearance of Winston's smile, Norm had caught another glimpse of his guest's beauty. This time it touched him profoundly, for he found that now he could see quite clearly in his mind's eye the man as he had been in the sunlight, smiling, rosy, and golden, with lips that so much wanted to be kissed.

"So," Norm said. "You work for Hydro long?"

"A year."

"Ah." A pause. "You like the work?"

"Oh, it's okay."

Norm wondered at the fellow's response. It didn't fit with what he had seen in the guy when he was outside—the exhilaration, the joy.

"I envy you," Norm said. "Working outside, I mean."

"You work inside?"

The question was merely polite. The guy was still uncomfortable. Norm pulled a face and pointed toward the ceiling with his fork. "I work upstairs."

"Oh? What do you do?"

"I do tech work for people's websites."

"Does that sort of thing pay well?"

Norm laughed. "Yeah, if you're good enough."

Winston looked at him speculatively. "I'm guessing that you are."

Norm felt his face heat up. He laughed. "You're too kind." He took another large sip of wine. "But between you and me—yes, I am."

At last Winston chuckled at this—and showed his pearly teeth again for a moment. *Yes*, Norm told himself, he could definitely see that something there again, that beauty—and he felt a return of his interest. The feeling was richer now, for he had seen the guy's vulnerable side, and he was getting to know the man himself. And Norm decided that he liked the guy, apart from anything else.

Something of his host's change in attitude must have communicated itself to the guest—or maybe it was the wine—for Winston's demeanor began to be less constrained. The conversation flowed more easily. Winston even talked about his work at Hydro with more enthusiasm, which made him more attractive. He also showed a real, if naïve, interest in Norm's web-support work.

When they had finished the meal—and the bottle of wine—Winston leaned back and said, "You know, that was about the best meal I've ever eaten."

Norm's face heated up slightly, but he smiled. Appreciation was never unwelcome. "Thank you," he said. "Why don't we go into the living room? It's a bit cold down here with that wind, and there's a heater in there." They rose, and he opened a second bottle of wine and poured them both glasses, which they carried into the other room.

Winston sat on the couch. Though Norm longed to join him there, he sat in the big armchair after turning on the electric heater that sat inside the barren fireplace.

"The fireplace doesn't work?"

"Yeah, it does." Norm shrugged. "Chris doesn't like using it. He's the guy—a friend—who owns the house. I just rent two rooms. He says fireplaces are inefficient."

Winston nodded. A cell phone sounded and Winston fished it out of his pocket. Looking at the display, he got up. "Excuse me," he said. "I've got to take this. It's my sister."

"No problem." Norm went into the dining room and carried some dishes into the kitchen to give his guest some privacy. At first he couldn't hear any words. Then the volume rose.

"I don't think that's fair!" Pause. "I'm *not* disrespecting you, Sue." Pause. "I *do* appreciate what you're doing for me." Longer pause. "Fine. Okay."

Norm dried his hands and went back to the living room. "Everything okay?"

"That was my sister," Winston said. He looked embarrassed and dejected. When they had reseated themselves he sighed. "She's angry I didn't phone and let her know where I was or when I was coming to her place."

"Oh, you live with your sister?"

Winston shook his head. "No," he said. "Only—well—I lost power at my place yesterday, and I'm staying with her." He paused, distracted, punched the arm of the couch and added, "And I *do* appreciate her putting me up." Then he caught himself and smiled embarrassedly. "Sorry," he said. "But Sue and me—well, we don't get along that well in close quarters." He shook his head and sighed. "Never did."

"Why don't you stay here, then?" Norm said. The words were out of his mouth before he realized it.

Winston started, then frowned and colored. He looked at Norm a little sideways and shrugged uncomfortably. "I wasn't angling for that."

"I know you weren't." Norm forced a laugh. "You should see me and my brothers get along."

"Bad?"

"Worse than bad," Norm said. Painful images arose and he shook his head. "Not pretty at all. And not just because I'm gay, either."

V.

AGAIN THE words had slipped out before Norm realized it, and afterward he felt his face heat up.

Oh great! Now you've outed yourself to a near stranger—who you've just invited to stay over. He's going to think you're trying to get into his pants.

Norm looked at Winston cautiously, but the man seemed caught up in his own thoughts, staring into the fireplace. Perhaps he hadn't even heard, which made Norm feel both relieved and slightly annoyed as well.

"Sorry there's no real fire," he said.

Winston didn't respond for a second or two. Then he shrugged. "Heat's heat." A pause, then he added, "Family's difficult."

Norm was silent for several seconds. Then he said, "Hey! I have a riddle for you. What's the best definition of 'friends'?"

Winston shook his head without looking at him. "What?"

"God's apology for family."

Winston stared for a second, then burst out laughing. He went on so long that Norm started laughing as well. He felt giddy just watching the guy laugh, those teeth.

"That's a good one!" Winston said at last.

Into the silence that followed, Norm said quietly, "The invite is still there. You could sleep in my room. I'll sleep in my friend's room—he's away for two weeks."

Winston nodded noncommittally. Then he changed the subject. "So you work at home." He considered this, then added, "I like working outside."

"You know, I saw that when I first spoke to you. Looking at your face was like looking at the sun—just radiant."

Winston ducked his head in response, evidently embarrassed. Norm wondered how his remark had come across.

"Gotta go to the washroom." Winston got up and went downstairs. Norm wondered whether he had effectively driven the guy from the house, and after a few seconds decided to go upstairs and get dressed.

Winston was back on the couch when Norm came back downstairs. He didn't seem to be in any hurry to leave, however, and didn't object when Norm refilled their wine glasses. They both took a sip.

Winston looked directly at him. "So you're gay."

"Oh. Yeah."

"That's cool." A pause. "I saw a lot of exercise equipment in the basement. You use it a lot?"

"Some. I used to go to the gym when I lived downtown. It's harder to work out by yourself."

"Everybody seems to go to the gym these days," Winston said mournfully. He looked Norm over. "I kind of figured you work out."

Norm laughed incredulously. "Me? You're kidding. Sure, I work out, but, well, not too hard, perhaps. But here I am—" He stood up and flexed while making a pathetic face. "—still skinny as hell. I just don't seem to be able to bulk up."

"Don't they call that—what—compact or something? Tight? You look tightly muscled, I would say."

Norm couldn't suppress as smile as he sat down again. "Thanks."

Winston shook his head and sighed. "I tried working out," he said. "But I'm just naturally chubby. I was all my life, even when I was a kid." He colored. "I got teased a lot. 'Fatty, fatty!' You know, that kind of thing."

Norm nodded. "I was called 'the stick man' and 'Twiggy,'" he said. "Also faggot, sissy, and Mary." He laughed briefly. "High school was hell."

Winston glanced at him and nodded.

"Anyway," Norm said, "I don't think you have a bad body. Sure, you're not Charles Atlas, but who is?"

Winston frowned and shrugged. "I don't like it."

"Really?" Norm paused. Then he went for it. "Well, what does your girlfriend say about your body?"

There was a brief pause. "Don't have one."

"Oh, I'm sorry. It's just—well, I mean, you're so good-looking—" He stopped. Winston was staring at him, openmouthed.

"You're joking!"

Norms felt his face heat up. "Sorry!" he said again. "I wasn't—I mean, I wasn't trying to come on to you or anything."

Winston waved this away impatiently. "That's not what I meant."

"What? You really don't think you're good-looking?"

Winston shook his head.

"Well, sorry—but, well, you are. And I have to say, my opinion of the women of this city has really suffered if one of them hasn't snared you." The funny thing was, as he heard himself say these words, Norm really meant them. He thought Winston *was* good-looking. He'd seen him smile enough now that the radiance of those moments had become part of his overall impression of the guy. He now saw a good-looking, solidly built man, someone he found very attractive.

"Anyway," Norm continued, "you're only, what? Twenty-one? Twenty-two?"

"Actually, I'm twenty—last month."

"Oh."

"And I'm fat."

The starkness of this statement took Norm aback for a second or two. Then he said, "No, you're not. You're a—what is it—an endomorph, with a few extra pounds. And I'm an ectomorph. A doctor told me I must have a highly active thyroid." He shrugged. "People are just different. And, I don't know, society teaches us we should all be the ideal." He paused. Then he added, "If you want the truth, I hate my body. When I look at myself in the mirror, all I see is scrawny."

"But you're well muscled."

Norm laughed a bit bitterly. "Not so much that it shows!"

"It does. It's just not… well…."

"Showy?"

Winston shrugged. Then he shook his head and murmured, "I would kill for a body like yours."

Norm almost laughed. He wanted to say *Well, just say the word, big boy! I'm yours!*

Winston, following his own train of thought, said, half speaking to himself, "I tried to lose weight all through high school. I took up sports, joined the football team. But they wanted me to stay heavy—a better blocker, they said." He made a disgusted noise. Then he grabbed at his midriff through the shirt, clutching a handful of flesh, and worried it. "See? Flab."

Norm shook his head. Winston saw this and raised his eyebrows questioningly.

"Well," Norm said, speaking with difficulty, "I suppose it's none of my business, but, well, it just seems a shame. I mean, here you are, a big, brawny buck—handsome to boot—and all you see is flab. *I* got flab." He lifted his shirt and pulled at a bit of his belly flesh. "Here," he said. "See? Flab too."

"Lift it higher?" Winston said.

Looking, Norm saw the guy was just curious, so, though his face warmed slightly, he took a breath and removed his shirt and undershirt, running his hand up and down his torso. "See?" he said. "That's about ten years of going to the gym. Not much muscle."

Winston, still looking a little surprised, shrugged. "You're fit. That's what important. No fat at all. Toned."

Norm laughed and recited, "Jack Spratt could eat no fat. His wife could eat no lean."

Then he suddenly leaned forward and rubbed Winston's belly. "That's not fat," he said aggressively. "It's meat. *Man* meat." He sat back, grinned, and laughed, totally embarrassed. But he also felt a bit intoxicated by the sexual excitement, the frisson that had passed from his hand into his body at the contact, so much so that he was half-hard in his pants.

Winston seemed to be experiencing several conflicting emotions due to this contact. Norm, uncertain how this would go, felt reckless enough to stand up, point at his guest, and say, "Take off that shirt!"

Winston looked at him, incredulous.

"Look, I showed you mine. Fair's fair."

Winston gave a small laugh and reluctantly removed his shirt, then his undershirt. It was a slow business, but Norm found to his delight that the gradual reveal was hot as hell. And when Winston finally doffed his T-shirt and showed an unexpected growth of dark golden chest hair, with a line of it going down into his pants, Norm felt like he'd been hit by a brick.

Winston was heavy, no doubt about that, but *man*, those *curves*! The rounded pecs, the bulge of belly, at the front and even the sides, somehow to Norm they seemed more masculine than the most chiseled, muscle-bound gym jock Norm had ever met. And in that moment he realized that all his years pursuing the "hottest" tight body had been utterly misguided. He'd been going in the wrong direction.

Winston looked up shyly. Seeing Norm staring, he ran his hands protectively over his chest and belly—at which Norm almost whimpered. *The action was so hot!* His face was burning and his dick was hard as a rock. What saved him from mortification at this, however, was the feeling of awe that accompanied his arousal. He whistled slowly.

"And you're ashamed of *that*?" he said.

After staring incredulously for a second, Winston colored, but there was also a slight smile on his face, innocent gratitude and perhaps some gratified masculine vanity. Norm meanwhile was fantasizing running his fingers through that wiry golden hair, or even dragging his dick through it. At which point he had to look away—it was just too much. His head was swimming.

After a silence Winston said, "About my staying over…."

Norm looked back at the man's solemn face. *He's going to say no—*

"I accept."

"Oh! Uh…." A rush of joy flooded Norm. "Great!"

"Besides, Norm, I'm pretty tipsy. I don't think I should drive, especially in this weather."

"Okay. Sure. I'll show you my room."

Winston shook his head. "Actually, I'd rather sleep on the couch, if it's okay with you."

"Oh." Norm struggled with an urge to argue the point. He shrugged. "Sure. I'll get you blankets."

As he went upstairs, walking with a certain amount of awkwardness due to his erection, Norm wondered at the feeling of disappointment that was diminishing his initial excitement. Maybe it was just a wish to have that body in his bed, even if he wasn't there. He wondered whether Winston slept in the nude, and there it was again—the rush of excitement, and his dick hardening even more.

They made up the couch and exchanged slightly awkward goodnights. Norm performed his evening ablutions and went to bed, where he fell asleep with the fantasy of Winston's solid warmth pressing against him.

VI.

AT SOME point in the night, Norm found himself getting cold. Half-awake, he pulled the covers around himself more tightly. Finding that didn't help, he swam to full wakefulness—and realized he could smell wood burning.

He leaped out of bed, heart pounding, the thought filling his mind that the house was on fire. The room was totally dark. The clock radio was off. He stumbled to the light switch, flicked it—nothing happened. The power was off!

Making his way into and along the hallway, Norm saw a dim reddish glow coming from downstairs. The smell of wood burning was stronger here, and he heard the quiet crackle of logs burning. It came to him with a wave of relief that Winston must have lit a fire.

Norm cautiously descended the stairs and saw Winston sitting in front of the couch, feet toward the fire that was burning merrily in the fireplace.

Winston must have heard him, for he turned and said, "Oh, hi. I hope you don't mind." He gestured toward the fire. "I know your friend doesn't like using the fireplace, but it was getting cold."

That made Norm realize how cold he was. He shivered, went over to the couch, and sat down, holding his hands toward the fire.

"Better get closer. Sit on the floor, here." Winston made a hole in a pile of blankets to his left. Norm settled into it and pulled them around him. Covered up and with just his face and hands exposed to the fire, he began to feel better.

"I didn't want to wake you," Winston continued. "But the storm's back." He shook his head. "There'll be more limb damage by tomorrow. Lots of work for yours truly—big time."

Winston's face was half lit by the ruddy light and half in deep shadow, and Norm thought it very beautiful.

"Where'd you find the wood?" he asked.

Winston grinned. "I used the wood we cut up last night. It turns out that limb was dead—must have been dead six months, at least. Anyway, the wood was dry enough, though it still wasn't easy to start, with the ice on it and all. I knocked most of that off outside."

"Well, thanks."

"No problem."

They were silent for a while. "Best get comfortable," Winston said, yawning. "We're going to have to sleep here. Not just because it's warm—you don't have a fire screen, and there's the danger of sparks. Don't want the house to burn down." He grinned at Norm.

"No, we don't." Norm shuddered at the thought.

"If anything catches, the smell will wake me," Winston continued. "I'm a pretty light sleeper."

Norm nodded, and they sat in silence, staring into the fire. Then Norm noticed a pot that was suspended just to the side of the flames. It was hanging from what appeared to be an opened hanger connected to a large piece of metal. He pointed to this.

"I got that stuff from the basement," Winston explained. "I hope it's okay. That steel bar is from one of the exercise machines. The heat won't hurt it, though it might blacken a bit."

Norm shook his head.

"I'm heating water."

"Great."

"Making tea, or soup if you like."

"Tea would be nice."

Winston reached to his other side and lifted two mugs, setting them on the floor between them. In another minute there was the quiet sound of boiling. Winston got up, lifted the pot with an oven mitt, and expertly poured the water into both mugs.

Norm, watching him, was again impressed. The guy did things so simply, so capably. Norm hadn't realized before what a turn-on that was.

Winston held up a can of condensed milk and, when Norm nodded, poured.

The hot tea was better than anything Norm ever remembered drinking. As he drank he began to feel cozy and warm—and just slightly intoxicated sitting next to this marvelous man. Winston, he noticed, had his shirt open, exposing his T-shirt, above which several golden curls of chest hair showed. Norm fantasized running his hand under the T-shirt.

"You're going to have a lot of work tomorrow," he said.

"Yeah. That's for sure. But I really love the work. I don't know. It's kind of exciting being out there battling the elements, getting things working so people can go on with their lives again. Makes me feel good."

"I can see that. Is that different from what you ordinarily do—I mean, when there isn't a storm?"

"The work is similar. There's always problems, but right now, well, there's a sense of excitement." He laughed. "How to put it? There's a sense of crisis—it's like we Hydro workers are being tested." He laughed again and shrugged. "I don't know, but I kind of like that."

Norm nodded. He understood.

He asked more questions about Winston's work, partly to learn about him, partly just to hear him talk, for there was something reassuring about his gentle baritone voice. As Norm listened, sleepiness slowly overcame him. He slipped sideways onto Winston's shoulder and fell asleep.

Twice in the night, Norm came partially awake. The first time was when Winston got up to add a log to the fire. The second time was to feel Winston's solid warmth pressing against him from behind, no blankets between them, so the warmth of the bigger man seemed to flow around him. One of Winston's arms was loosely draped over Norm's chest, the fingertips just touching his arm, which gave Norm a sense of warmth and security. As he sank back to sleep it came to him that he'd never felt like this before, so content in the arms of another man.

VII.

Norm awoke the next morning to the sound of wood being chopped. The fire was going as strongly as ever, and sunlight streamed in through the living room window. Filled with a sense of well-being, Norm stretched luxuriously beneath his many layers of blanket.

The chopping stopped. A minute later the back door banged. There was a waft of cold air through the room, making Norm huddle up more tightly, and a minute later Winston appeared, in his coat and carrying a load of wood.

"Good morning!" he said. "Did I wake you?"

Norm smiled. "Yeah, I guess you did, but that's not a problem."

"I had to chop wood for the fire." He knelt, stacking wood against the side of the fireplace.

"Oh. Well, thanks for taking care of the fire." Norm looked up at the mantelpiece clock, which ran on a battery. Its ornate hands read 6:41. "You always get up this early?"

"We're starting early this morning." Winston carefully put one of the wood pieces onto the fire. "I got a message. Twelve-hour shift."

"Oh. Of course."

Having adjusted the fire, Winston rose. "I made breakfast." He nodded toward a large stew pot sitting on several bricks next to the fire. "I found bricks in the shed. In a minute I'll have coffee ready. No need to move." He went to the kitchen and brought plates, cutlery, and napkins.

Norm found it to be a delightful breakfast—scrambled eggs with a spicing that he didn't recognize but liked, with bacon, toast, and coffee.

They ate ravenously. Then Winston looked at his cell and got up quickly. "I gotta go," he said. "There's more wood by the back door." A half minute later, the back door closed and Winston was gone.

Norm, sitting with a half mug of coffee between his hands, remained where he was in front of the fire, thinking about Winston, a man with such a beautiful smile who was so kind and capable. Then he remembered the sight of his torso, the feel of his body in the night, and felt the return of sexual heat. After several minutes of these pleasant feelings, his mind stumbled against the old roadblock—the guy was probably straight.

Norm chided himself. *Don't get ahead of yourself, boy! Just accept what comes.*

He sighed and then realized that there was something else, something important that hovered just beyond his conscious awareness. He sought it for a minute or two without success. Then it came to him. He remembered that he had discovered something about himself last night, discovered what really turned him on.

He was into bears!

What did they call people like him? Bear chasers? He ran a hand under his pajama top, over his own belly and chest. He had some hair, not so much "hair" as "hairs" though; he felt he could count them if he wanted to. They were dark like the hair on his head, and certainly nothing like the wonderful golden fur that Winston had.

After a while his thoughts turned to whether Winston would return that evening. The guy hadn't reacted badly to Norm telling him he was gay, but you never knew. Frustratingly, Norm realized he didn't have the guy's number, or even his last name.

"Well," he said to himself, "then I guess it's up to him." He tried to accept this, but he felt agitated enough that he had to get up and moving.

He spent the day doing various minor household duties. Without a water heater, doing the dishes was a bit of an adventure. He had to heat water over the fire and carry it into the kitchen. There was something exciting about doing it like this, without power.

In midafternoon he got a call from Chris, asking how he and the house were. Keeping it brief to save on the phone's battery, he explained about the loss of power, that he was coping, and that the house was fine.

VIII.

THE LIGHT was almost gone, and Norm was beginning to find being alone in the house without power a bit creepy despite the fire, when there was a knock on the front door. He ran to the door and almost sobbed with relief when he saw Winston through the glass, standing on the front porch with a number of bags in his arms.

Inside, Winston put the bags down and grinned at Norm. "I thought I'd get a few things to make—uh, you—more comfortable. You said you didn't have a car, and it's really icy out there."

"Oh, thanks!" Norm wanted to hug the guy and scamper about.

They unpacked. The refrigerated goods went into the fridge, which was still pretty cold—along with the rest of the kitchen. "You know," Norm said, "you're welcome to stay here tonight too—although I guess your sister has power."

Winston paused in lifting cans from another bag. "Well... if it's okay with you. I hate imposing on her."

A rush of joy made Norm feel giddy. He said jokingly, "But you're okay imposing on me, is that it?"

Winston, who had been turned away, turned back, his face mortified. "Oh—" he began. Then he saw Norm's expression and burst out laughing. Norm joined in.

Afterward, Winston said, "Actually, that's why I brought these groceries. You know, doing my part."

Norm stared at him. "You're kidding, right? It seems to me you're doing everything."

"You're providing the house."

Norm laughed and shook his head. "I was kind of getting creeped out being all alone here. It's a big house." He grinned and shrugged. "So, anyway—I'm happy to have you."

Winston smiled shyly. "Well. Thanks."

Norm looked at the food they had unpacked. "I guess we should decide what we're going to have for dinner."

Winston turned away and turned back holding up another bag, with the words Swiss Chalet printed on its side. "How about this?"

"Wonderful!" Norm cried, clapping his hands. "Thank heaven we don't have to cook!"

They ate in front of the fire. Conversation was desultory at first. Then, as if he had planned it, Winston brought up the topic of body image again.

"My brother was always a star athlete," he said, speaking casually. "He used to tease me about being chubby, and call me Winnie—you know, after Winnie-the-Pooh?" Winston smiled ruefully. "He said I looked just like him." He sighed and shook his head. "And I *was* chubby," he admitted, "right from the start, as far back as I can remember." He paused, seeming to think about this. Then he shrugged dismissively. "I guess I always lacked self-confidence. But who doesn't?" He gave an attempt at a light laugh, the sound of which squeezed Norm's heart.

"Speaking of Winnie-the-Pooh," Norm said suddenly, "have you ever heard of the concept of the bear? It's something in the gay community, guys who are heavy and hairy. They're kind of anti this slim-and-trim and fit-as-hell ideal that has come to so dominate gay culture."

"Heavy and hairy."

"That's right."

"Huh."

"Anyway, the bear is about appreciating the male body in its natural form, rather than trying for an ideal." He paused, and then said, "And let me tell you, some of those gym rats I've been chasing for years have got very little in the way of real character." He paused again. "You know, I never thought about it before, but now I think it's because they're not just being themselves. They're trying to be something else—some*one* else."

He stopped suddenly. "Oh, I'm sorry," he said. "I'm talking about the gay community like it's the entire world. I want you to know that I'm not making any assumptions."

Winston shrugged and scratched his head. When he looked up again, his face was red. "Actually," he said, "since it's come up, I guess I'm bi. Bisexual, you know?"

"Fuck anything that moves, eh?" Norm blurted, and then felt embarrassed by the coarseness of the remark, made to cover up his discomfort. But Winston laughed, and Norm felt relieved.

Winston lowered his head and scratched it again. "Well, not anything," he said.

"Good," Norm said, still feeling a little off balance. "Good to know I'm safe, then."

There was a slight pause. "Oh," Winston said in a quiet voice, "I wouldn't go that far."

Norm experienced a wave of intoxication at this remark—which made him feel panicky. He got to his feet.

"How about some wine?" he said. "I forgot to offer anything, and you bought dinner."

Winston looked up at him in the dim light and smiled his beautiful smile—which went through Norm's system like a bottle of wine all on its own.

"Love some."

The wine made conversation easier. By the time they were on their second bottle they had gone through topics ranging from Norm's love history, Winston's lack of same, the nature of relationships, of love—and incongruously, the different kinds of work occupations. It struck Norm how easy and natural it was talking like this with Winston. They seemed to really connect.

Thinking about this, he reached out to refill Winston's glass, but the wine made him clumsy and he lurched, spilling wine onto Winston's T-shirt.

"Oops! Sorry!"

Winston stared down at his chest. "No problem," he said. "Not much."

Norm stared at the stain and shook his head. "No. You gotta take it off. I'll wash it."

Winston laughed. "No washer. No power."

"Oh, right. But still—it'll stain."

Winston hesitated, so Norm started to lift the T-shirt himself, whereupon there was a little struggle, and Winston took the shirt off himself. Norm carried it to the kitchen and ran icy water over it. After scrubbing it with soap and rinsing it several times, he wrung it out and brought it back.

"We can… can hang it by the fire," he said. He positioned the garment on the wire so that it was close to the fire but wouldn't burn.

"There," Norm said, leaning back again. He looked over at Winston, saw his bare chest and, without thinking, reached out and ran his fingers through the guy's wiry chest hair. It was a second before he was fully aware of what he was doing, but by that time he was also aware that Winston wasn't objecting. And it felt *wonderful*. He looked up into Winston's eyes.

"I've been wanting to do that for a while."

Winston looked at him and chuckled. Then he reached out, grabbed Norm's T-shirt and, pulling him forward, kissed him gently on the lips. Just a polite, closed-mouth kiss, but very sweet. It took Norm's breath away.

When they separated, Winston said, "And *I've* been wanting to do that since I first saw you on the street."

"Really?"

Winston nodded. Then he pulled Norm gently to him and wrapped his arms around him.

They had been wrapped in blankets on the floor in front of the fire when they began to eat, for the fire didn't warm the house very well. But by this time, the warmth of the hearth had made them discard the blankets and even shirts. Norm felt his T-shirt press against Winston's chest hair as they kissed. This wouldn't do. He pulled back and doffed the garment. Winston was looking at him with happy eyes. Norm put his hands gently to either side of Winston's head and stroked his silky golden hair. Feeling like he wanted to melt, he let his hands drift down to Winston's beard and then to his wonderful chest hair.

The touch of Winston's flesh was extraordinary. It was soft and solid at the same time. Yes, there was a fullness of flesh, but there was also muscle, the muscle of a guy who was physical and capable to a high degree. The extra padding just made him real, made him genuine. It was so wonderful, intoxicating.

Winston pulled Norm to him. They kissed, and Winston slowly initiated a turn so that he was on top. Norm found he liked the sense of being borne down by Winston's weight. He began kissing Winston's neck, then his upper chest, scooching down until the swell of Winston's belly overtopped his face. When he'd been sitting or standing, Winston's belly, while not ripped, had neither been a full beer gut, but now the force of gravity accentuated its curve—which Norm found a real turn on.

There came the clank of metal, and Winston was undoing his pants. He pushed these down, along with his shorts, and there, below the curve of his belly, was his erect cock. Scooching down further, Norm took the fat cock head into his mouth. Winston moaned quietly.

The curve of Winston's belly pressed against Norm's forehead, which he found incredibly hot. He let the swollen cock slip from between his lips and lifted his head to kiss the curving mass of that wonderful belly. Winston pulled away self-consciously at first, but Norm reached around and pressed his hands against the small of Winston's back. The guy got the message. He pushed his belly out and down, pressing hard against Norm's head and face, which made *Norm* moan with pleasure.

As Norm alternated between Winston's belly and cock, he undid his own belt and pushed pants and shorts down to his knees. Meanwhile, Winston began pushing forward with his hips, so that his cock's head slid up Norm's cheek. When Norm turned his head to take the cock into his mouth, Winston pulled back, sliding the slippery head out of the reach of his eager lips. Being teased like this was something Norm found especially exciting, and the heat between his legs was almost continually on the verge of exploding, a kind of exquisite torture that drove him wild.

He had, he realized, *never* experienced anything as hot as this before.

He felt himself letting go completely. There was no thinking now, just being—just experiencing this intensely satisfying situation, the mass, curves, and weight of Winston's body, the sense of his virility, his passion. While Norm's mouth was busy, so were his hands. He kept rubbing Winston's belly, savoring its curve, then moving up to the hairy chest and down to the thighs, but always, always, back to the belly that bore down on top of him. Its proud, solid softness, curving just above Winston's cock, which stood out, hard as anything and glistening with Norm's saliva, was perfection, pure erotic perfection.

The thrusting cock became gradually less elusive. Norm wrapped his lips around it and sucked lustily. The sense of pleasure doing this was so great that molten heat rose inside him, filling his entire body. He felt Winston's cock head swell even further, become taut. Then, pulse after pulse of thick, hot, sticky cum spewed into his mouth. For a second he gagged, but then he swallowed and allowed the thrusting cock to press the back of his throat. Surrender made it easy and wonderful. And at the same time his own heat overflowed into orgasm, which made him feel like his veins were filled with butter. He arched his back and felt the wonderful spasming of his own cock while his hands, fingers spread, pressed against the heavy curve of Winston's belly.

A minute or two later, Winston rolled off of him and held him close.

"Oh man!"

Norm raised his head and looked at Winston. "Was that good for you?"

Winston looked back at him, slightly dazed, and laughed. "You're kidding, right?" He breathed several times. Then he asked, "Uh, how was it for you?"

Norm smiled the smile of a fulfilled cocksucker and shook his head. "Don't ask," he said. "I came without touching myself."

"Wow! Yeah, I felt it hit my back, all the way up to my shoulders and neck. You came like a stallion!"

"So did you. And I swallowed it—every drop." Norm smiled sweetly at Winston.

Winston leaned forward and kissed Norm, a long, lingering kiss, and Norm reached out, taking hold of Winston's cock, which was still erect. It even swelled when he squeezed. "You got a repeater rifle?" he said.

Winston grinned. "Almost. If you give me a few minutes."

"I forgot," Norm said. "You're twenty. Ah, youth," he added wistfully. They both laughed.

"It's your fault," Winston said. "The way you touch—it's, it's electric."

"Great! Terrific! Now all you have to do is move in, and I'll suck your dick every time you get hard."

"Then you'll be doing a *lot* of sucking."

Norm pulled a mock straight face. "Hey!" he said. "I was serious."

Instantly, Winston looked mortified. "Hey," he said quietly. "Don't talk like that."

"Why not?"

"Well," Winston didn't meet his gaze, "I don't like to think it's something to joke about."

"Oh. Sorry."

"That's okay." Winston traced the curve of Norm's chest with a finger.

After a pause, in a more sober voice, Norm said, "Actually, I wasn't completely joking."

Winston's reddened, but he didn't look mollified.

Norm sat up, his own face heating up. He felt he'd messed up somehow.

"Sorry if I've said anything I shouldn't have," he said, speaking cautiously.

Winston shook his head but didn't look at him.

"Maybe you could stay for the remainder of the blackout."

Winston looked at Norm finally, eyes searching his. Then he leaned forward and kissed him gently, a sweet kiss that lasted almost a minute.

With Winston's arms around him, just being together like this, Norm felt something inside his chest wrench itself loose. It fluttered and ached—and after a period of confusion, with a kind of awed mortification, Norm realized that he had fallen for the guy.

He decided that he wasn't going to say anything. Not yet, anyway.

After the kiss, Winston smiled his shy smile and nodded.

"Yeah, okay," he said. "At least for the remainder of the blackout." And then they were kissing once again.

G.P. KEITH lives in Toronto in a household dominated by two opinionated and irresistible miniature pinschers. His worldview is defined by two personality traits: being an irrepressible romantic and having an insatiable curiosity about how things work, both within and beyond his skin.

This curiosity has led him in stages from studying the purely objective reality, through the field of physics, examining the principles by which the universe operates; on to the practical application of these principles, working on engineering control systems using real-time computer programs; and finally to studying of how human beings themselves function, both in general (psychology), and specifically how they subjectively experience and interact with the external world (neuroscience).

At the same time G.P. Keith nourished his abiding interest in the arts—dabbling in drawing and piano, but writing in particular. He has always been a passionate reader, mostly of science fiction, fantasy, and horror, but with sojourns into literature proper and plays—basically anything with a compelling story and sympathetic characters.

G.P. Keith has published a number of articles and stories for gay magazines in the past, along with some historical nonfiction, and he welcomes the rising world of m/m romance fiction, which provides the opportunity for exploring what he now believes to be the ultimate secret of human existence: the mysterious operation of the human heart, and its ability to grow when broken.

Contact him at g.p.keith14@gmail.com.

Banyan Court
Samuel scott Preston

AUTHOR'S NOTE: *The translations from Zeami's* Atsumori *are by Arthur Waley and are in the public domain. His version of the whole play can be read at http://www.sacred-texts.com/shi/npj/npj08.htm (accessed June 7, 2014). The video of the Noh play Kenji shows Hank can be seen at http://youtu.be/3mXuGC16ix4 (accessed June 7, 2014).*

"I SHOULDN'T complain," Dan Kumagai said, setting his coffee cup down with a clatter. "She means well. She just can't stop fussing. She seems to think I'm going to turn into a lonely old misanthrope as soon as I hit sixty."

"She couldn't be more wrong," replied Ann Burleson. "You were already that when I met you, and you were only thirty-two then. But you may turn into Pantalone, perhaps," she added thoughtfully. Kumagai had known he could count on Ann to cheer him up. She was good at putting things, and people, in their proper places. Her tidiness was what made her such a good papyrologist and departmental colleague. He made a harrumphing noise. "Pantalone indeed," he muttered, feigning indignation.

The "she" Kumagai meant was his older sister. Like her brother, Kazuko was a college professor, of Japanese language and literature at the University of Hawaiʻi at Mānoa. Kazuko had chosen the path well traveled, staying in Honolulu, marrying, teaching her ancestral language—which, however, as with most Hawaiʻi *sansei*, or third-generation Japanese-Americans, their war-generation parents had refused to teach them at home. Kumagai, on the other hand, couldn't get away soon enough. He went to college on the mainland and stayed there, earning his PhD in classics and taking a very satisfying job at a small

Midwestern liberal arts college. He was more Roman than Japanese. He even affected a Hadrianic beard that Ann always teased him about. He secretly agreed it didn't look exactly Roman on him, but at least it hid his face, and it most definitely distanced him from most people's mental image of an Asian.

Kumagai wasn't ashamed of his Japanese heritage, but he'd never been attracted to Asian men. Accordingly, he assumed that few men could be attracted to him, and did what he could to counter the stereotype of effeminacy. He considered himself lucky to be hairy, although he hated that it cast him as a "bear," another type of man he was not attracted to. He knew facial and body hair were more common among Japanese than most people realized. So he used his fur—or, rather, he had when he had still been on the prowl. That had stopped in his early fifties, when, he had told himself, it was time to admit his chances were going from slim to none—past time he should get used to being single.

A cup clicked on a saucer. "So, will you go?" Ann broke in on his thoughts. He didn't answer. He didn't really know yet. She waited quietly. Another of her virtues, one Kumagai envied her, was patience. When he was growing up, he kept hoping he would eventually acquire some kind of innate Japanese Zen thing that translated to patience. He hadn't.

"I suppose I have to," he finally said. "I haven't been back in a while. But I know she's going to go with the whole Japanese shtick about starting over a brand-new sixty-year cycle, make me wear a baby cap and a bib, probably." Ann laughed. He knew she'd be trying to picture it. He gave her time to enjoy it before going on. "I suppose, if I'm going to go at all, I'll try to persuade her to put it off until after commencement. Maybe by then she'll have forgotten, or something will turn up to get me out of it."

"You see? You *are* a surly old misanthrope." She continued to grin.

"I didn't say 'surly,' I said 'lonely.'" And Kumagai deftly turned the conversation. "What do you think of the candidates to replace Thompson for the Latin side?"

Professor Burleson was too tidy to leave her former question hanging. "My publisher expects the final draft of my book by August. I'll be around, and I'll take care of watering your plants and feeding the cat," she said. "No need to thank me. Just make sure to send me a picture of you in that bib and baby cap. There could be no more priceless reward. Now, I think the specialist in early Roman religion would be most versatile for our purposes...."

KUMAGAI'S WIDOWED sister had moved into a smaller house when she retired a few years back, so she arranged for Dan to stay at the Moana Surfrider Hotel, the Edwardian pile that was one of the oldest Waikiki hotels. Her husband had been a successful lawyer and left her well off. She could afford it, Dan reflected as his cab pulled up to the porte cochere. He savored how the sunset colors shone on its white columns. He was warmed by her remembering how much he had always loved the place and wanted to stay there, even though he had never treated himself to it. He guessed he had only been about ten when he first heard of the Moana's lasting mystery, the death, perhaps by murder, of Jane Stanford, cofounder of the famous university. For months afterward, Kumagai had bored Kazuko with his latest researches and discoveries about the ancient scandal. He had roamed the hotel as completely as he dared—sadly, the fatal Room 120 had vanished in some renovation or other—and as an adult still made a point of going there to eat or have drinks with friends in the Banyan Court whenever he was in Honolulu. He remembered vividly the first time he saw the hotel, just a few years after statehood, when Waikiki was a lot emptier. He had been visiting a classmate, Sidney (a not-very-happy substitute for his Japanese name, Sadao), who lived in a modest back street nearer the Ala Wai canal than the beach. He was supposed to be taking calligraphy lessons from his schoolmate's father. He didn't care much about calligraphy, but as he turned thirteen, he was learning he cared a lot about Sid—and that made him punctual and faithful in attending his lessons. They had discovered *The Lord of the Rings* together, and more important, the novels of Mary Renault, whose romantic depiction of love between men in ancient Greece had set Dan on his career path, while also giving Sid and Dan permission to explore their feelings for one another.

He had infected Sid with his enthusiasm for solving the Stanford mystery, and they had saved their allowances to be able to afford tea in the Banyan Court. This noble tree was a far cry from the more democratic banyan at the International Marketplace just down and across Kalakaua Avenue, their usual haunt. That one was carved with initials and various equivalents of So-and-so Was Here. In fact, they had been so daring, one day, as to leave their own initials there, surrounded by a heart. At the Moana's Banyan Court, after tea, they had both risen and touched the smoother bark of the banyan tree there, at first separately, then, gradually, hardly knowing it, entwining their fingers against the strong, smooth wood that felt so much like skin over muscle, until Sid's hand rested on Dan's, and they let it linger as long as they dared, loudly discussing the surfers off the beach to distract any onlookers. A year later, Sid was killed in Vietnam.

Dan didn't even bother to unpack once he was shown to his room. Sid might not have been replaced in his heart, but he couldn't help noticing how handsome the bellhop who carried his bag was—Samoan, he thought, built like a football player. His tip was generous, and the Samoan grinned knowingly. Dan took only enough time to wash the travel grime from his face and arms and to change into khaki shorts, a tent-sized aloha shirt—brick colored, with only the most discreet white outlines of hibiscus blooms—and hiking sandals that made his feet look even more like bears' paws than usual. *Well*, he thought, as he often did when trying and failing to bring himself to some acceptance of his looks, *Kumagai does mean "Bear Valley."* As he took the elevator down to the ground floor, he found himself hoping Samoans liked their men as big as they seemed to like their women. The bellhop was solid muscle. Dan would have been less willing to entertain such questions had he met him in the street after dark. He scolded himself silently, in words that had become a mantra for him, albeit unconsciously. He was sixty now. Time to admit his chances were going from slim to none—past time he should get used to being single.

Within fifteen minutes of his arrival, he was seated before a lavish tea in the Banyan Court. His order given, he had walked slowly, hoping to avoid notice, to the banyan tree. As he always did when he was there, he reached out and laid his palm against it in that same spot, remembering the feel of Sid's hand over his nearly half a century ago. If nobody had wanted to take Sid's place in all those decades, it was time he accepted nobody ever would. He touched the tree bark a long time, feeling Sid's muscular body in the wood. Then a tourist couple, plainly honeymooners, politely asked if he would take their picture standing in front of it. Embarrassed at being caught in so sentimental a gesture, he assented eagerly.

ANN BURLESON would have to do without the baby-cap-and-bib photo, Kumagai wrote in his e-mail to her after the birthday party the next day. Kazuko had been talked out of it by the others. Kumagai was inventing here—he had no idea whether his sensible, if occasionally overliteral, sister had actually ever intended such a thing. Ann, however, deserved his most artfully improved version of events. She would want to pass it on to her spouse Jillian, a lawyer. His grandnephew Kenji, however, had been a diligent photographer, both during the formal banquet at one of Honolulu's most expensive Japanese restaurants and at the smaller after-party held at Kenji's father's rather grand residence near Koko Head. Apparently he had a new iPad Mini and wanted to test its camera. Kenji was Kumagai's favorite relation in the newest generation. He was soon to graduate from UH and had already been accepted into law school. He would go into his father's law office, which had been founded by Kumagai's father and continued by his brother Gerald and Kazuko's husband, and now was headed by Kazuko's son, Kenji's father. The firm specialized in real-estate law, with a sideline in politics. Kenji, according to a quiet conversation on the lanai with his great-uncle, would keep the tradition. Of course, being Kenji, he kept it in his own way, by writing a senior thesis for his political science degree on disputes over the legal sleight-of-hand by which so much of the land in the islands had passed from its Hawai'ian owners into the hands of the white planters.

Kumagai was pleased, and said so. Kenji basked in the approval. Ever since he had come out to his gay great-uncle a few years before, they had been close. Dan assumed Kenji was glad to have at least one family member who hadn't plotted out his life for him like an escalator. To his surprise, Kenji had handed him an envelope out on the lanai. Dan assumed it was a card that Kenji, for some reason, didn't want mingled with the other cards and small gifts from family and friends. He had started to open it, but Kenji stopped him. Just then Kazuko bustled out and insisted Dan return for his brother's star turn, and Kenji told him to wait till he got back to the hotel.

This, Kumagai reported to Ann, was the same star turn he used at every family gathering. Nevertheless, it was always welcome, and not just from indulgence. Gerald really did get a little better each time, especially now he was retired and had time to practice, and by now the rest of the family could back him up. Every Japanese man, decreed Kazuko, must have a hobby—though Kumagai had refused to touch a calligraphy brush since Sid's death, and Kazuko had delicately let the omission slide—and Gerald's was Noh chanting. Dan digressed enough in his explanation to Ann to report what Kazuko had said to him once in private—"If they don't have hobbies, Japanese men drive their wives nuts when they retire. That's when most divorces happen in Japan."

Gerald's party piece, appropriately enough, was the climax of Zeami's *Atsumori*. The play tells how the Genji warrior Kumagai, now a Buddhist priest with the name Renzei, encounters a reaper on the shore where his most famous battle was fought. The reaper turns out to be the ghost, or reincarnation, of the young and beautiful Heike enemy Atsumori, whose flute playing Kumagai had admired at a distance on the eve of the disastrous final defeat of the Heike at Ichi-no-tani, but whom now Kumagai's duty, and Atsumori's own pride, required him to slay.

Despite his noisy proclamation of the superiority of Greek and Roman culture, Kumagai loved Noh, and even more, Kabuki. One of the treats of his childhood had been his walk-on part in the University's English-language Kabuki production of *Kumagai's Battle Camp*, in which he had mimed Atsumori to a slightly taller boy's Kumagai, a traditional stage effect to make the action appear far off in the distance. In the more flamboyantly emotional Kabuki version, Kumagai substitutes his own son for Atsumori, and lets the enemy escape. Then Kumagai and the boy's mother must go through the painful business of pretending not to recognize their own child's head and identifying it as Atsumori's. It was a crowd-stopping scene, the kind of three-hanky operatic moment that Dan secretly loved, though he always disclaimed any such thing when watching it. He had learned to position himself so nobody could see his wet eyes.

Professor Kumagai had often played video of both plays for the students in his popular Greek Tragedy course. His PhD dissertation had been on stagecraft in the Athenian theatre, a topic chosen both because of his early adoration of Renault's *The Mask of Apollo* and because of the haunting beauty of the Noh. So he knew the lines and the dance that his brother now repeated with even more mastery and control than the last time Dan had seen him. "But truly a generation passes like the space of a dream," chanted Gerald.

The leaves of the autumn of Juei
Were tossed by the four winds;
Scattered, scattered (like leaves too) floated their ships.
And they, asleep on the heaving sea,

Went back home.
Caged birds longing for the clouds,
Wild geese were they rather, whose ranks are broken
As they fly to southward on their doubtful journey.
So days and months went by; Spring came again,
And for a little while
Here dwelt they on the shore of Suma
At Ichi-no-tani....

Dan also joined Kazuko and one or two others—Kenji included, to Dan's amazement, though he had to drop out at one or two points where his memory failed him—in the final chorus, while Gerald danced. By established family custom, they substituted their own names for the priest Kumagai's Buddhist name Renzei:

So Atsumori fell and was slain, but now the Wheel of Fate
Has turned and brought him back.
"There is my enemy," he cries, and would strike.
But the other is grown gentle
And calling on Buddha's name
Has obtained salvation for his foe;
So that they shall be reborn together
On one lotus-seat.
"No, Kumagai is not my enemy.
Pray for me again, oh pray for me again."

The haunting lines always cast their spell, and had become a traditional signal that a party was ending. Dan made no protest when Kazuko and her daughter-in-law pressed on him the majority of the leftover Japanese delicacies from the banquet and the after-party. They knew, mainly because Dan continually reminded them, that it took an hours-long drive to Chicago among deathly flat cornfields to find even a half-decent Japanese restaurant. Trips back to Hawaiʻi always meant gorging on proper Japanese food. Kenji drove him back to the hotel, and they chatted about inconsequential matters. But before he got out, Dan commended Kenji for learning the lines from *Atsumori* and was glad to discover that Kenji had once seen a video of the Kabuki version as well. As they sat in the dark car, Dan recited a passage in Greek from the *Iliad*, describing Achilles mourning for Patroclus, and then recited Dryden's translation.

Now, composing his e-mail to Ann, he felt somehow shy of describing his conversation with Kenji. Instead he wrote about the food.

IT WAS the next morning when Kumagai opened Kenji's envelope, only to discover that he should have done so the night before. There was more than just a card in it. Taking seriously the new start expected at sixty, Kenji had arranged, and paid for, an unlikely gift—a daylong private surfing lesson. Dan had slept in and now saw he had only about half an hour before he was scheduled to meet the instructor. Kenji had been thoughtful enough, at least, to specify that Dan would do so on the terrace by the Banyan Court, overlooking the beach where the lesson was to take place. The instructor would have his sandwich-board sign with him so he could be identified, and Kenji apparently knew the man, to whom he had given what the note described as "a detailed and thorough" description of his great-uncle.

Much as Dan liked Kenji and appreciated his thoughtfulness, this was awkward. He vaguely remembered a conversation last visit in which Kenji, who had been an avid surfer for years, was appalled to discover than Dan had never surfed. In fact, this was a half-truth at best; Sid, who as a Waikiki boy had surfed as soon as he could walk, had tried hard to teach him. But Dan had even then been so out of touch with his body that he had never been able to get the knack, and Sid had given up once he saw it was more like torture than friendship to continue. Dan could swim, of course, and was perfectly at home in the water. He swam every noon in the college pool and regularly longed for a proper beach with proper warm salt water to swim in. But surfing had been beyond him.

Kenji's note was persuasive, though. The boy would make a fine lawyer, Dan thought idly as he read his grandnephew's argument for learning something new. He knew Kenji would be checking up to make sure the lesson took place. Well, a day in the water would do him no harm, and he consoled himself by composing a little speech on his way down to the Banyan Court in which he would warn the poor instructor that he probably had a hopeless pupil on his hands. No doubt the young man would have his doubts about teaching a sixty-year-old anyway. He would do his best to diminish how distasteful it would be for the instructor. Kenji described him as experienced and good at his job—probably Kumagai wasn't the first dotty old man whose age-inappropriate behavior he'd had to deal with.

His beard saved him shaving time, which he used to decide how to dress for the lesson. Dan knew better than to ruin the scenery all the tourists had paid good money to see by exposing his bearish old body, so he chose one of his usual XXL T-shirts, so loose that the sleeves came halfway down his forearms and the shirt covered his overlarge butt. At least the board shorts he usually swam in concealed how hairy that butt was. He didn't have any reason to be ashamed of his legs, at least—any errands at home that took him farther around town than walking distance he usually did by bicycle. And there was nothing to be done about his bear paws.

Kumagai realized he was hungry and decided he would offer the instructor breakfast at the Banyan Court, assuming he wasn't too scruffy or salt-encrusted. It would kill some time and let him warn the poor guy—Hank Ross, according to Kenji's note—what he was in for. Fortunately "all day" was general enough to permit both sides to end the disaster gracefully without hurting Kenji's feelings.

Then Dan Kumagai got his first look at Hank Ross.

The instructor was older than he expected, not Kenji's age at all, more likely at least thirty. He was in one of Kenji's classes, but of course not all students at UH were young. Nor was he the usual longhaired "dude" of questionable personal hygiene the fastidious professor had somehow expected. He was staring out at the surf, his back to Kumagai and backlit by the late-morning light. It showed off broad shoulders and a sharp taper to a narrow, lithe waist. He was muscular, but in the lean style of a greyhound. His flawless skin was the color of honey, and his short-cropped hair only slightly darker. The contrapposto of his stance gave prominence to strong round glutes.

Kumagai took all this in, but that wasn't what stopped him in his tracks. Hank was leaning with his palm against the bark of the banyan, right where Sid and he had so long ago. Dan found he couldn't breathe. He nearly fled, but the man's beauty was too powerful a force to let him.

He was saved from making a fool of himself by the waitress asking him where he would like to sit. Dan cleared his throat. "Next to the tree, please." A couple—he recognized the newlyweds from the first evening—were just vacating the table nearest the banyan, a few steps this side of where Hank was standing, and Dan took the opportunity offered by waiting for the table to be reset to gaze on the surfing instructor. The exchange with the waitress, and a cheery greeting from the honeymooners as they walked by, brought him back to some degree of reality. He strode over to the instructor and, standing by the table as the busboy cleared it, cleared his throat again, and asked, "Hank Ross?"

He caught the tail end of a pensive look as the latter turned to him, holding out his hand and saying with a cordial smile, "Mr. Kumagai?" Dan could only nod and smile back. He was glad of the handshake, both for the way it filled in a few moments before he could find his voice and his composure, and because of the unaffected good manners it showed. Hank's face was even handsomer than his body. A welcoming smile just barely disclosed perfect teeth, but the eyes seemed old, somehow. The step he took to meet Kumagai's outstretched hand showed off powerful lean thighs and calves and long-toed, high-arched bare feet. Hank's grip was strong, his palm somewhat calloused but not rough. This was no overaged teenager putting off adult life, as Kumagai had unconsciously expected. He was relieved. Hank Ross might not regard him as decrepit after all.

Hank accepted a coffee and half a grapefruit but declined more, saying he had eaten already. He seemed not at all bothered by Dan's lateness or the time spent over breakfast—it turned out he wanted to find out more about his client's expectations and experience anyway. This seemed to be his usual procedure, and it put Dan a bit more at ease, although he found himself losing the thread of the talk when those knowing hazel eyes were turned on him. He felt ungainly, clumsy even, in this man's company. He concentrated on every movement he made, even on his table manners, as if he were trying to convince his parents they'd been right to let him eat at the grown-up table.

Dan played for time by taking a second cup of coffee after he finished his granola with yogurt and an English muffin—far less than he usually had, but then he was about to engage in some vigorous activity, he told himself—and asking, "So, how do you know my nephew?" He couldn't think how the "grand" had vanished.

"I'm taking a few classes at the university," he said. "GI bill." That explained the ancient eyes. "One of them has to do with the history of land tenure in the kingdom, then the territory and state. Kenji's in the same class. I'm interested in history."

Kumagai felt, for the first time, as if he might survive this day. "I'm a classics professor," he returned. "I know less about Hawaiian history than I should, except what they taught us in school. But ask me about the battle of Thermopylae or the Peloponnesian War and I can bore you for days. My real specialty is performance practice in the Attic theatre, though, and its antecedents in choral song and dance." He could hear the pedantic tone creep into his voice and decided to quit while he was ahead. "So you were in the military?" he asked, to deflect the subject from himself.

"Marines. Iraq, mostly." Hank didn't elaborate, and Dan didn't dare pursue the matter. Sid had been a Marine. After a pause, not quite long enough to be awkward, Hank continued, "So you may need to tell me more about the Peloponnesian War sometime. I've read my Thucydides, though."

"I'd better stick to the Trojan War, then," Dan replied. "I haven't taught Thucydides in almost ten years." His grin brought forth an answering chuckle from Hank, and Dan's heart skipped a beat. "I should warn you I'm not as good a pupil as I am a teacher. I can swim at least, but I have my doubts about surfing."

"And you call yourself a Hawaiian," teased Hank.

"I'm one hundred percent Japanese-American, a *sansei*," countered Dan. "My father was a lawyer, and his father was a pineapple worker. Neither had much time for hanging out on the beach. I only came to Waikiki for my calligraphy lessons."

"Kenji's an excellent surfer," Hank said. "I'm sure you'll do fine."

"You've only survived IEDs and suicide bombers, what do you know about difficult jobs?"

Dan had no idea how he had dared ask that—the privilege of age?—but to his relief, Hank laughed and said, "Touché!" Then he said, serious again, "We really ought to get started, though, while the waves are right for beginners. If you're finished with your coffee, that is."

Dan signaled for the check, signed it, and followed Hank out to the beach. Another sandwich board like the one he had used for identification guarded a small array of surfboards of different sizes jammed upright in the sand. He waved to a young woman at a shave-ice stand a few yards away, signaling he was back and her sentry duty was over. He didn't touch any of the boards, but lay down in the sand on his flat, lean belly and motioned Dan to do the same. The lesson had begun.

There was no banter for the next few hours. Hank wasn't a harsh instructor, but his concentration was fierce and it was plain he expected the same from his pupil. Dan's professional judgment approved. He knew this meant Hank respected him and wasn't belittling a fat old polar bear's abilities. Instead, Hank looked past the surface to find the teachable points. He returned the compliment with his undivided attention. But when they were out in the lineup—safely away from the real surfers, he noticed—his best efforts weren't enough to get him upright on the board, much less to catch a wave. Hank never lost patience, but in the end he decreed it was time for a break. They paddled back onshore. Dan realized he was more tired than he had imagined.

They sat side by side between their upright boards, looking out to sea. Hank said nothing, but Dan could tell he was trying to figure out what to say or do next. When it came, Dan was surprised at its irrelevance. "Why do you wear a shirt to swim in?" Hank asked.

Kumagai didn't know what to say. He knew why, but he wasn't about to tell Hank Ross. He felt as if he were the young one, and Hank the wise old man.

"I think I can guess," Hank said. "I hope you don't mind my asking, but is it because you're ashamed of your body?" Kumagai dug his toes into the sand and said nothing. Hank nodded to himself, apparently taking silence for assent, and went back to staring at the ocean.

After a bit he stood, in a single fluid motion, and began to dance a traditional man's hula, slowly at first, but with the strength of the warrior he was. It was nothing like the tourist shows, neither the soft hand gestures that most people think of as "hula," nor a vigorous war dance. He seemed to be immeasurably older as he danced, moving with all the grace he had shown on his surfboard but within a much narrower range. He went on for about five minutes, responding to some internal chant that from time to time escaped him in a low murmur, then sat down, still without a word.

Kumagai suddenly was reminded of the final dance of *Atsumori* that his brother had sketched the night before. It had the same solemnity, the same inner stillness that almost made "dance" seem the wrong word. Gerald wasn't a dancer, of course—his attention was on the singing. Hank *was* a dancer, and a very good one. When he spoke, it was nothing to do with surfing. Or so Kumagai thought at first.

"My Auntie was a well-known *kumu hula* in Kailua. I live in the house she left me in Kāne'ohe. She was my great-aunt, really, but I never knew her sister—my grandmother—and hardly knew my mother. Auntie really raised me. My father was a Marine too, and was gone a lot—don't get me wrong, he was a great father when he was home—and my mother left when I was so young I barely remember her. Auntie took her place. So I danced from an early age. I still do, in fact, from time to time. I may look like a haole, and I guess I mainly am, but Auntie and my grandmother were half Hawaiian. That's why I'm taking the course where I met Kenji." He paused. "Have you ever been to the International Marketplace?" he asked.

The memory of his hours and days spent there with Sid rushed back in on Dan, and for a moment he couldn't breathe. "Yes," he said, and the questioning look on Hank's face told him he had freighted the short syllable with more than he meant to.

Hank looked as if he were going to pursue the opening, but he apparently thought better of it. He went on, "I sometimes dance there for extra cash. The Samoans who mostly perform call me when somebody needs a night off. They tease me about being blond, but they know I was in combat and that's good enough for them." Another pause. "Well, I guess that's all over now. You know they're closing it and tearing it down?"

Dan cried, "No!" It was impossible. It had been there forever. To many it was a tawdry tourist trap and eyesore, to others, land wasted in low-rises. To Dan, who still saw it through the eyes of childhood, through memories of Sid especially, it seemed impossible it could go. "I used to spend a lot of time there in my early teens," he said, "hanging out with—with my best friend." Hank looked at him hard and nodded, as if he somehow intuited that by "best friend" Dan really meant something more.

One revelation deserves another. Hank had let him into his life, in a small way. Dan decided he owed as much back. "You actually reminded me of him for a minute this morning, under the banyan tree. He used to stand that way, touching the tree with a kind of… tenderness." He couldn't go on. He had said too much already.

Hank left a space to honor the confidence, but when he spoke again, he returned to his theme. "Do you dance?" he asked.

"Not really," Dan said. "Not for years. And never well."

"But you know about dance? Kenji says you're a fan of Noh and Kabuki. I actually know something about Kabuki, but not much about Noh."

Dan wondered how Kenji even knew this, other than the family tradition. "I know a lot more about Western opera and ballet."

Hank nodded, paused a moment, considered, and made a decision. He said, "I think the reason you had trouble this morning is that you aren't in touch with your body. You're at home in the water—I can tell that—but you just don't *like* your body, and that means you can't feel what it's like to be *in* it, the way a dancer or a surfer does. Am I right? I'm not criticizing, just asking," he added, after Dan didn't answer. Another pause. "Take that shirt off," he said, in a quiet voice. Dan did as he was told.

Hank looked him up and down, then reached out and touched Dan's chest and ran his fingers lightly down to his belly, where he ruffled the hair, then twined his fingers in it. "I envy you that hair," he said, stroking his own sleek belly with his other hand. "Silver. It shimmers like a mithril coat."

Dan was stunned, by the touch and by the simile. He stood, unable to think of anything to say as Hank continued to stare at him, not taking his hand away. Its touch grew hot against Dan's skin.

Kumagai had no idea how much time passed before Hank stepped back again and broke eye contact. "If you're not doing anything tomorrow, I'd like to try again. On me." When Kumagai didn't reply, he said, now with a grin, "I hate to fail. I've never yet had a pupil who didn't surf like Kelly Slater when I was done." More silence. "Or the next day, if that's better."

"Tomorrow is... fine."

"I'll come get you. Earlier than today, though. We have to go to my place. I know a cove where it will just be the two of us, nobody watching to make you self-conscious. Nine o'clock, okay?"

"Eight if you want breakfast here," Dan said, looking at the banyan tree. "On me."

"Deal." And Hank strode away, leaving Kumagai gaping after him. When Hank was out of sight, he turned to go back in. Before he left, he reached out and touched the banyan lightly. For luck.

THE LITTLE bungalow in Kāneʻohe was a few blocks from the beach, in a modest neighborhood of small lots. There was a carport with hardly enough room left in it for Hank to park his battered Sidekick. The rest was taken up with surfing paraphernalia and a small but exquisite war canoe, with its outrigger detached and hanging from the ceiling. It only had room for two or three people, Dan guessed. "I take tourists for rides, sometimes, when the waves aren't good enough to surf." He led Dan past the side door and onto a small lanai in back of the bungalow. A few bananas marked off the property line on two sides, and the whole area was shaded by a noble old mango. "We need to talk," said Hank as he hooked a garden chair with one handsome bare foot in Dan's direction and sat in another. He crossed that same foot over his knee and played idly with his long toes while he thought about where to start. Dan couldn't stop looking. He nearly stopped breathing when Hank grasped his own big toe in one fist—Dan knew this to be a coded erotic sign in a Kabuki context, the equivalent of grabbing his cock. Surely Hank could not know what he had just "said," much less what Dan "heard"? Dan forced himself to breathe normally. Every inch of this man was beautiful. But he was half Dan's age. He shifted his gaze to Hank's eyes.

"How did the Greeks dance? Teach me," he said.

"We don't really know," Kumagai said. "There's no evidence except on vases and they're stationary and two-dimensional."

"Show me."

Dan struck an awkward pose. "It's really not easy to imagine," he said lamely.

"How about Noh? It's mainly dance, right? Show me what that's like."

"Well, you have to study forever to learn it." Seeing that this would not get him off the hook, he added, "I can only give you a general idea." Hank waited.

Dan thought back to the deceptively simple-looking movements that had accompanied Gerald's chanting two nights before, trying to remember how they went. He stared off into space as he tried to recall the shape of the dance. Suddenly he was back in the classroom, a teacher again, determined to awaken his students to the beauty of performance, how the emotion of a story lies in the dance and music. His voice slid unconsciously into teaching mode as he explained. "It's part of a play, a story," he said, "so you need to know what's going on. This is the very end of the play. My brother is the one who really knows it, but I've watched him often. So has Kenji, actually. Gerald performs it a lot, in an amateur way of course, because the main character is called Kumagai, only in the play he now has a Buddhist name because he has given up fighting to follow the way of compassion and expiate his sins. He was forced to kill a beautiful young man, Atsumori, in battle—it's a civil war, back in the 1100s—and just as he's about to do it, he realizes that this enemy was the person playing an exquisite melody on his flute on the eve of battle. Kumagai could hear it from the opposing camp. So now he is back at the scene of the battle, many years later, and meets an old man who turns out to be the ghost, or the reincarnation—in Noh plays it's all sort of the same thing—of Atsumori, who begs Kumagai to pray for his salvation, which he does. It ends with Atsumori singing and dancing." And Dan chanted the lines first, translating them as he went, then combined them with what he remembered of the dance, clumsily, ineptly, possibly mistaking the simple steps, but absorbed in the story, almost a love story between two men, filled with the beauty of reconciliation and reunion in the next world. As he danced, he thought of Sid.

When he was done, he stood still, then without thinking turned to exit the stage that he had built in his mind, using the banana trees as if they were the three pines that mark the entry and exit ramp of a Noh theater. At the end of the backyard, he stood for a long time with his head bowed. When he came to himself and turned to Hank, he saw tears on the handsome cheeks.

"I know how both of them felt," Hank said at last. "I know." And he put his head in his hands and wept. Dan, who remained true enough to his training as a Japanese man to suppress displays of emotion, was shocked. Then, almost immediately, a wave of warmth and tenderness broke over his shock, sweeping it away with the memory of his losses and missed chances. Feeling his own cheeks wet at thoughts of Sid, Dan crossed to Hank and put his arms around those broad shoulders, timidly at first. He had already begun telling the story before he realized he was speaking aloud—how they had cut their initials in the banyan at the International Marketplace, and then, years later, how they had met one last time before Dan went off to college and Sid, also a Marine, to Vietnam. As he spoke, his arms tightened around Hank's shoulders.

"We ate supper at the Banyan Court, where you and I met. We avoided what was on both our minds, the chance—it suddenly seemed more like a certainty—that Sid would not come home except in a body bag, that this would be our last meeting in this life. Saying it aloud would have made it come true, I guess, but we should have said more than we did. It came true anyway, and we wasted our last chance. Before we said good-bye, after we had finished eating and were on our way out, we both touched the bark of the banyan tree one more time. It seemed as if the idea came to both of us at the same time, spontaneously. Our little fingers just touched, no more, because now we were too old to hold hands anymore. Or thought we were."

Dan could feel through Hank's body that he was still crying. Dan stood waiting for a long time, until Hank lifted his face, streaked with tears, and gazed at Dan. "You are a beautiful man," Hank said. "You don't know it, but you are. Even more so when you dance. If you can dance like that, you can surf. But you don't need to."

Dan leaned down and slowly, gently, bit by bit, rubbed away Hank's tears with his thumb. Hank turned his head, then grasped Dan's wrist in his strong hand and pulled it away. He looked at it, murmured to himself, "So soft," and spread his own larger, harder hand over it. "So small." He left his hand resting on Dan's but said nothing more.

Dan felt the blood rush to his face. He was mortified. He was ashamed of the soft hands of a scholar who never used a harsher tool than chalk, and he hated his short-fingered bear paws. He hated them. Surely Hank must be despising their softness, their uselessness, and him. Fat, disgusting old bear of a man, how had he been stupid enough to let his guard down before this young Alexander?

But he knew Hank was in pain too, from memories Dan dared not probe, so although he dreaded continuing the physical contact, he didn't move. After a time filled only with the distant sound of surf breaking, Hank let go, wiped his eyes, and made as if to stand. "I'm sorry," he said, and leaned forward. Dan felt a sudden desire to kiss Hank. No sooner did he recognize the desire than he knew following it through would ruin everything. Panic choked him. He turned and fled.

DAN STARED out the window of the bus that took him back toward Waikiki. He saw nothing. Nor did he hear himself muttering, "You're sixty, your chances are all past now. Time you get used to being single." He felt foolish. Why on earth would he have assumed Hank was leaning forward to kiss him? He, at least twice Hank's age, and so physically inept he couldn't even learn to surf, despite a handsome and attentive teacher. Hank reminded himself, coldly and methodically, of all the times he had mistaken kindness or generosity for love, of all the times he had let himself believe in the impossible, and of all the times he had fallen in love with wildly inappropriate, out-of-his-league men. If sixty was the age to start over, that should be his birthday resolution.

He realized, as he walked back to his hotel from the bus stop, that he was talking to himself. *Hank is not in love with you.* However many ways he phrased it, however many times he tried to make it mean something else, that was what he was saying.

He realized all this about the time he woke up to the fact that his feet had taken him to the International Marketplace and brought him to stand before the banyan tree there, the one he and Sid had carved his initials into. *You have these memories. You had Sid, and nobody else ever did. Can't you be satisfied with that?*

Thinking of Sid, and of his calligraphy lessons with Sid's punctilious, old-school father, brought him sharply to the realization of how rude he had been in simply running out. He owed Hank an apology at least. Stroking the bark of the banyan one last time, he turned resolutely away and crossed Kalakaua to the hotel, went to his room, and found Hank's business card on the nightstand, tucked into Kenji's birthday card. Taking a few minutes to frame his apology, determined that he would at least make it up to Hank by inviting him to dinner the next night, he picked up the bedside phone and dialed.

In the end, they talked for over an hour. Dan's apology and his awkward attempts at explaining himself, half excuse, half evasion, only took up the first ten or fifteen minutes of the time. Hank was gracious, more so than Dan felt he deserved. Even more, Dan could almost believe Hank was glad to hear from him, although as usual he cautioned himself silently against once again yielding to wishful thinking. Somehow Hank turned the conversation to the dance from *Atsumori*, telling Dan of a legend his auntie had told him that resembled it. She had even choreographed a hula to tell it, for Hank to dance.

Dan could hardly recall a conversation that had been so easy, at least not with another man, although of course he and Ann and Jillian could talk this way for hours. He found himself holding up his end much better than he had with Hank earlier that day, let alone the day before. Hank had a way of drawing him out, almost as if he wanted to hear Dan's voice. Hank's questions were intelligent, and his reactions as they discussed storytelling in dance were respectful but not at all as if he were humoring the older man.

Dan enjoyed the conversation so much that he nearly forgot the purpose of his call, to invite Hank to dinner. When he did, Hank's reaction was sweet beyond his best hopes. "I was hoping to see you again," Hank said, "but I hardly dared hope for it." This started Dan on another round of apologies, which Hank cut off by asking about time and place. When these details were settled, he said again, simply, "I'm so glad." Filled with a rush of gratitude, Dan found himself, completely on the spur of the moment, saying, "I think I'll stay another week. There's no rush to get back to the mainland, after all. I've come all this way, so why not? That is, if you aren't too busy. I want to spend it with you, as much as we can." A moment's renewed panic seized Dan. Had he pushed too far again? But before he could take it back or jolly it over, Hank's voice, rich and low, came back. "I'd like that. Very much."

HANK CAME to the Moana Hotel for dinner the next night, looking dashing in a seersucker blazer and open silk shirt that showed off just a tantalizing glance of his pectoral muscles. Dan was wearing a bright new aloha shirt, for once not in a subdued or solid color. He had gone to the International Marketplace to make one last visit to his doomed childhood patch of heaven, and had yielded to an impulse to buy a shirt that would show Hank he wasn't afraid to be noticed anymore.

Avoiding the Banyan Court, Dan had made reservations at a sushi place nearby—not one of the grand ones along Kalakaua, but a quieter one on Kuhio, where most of the customers were either tourists from Japan or locals. Kazuko always brought him here to eat when he was in town, and he had invited Kenji to meet them there. He explained as they walked to the restaurant. "It's too expensive for a college student, and if it hadn't been for Kenji I wouldn't have met you," Dan said. Dan wondered if he was implying too much, but Hank didn't object.

Kenji was waiting when they arrived, and knowing Dan's habits, had bagged them a quiet tatami corner where they'd have a little privacy. Hank seemed to have no trouble sitting on the floor, to Dan's relief. Dan thanked Kenji for the surfing lesson, hinting that it had turned into something more, although he still didn't know how to surf. Kenji seemed to know all about it in advance. "You little *nakōdo*, you!" Dan scolded, not very seriously, secretly hoping Hank didn't know the Japanese word. Kenji laughed. "Not all go-betweens are little old ladies or company bosses," he retorted.

They spoke of this and that during the meal, eventually turning to hula. Kenji seemed to want to know all about Auntie and her *hālau*. "Is it still going?" he asked.

"Her cousin has it now," Hank said. "He's a lot more into Hawaiian independence than she was, but he still says most of what he knows he learned from her."

"Would they take a Japanese?" Kenji asked.

"Never hurts to ask," Hank returned. "I may be able to pull some strings. Speaking of dancing, I'm filling in at the International Marketplace tomorrow night. Probably my last gig there. You want to come watch?" Dan explained to Kenji, who, to the others' disgust, turned out never to have gone to the International Marketplace.

"I thought that was just some crummy tourist trap," he protested, to which Hank and Dan exclaimed simultaneously, "Bite your tongue!" then to each other, "No respect for tradition!" Dan narrated his and Sid's history with the place, discreetly omitting the carved initials. That seemed a bit cheesy for today's youth. Hank noticed the omission, and with a wink at Dan, spilled the beans.

"No way!" Kenji said. Oddly, it seemed to add to his respect for his great-uncle.

But Dan, for some reason, felt something he had offered to Hank alone had been passed on too lightly. He liked Kenji, but he wasn't sure he wanted Kenji to know everything about him, certainly not before he had decided himself to tell it.

The silence that fell lasted a few beats too long, until it was broken by the waiter bringing refills of green tea. When they were replenished, Kenji began to scramble with the messenger bag he always carried, saying, "I almost forgot!" He pulled out his iPad Mini and said, "This is the dance I was telling you about, that goes with Dad's party piece," he explained to Hank, as he booted the thing up and swung it around in Hank's direction. It proved to be a video of *Atsumori*, cued up for the dialogue between the priest Renzei and the Reaper in the second part, just before the revelation. "Baa-chan showed me where to look," he explained, leaving Dan to interpret for Hank.

"Kazuko, my big sister, Kenji's grandmother."

"We'll skip the first two-thirds for now. I'll send you the link later. You remember the story? That I told you on the phone?"

Kumagai was startled. *Kenji and Hank had been talking? Without him knowing? When?* Some vague unease nagged at Kumagai's gut. *Calm down*, he told himself. *They knew each other before you met Hank—after all, it was Kenji who brought you together.* He wasn't soothed. He had tried to dance this for Hank the day before. Now he was learning Hank had gone behind his back to Kenji to find out what it really looked like. Obviously he, Dan Kumagai, was so clumsy and ugly that Hank had, despite his protestations, gotten no impression of the dance from so feeble a sketch of it. Dan knew now he should never have even tried.

Kenji started the clip. A few of the other patrons looked around at the sound, but since it was clearly some kind of Japanese music, they seemed to think it wasn't out of place. Kenji put his head near Hank's as they watched the video, leaving Dan to look over their shoulders. Kenji occasionally murmured a paraphrase of the text for Hank's benefit. Dan couldn't help thinking how different these *yonsei*, fourth-generation kids, were from his generation, how much more attuned to their Japaneseness. Feeling excluded from Kenji and Hank's close perusal, his thoughts drifted back to Hank's question about dance in Greek tragedy.

Kenji was saying, "Notice how first they alternate speeches, and then as the action builds they gradually take up each other's lines and finish them." Kumagai's mind immediately supplied the Greek term for the same technique, stichomythia. That set his mind veering off into a consideration of an article on classical Japanese and classical Athenian dramatic construction.

"The final dance begins here," Kenji was telling Hank in a low voice, who noted the time on the back of his hand. Kumagai noticed that he was now out of their thoughts altogether. The chanting ceased and the flute dominated, while the masked dancer opened his fan and began to circle and cross the polished wooden floor, seeming to feel his way by his toes. *Makes sense,* Kumagai thought. *He probably can't see much, and the Greek tragic actors would have had the same difficulty.* The dance looked easy, but Kumagai knew enough to guess how many years of training it took to make it look so, controlled and yet unfolding as if spontaneously. Twice it rose to a climax, then relaxed twice as the actor stood motionless and stamped before resuming, each time at a higher level of tension. Back and forth, turning in place and rising on his toes, several times raising his arms like a raptor about to take wing, his fan opening and closing—and then the actor began to chant again, in the third person now, relating the final moments of his earthly existence, how the departing boats had left the young warrior alone on shore with no way to escape. The chorus spelled him as his dance covered more and more of the stage. Then he chanted again, telling how Kumagai spurred his horse to follow him into the waves. The chorus narrated how they exchanged sword strokes, and the dancer demonstrated with his closed fan. They fought in the surf, but the boy was bested—the dancer went down on one knee, then both, then dropped his fan as Atsumori gave up his life. But this was a Buddhist play; it was not the end of his soul's existence, as we already knew by now, so it was not the end of the dance. Overwhelmed by long-past emotions not yet purged, the dancer drew his sword, crossing the stage toward the man who had killed him and who now prayed for him. Running into that wall of prayer, he dropped the sword with a clatter and the chorus concluded the play: "They shall be reborn together/ On one lotus-seat."

In spite of himself, Dan Kumagai was moved. Kenji and Hank were silent, motionless, heads nearly together. A sudden hot rush of shame broke over Dan as he saw clearly that the bond between his nephew and this soldier to whom Dan was so powerfully, if unexpectedly, drawn was far deeper than he had any right to wish for himself. He was old, he was fat and ugly, he couldn't even learn to surf—*And you call yourself a Hawaiian,* Hank's remark leapt from his memory—much less hold the attention of such a splendid, handsome, talented young man as Hank. As the pair watched the silent departure of actors and musicians from the stage and the video cut off, Dan silently rose, paid the cashier, left extra for a tip and any desserts the two lovebirds might still want, and then left the restaurant. They hadn't even seen him leave the table.

A few hours later, on the midnight plane that took him, a week early, back home to the Midwest, Dan Kumagai gave himself over to jealousy. He had checked out of the Moana and changed his flight without telling anybody. For all he knew, Hank and Kenji were still talking over the Noh play. He would call Kazuko when he got home and make some excuse.

He could never sleep on the red-eye. In fact, he had long since given up taking it. But this time he couldn't stay an extra minute, much less wait till morning. As he sat, wide-awake, Kumagai scolded himself, as he had so often before, for letting himself be lured into thinking any other man would find him attractive. He cursed himself for a Pantalone, and thought bitterly of one of his favorite comic operas. *You'd make a perfect Don Pasquale, if only you could sing.* Hank would not miss him. He had only been a pupil, after all, and a spectacularly unsuccessful one at that. He still had colleagues and friends, like Ann Burleson. He knew he would find a way to tell the story so that it would be funny instead of sad, and that would cure him. He could turn it into a scene from Plautus, perhaps. Besides, he had a good idea for a new research project, something he had been looking for to keep him busy over the summer.

He pulled a couple of Kazuko's homemade *okaka musubi* from his carry-on, gently tilted his seat back, and idly ate as he began to map out his research plan.

KUMAGAI WAS still working on the article, starting to sketch his thesis in rough outline, during the long winter break the following January. Kazuko, after a frosty exchange or two, had forgiven him for leaving without saying good-bye, as she always forgave her incorrigible brother. Kenji was applying to law schools, she reported. Ann's book would come out in June or July. They still met every other day over lunch or coffee, and traded off hosting dinners for their department colleagues, or Sunday afternoon "teas"—not that tea was the beverage served—for students. The fall semester had gone well. Their new colleague, the Roman religion specialist, was working his way into the department culture, occasionally threatening to upset venerable applecarts, but then that was what they had brought him in to do. Academic life was moving along in its quiet way, all the quieter today because it had been snowing since yesterday afternoon, bringing the silence that a slow but heavy snowfall always does. Dan was enjoying the quiet.

He worked in his office, preferring to keep his house free for other things than work, although he lived only a couple short blocks from campus. Not long after returning he had pinned Hank's business card to the corkboard over his desk. He had found it in his pocket and could neither throw it away nor think of anything else to do with it. At least here it was not a constant reminder. The corkboard was so crammed with items that he could ignore it, and when he couldn't, he would pin something new over it, for a few days. At some point he had pinned up Kenji's birthday card next to it, with its description, for easy identification, of Hank. It was scanty, but Dan had no photo of Hank and wasn't sure if he would have posted it where he could see it if he had. Twice Hank had tried to call, in the first weeks after Dan's return, but Dan had kept his end of the conversation frosty, brief, and uninformative—as much from shame as anything else. His attempt to discourage Hank had apparently succeeded. Fine.

Kumagai was checking a reference for the article when he heard a quiet knock on the frame of his open door. A few seniors were always around during the break, if they lived off campus or had friends who did, getting a head start on their senior projects. The knock was so faint at first he thought it was on Ann's door instead of his own, but when it was repeated he grunted a vague invitation to enter.

"*Nani shi ni yume nite arubeki zo?*" came a quavering voice chanting in Noh style.

Kumagai looked up, startled, exclaiming as he did, "Gerald?" Who else would greet him with the familiar line from *Atsumori*?

"It is to clear the karma of my waking life that I am come here in visible form before you," continued the voice. But it was not Gerald, who in any case hated snow and never came to the mainland in winter.

Kumagai just stared at the blond man standing in the doorway. Neither spoke.

"May I come in?" Hank finally asked, in an almost timid voice. Dan could only gesture vaguely, then realizing, stood up and moved a heap of papers and books from the only other chair, looking about for an empty spot on the floor to park them.

Hank sat. Neither spoke. Hank looked around the cluttered room with its tall windows, high ceilings, and woodwork under generations of varnish. Through the window behind Dan's head, snow accumulated on the boughs of a huge pine. Hank stared at it as if he'd never seen snow before.

Dan realized he had not even greeted his visitor. He rose and plugged in the electric kettle perched precariously on a small, book-laden table at his elbow, desperately trying to figure out how Hank had gotten here, and what to say to him.

He heard how feeble his attempt was as soon as it was out of his mouth. "Ski trip? Snowboarding, maybe? It can't be surfing, around here."

Hank smiled as if the remark had been more amusing than it was. "No banyan trees on campus either, I suppose."

The sound of water beginning to boil pointed up the renewed silence. Dan hoped he had some tea bags left, then realized he had only one cup. That gave him another thing to say.

"I don't need anything," Hank replied. "Nothing to drink, that is." He fell silent again. Finally he said, in a lower voice, "You never even said good-bye."

Dan turned away, lifted a random pile of papers as if hoping to find a second cup underneath, and said nothing.

"You told me you were staying an extra week," Hank went on, hesitantly, as if fearful it would sound like an accusation. After a pause, he added, more quietly still, "You said it was to be with me."

That gave Dan the straw he needed to clutch. He cleared his throat. "I realized it was Kenji you wanted to spend time with, not me."

Now it was Hank's turn to look surprised. He said nothing but turned his head to look out the office window at the snow. Dan had never forgotten Hank's pensive look—brows drawn together, lips pursed. Dan quietly unplugged the electric kettle, useless if there was no way to offer tea. Hank started for the door. Dan said to the tapering back that had haunted his dreams for months, "I don't blame you, you know. You have interests and activities in common, dancing, and surfing. You don't live three thousand miles apart, and you've known each other longer, and of course there's the age problem. One afternoon of trying to help a clumsy old man feel better about himself doesn't...." He stopped when Hank whipped around, still with his unfailing grace, and stared at him openmouthed. He seemed about to say something, but plainly thought better of it.

To break this latest awkward silence, Dan apologized for not being able to offer him something hot. "I don't live far from here, less than five minutes' walk. Oh, and I didn't think to ask—do you have a place to stay?"

Hank named a local bed and breakfast only a block from Dan's house, and said he knew the way back to it. "But maybe you could walk with me back there? I won't keep you, but I did want to show you something."

It was the least Kumagai could do, and in any case it would only prolong the suffering of seeing Hank for another five or six minutes, ten at the most. He struggled into his snow things, which made him look even more bearish, put his computer to sleep, pressed the old-fashioned button switch for the lights, and locked his door. The empty stone-floored corridors and stairwells echoed in a silence made deeper by the two men's separate thoughts.

He tried to leave Hank at the door of the B and B, indicating his own house visible a block away. But Hank insisted he come inside, into the parlor of the Victorian pile, lovingly restored and famous for its breakfasts. They stomped their feet outside the heavy door with its oval window of beveled glass and its ornate brass knob, and left their coats, hats, and other impedimenta on the coat tree inside. Someone had laid out newspapers inside the door for wet footgear. They both pulled off their wet boots and left them there. Dan could not help noticing once again how beautiful Hank's body was, how delicate yet powerful his feet were through his socks, too thin for a Midwestern snowstorm. He glided on them into the parlor, across a polished floor studded with small rugs.

There was a large thermos of hot spiced cider ready for guests, just inside the double pocket doors of the parlor, with a tray of cut glass cups beside it. Without asking, Hank drew a cup for Dan, placed it firmly in his hand, and all but shoved him to a large wing chair upholstered in russet, itchy-looking horsehair.

When Hank next started moving aside the throw rugs and a couple of ornate tea tables, Dan couldn't imagine what was going on. Had he prepared some kind of speech? What could he possibly have to say? Dan had forgiven him, truly he had—and really, they had known each other for only three days, met only three times, and Dan had never expected to see or hear from him again.

Instead, with a quiet, high-pitched humming, Hank took up a place at the far left corner of the parlor from where he had installed Dan. He stood, beautiful, generating a stillness that was beyond mere lack of motion. Then he began to glide across the floor, holding a folding fan he had picked up off one of the tables, and less than a minute later Dan recognized the final dance of Atsumori, interspersed with bits of the chant—not complete, but enough to remind the dancer where he was. Dan seemed to hear the drumbeats and punctuating cries of the musicians, and the shrilling of the flute to build tension. It was so vivid he scarcely knew the sounds weren't in the air of the parlor. For twenty minutes Hank danced, perfectly controlled, defying time, showing no strain, his face as distant as the mask of the Noh actor, until he knelt, dropped his fan with a clatter that made Kumagai start, drew an imaginary sword, and began to chant, louder now, and in English, "No, Kumagai is not my enemy. / Pray for me again, oh pray for me again." Opening his hand, he made Dan see the sword drop. He could almost hear the noise of it, and then, once again all stillness, Hank glided into the far corner, where he stood with his back to Kumagai, head bowed.

Dan Kumagai could barely breathe. He sat still, feeling as if he could weep, but dry of eye. Finally, how much later he could not say, Hank stood, turned, and looked him in the eye.

"I learned that," he said, "so I could dance it at our wedding. Yours and mine." Then, turning his face away, he made as if to leave the room. No longer erect, no longer certain of himself, he seemed defeated and weary. He stopped when Dan stood and blocked his way, causing the chair legs to grate across the beautiful floor. Hank stood half-turned to one side.

Dan took Hank by the shoulders and turned him so they were face to face. As he did, whatever he had meant to say went out of his head. He hesitated and then repeated, "Yours? And... *mine*?" When he saw the almost imperceptible nod, as well as the effort it cost Hank's pride to offer it, he pulled the handsome head down to his level and kissed him.

Hank yielded, but only briefly. He pulled back and looked at Dan, as if waiting for an explanation. It took Dan a few minutes—they seemed like hours—to frame his words. To his horror, they came out in his lecturing voice, dooming them to ring hollow.

"I have never been handsome, like you, or graceful, like Kenji. I grub around in the past, the past of my scholarship and the past of my youth. I didn't only carve my initials on the banyan tree with Sid's—I seem to have carved his into my own ridiculous flesh. But there is no Sid, has been none for decades. I have had to learn to push any hope of being loved into the dark corners of my dreams, although I could never manage to do the same with the idea of loving. Then I saw you in the Banyan Court. Your hand was resting exactly where ours had rested before he left me to die. It was as if finally he, or rather an adult, more beautiful, more deeply feeling version of him, had reappeared. And I made a mess of it. So when I saw you and Kenji together, well." He shrugged his shoulders.

After yet another silence, but somehow a less awkward one, Hank replied, "You made a mess of what? I don't understand. I love you. From the moment you told me the story of Atsumori and Kumagai, I loved you. No, sooner. From the moment you were brave enough to give me the gift of taking off your shirt—which I know cost you beyond anything else you could have done—I knew I loved you. First, I knew you trusted me, which hardly anybody ever has since I left the Marines. I've missed that closeness with men, more even than I knew until you showed me... till you gave it back to me. No, let me finish," Hank held up a hand to silence Dan, who had opened his mouth to speak. "I won't let you make some crack about your 'ugly body.' I like your bear body. It's what I'm attracted to, that fullness, so different from my body. Maybe that's the Polynesian side of me," he said to himself, and a grin fluttered over his features and was gone again. "And more important even than that was what you gave me with Atsumori and Kumagai, and telling me about you and Sid. It opened a secret place, full of grief, that I've known since

Iraq, but could never dare to open. Grief of war, and its loss, its cost not only in the comrades you love and see killed beside you, leaving you to survive, but in the fighting men you have to kill yourself, knowing it's your duty, but knowing nothing of what you have robbed or who you have robbed them from. Kumagai survived the battle. He knew how awful it can be to survive. He knew also what he had robbed from the world, though he had no choice—he had heard the flute, and it changed his life." Hank seemed to recede into himself for a while; Dan didn't know how long. "And you changed mine."

He stopped speaking then, and looked at his sock feet.

Dan dropped into the chair, hugged his knees to himself, and began rocking and moaning. Hank looked up, surprised to see the tears on Dan's face. "What?" he asked.

"And now I've ruined it" was all Dan could get out.

"Ruined it? I don't understand," Hank replied.

"And I'm so old, too old," Dan said, not realizing he spoke aloud.

Hank moved to kneel in front of the overstuffed wing chair. He reached out and with a thumb wiped away the tears on Dan's face.

"I'm the one who has been to war," Hank said slowly, as to a child. "You may have had more birthdays, but you cannot be older than I. Do you think I am Atsumori, here? No. I'm Kumagai. I'm not even Renzei, yet. Just Kumagai, the old warrior, trying to get free."

Dan was as ashamed of his tears as he had ever been of his body. He sat still, accepting Hank's touch, and accepting the growing silence, until he was ready to speak.

"Then you'd better have the name too," he said.

"Is that... yes?" Hank asked.

HANK ROSS Kumagai did not dance the final scene from *Atsumori* at the wedding. That was Gerald's, and he would not steal it. Instead, he danced a hula his auntie had taught him, an ancient courting dance. The ceremony, at the Moana Surfrider's Banyan Court—for where else would they wed?—was a hybrid affair all around, making it thoroughly Hawaiian.

They had waited a year, which had meant plenty of time for negotiations among the relations on both sides. Dan suspected Hank had agreed to the delay to allow plenty of time for Dan to run away if he panicked again. They had needed the time to be at home with one another, anyway. Kazuko insisted on the ninefold exchange of sake cups, not that she had to insist very hard. Dan Ross Kumagai wore formal kimono robes and *hakama* trousers with white *tabi* socks and *zōri* sandals, for the first time since he was eight or so, while Hank wore the formal *tapa* cloth he had been vested in by his auntie as an ʻ*olapa*. He had, as tradition demanded, made and painted it himself. He had also used the long engagement to make and paint the new *tapa* that his uncle, Auntie's successor, put over his and Dan's shoulders after the ritual sake was drunk, chanting as he did so a long *mele* of blessing. The uncle had made the leis and wristlets for all the wedding party, which included Ann Burleson as Dan's attendant.

To start things off, the couple advanced to the banyan tree under the swords of some of Hank's Marine buddies. They placed their hands, fingers interwoven, on the warm bark, and left them there a moment, honoring the past, calling up the future. The blast of a conch shell opened the formalities, but before they turned away from the tree, Hank murmured in Dan's ear, "I'll teach you to surf yet. I never give up on a pupil." Dan grinned and shook his head. He felt no panic anymore. They had a lifetime for it.

Kenji, as he deserved, having been the *nakōdo* or go-between, was the master of ceremonies. Interspersed among the speeches required by Japanese etiquette, members of Auntie's *hālau* danced, followed by the Samoans from the now-shuttered International Marketplace. The climax was the hula Hank's auntie, the *kumu hula*, had made for him. Hank had taught it specially to his uncle, who danced it beautifully as Hank murmured a quiet narration into Dan's ear. For the less formal part of the evening, more of Hank's comrades, surfer buddies this time, were the band.

But as the evening wound down, under the fairy lights on the banyan tree, Gerald, with Kenji, his pupil now, shadowing his steps and chanting Kumagai's lines as his newlywed great-uncle chanted Atsumori's and the chorus's, danced once again the family dance. The *hālau hula* members watched in attentive silence. Kenji, who was studying with them now too, had taken care to teach them the vital last lines of the play, however, and when the time came they joined the Japanese in chanting together,

They shall be reborn together
On one lotus-seat.

SAMUEL SCOTT PRESTON is the pseudonym of a technical writer currently located in the Eastern Caribbean. The name does honor to three of the author's most admired gay male writers: Samuel Steward (1909-1993), Scott O'Hara (1961-1998), and John Preston (1945-1994). S.S. Preston has worked in a variety of jobs in his sixty-odd years: Federal civil servant, soup kitchen volunteer, editor and proofreader, educator and activist on LGBT issues, civil disobedience trainer, teacher of English as a second language, and Japanese-to-English translator. He has published a book of gay male theology under his own name and is an ordained priest in the Eastern Christian tradition. He lived off and on for some nine years in Japan and has a Master's degree in Advanced Japanese Studies from Sheffield University in the UK.

The Bear at the Bar
J. Scott Coatsworth

Dex walked into Ransom on a Thursday night like he owned the place, grinning at the bouncer, who sneered at him even as he waved him past the door. Jealous. They were all jealous. The music was the usual *thumpa thumpa* beat—a mix of house techno and the latest hits this week from the youngest, cutest artists.

Dex was born for this life—tall, blond, blue-eyed, a beautiful athletic build with six-pack abs, and a body that everyone in the club acknowledged was gorgeous. And he hardly had to work for it at all.

And so what if he didn't have a boyfriend? Who needed to be tied down like that? He was still well on this side of thirty and had a virtual lifetime of casual sex ahead of him.

He flashed a perfectly white smile at one of the go-go boys on the bar, and the boy blushed and grinned back. Dex had a certain kind of sexual power, and he wasn't ashamed to use it.

He slipped onto a barstool and grunted "beer" at the bartender. The man set down a pale ale, a local brew, his favorite. They knew him here. They knew him well. Many of them knew him *very* well.

Someone sat on the stool next to him, one of the fatties everyone was calling bears these days. Far as he was concerned, they were just fat. Fat and ugly, men who didn't care enough to take care of themselves.

"Buy you a beer?" the guy asked.

"Sorry, dude, got one."

"I've seen you in here before…."

"Not interested. Fuck off." He pushed away from the bar and took his beer with him, ignoring the muttering of the man behind him.

He approached the go-go boy on the bar, a cute young twink with golden eyes who was maybe eighteen, and the guy leaned down to talk to him. "What time you get off?"

"That depends on you," the boy said with a grin. "I finish work at one."

"I can wait." He slipped away into the crowd, finding a group of his friends dancing in the middle of the floor. Well, fuck buddies, anyway. He slipped in among them, sipping his beer and dancing his ass off, forgetting all about work tomorrow, his bills, and the rest of his life.

Someone tapped him on the shoulder. He turned around and saw the bear from the bar.

"Look, I just want to talk," the bear said.

"I thought I told you to fuck off," he said and started to turn away again.

The man grabbed him by the arm, and he felt an electric shock, like the worst static ever. "You shouldn't treat people like that," the bear said, sneering. "You don't know who you're messing with."

And with that he let go of Dex's arm and disappeared into the crowd.

Two hours later, Dex left the bar, go-go dancer on his arm, and forgot all about the bear at the bar.

DEX WOKE up the next morning feeling thickheaded and groggy. He rubbed his eyes and turned over to find the bed empty. The go-go boy from last night was long gone. *Man, I must have been drunk last night.*

Something was off—he couldn't quite place what it was. He rubbed his eyes, and his hands felt heavy. *Shit, what did I drink last night?* He wasn't usually so fucked up the next day. He sat up and looked around.

"What the hell?" He wasn't home. Not his home. He was sure he'd taken the trick back to his place, but this place was nothing like his own. Instead of Scandinavian modern, the room was stuffed with dark, bulky furniture. And there were books everywhere—piles of books, shelves of books, books on the nightstands and stuffed into drawers. It was a professor's wet dream.

This didn't look like a go-go boy's place, either.

Dex eased himself out of bed. He felt heavy, strange. He looked down at his arms. They were thick and covered with coarse black hair.

What the...? These weren't his arms. His arms were strong, corded with muscle, and smooth. These arms....

He ran toward the nearest door, praying it was a bathroom. It was, and it was empty. He glared at the bathroom mirror.

A stranger looked back at him.

He pinched himself, but nothing changed, and he didn't wake up from this strange nightmare.

His beautiful blond hair was gone, replaced with a badly balding pate surrounded by a fringe of black hair that was cropped close. His face looked swollen, and he'd sprouted a thick black beard. Worst of all, his stomach stuck out before him as though he were pregnant. And his entire body was covered with thick black hair.

This had to be some kind of sick joke. His friends had broken in during the middle of the night and had done this to him. It was some kind of makeup... a costume... something.

He tried to pull off the mask, but his fingers met only skin. He wrapped his hands around his belly, but it was as much a part of him as his cock. Which was about half the size he remembered it.

"Shit shit shit shit shit...."

"Honey, you okay up there?"

Dex froze. He wasn't alone in the house. Worse, the other man thought he was someone else. His mind raced. "I'm fine," he called, stalling for time. His voice sounded deeper, more masculine than he remembered.

Footsteps up the stairs. He looked around. No place to hide. Except....

"COLIN?" A man's voice called from the bathroom doorway. "Are you in here?"

Dex huddled in the bathtub, the heavy shower curtain (covered with fish!) drawn to hide himself. *Don't hear me breathing, don't hear me....*

The curtain was pulled back with a whoosh. "There you are."

The voice came from a young man, probably Dex's own age, what he supposed the guys at the bar would call an otter. Slimmer than a bear, hairy but in kind of a sexy way. Dirty blond hair and a neatly trimmed beard, with blue eyes.

And he apparently knew Dex—or at least the guy whose body Dex was wearing.

"What the hell is going on?" he demanded, scared shitless. He squeezed his eyes shut. *This isn't right. This isn't right.* But when he opened his eyes again, nothing had changed.

"One of the nightmares again, huh?" the man said, his voice kind.

"I guess so," he managed weakly.

The man laughed, a pleasant sound. "Come on, get yourself out of there. I love it when you play games, but I've got breakfast on, and then I've got to run."

He took Dex's hand, and Dex felt a strange warmth. He allowed himself to be helped out of the tub.

"Get yourself dressed and hurry down," the man called from the doorway.

Dex found the closet, pulled on a pair of jeans and a flannel shirt, and followed his host downstairs. He'd bide his time and figure out what had happened. For now, he'd pretend to be this Colin guy. What else could he do?

The whole house was decorated in earth tones—pottery barn colors on the walls and tasteful sculptures, vases, and wall art in ruddy oranges, chocolate browns, and the occasional fiery red.

There was a wonderful smell emanating from the kitchen. As he entered, the man gestured to him to take a seat at the bar. There was a pile of mail there, and he glanced at it surreptitiously. Colin and Alvin, one of the pieces said.

"Alvin," he said, tentatively....

"Yeah?"

"I-I feel a little out of sorts today. I think I might stay home." He sat down, but his belly wouldn't let him get his chair all the way under the counter.

Alvin laughed again, serving him a plateful of eggs and breakfast potatoes with a side of bacon. He hadn't eaten a breakfast like this since he was a fat kid in high school. He usually had a slice of dry toast and a glass of Powerade. *Oh my gawd, it smells wonderful.*

"Funny. Like you ever leave the house." He slid over a glass of orange juice. "You gonna get some writing done today? You know the publisher wants your first draft in a couple weeks."

Alvin sat down next to Dex and started eating.

"Um, yeah, I'll try to do some today." A strange feeling was swelling inside him. It wasn't sexual. Not exactly. He felt a strange affinity for this man, some kind of connection that made him feel safe and warm just being next to him.

It was weird. But kind of nice.

They finished breakfast together in silence. At some point, Alvin's hand strayed over to his.

Finally Alvin turned to him. "I've gotta run, really. Tony is waiting for me—we're doing the June layouts today. I left you a little surprise in the oven. Can you clear these plates?"

Dex nodded. "Thanks," he said, pushing away from the table.

"For what? I do it every morning." Alvin gave him a quick kiss on the lips. "I'll be working late—maybe we can catch a bite when I'm done?"

"Sounds good," Dex called after his sudden partner. "See you tonight."

He waited until he was sure Alvin was gone and then put away the dishes and set about exploring the house. But not before having eaten the fresh cinnamon roll awaiting him in the oven.

Whatever this thing was, it did seem to have its perks—eating like this and no guilt.

WHAT HE learned in his explorations was this: Colin was a gay writer of some renown. He had a shelf full of his published books and anthologies, mostly gay romances. He and Alvin Alvarez had been together for at least five years, based on the photos he found, which included a Christmas Eve shot under the mistletoe.

And Dex was most definitely playing the part of Colin. To be sure, he'd taken one of the books into the bathroom and compared the photo on the dust jacket to his own new face.

Although he'd never read any of Colin's books, the face seemed vaguely familiar. He itched at it in his mind for a bit, but no answer was forthcoming.

He tried pinching himself again. He tried slapping himself too, hard. He even tried jacking off, just in case, but he couldn't quite get a handle on his new equipment.

But none of it seemed to matter—he continued to be, stubbornly, a bear.

It was still early—he wasn't due to be at work for another half hour. Well, obviously, that wasn't going to happen.

He found Colin's cell phone, and called his office secretary. "Jenny, this is Dex."

"Dex? You sound weird."

He brushed her off. "Whatever. Let Alex know I won't be in today. I think I've come down with something."

"You've got a meeting with Applied Dynamics at ten...."

"You must have that wrong," he said. "I met with them yesterday. Just tell Alex. I can't come in today."

"OK, see you tomorrow. Hope you get better."

He threw the phone down on the counter and sat down on the barstool. *What the hell is going on?*

David. David would know what to do.

David was his ex, his first—they'd been together for two years after Dex had come out, and even though they'd been split up for five years, David still answered when he called.

He called David's number—thank God he still remembered it. Who knew where his own cell phone had gotten to? "Hey David, it's Dex? I need your help. No questions asked. I'm at—" He grabbed a piece of mail from the kitchen counter. "—1432 Walden Avenue. Just come over here, now."

"Dex, what's wrong? Your voice sounds funny—are you feeling okay?"

"Just get over here. And David...."

"What?"

"Keep an open mind."

DEX PACED back and forth across the living room, which was filled with issues of *National Geographic*, solid mission furniture, and Tiffany lamps, waiting for David to arrive. This whole situation made no sense.

It was like some kind of body swap thing—but that never happened in real life, did it?

He racked his brain for other possibilities. Some kind of strange illness that had come upon him during the night? *God, maybe it's a new STD.*

But surely no disease would work this quickly. Even that flesh-eating virus took days to kill you. *Am I dying?*

Finally there was a knock at the door. He went to open it and then thought better of it. "David, is that you?"

"Yeah, Dex, open the door."

"Not yet. Something weird happened to me last night." He searched for the right words. "I don't know how to explain it."

There was a long silence. "I can't help you from this side of the door," David said finally.

This time it was Dex's turn to be silent.

"Are you there?"

"I look… different."

"Different how?"

"Umm, not like me."

"Come on, open the door. I don't have all day. Stop fucking around with me, or I *will* leave."

"Okay, okay. But just let me explain." He opened the door.

David started to enter, took one look at him, and jumped backward. "Who the fuck are you?"

"It's me. Dex."

"You're not Dex. You don't look anything like Dex. I'm calling the cops." He pulled out his cell phone and started dialing.

Dex grabbed his arm and pulled him inside, slamming the door behind them. "Ensenada, 2004. You in a yellow Speedo. Three nights, one hotel room, too many margaritas."

David's mouth dropped open. "No one knows about that."

"The day we met, it was the third of July. I remember, because—"

"Because you wanted it to be the Fourth of July. So you would always remember it."

"And I always have."

David's hand came up, two fingers raised, and Dex met it with his own, unthinking. Together they drew the two sides of a heart in the air, something they'd always done as an unspoken *I love you* when they'd been together.

David sank into one of the mission chairs. "Shit, Dex, it *is* you. What happened to you?"

Dex shook his head. "I don't know. I brought a guy home last night—cute go-go boy, you would've liked him. When I woke up this morning… this." He spread his arms.

David started dialing his phone again.

Dex hissed, "Come on, David, don't call the police…."

"I'm not calling the police."

"Hello?" a voice said at the other end of the line. Dex could hear it through the phone's speaker. It was his own.

David hung up. "Seriously, *Freaky Friday*." David shook his head. "This is weird. I'm gonna need coffee before I can take this all in. Come on, there's a coffee shop at the corner.

Dex shook his head. "No way. I'm not going out like this."

"Come on, Dex, if that's really you—no one will be able to tell who you are anyway." He opened the front door and started down the stairs.

With a frown, Dex grabbed Colin's keys and wallet and headed out into the world that had suddenly turned upside down.

DEX FOLLOWED David down the street to the coffee shop on the corner—the Everyday Grind. *Cute*, he thought without much humor.

It was quiet inside, thank God. David ordered a skinny vanilla latte, getting a sly smile from the barista.

Dex flashed the boy his trademark smile, but the barista avoided eye contact. "What can I get you, sir?" he asked, staring at David's retreating ass. Dex felt worse than invisible.

"A no-foam skinny chai latte, extra hot," he said sheepishly.

"Name?"

"De… Dennis."

"Ok, Dennis, that'll be three fifty."

He paid in cash from Colin's wallet, not wanting to have to show his ID. He hadn't worked up the courage yet to look at it—it would match his new face, he was sure, and he wasn't quite ready to deal with that.

He retrieved his coffee and joined David at a semiprivate table by the window. He watched a group of young guys walk by outside. Not one gave him a second look.

"Ok," David said. "Tell me what I said to you the night we broke up."

He sighed. Another test. He supposed he would have done the same in David's shoes. "You said, 'you'll never find what you're looking for until you know what you're worth, and I can't do that for you.'"

David shook his head. "Shit, Dex, I always thought you were a little too devoted to the gym, but this is ridiculous. What happened?"

"Hell if I know. So you believe me?" He drank David in like a man dying of thirst—all of him, his warm brown eyes and skin, the concerned look that made his face look so sweet.

"I still think this could be some elaborate joke, but let's say yes for the sake of the argument." He stared out the window as if collecting his thoughts. "Walk me through the last twenty-four hours."

Dex nodded, grateful. He could feel the weight of his stomach pressed against the table. He tried not to look at his hairy, beefy arms. "I went to work, got sucked off in the copy room at lunch by one of the new interns, went home, hit the bars, and brought this cute go-go trick home for the night." He sighed. "Then the next morning, this!" He indicated his ridiculous new body.

"Did anything unusual happen?"

"Um, I had a bad salad for dinner at Pronto. And the go-go boy wasn't all that great in bed. Nothing else I can think of…. Wait."

"What?"

"The bear at the bar!"

David smiled. "That sounds promising."

"This bear came on to me—really out of shape—a fatty."

David looked him up and down. "Like you're one to talk."

Dex blushed.

"So what happened?"

He snorted. "What do you think happened? I blew him off."

"Like 'sorry, not interested'?"

"Like 'fuck off.' Twice."

"Ouch. That's harsh."

Dex didn't like the way David was looking at him. "I know. I just hate when they think—"

"Think what?" David's rich brown eyes bored into his.

"That they're good enough for me." Even as he said it, he realized how stuck-up it sounded.

David laughed. "I believe you now—you're definitely Dex."

"You do?" The place was busier now, one of the morning rushes. Dex looked around nervously, hoping not to see anyone else he knew.

"Yup. No one else I know is such a conceited ass."

Dex blushed. "Guess I deserve that. So what do I do?"

"What, do you think this guy put some kind of curse on you?"

"I don't know. I mean, that's crazy, right?" He'd missed this back and forth with David—it had always been one of their strengths as a couple.

"No crazier than you in a bearskin suit. Where did you see him?"

"At Ransom. It's where I pick up some of the best tricks."

David arched an eyebrow.

"Where I used to pick them up. I mean, look at me." He stared out the window, wondering once again how he'd gotten here. And remembering how things had been before, with David. "Can I ask you something?"

"Sure, hit me."

"Where did we go wrong?" he said at last.

David laughed ruefully. "How long have you got? Geez, it's weird seeing you like this."

Dex took David's hands in his and said, "I mean it, what happened between us? We were happy for a while, right?"

David looked serious now. He took a deep breath and turned away before speaking. "I was happy, for a while. I'm not sure you ever really were. You always wanted the next guy in the bar, the open relationship, the thrill of the conquest. That was fun for a while, but after a couple years, mostly I just wanted a romantic dinner together, a night in front of the TV, in bed by ten."

Dex grinned. "I can't remember the last time I was in bed by ten."

"But are you happy?"

Dex stared at him as if he'd just been asked if he liked to breathe. *Of course I'm happy. Aren't I?* But the words wouldn't come out.

"Being a gay guy is an amazing gift. And don't get me wrong. The sex is one of my favorite things. But it's not the only thing. We went wrong because it was the *only thing*, for you." He squeezed Dex's hands. "So did it make you happy?"

Dex wanted to say "This makes me happy, being with you, right here," but he couldn't bring himself to admit it. "Yeah, it makes me happy." He let go of David's hands. He could see a change in his ex's eyes, like a light had gone out.

"So, Ransom?" was all he said, his tone businesslike.

Dex nodded miserably.

"OK, if that's where this all started, that's where we have to go. Here's what we're gonna do."

HALF AN hour later, Dex was walking down Queen Anne dressed in a heavy sweater, a baseball cap, and sunglasses. He didn't want anyone else to see him like this, even if they didn't know who he was. *He* would know.

He stopped at an ATM to get some cash. The screen asked for his PIN, and he automatically entered his usual four-digit number. It flashed "wrong PIN entered, try again." *Crap. This isn't my card.*

There was a convenience store at the corner. He grabbed a pack of Altoids and slid Colin's ATM card through the reader at the register. "Credit or Debit?" the clerk asked.

"Credit," he said, and breathed a sigh of relief when the transaction went through. He scribbled something on the receipt and handed it back to the clerk, who shoved it into his drawer disinterestedly. He pocketed the cash.

He was supposed to meet David at the bar later—he wasn't sure how he was going to get in like this. But cross that bridge later.

For now, he suddenly had a free day, and David had suggested he get outside and forget about his strange dilemma for a few hours.

His new body felt profoundly unnatural. He found himself out of breath climbing the slightest hill, and Seattle had a lot of those.

He made his way down to Pike Place, where he would blend in with the crowd. He wandered through the aisles aimlessly, finding he almost enjoyed the anonymity of looking average. Few people gave him a second look.

He did catch the eye of one of the vendors, a man tossing fish in one of the seafood booths. Their eyes met, and Dex smiled sheepishly, as if in apology for the way he looked. But the man shot him back a broad smile, and waved between tosses. *Stranger and stranger.*

He spent so much of his life taking care of himself. Every morning, he was at the gym before work for an hour. He drank only protein shakes for breakfast and lunch. He did crunches at lunchtime in the company gym. He'd even had a secret procedure or two to enhance his gym-toned body.

And everyone around him was always jealous of him. He could see it in the way they looked at him. He was better than them, and they all knew it. So maybe it separated him a bit from the crowd. Maybe he was just a little lonely, sometimes. But he had the life—and whomever he wanted, whenever he wanted them. What more could he want?

He found a seat at the original Starbucks and watched the people go by out on Pike Place. Somehow today, in this strange new body, he felt more connected to the ebb and flow of life all around him. It seemed to include him, not exclude him. Instead of the jealous sneers and whispers he was used to in his own body, Colin's body and demeanor seemed to elicit smiles, real smiles, from many of the people coming into the store.

He even broke down and ordered himself a frapp.... God, he hadn't had one of those in years. He nursed it like a tequila as he took in the scene.

The folks who came into the café were so much more varied than the gay bar crowd—tall and short, exceptionally thin to grossly overweight. Black, brown, white, and yellow—so much variety. And of course, men and women. Not just fag hags but mothers and sisters and lawyers and nurses and policewomen.

For an hour or so, he forgot about his new bearhood—and just lost himself in the flow.

"Anyone sitting here?" a male voice said, and he looked up into the go-go boy's eyes from last night. They were like liquid gold—hazel, he supposed—and huge. Like anime.

"No, go ahead—you can have the chair. I'm not using it." The man had a Starbucks apron on—one of the baristas, apparently. And those eyes....

"I'm sorry." He looked a little taken aback. "I just finished my shift. I was hoping to sit here with you. I've been watching you."

Dex blushed. "I know, I know, I'm not the prettiest thing in the room. Look, I'm really not myself today...."

The man shook his head. "No, that's not what I meant. I just... you looked a little lost." He extended his hand. "I'm Simon."

Dex laughed, embarrassed. "Dennis," he said, taking the man's hand in his. It was warm.

"Can I be a little forward?"

Dex nodded. "Go ahead."

"I think it's great that you're not a gym bunny, that you're down to earth." He shook his head. "You don't find that often in the scene here." Simon gave him *the look*.

God, he knew that look. He had used it himself for years. He followed Simon out of the bar and up the hill to his place, a small apartment in a low-rent building. About what he'd figured the man could afford.

They climbed into Simon's bed together, Dex's thick belly pressed against his lithe one, their bodies intertwining, the man's mouth hot on Dex's neck.

He made love like a bear. He thought about his hairy, heavy body and what had been done to him, and suddenly the shame at what he had become turned into something else, channeled into a passion for this man who wanted him *even like this*. Or maybe *because* he was like this.

For the first time all day, he embraced who he was, not who he thought he ought to be.

He sought Simon's mouth with his own, hungrily, eager to explore his new form, this unfamiliar body, so different from the gym-toned muscles he was used to.

But it was more than simple lust. He saw those eyes again, and this time they were filled with compassion. With something close to love.

They climbed and climbed together on a wave of ecstasy-excitement-love, gasping aloud at the intensity of it.

When he found his release, it was the most intense orgasm he'd experienced in months, if not years, and he lay there next to Simon for a long time afterward, without moving, wondering what this all meant. Why was it so different? Same guy... but different Dex. He realized he'd spent far less time worrying about his own body—Was it perfect? Should he have spent ten more minutes at the gym that morning?—and far more time being in the moment with Simon.

When they parted, Simon hugged him affectionately, kissing him on the forehead. "See you again sometime?"

Dex could only nod.

For the first time in years, he began to wonder what a life might be like shared with another man.

DEX RETURNED to Colin's house and gathered a few things. After a moment's thought, he left Alvin a note: *Had to go out for a bit. Late dinner when I get back?* Alvin had been so nice to him, and he didn't want to screw up Colin's life any more than he needed to. Eventually he made his way back to Ransom.

He waited for David in an alley behind the bar, hidden away from the street where no one would see him. He didn't want to take a chance on being turned away at the door, and as much as it galled him to admit it, his ex was now much hotter than he was.

Especially in his "disguise." God, he must look like Mama Cass in this get-up—head scarf, big dark sunglasses, heavy wool coat.

He peered out from the alleyway and was spied by a couple of queens who started at the sight of him and hurried away.

"David, where are you?" he hissed, and sent his ex a quick text.

On my way! came the reply.

What if he was stuck like this? What if he had somehow offended the gay gods—Dance, Fashion and Style? Well, if not, he was certainly offending them now.

Finally he saw David walking down the street toward the bar. "David, over here," he called. David looked good—tall, slender, his gorgeous eyes dancing with laughter at the sight of him.

"I know, I don't look so hot."

"It's not that. What are you wearing?"

"You said I should wear a disguise."

He laughed out loud. "You look like an out-of-work silver-screen film goddess—twenty years past her prime."

"It's all I could find at… at Colin's house," Dex hissed. "It's not like I could go out shopping."

"Well, give me your scarf, glasses, and coat. You can't go in there like that."

Dex complied, and David stuffed them behind a trash can. "Come on. You remember what we planned?"

Dex nodded. "I'm going to chat my old self up at the bar. That is if I—if he shows up...."

"You always end up here eventually, Dex. You'll—he'll come."

"And if he really is the old me, I'll ask him what the hell he did to me."

"That's about it." David grinned.

They reached the bouncer, who smiled, *actually smiled*, at Dex as he waved them through.

David sat at one end of the bar for moral support while Dex waited near the middle, nursing a beer. An hour passed, then two, and he was almost ready to call it quits when he felt a hush come across the bar.

In strode a beautiful man. It was strange, terribly strange, to see himself from outside. But it was stranger still to see the reactions his old self engendered. People cleared out of his way, but behind the casual lust in their faces was something else. A mixture of jealousy and disgust.

And the unmistakable arrogance on his old face was shocking. Why had no one ever told him that?

This other Dex reached the bar next to him, grunted something at the bartender, and turned away, missing the look of anger that crossed the bartender's face. But Dex saw it.

Be tactful. "Buy you a beer?" he asked, keeping his voice carefully neutral.

"Sorry, dude, got one."

"I've seen you in here before...," he tried again.

"Not interested. Fuck off." His words almost dripped with venom. He pushed away from Dex, moving toward the go-go boy on the bar.

And then it hit Dex. This wasn't just another night. This was *the* night. *Last night.* And this time he was cast in the role of the bear at the bar. God, he'd been such an ass.

With a growing sense of déjà vu and inevitability, he followed old Dex out onto the dance floor. He tapped himself on the shoulder, and old Dex turned to face him.

"Look, I just want to talk," Dex told his old self.

"I thought I told you to fuck off."

"You shouldn't treat people like that," he said, and thought he saw a twinkle in old Dex's eye. He wasn't the only actor in this little drama.

"You never know who you're messing with." God, he sure hadn't known.

His old self put his mouth to Dex's ear and whispered, "It was fun being you."

"Colin?" he whispered, seeing now what had happened. It really was *Freaky Friday*.

He grinned and grabbed Dex's arm, and Dex felt an electric shock go through him. That was the last thing he remembered before he fell to the floor, unconscious.

DEX WOKE up. The morning light was filtering through his bedroom window. *His bedroom window.*

His hands went to his face. And it really was his face, the one he had grown accustomed to over the years. He grabbed his phone—right there on the nightstand, where it was supposed to be. It said Friday.

Letting out a sigh of relief, he turned on his side, and there was David. All glorious six feet two of him. Simon the go-go boy had opened Dex's eyes the day before, but he was no David.

David's eyes flickered open, and he grinned a lazy smile.

Dex brought his hand up, and together they inscribed a heart in the air.

"Guess you owe the bear at the bar a thanks, huh?" David said with a grin, his eyes alight.

"I'll thank him later," he said. It was time for Dex to see if he could be happy making someone else happy. Judging by the way he felt right now, the answer was yes.

Things were going to change. He was going to change.

He could feel it.

He kissed David's lips, and they made love like bears.

J. SCOTT COATSWORTH has been writing since elementary school, when he and won a University of Arizona writing contest in 4th grade for his first sci-fi story (with illustrations!). He finished his first novel in his midtwenties, but after seeing it rejected by ten publishers, he gave up on writing for a while.

Over the ensuing years, he came back to it periodically, but it never stuck. Then one day, he was complaining to Mark, his husband, early last year about how he had been derailed yet again by the death of a family member, and Mark said to him, "The only one stopping you from writing is you."

Since then, Scott has gone back to writing in a big way, finishing more than a dozen short stories—some new, some that he had started years before–and seeing his first sale. He's embarking on a new trilogy, and also runs a support group for writers of gay sci-fi, fantasy, and supernatural fiction.

He lives in Northern California with his husband of twenty-three years, and is thrilled that writing is once again a regular part of his day.

The sky's the limit!

Amped
Zoe X. Rider

Toby shouldered through the crowd, heading for the back of the arcade-turned-heavy-metal-club. A local band was on stage, and they sucked. Hell's Hornets, or some crap. A month ago, they'd been calling themselves Masters of the Disciple. In between the two names, they'd broken up, reformed with a different guitarist and drummer, replaced the guitarist with the original jerk-off, and kept on going, without the music getting much better along the way. Just faster, with more jarring rhythm changes. Next up would be Scar Horse, the band supporting the headliner. Them he'd never heard of. And after that, the band everyone had come for—Firesiren. Toby couldn't give a shit less about any of them. At some point in the evening, he'd tripped and fallen into a rotten mood.

Dickhead at the beer table refusing to sell to him hadn't helped.

Dickhead at the beer table refusing to sell to his twenty-three-year-old friend Max because he (rightly) suspected that Max would turn around and hand him the beer had only made it worse.

One fucking month. Not even—twenty-nine days. You'd think a guy could give you a break.

He found Wolf on the back wall, elbow propped on a video game console that had been unplugged and shoved out of the way to make room for the show. Wolf stuck out from the crowd in a lot of ways, not the least of which was his age—a good twenty years over most of them—or his appearance. "Imposing" was a good word for it. "Big" another, but don't get the wrong idea. He was solid, but not muscular. Large, but not fat. His shirt, a thin button-up with only the bottom few buttons done up, showed a triangle of hairy barrel chest and the slight swell of stomach beneath it. His thighs, encased in tight, dark jeans, were solid. He had hands like ham hocks, one of them braced on his hip right now.

"'Sup?" Toby said, turning and putting his back to the wall.

Wolf didn't answer.

"Hey, man." Toby elbowed him. "You got any speed?"

Wolf reached with two fingers into the breast pocket of his shirt and pulled out a plastic baggie about a third full of what looked like confectioner's sugar.

"Yeah, man," Toby said, watching Wolf open the bag.

Then he watched Wolf stick a meaty finger into his mouth, wetting it. Wolf plunged the finger into the bag and twisted it, like it was a bag of Fun Dip. When he pulled his finger back out, it was coated up to the first knuckle with white powder. He offered it to Toby.

Toby's focus shifted from the finger to Wolf's eyes, which weren't even looking at him. They were on the band. Toby glanced toward the crowd. No one was paying attention to the two of them up against the back wall.

"You want it or not?" Wolf asked, glancing at him.

Toby looked back at the finger. Back up to Wolf's face. Wolf pushed his finger forward and, yeah, wanting the speed, Toby let his mouth fall open.

The stuff dissolved on his tongue. He closed his lips around Wolf's finger to suck the powder off. Wolf gave his finger a twist, even crooked it for a second toward the roof of Toby's mouth, then pulled it out with a moist pop.

Toby meant to say thanks. Instead, he rubbed his tongue along the back of his teeth and savored the taste of the speed, of Wolf's skin. The roughness of it.

He'd die if anyone found out he'd gotten wood from sucking Wolf's finger.

"Anything else, kid?"

"Buy me a beer? I've got the money."

Wolf shook his head but held up a hand, rubbing his fingers together, waiting for the cash. Toby pulled it from his front pocket, a few crumpled bills.

Taking it, Wolf walked away.

Toby leaned against the wall and watched the sea of heads in front of him bob. His heart kicked up its pace, keeping time with the music Hell's Hornets was playing, thanks to the speed, and that made it a little more bearable.

Wolf's speed.

At first, Toby had thought "Wolf" was a nickname. Maybe he'd been leaner when he was younger, rangier. His face could have had wolf-like qualities, those eyes turning on you, fierce if you rubbed him the wrong way, his teeth showing, dangerous under that brown mustache. Someone—Max, maybe—had told him it was his actual name. Wolf McCandless. How fucking cool were parents who'd name their kid "Wolf"? Toby doubted young Wolf McCandless had had much trouble from other kids at the playground, though imagining it was hard. In Toby's head, ten-year-old Wolf had his shirt half-buttoned, hair on his chest, and a cigarette dangling from his teeth.

When Wolf returned, Toby's head was banging against the wall behind him, and he hardly noticed that the singer was thanking them for turning out and telling them Scar Horse would be up next.

"Thanks, man," Toby said, taking the red plastic cup. It was cold in his hand. He took a thirsty draught off it, then wiped his mouth with the back of his arm.

Wolf took up his place against the video game machine.

Toby elbowed him again. "Ever heard of Scar Horse?"

Wolf shook his head.

Wolf came to all these shows, lame as most of them were. Toby had asked him once what an old fuck like him was doing coming to these things. Admittedly, he'd been more than a little drunk—and thought himself more than a little cute—at the time he'd asked that question. Wolf hadn't answered him, much like Wolf didn't answer most questions.

"Want some?" Toby asked, offering his beer. Not that he thought Wolf couldn't have bought his own, but he was out of cash himself so maybe if he seemed generous, that generosity would be repaid in the form of future free beers.

Wolf started to shake his head, but appeared to give it another thought. Shrugging, he took the cup.

Instead of wiping his face after he was done, as Toby had, he pulled his bottom lip up over the top one and sucked out the beer that had sopped in his mustache.

Toby had never had a mustache. Oh, he shaved. He had to—the soft, fuzzy stuff that grew on his face looked ridiculous. Peach fuzz. *Still.* At nearly twenty-one. Not that he could imagine himself with a 'stache, or a beard. Five o'clock shadow, even. But if he could have one, he'd want it to be the thick, coarse kind, like Wolf's. Like a little bit of wolf pelt.

His face felt hot suddenly. He'd wanted to ask Wolf if he could touch his mustache, which made his mouth remember the taste of Wolf's finger and made his upper lip wonder how the mustache would feel against it, all the little hairs damp from the beer. He drained the red cup and glanced around for a trash can.

Wolf took the cup from him and set it on top of the video game.

"Are you married or anything?" Toby asked, the words rushing out while Scar Horse fucked around onstage with their instruments, setting up, plugging in cables, bickering a little as they moved mic stands around.

"Nope."

"Girlfriend?"

"Nope."

"So that's why you can come to these things all the time, huh? No one to nag you about it or say you can't go."

"Okay."

"What?"

Wolf shrugged.

Toby shook his head. "What do you do the rest of the time, man? I mean work and shit, and don't you have friends or anything?" Toby pictured him going home, some small place, sitting in an old easy chair in front of the TV, smoking a cigarette, watching the set in exactly the same way he watched the stage.

Wolf patted a pack of cigarettes and a lighter from the breast pocket of his shirt. The pack was soft, half-empty and flattened. He tilted its open end toward his hand and tapped the bottom, plucked one of the cigarettes that started to slide out. As he lifted the cigarette to his lips, he said, "Yep."

"Well?"

Wolf shrugged, lit his cigarette. He let out a stream of smoke as he dropped the pack and lighter back in his shirt pocket.

Toby bounced the back of his head against the wall. He was warm. His upper lip was wet with sweat. He licked it.

"Wolf?"

Wolf took another hit off the cigarette.

Toby chewed his bottom lip for a second, but the speed won out over good sense. "You ever been with a guy?"

A smoke-filled laugh rolled from Wolf's throat like he'd been nudged in the gut with the question.

"I'm not coming on to you," Toby said quickly, his neck heating. "Don't take it that way. I just never see you with a chick, so I'm just asking. You don't have to answer." He pressed his damp palms against the wall, by his sides. He could use another one of those beers. Just the one had done nothing for him. And yet—look what was coming out of his mouth. Jesus. And he just kept going. "I was just making conversation, anyway. Wish Scar Horse would hurry the fuck up. And they'd better not suck."

"It sounded like coming on to me," Wolf said finally, without looking over at Toby. He seemed to be smiling a little under that mustache, as he brought the cigarette to his mouth again.

Up on stage, a gangly guy in a ripped Lamb of God shirt grabbed the mic, leaning toward it from three feet away, and said, "Hey, we're Scar Horse and this first song is called 'Flesh Pipe.'" He barely got the last word out before the guitar jumped over his voice and screamed out the speakers, drums pounding in right behind.

The music was loud. Toby would have had to yell his rebuttal, if he could have thought of one. Instead his face prickled, the back of his neck itched, and he rocked his body in time with the music, hoping the topic would get drowned out by the noise.

"But maybe you're just curious?" Wolf yelled in his ear. Toby smelled smoke and Irish Spring. He felt like he was going to hyperventilate.

And his cock was hard.

Just... really fucking hard. Aching hard. Ever since the fucking finger thing, the taste of which he could still call up, even after the beer.

"It's okay to be curious," Wolf yelled, the vibrations of his words tickling Toby's ear canal. "I get curious sometimes." His shoulder pressed against Toby and stayed there, even as Wolf turned his attention back to Scar Horse, who were more polished than Hell's Hornets, but that was about all that could be said for them. What was happening to music anymore?

Wolf's weight against him was a solid thing. And he could smell him now, this close. The Irish Spring, the cigarettes. Something else too. Something dark and musky—like a wolf's den—that deepened the ache.

Fuck it. Fuck it fuck it fuck it.

Without looking at the man, he hooked a finger in the waistband of Wolf's jeans, Wolf's belt cool against the knuckles of his other fingers, and pulled himself off the wall, tugging Wolf along with him for a few steps before dropping his hand and just leading the way through the crowd, through the thick of the thrashing bodies, past the restrooms, past the security yahoos who tried to stop him from going any farther until they saw Wolf behind him. With a nod they let them both pass, out into the cool, brisk air of the alley behind the club. When he turned finally, Wolf was there, the door closing behind him, cutting off the music from inside.

They were hardly alone. Scar Horse's van was backed almost to the stairs, ready for them to unload their gear at the end of the set. The Firesiren bus sat parked nearby, sleek and dark and quiet, all its windows shaded. Five or six people hung out by the bus door waiting for someone—anyone—from Firesiren to poke his head out. Talking loudly about this cool thing Firesiren's singer had done, that badass thing the bass player had done. How crazy the drummer was.

Toby swallowed.

Wolf stood, his back to the door, thick fingers pushed into his jeans pockets, waiting. His face was unreadable, but the bulge between his pockets wasn't. Everything about him was thick, solid. Heavy.

Licking the corner of his mouth, Toby glanced toward the dark strip of alley between the far side of the bus and the building, then back to Wolf, who lifted his eyebrows.

Toby wiped his palms on his jeans. Okay. Okay, he could do this. He hopped down the steps and ducked between the bus and the wall. When he'd gotten halfway down the length of it, he stopped and turned. Wolf was right there, his hands already on his belt buckle. In a second, his fingers had worked the tongue free.

Heart beating wildly, Toby reached for Wolf's fly, popping the button. He ran his hand over the bulge, the huge fucking bulge, before working the zipper pull down over it. Wolf put his hands on Toby's shoulders, his head bent, watching him reach into the heat of his jeans and find what he was going for.

He looked up and Wolf's eyes met his.

Toby licked his lip again, staring at that mustache. At the teeth that were starting to show beneath it, Wolf's lips pulling back in a trace of a smile.

Toby rose up on his toes, going for it, pressing his mouth against Wolf's, finding out what a real mustache felt like. What a man's mouth felt like. Everything till now had been furtive hand jobs with kids his own age or younger. Shit that happened and they didn't talk about it—and that was easy, because a lot of the time Toby just didn't run across those guys again. He stayed away from the regulars at these shows—they wouldn't be interested. Stayed away from his own friends with this shit. Didn't want to lose them, and all it took was one of them saying to the others, "You know what that asshole Toby tried to do when I was at his house last night?" All it took was that, and he wouldn't be able to show his face again. It was probably okay to be gay… it just wasn't okay to be gay all over Max or Skeez or Albee. That wouldn't be cool.

Wolf's mustache was like coarse fur, rubbing his upper lip, the blunt ends of hairs poking his skin. Clutching Wolf's thick cock in his fist, he thought he could feel its veins throbbing in his palm, but it might have just been the speed. It probably was the speed. Toby's leg was jiggling—*that* was definitely the speed. How did Wolf always have speed on him but never seemed to be *on* it? God, what was he like off the stuff? Comatose? Their lips pressed together, hard, Wolf's breaths heavy and short against Toby's face as Toby slid his thumb through the slick precum seeping from the head of Wolf's cock.

Wolf's mouth opened and Toby tilted his head for it, Wolf's mustache scraping the side of his lip as he pushed his tongue into Wolf's mouth. Cigarettes and beer and the long exhale of Wolf's breath as Wolf pressed the considerable weight of his body forward, backing him against the bus, trapping Toby's fist against his own stomach, Wolf's cock throbbing like a heartbeat in his hand.

Wolf pushed his big paw down the back of Toby's jeans, making the front pull tight against his stomach, against his cock. It felt incredible. He pushed his crotch against Wolf's wide thigh and Wolf pushed back. Solid. Unmovable.

A groan left Toby's throat as Wolf clutched his ass in that big hand of his, squeezing it as he pulled Toby against him, pushing his tongue deep into Toby's mouth. Breathing in long and hard like he was sucking the life right out of Toby.

It made Toby's knees weak—something he thought was just bullshit from chick books, but the bus was the only thing keeping him on his feet. The bus and Wolf, who'd backed off a little, giving him room to work his cock.

Precum oozed in a warm trickle toward his wrist. He flattened his other hand against Wolf's chest, curled his fingers into Wolf's pelt.

Panting against his mouth, Wolf said, "Yeah," as he thrust his thigh against Toby again and lifted him onto his toes with that big paw of his.

Toby's hand slipped underneath Wolf's shirt and around, pulling Wolf's barrel chest against his own smaller one.

His teeth found Wolf's neck, ruddy and rough and tasting like cigarette smoke and sweat, and he ran his tongue over the muscle there while he pumped Wolf's cock, his hand sliding easier now with the lubrication he'd worked up.

"Yeah," Wolf breathed again with another thrust. "Yeah, that's—Hunh. That's it. Yeah." Wolf's head rested against Toby's and Toby tipped his head back against the side of the bus, Wolf's hips jerking, his own hips jerking—he realized he couldn't tell which of them was coming until suddenly he came for real, bucking against Wolf's thigh helplessly, digging his fingers into Wolf's wide back.

Wolf stopped moving, his body heavy, holding him against the side of the bus. Had anyone up there peered down from the window? Had they heard the noises against the metal wall?

The door to the back of the arcade/club opened and the both of them—Toby with the side of his hand in his mouth, tasting Wolf, and Wolf with his fingers refastening his belt—looked in its direction.

Heavy, thumping music spilled out. A cigarette butt flew onto the steps, and then the door fell shut.

"Shit," Toby said.

"Want another beer?" Wolf asked.

Toby wiped his mouth with the back of his arm, acutely aware of the warm stickiness against his thigh. He wanted to look down and see if it was visible, but he didn't want Wolf watching him look down at his crotch like some kid who'd pissed his pants.

Beer was tempting.

Wolf was waiting.

Someone inside the bus called something to someone else inside the bus.

Shit. What had he just done?

Shit.

Wolf's eyebrow arched slowly, his fingers digging in his shirt pocket for his cigarettes.

Toby looked down the side of the bus, toward the arcade's back door. "Give me a minute, okay?" he said finally. He braced his hands on his knees, head bent. If nothing else it gave him a chance to check his crotch. And let him avoid seeing Wolf's face.

He sensed a shrug.

He listened to Wolf's boots stride up the strip of pavement.

Toby rubbed his forehead against his arm, still bent over. There was a little bit of a damp spot on his jeans, but the denim was dark. It hardly showed. It *felt* like it showed a lot, but no one was gonna notice it. They'd think he just spilled a little beer, maybe splashed a little water over the edge of the counter when he was washing his hands in the bathroom.

Shit.

To go back in or not? And if he did go back in, what was he supposed to do? Find Max, see what he was up to? Ignore Wolf? Pretend nothing happened?

He heard talking, and looked over to see a couple roadies climbing the steps to the back door. One of them—big shouldered and bald with half his skull tattooed dark blue—flicked his gaze toward him, registered there was some kid with his ass to the bus, and said, "Hey. Offa the bus. You sick or something? Go puke somewhere else."

Nodding, Toby straightened.

"Don't hang around back here. I catch you again, your ass is out of here."

Toby lifted his hand, nodding again, his Day-Glo orange underage wristband slipping down his wrist. He started to turn away, then back—what the fuck? He wasn't walking away from the show. The bald roadie had the door open, watching Toby as the other guy with him passed into the building.

"Almost forgot which direction the show was in," Toby said with a crooked smile.

"It's around the other side of the building. No entrance through the back. Go on."

With a sigh and a roll of his eyes, Toby turned on his heel and headed the other way after all, all the way down to the end of the strip mall, around the building, and back up to where a few groups of people hung out just outside of the arcade's doors. He had to wait in line to show his wristband and hand stamp to get back inside, just in time for Scar Horse to start dismantling their setup.

"The fuck have you been?" Max asked, yelling in his ear even though the crap they were playing over the PA system wasn't nearly as loud as the band had been.

Toby just shook his head. Max had beer on his breath, just a swallow left in the cup in his hand. Not worth asking for some. Beer sounded *really* good right now, though—and he couldn't even buy a *soda* with the lint in his pockets.

The bathroom would be packed between bands. No point in trying to get in there to clean himself up. He could feel the stickiness drying against his thigh. At least it was drying.

Max didn't even tag him when he started walking away—Max was up on his toes, searching over the heads of the crowd, looking for Albee or one of the metal skanks he talked up from time to time. Toby wasn't interested in the girls. He wasn't all that interested in nonskank girls either, but calling these ones skanks took the pressure off why he didn't hook up with any of them. These ones were skanks—the other ones were out of his league. That's all the story he needed to stick to when his friends got on him about it.

As he pushed through the crowd of sweaty bodies, Toby's gaze fell on Wolf, back at the far wall again, elbow propped on the game machine, again. One beer in hand, two new red cups set on top of the machine. Had he been outside long enough for Wolf to go through two beers?

Wolf was watching the stage as usual, even though it was nothing but Scar Horse dragging their gear off the stage while Firesiren's roadies worked around them. Toby'd been thinking it'd be cool to be a roadie, that maybe he could volunteer for one of the local bands, get his start. But right now he was thinking roadies were dicks. He scowled as one of the stage lights hit the skin-colored side of baldy's skull, the guy walking around up there like he was in charge of everything.

Toby turned and headed for Wolf.

As he approached—and without even turning his head—Wolf lifted one of the red cups from the top of the video machine, carrying it like it was full. When Toby was within reaching distance, he held the cup out.

A smile jumped to Toby's face. "Shit. Thanks."

Wolf shrugged a little.

Toby thumped against the wall and took a long pull off the plastic cup. "You coming to the Dynodriver show Saturday?" he asked after he wiped the foam from his lip.

"Sure."

Toby took another long swallow off the beer, crisp and cold and just exactly the thing he'd needed. "I don't really like Dynodriver much," he said.

Wolf didn't respond, just tapped the top of the game machine with two fingers that held the stub of a cigarette.

Toby said, "I was thinking of coming anyway, though." He stole a look at Wolf over the rim of his cup as he took another swallow, but with Wolf you could never tell *what* the fuck he was thinking. So Toby kept on talking. "I figure they're worth a second chance and all, right?"

The corner of Wolf's mustache rose a little. He tipped his chin up and took a last drag from that stub of a cigarette. Still smiling a little, as if at some private joke, he said, "You may be right." He ground the butt out under the toe of his boot.

Toby leaned back against the wall, watching Wolf watch the stage, which was empty now of everything but Firesiren's gear, just waiting for them to get their asses off the bus and start the show. Wolf dragged his lower lip under his teeth and held it there till it slipped free. He took a drink from the red plastic cup dwarfed by his hand. After another half minute or so of studying the empty stage, Wolf said, "What?" and turned his head.

Toby was biting his own bottom lip. He rubbed his tongue across the inside of it as he slowly shook his head, eyebrows up, all innocent. Thinking about Wolf's mouth on his. Wolf's thigh jammed against his crotch.

Wolf smiled—it was a wolf's smile, like he *knew*—and turned his attention back to the stage.

A low guitar sound came over the PA, just one note, reverberating against the wall at their backs. The crowd yelled and whistled. Toby imagined the band walking out on stage, casual like it was no big thing. That was how the crowd sounded, mixed in with the one never-ending guitar note, like the band was finally fucking here.

Wolf lifted his big hand and dropped it on Toby's head to turn his face toward the stage. He ruffled Toby's hair before hanging his arm around Toby's shoulder.

Toby snuck one more look at him.

Wolf's weight leaned closer, Wolf taking his eyes from the stage only once he was close enough to turn his mouth against Toby's ear. "Want to go to my place after this?"

Without a word to the audience, the band kicked into probably their heaviest song on the latest album. It hit Toby full-on, like stepping outside and having the wind snatch the breath from your lungs.

He grinned like his face was being blown off.

Firesiren was *insane*. There was a reason Scar Horse was just a support act and Hell's Hornet, or whatever the fuck they were going to be calling themselves next week, only *wished* they were even a support act.

Still grinning, he closed his eyes and let the music blast him against the wall, the weight of it hard, solid, relentless. Like Wolf earlier.

Like Wolf.

He ran his tongue along the corner of his lip, where he could still feel the memory of a mustache prickling against his skin. Where he could still *taste* Wolf, the bitter tobacco on his tongue, the saltiness he'd licked off the side of his hand. He drew his tongue along his upper lip, tasting the salt of his own sweat, and edged closer to the man, his mouth dry. His head fuzzed up like he'd taken a hit off a joint.

Wolf propped an elbow on his shoulder, throwing his other arm in the air with a yell as the wild part of the song kicked in.

Toby's cock was trying to bust through his jeans again. *Wolf's place later*. He wanted to bury his face against Wolf's armpit and breathe him in. He wanted to push his hand in Wolf's jeans again, feel him throb against his palm. But he just kept his eyes closed, carrying the weight of Wolf's elbow. Trying not to drown in the smell of him—Irish Spring and cigarette smoke. And underneath that, the real smell of the wolf.

God *damn*.

Firesiren was *insane*.

ZOE X. RIDER spent her malleable late-teen/early-twenties years never very far from a pool table—billiard halls, rec rooms, dorm common rooms, or barracks. At one point, she lived upstairs from a pool hall, which is pretty much what she imagines being in heaven is like. She has a pool table in her living room these days, which is almost as good. When she's not practicing rail shots, she writes fiction, sees her favorite bands at small dark venues, and loses herself in other people's books.

Twitter: @zoexrider
Facebook: https://www.facebook.com/zoexriderfiction
E-mail: zoexrider@gmail.com

The Bear Next Door

Jack Byrne

"I'VE BEEN wanting to ask you something."

Rob Johnson looked up from his computer and frowned. In the doorway stood his new young neighbor, Bryce Philipson. Rob raised his eyebrows and waited, having no idea what the boy wanted. Well, he wasn't a boy, he was a young man. Bryce was about twenty-two. He looked sleek and tanned and golden and self-assured, the opposite of Rob's massive beer-barrel, hirsute frame. Bryce didn't look that self-assured now, though, Rob noticed. He was hovering above Rob, looking nervous.

"Yeah?" prompted Rob, wondering what was so important it had to impose on his office time. He did not enjoy office work, and it always put him in a bad frame of mind. He preferred to get it over with as soon as possible, and therefore looked upon interruptions with a jaundiced eye.

"Do you ever... um, go out?"

Rob looked up at Bryce and took off his glasses, twirling them in his hand absently. He considered asking why in the hell Bryce would ask him that, or whether the youngster was blind, but he looked up at the nervous face and took pity.

"No," said Rob, and went back to registering the calf drop for the season.

"Oh... okay."

Bryce wandered a little about the office, stopping by a photo on the wall of a tall auburn-haired boy about sixteen to ask, "Is that your son?"

"I don't have a son!" growled Rob angrily. He started again at the top of the page, because Bryce's comment had made him lose count.

A few minutes later Rob looked up from his computer and realized that the lad was gone. He took a sip of his coffee and e-mailed his agent to book the calves into the early fall sale. He glanced longingly out the window at the beautiful Nebraska landscape and sighed. The quicker he had this paper work done and could get back outside, the better.

IT WAS a week later that Rob had a curious sense of déjà vu when he logged onto his computer again. A voice from above him said, "Hi, Rob."

Rob looked up to see Bryce standing there, incongruous in a ten-gallon hat. He began to wonder if Bryce was a holographic projection somehow generated every time he logged on to his computer. Remembering his manners, Rob grunted.

Encouraged by this show of interest, Bryce spoke again in a rush. "A few of us were going to ride out tomorrow to the old creek behind Cat Mountain. You wanna come?"

Rob skewered the hazel eyes of his guest with a look of disinterest. "What for?"

"Just… just for fun," replied Bryce.

Rob squinted up at Bryce's young, smooth, earnest face. "Can't see the point. You bringing cattle in?"

"Well, no, just…."

"Well, no." Rob slammed his laptop shut, but to his disappointment Bryce did not disappear in response; so much for that theory. Rob heaved his huge frame up with a hand on each chair arm, grabbed his hat off the top of the well-polished piano, and stepped toward Bryce, who looked up—and up—as the big man approached him and stared down at him.

Rob hesitated. "You gonna move, or am I gonna walk over you?" Bryce looked up at him but did not budge, then said suddenly, "Is it true, what they say about you?"

Rob felt the peculiar stillness come over him that he usually noticed before a fight. He let his fists curl at his side and glared at Bryce. "What people say about me ain't necessarily true. And in any case, what I am ain't none of your goddamned business. So kindly step out of my way and off my property."

The golden face did not move, and the golden body straightened up in an impressive display of courage. There were not many men in the county who would stand up to Rob Johnson.

Bryce said, "So it's true, then? That you like men?"

Rob was reaching out to pick the young pup up by the scruff of the neck when Bryce spoke again hastily. "Because if it is, I'd like to know if I'm your type."

Rob's hand fell to his side and he blinked stupidly at Bryce. "You?"

"I have asked you on no less than two previous occasions to go out with me, Rob, and I'm asking you now straight up."

"You have?" Rob's reply was indignant. Then he snapped, "You... you scrawny little piece of gold dust, what makes you think I'd want to go out with you?"

Bryce pursed his lips and said, "Right. That sorts that out, then. I do apologize for interrupting your working day, Mr. Johnson. Good day." He turned on his heel and strode out.

Rob blinked again, staring after him. Eventually he sighed quietly. "Well, I'll be goddamned."

IT PLAYED on his mind.

As he went about his chores for the next week, Rob kept thinking about the young—very young!—man's invitation. Rob could not for the life of him think what Bryce, spoiled rich boy as he seemed, would see in a gruff, middle-aged cattleman like Rob. He had to admit, though, the kid had nerve, to stand up to him like that and ask straight out. And Rob admired people with gumption.

But Rob was too old for this sort of thing, he thought, as he grabbed a roll of new barbed wire to replace the rusty lowest strand on the east paddock. The free end of the wire almost immediately flicked loose and took a nick out of the webbing between the index and middle fingers of his right hand. He cursed himself for getting distracted and forgetful and went to grab his roping gloves out of the glove box of the old pickup. On second thought, he jammed on a hat and some sunglasses too. No sense losing an eye.

Rob glanced at the untidy mess of old barbed wire on the ground that he had cut off the fence the day before. Then he set to work with the truck and the new wire. He set up a roller on a steel rod, which he fastened crosswise in the bed of the pickup. He pulled out the loose end, walked with it over to the fence, and used his fencing pliers to tie the end of the new barbed wire roll to the corner post of the fence. Then he climbed in behind the wheel and started off slowly along the fence line, listening closely to the god-awful racket of the barb scraping across the lowered tailgate of the pickup, tugging harder and harder with the weight of the wire as he paid out more and more.

Rob reached the end of the fence line without incident, jumped out, and took the roll off the pickup. He passed the almost empty roll easily around the end post, put the roll back on the rig, jammed a shorter steel rod through the rig to stop it rolling, and drove carefully until the wire was pulled taut along the fence line.

Rob used a short strand of scrap barb to tie off the strained wire securely before cutting the wire. It gave with a dangerous "twang" but held because the barbs caught on each other and prevented the wire from slipping past it. He had learned that lesson the hard way when he first started fencing and used plain tie wire to fasten a strained fence. He had the long scar across the underside of his right forearm to remind him of that. Luckily it didn't show because of the thick hair on his arms.

Now came the tedious work. Rob grabbed a bucket of tie-wire shorts that he had cut in the shed and started fixing the wire to each post along the run. Only seventy-five to go, he thought ruefully. He started sweating almost immediately in the hot morning sun, and looked around quickly before stripping off his shirt and throwing it on the back of the pickup. Having hair on your chest sounded great, but having hair over your chest, shoulders and back was not so great during the hot Nebraska summer because it acted as a sort of insulating layer under the shirt, trapping the heat. Rob usually worked shirtless whenever he was alone in the autumn and spring, because he had very little risk of getting badly sunburned through his thick layer of hair. He was quick to cover up in company, though, because he had heard people's expressions of astonishment when they saw his hirsute form, when they didn't think he could hear them. He knew his body was uncommonly hairy, so much as to be unsightly to most people. Whenever he brushed his hair, he kept brushing down over his shoulders and back as far as he could reach, to smooth the hair under his shirt so it didn't bunch and itch during the day. It was just one of those things.

He worked his way slowly along the fence line, farther and farther from the pickup. When he was about 150 feet from the pickup, groaning as he straightened up from squatting down to the lowest part of a post to tie off the wire run for about the sixteenth time, he was startled to hear a voice behind him. "Could you use a hand?"

He spun around to see Bryce standing there.

Rob, covered in sweat and without his shirt, felt his face warm up with embarrassment. "What are you doing back on my property?"

"If you like, I'll jump back over the fence, so then I'd be on my property. Which raises the question, why didn't you ask for my help to fix this fence? It's a big job, and a bit of neighborly help wouldn't have gone astray. Plus it's my fence too."

Rob didn't know what to say, so he characteristically said nothing and turned back to his work.

To his surprise, Bryce produced a pair of thick leather gloves out of his pocket and reached into the bucket of ties, bringing out a fistful, and said, "We'll take turns, okay? It'll halve your workload."

Rob nodded curtly, acutely aware of his lack of shirt and the other man's occasional glance at his exposed body.

They worked away, and soon Rob noticed Bryce's shirt begin to darken with sweat. As he walked past, Rob said, "You should take your shirt off. You'll get heatstroke."

"I would, but I'd sunburn."

"Oh. Yeah, right." Rob hadn't considered what it would be like to not have a protective pelt over your body.

"I don't suppose you sunburn. Lucky devil."

"Lucky? Jesus." Rob half-smiled.

"What?" Bryce's voice was mild and curious, not judging at all, and Rob felt himself relax a little.

Rob volunteered, "I don't burn easily, but I don't tan either. Never look like you, all...." He stopped himself.

"All what?"

"Nothing."

They worked on in silence, and the job passed surprisingly quickly. Rob tied off the last post and reinforced the fastenings on the end post, and then they turned to walk back to get the pickup from the far end of the paddock.

"Thanks for your help, Bryce."

"My pleasure."

Rob couldn't help sneaking a look at his companion and was rewarded with a cheerful smile from Bryce, which just made him feel embarrassed all over again.

They walked in silence for a while. Then Rob ventured, "I didn't really think you'd be back here after what I said last time we spoke."

Bryce chuckled. "Yeah, what was that about? I've sure never been called a 'scrawny little piece' of *anything* before."

"Oh, you know," Rob said apologetically. "I just meant, you're awfully young to be… looking to someone like me to go out with."

"How about you let me decide that, Rob?"

Rob subsided into what was rapidly becoming a habitual embarrassed silence around Bryce. After a while, noticing Bryce glancing at him several times, he said quietly, "Well, I'm sorry I spoke to you like that."

"Would you go out with me?" asked Bryce suddenly. "I mean, now that you've got over the shock of it, me asking you?"

"Shock? No." Rob scratched his neck thoughtfully. "I just—you're so young. Why wouldn't you go out with someone your own age? Surely you'd have more in common?"

Bryce stopped walking. They were still about 150 feet from the pickup. Rob stopped and turned reluctantly to face him, impatient to get back to his shirt and hide his unsightly, hirsute body from the smooth-skinned Bryce.

Bryce looked at him with unsettling sincerity and asked, "What if I said I find you incredibly attractive, and that I don't care about your age?"

Rob, dumbfounded, just stood staring at the splendid young man with the earnest face and decided he'd better get his hearing checked at the first opportunity.

"Attractive? Me?" he said stupidly.

Bryce took a step closer and raised his hand to brush his fingers along Rob's forearm. It tickled like hell, and Rob sucked in his breath but then couldn't think of anything to say. Bryce looked at Rob's hairy torso and said quietly, "I happen to find this an incredible turn-on, the hair. Up until an hour ago I could have lived with you rejecting me. But seeing you like this, in all your glory, I'm not gonna give up that easy anymore."

Rob looked down at himself incredulously. "This? Me? You like this?" He frowned.

Bryce smiled and stepped a little closer, giving his right hand an opportunity to drift down the downy surface of Rob's chest. Rob found it a little hard to breathe all of a sudden, and looked down into soft hazel eyes. It dawned on Rob that they were having a moment.

Bryce spoke again in that quiet voice. "I do like this, very much. I think you are one of the hottest men I have ever clapped eyes on. So powerful, so utterly masculine." His fingers closed on the dense, curly hair over Rob's chest and tightened, and he pulled Rob closer to him, tilting his handsome, golden face up to meet Rob's gaze. "I could tap this."

Rob didn't quite know what to do, so he put a hand over the fist curled tightly on his chest and said, "You don't know what you're getting into."

"Don't I?" There was a challenge in Bryce's hazel eyes, and Rob couldn't help but respond. He leaned down and hesitated, surveying the handsome young face. Then, to his surprise, Bryce stood up on tiptoes and met his mouth in a warm, inviting kiss.

It was nice. It was extraordinarily nice, and Rob blinked as Bryce pulled away. Bryce looked up at him, the doubt creeping back into his expression. There was a moment, and Rob said softly, "Could you do that again, please?"

Bryce's face lit up in a million-dollar smile, and he reached up to kiss Rob again, more enthusiastically this time. Rob felt surprisingly strong arms come up around his neck and pull him close, and he dropped the pliers and bucket of gear he was carrying, not even hearing the thumps as the items hit the ground. He was too busy claiming those warm, silken lips and putting his powerful arms around Bryce. He pulled Bryce tight, making him gasp and struggle a little, so Rob loosened his grip and said, "Sorry."

Bryce shook his head and whispered, "It's fine. You're just a lot stronger than I expected, that's all."

Rob could feel his cock begin to thicken in response to Bryce's hard, slim body against his, and his jeans were getting pleasantly uncomfortable and tight. Bryce must have felt it too, for he reached around Rob and pulled him closer so he could rub his body against Rob's as he tilted his head up for another kiss. Rob was getting hot and bothered in more ways than one and suggested huskily, "Let's go back to the house."

Bryce kissed him again and nodded. They pulled apart, and Bryce bent down to pick up the bucket and pliers. Rob gazed admiringly at the taut body before him and counted his blessings.

The trip back to the house was a little awkward and quiet, but as Rob strode in and kicked the front door shut behind them, Bryce was back in his arms in a second. He kissed Rob and worked at the buttons on his shirt front, then pushed his hands into the coarse blanket of hair over Rob's chest. He tugged at Rob's skin and pinched his nipples through the mat of hair. Rob made a gruff noise and Bryce smiled. "You like it a bit rough, don't you?"

Rob surveyed him, panting and considering Bryce. He could feel the heat in his body and smell the sweat of the morning's work in his shirt. "I need a shower."

He turned away abruptly, embarrassed at the way Bryce made him forget himself. Rob knew that he must look and smell a mess, and felt the urgent need to get cleaned up. He called back over his shoulder, "Make yourself at home. There's cold water in the fridge." Rob walked into the bathroom, turned on the shower, and discarded his clothes into the basket in the corner. He heard the fridge open out in the kitchen.

Rob stepped into the water. He had set the taps to what he knew was a tepid temperature, but the water felt freezing at first on his overheated skin. He turned the tap on full and tipped his face back, letting the water rush down over his head. The water ran through the hair on his back, cooling him and weighing him down at the same time. He reached for the shampoo and lathered his head, shoulders, chest, and back.

Eyes closed against the shampoo, he jumped when a quiet voice asked, "Want a hand?"

Rob opened his eyes and they immediately stung with shampoo, but he could not close them. Bryce was standing naked in the shower door and then stepped in to join him. Rob stared at his sleek, muscled torso, the broad shoulders and muscled stomach, the slightly pink shaft hanging down along the long, golden thighs, the strong arms coming up to wrap around Rob's neck. Rob managed to choke out "Yes" before the pain in his eyes forced him to close them.

Through the water, Rob felt strong lips press to his. He gave a short moan of appreciation and reached out to take Bryce's smooth torso in his arms and pull him close. Bryce's hands moved down and massaged his shoulders as they kissed—then Rob felt them slide down and under his arms to take a firm grip around his back. Rob moaned and pressed his thighs against the warmth of Bryce's legs. Bryce's warm body was a contrast to the water, which still felt a bit chilly to Rob even though his body had cooled down a little from the hot sun. An eager, hot tongue invaded Rob's mouth, and the hands at his back fisted into the hair there as Bryce slipped slightly on the shampoo suds on the shower floor. The sudden pain of having a handful of hair tugged nearly out of either side of his back made Rob gasp and move slightly forward, into Bryce's rigid erection. *He really does want me*, thought Rob, a little surprised.

He felt the sudden sensation of rough, wet cloth being pressed across his forehead, and realized that Bryce was mopping up the shampoo from his eyes. The cloth pressed firmly across his eyelids, and he managed to open them. Bryce was watching him with those hazel eyes, enthralled, from under a darkened mop of saturated blond hair plastered over his skull.

"Hey," whispered Bryce. "Turn around and pass me the shampoo."

Rob was a little surprised, unused as he was to being told what to do, but he turned anyway, being careful not to slip or step on Bryce's toes as he did so.

The voice came now from just behind his ear. "I'm not made of glass, you know."

Capable hands rose to his head and massaged his hair as Rob braced his hands against the shower wall and lowered his head to let the flow of water fall on his head rather than his face and chest. He stared down at his swollen sex, which was standing, thick and hard, almost horizontal in front of him. He started to worry that the feeling of Bryce's strong hands now massaging down his neck and out to his shoulders would make him come before Bryce even touched his cock. Bryce worked his hands into the thick hair covering Rob's upper back, pressing small circles into the skin below, and Rob moaned again, the unaccustomed touch welcome on his skin. His cock began to ache with fullness, so that he could feel each heartbeat throb through it. He could see beads of white moisture appearing at the tip briefly, only to be washed away immediately by the water.

Bryce whispered in his ear. "Okay?"

"Mm—hmm," managed Rob, and he heard a quiet chuckle and felt hot breath behind his ear. Rob looked down and saw Bryce's hands snake around his torso to find the base of his erection. Smooth fingers squeezed him, then slid over the taut skin covering his cock, and pleasure lanced from those fingers all through his cock into his belly. Rob felt himself become even more rigid. His cock bobbed upward several times.

He managed to whisper hoarsely, "You touch me much more there and I'm gonna come real quick."

"Good" came a husky murmur in his ear, and Rob felt his balls tighten up sharply into his body at the naked desire in that single word. Far from letting up, Bryce encircled Rob's cock with his hands and squeezed gently, pushing slowly up the slick, soapy surface until his hands were grasping Rob just behind the broad ridge of his glans. Then he released one hand and used it to thumb over the head of Rob's penis, which was slick with precome. The pleasure rendered Rob speechless, and his cock already felt like it was going to explode any second.

Bryce wasn't letting up. He set a regular rhythm, pumping Rob steadily. Rob could not see or hear anything; his world was reduced to the pleasurable sensations in his cock from those quick, firm hands. He managed a moan of approval.

"Christ, you're massive," murmured Bryce in his ear, and squeezed harder. Rob's body bucked forward, and he felt his face spasm as he squirted fiercely against the wall. Bryce's arms tightened around him as the younger man realized he had come, and Rob cursed his lack of control under his breath even as pleasure lanced through his whole body and left him supporting his suddenly limp form with shaking arms against the shower wall.

Rob managed to push off the wall after a minute and spun within the confines of Bryce's arms to face the drenched younger man. Bryce looked up, his lips parted as though to speak, but Rob bent down and captured his lips in a long, exploring kiss. When Bryce responded more eagerly than he expected, Rob remembered that Bryce had not come. Rob released Bryce's lips, slid slowly to his knees in front of him, and with practiced ease took Bryce's taut erection in his mouth, then sucked it down to the back of his throat. He heard Bryce make some sort of incoherent gasp above him, and his knees pushed into Rob's hips as his legs sagged. Rob brought his hands around to work the base of Bryce's shaft expertly, his fingers just tight enough to produce maximum friction as he worked the slick pink shaft. He fastened his lips over the tip and sucked vigorously, feeling the tip of Bryce's cock swell into a fat mushroom as Rob worked. The beautiful golden body in his hands tightened up, and then Bryce cried out. Rob drank the hot, bitter seed down and swallowed it while Bryce's hands tightened almost unbearably in the hair on Rob's head as he came. Bryce gave a series of choked moans as his thighs bucked again and again into Rob's rib cage.

Slowly, they collapsed down onto the shower floor together and sat until the water ran too cold for them. They stood up, turned it off, and toweled each other dry.

Rob steered Bryce in the direction of his bedroom and smiled when Bryce said, "Really?"

Rob led him into his room and took him in his arms again. "I sure haven't finished with you yet!"

IT WAS three weeks later, and Rob was sitting in his kitchen having breakfast when a sleepy figure appeared in the doorway. Rob looked up and smiled. "Hey."

Bryce wandered over to him and wrapped his arms around Rob's chest from behind. "Good morning."

Rob tilted his head up for a slow kiss. Bryce asked, "Coffee?"

"I've had one. I left the machine on for you."

Rob watched as Bryce moved over to the cupboard and pulled out a cup, then asked, "What do you have on today?"

"Mmm. Probably do some fencing. That lower paddock could do with a new top line."

"Never ends," observed Rob.

Bryce chuckled as he brought his steaming coffee back to the table. "Well, I did want to be a rancher. Could have stayed in the city and become a lawyer."

Rob reached up before Bryce sat down, took his coffee out of his hand and placed it on the table. "Come here."

Bryce looked a little surprised as Rob pulled him onto his lap, facing him. Rob felt the strong slim legs of his lover wrap around him and the warmth of Bryce in his lap as Bryce asked, "What?"

Rob pulled him down into a deep kiss. He took his time and captured Bryce's lips in his, then nudged open Bryce's mouth and explored it gently. By the time Rob released Bryce from the kiss, Bryce was beginning to moan a little with desire. He stared at Rob, his face inquiring.

Rob said, "I had an idea. If you want to leave the fencing for a day, I thought we could take the horses for a ride over to Cat Mountain and go swimming."

Slowly, Bryce began to smile. "I thought you didn't see the point of going riding unless there were cattle to be brought in."

"Maybe you changed my mind for me," said Rob with a smile. This time it was Bryce who pulled Rob into a long, deep kiss.

WEEKS PASSED, and Rob and Bryce drifted into a contented routine. On most nights Bryce slept over at Rob's ranch, and each morning they would head out together and work on both properties, helping each other with fencing, checking and moving stock around, and doing general maintenance work in the sheds.

By unspoken agreement they did not go into town together. If Bryce had any issues with that, he did not express them to Rob. Occasionally one or the other of them would announce that they were driving into town and disappear for an hour or so, coming back with supplies or groceries as they both needed.

Today was one of those days. Bryce told Rob, "I'm going to town to pick up some pour-on insecticide for the heifers in the yards. I'll come back over here after I've done them."

"Okay," replied Rob, and pulled Bryce into a tight hug.

Bryce kissed him and walked cheerfully out of the kitchen, snatching his hat off the hook by the door as he went. Rob watched him go and decided to do some office work. He was a little behind in his stock returns and was soon deeply absorbed in his task.

It took him a moment to realize that he could hear a vehicle in the drive. Rob glanced at the clock and saw that two hours had passed. That was plenty of time for Bryce to get into town and back, run the heifers out through the race, and drive back over to Rob's. But then Rob tilted his head. The vehicle didn't sound like Bryce's. The note of the engine was deeper, more powerful.

Rob stood up and walked to the front door. What he saw stopped him in his tracks. His lips formed the word "Michael" but no sound came out.

Slowly, Rob walked out of the house and approached the car that had pulled up. A tall, powerful-looking young man unfolded his length from the driver's seat, and he watched Rob as he walked toward him.

They stood facing each other for a long time. Then Rob said, "Michael—"

The blue eyes that met Rob's were older, a little wiser, but as familiar as ever. His face was handsome, a bit more rugged and weathered than Rob remembered it, but the planes of the cheeks and the strong cut of the jaw hadn't changed a bit.

Michael walked up and said, "Hey."

Rob stared at him blankly, then said, "I didn't think I'd ever see you again."

Michael, who was about Bryce's age, with thick, reddish-brown hair, pursed his lips and looked down at his feet for a moment, then looked back up into Rob's eyes.

Rob took a hesitant step forward, and Michael raised his arms. Encouraged, Rob closed the distance between them and took Michael in a crushing bear hug.

They hugged for a long time. Then Michael pulled back far enough to stare at Rob and brush away the tears on the older man's face. Michael said, "I couldn't stay away forever, could I?"

"Thank you," whispered Rob, and stepped back awkwardly. "But I thought you would."

"So did I, for a couple of years. Forgive me?" Michael asked, his eyes pleading.

"Forget about it."

"Can I stay here?"

"Of course, you can stay as long as you like," replied Rob. He put his arm over Michael's shoulders and led him into the house.

ROB DID not see Bryce's pale face withdraw back around the corner of the house, nor see Bryce stumbling back across the lawn toward his pickup, stopping several times to retch into the shrubs beside the fence line.

It was hours before Rob realized that Bryce hadn't returned as expected, and he called Bryce's house. There was no answer, so Rob excused himself and drove over to Bryce's property. There was no sign of the pickup, but the cattle had been released, and the opened box of pour-on stood on the back porch. Rob hefted it, but it was light—empty. Rob decided that Bryce must have gone back into town to get something he had forgotten, and went home.

As the evening progressed and Bryce still didn't return, Rob excused himself again and left Michael minding supper so he could check on Bryce again. As he pulled up at Bryce's, he was relieved to see Bryce's truck back in the drive. Rob hesitated as he heard music and voices inside, but knocked on the door.

A stranger answered the door, a young man of about twenty that Rob had never seen before. Rob, taken aback, asked, "Is Bryce here?"

"Bryce?" The sleek young man eyed Rob with knowing and slightly condescending eyes. "Course he's here. Who's asking?"

Just then Bryce came out to the door and stopped behind the stranger, his eyes locking onto Rob's. Rob frowned when he saw the hardness in Bryce's eyes. The sleek young man rocked his hips into Bryce's and slung a casual arm over his shoulder.

Rob snarled, his eyes locked onto Bryce's, "Nobody. Nobody's asking." He spun on his heel and left, revving his vehicle loudly and deliberately spraying the side of Bryce's truck with gravel.

Rob felt feverish and frozen at the same time.

The only positive of the evening was that he didn't have to explain to his son Michael that he had a new live-in lover. As for Rob's foul mood over the next few weeks, well, Michael probably thought that was normal for his father.

Rob took to buying a bottle of rum to get him through the week, and one evening, thanks to some recalcitrant calves and a broken gate, he was late into town to buy it, so he ended up going to the bar after the store had closed. He was walking back around to the parking lot in the rear, with a bottle each of rum and cola, when he heard snarling voices. He put the drinks in his pickup and walked over quietly to investigate.

What he saw made his stomach clench.

Bryce was backed up against his pickup, with two men holding him by the elbows as a third drew his fist back for another blow. Blood was trickling from Bryce's nose and he looked dazed but defiant.

Rob broke into a lumbering run, and three faces turned to him. He drew his huge, powerful fist back but was still ten feet away when they released Bryce and turned to run. Rob took a few steps after them but realized that he had no hope of keeping up with their adrenaline-charged flight, and that Bryce might need his help. Bryce was slumped back against the pickup, head tilted up, holding his nose to stop the bleeding.

Rob went over and took his free arm to stop him sliding down to the ground.

"You okay?" asked Rob.

"I'm fine," said Bryce nasally.

Rob nearly turned to go, but hesitated and said, "You'll be no good driving like that."

"I can go back into the bar."

"And get bashed up by someone else? Forget it, I'll drive you home."

"What about your truck?"

"I'll lock it up and leave it here. Nobody's stupid enough to lay a finger on my truck," said Rob drily.

"Ain't that the truth."

Rob led Bryce by the arm over to his own truck, made sure it was locked up, and then took him back to Bryce's pickup. "Where are the keys?"

Bryce patted his back pocket, but Rob growled, "Just hand them to me."

Bryce gave him a slow, pained, and angry look, pulled out the keys and handed them to Rob with a raised eyebrow.

"Get in," said Rob shortly, and went to the driver's side.

They drove in uncomfortable silence for a few minutes, until Bryce's glare spurred Rob into asking, "Problem?"

"Yeah. You're an asshole."

Rob, taken aback, spared him a cold glance and shrugged. "*I'm* an asshole?"

But Bryce didn't reply.

They drove on in silence until they reached Bryce's beautiful home. Rob saw the front door open, and a young woman came out.

"Who's that?"

"Oh, Mary, my sister. She's up for a visit."

"Oh."

Rob stopped and let Bryce out, then drove off without another word as the young lady fussed over Bryce.

A FEW nights later, Rob's mood being even fouler than usual for some unknown reason, his son Michael had decided to go into the bar in town by himself. He'd sooner be ignored by strangers than growled at constantly by his father. He wondered whether he had outstayed his welcome and began tossing up plans for leaving the ranch again.

Michael leaned up to the bar and called, "JD, straight up!"

He began to drink quietly, trying to blend in. It wouldn't do him any good to stand out; if people knew who his father was, they might decide to pick a fight. If they didn't know him they still might, just because he was an unknown face. In either case, he was better off keeping a low profile. He was pretty good at doing that, so he was surprised to hear a voice at his elbow just as he finished his shot.

"You want another one of those?"

It was a male voice, and Michael frowned as he turned around and looked at the handsome blond man about the same age as himself, staring intently at him. Michael asked, "Now why would you buy me a drink?"

A shadow of doubt passed over the other man's face, but he recovered quickly and said smoothly, "Just being friendly. I didn't think you'd mind. Seen you around with Rob Johnson." He looked at Michael as if that should explain everything.

Michael stared at the man stonily. Despite saying he was "just being friendly" there was nothing friendly about the look in his eyes. Michael wondered where this was leading, and felt his fists clench at his sides. He didn't know this person who obviously knew of Michael's father. Michael glanced around quickly, trying to ascertain if the other man had backup if things turned ugly.

"What of it?" Michael asked in a flat tone.

"Just friends?" asked the blond man, and Michael could swear he heard a suggestive tone in that question.

"How is that any of your business?" demanded Michael, his voice tight. *The last thing I need is to get into a fight because of who my father is*, he thought. He glanced around the bar again and realized, no, in this bar the last thing he needed was to be seen backing down from a fight.

He stood up, towering over the blond man, and looked down at him with what he hoped was a reasonable imitation of his father's best cold-blooded glare. To Michael's surprise, the other man's eyes narrowed, and he looked at Michael oddly. When he said nothing for a while,

Michael glared at him and asked, "You gonna move, or am I gonna walk over you?"

The stranger's eyes widened, and he stared at Michael and said in a horrified tone, "Wait. Are you related to Rob?"

Michael tilted his head, confused. "What, Dad? Well, yeah...." He trailed off at the look in the other man's eyes.

The blond man said, "He's your f...," then began to swear profusely. Michael and the bartender watched in confused fascination as the odd young fellow slammed a fist onto the bar, then spun and sprinted out.

Michael tilted his head the other way and watched him leave. He turned back to the bar and sat down, and the bartender said, "Scared him off real fast, didn't you?"

Michael just turned and stared at him for a second, shrugged, and went back to his drink.

OUT AT the ranch, Rob looked up as a familiar pickup skidded to a stop in his drive. Rob stood up from the porch where he had been sitting repairing a bridle and frowned as Bryce jumped out of the truck before it had even stopped. The young blond man raced up to Rob, looked as though he was going to hug him, then stopped and waved his arms around and said almost inarticulately, "Michael.... I thought, Rob.... He's? I thought he.... I saw you with him! You hugged him! You were... in tears!"

Rob gave Bryce what he hoped was his best thousand-yard stare.

After a few more false starts, Bryce managed to blurt out, "Michael's your son? You told me you didn't have a son!"

Rob said, "Well, for a long time that was true...."

"Look, Rob, you either have a son or you don't have a son. You can't lie about something as important as that to me! Look what's happened because of it."

"We weren't on talking terms."

"That doesn't mean he doesn't exist! Anyway, the picture on the wall is of a kid. And Michael's older than I am!"

Rob stared at him and said drily, "Well, that ain't exactly difficult, Bryce. But for your information, I hadn't seen Michael for six years until he showed up home a few weeks ago."

"Well, I, yeah, I thought you were too young to have an adult son… I thought he was… I thought you were cheating on me."

Rob sighed deeply and looked sadly at Bryce. "You thought that, did you?" There was a long, awkward silence, but then Rob spoke again, a world of reprimand in his deep, gravelly voice. "I'm a bit steadier than that. And, you know, you could have asked me."

Bryce hung his head. "I'm sorry. It was stupid."

Under the blond locks, Rob could see the young man biting his bottom lip. He stepped closer to Bryce and peered at his face. "You bawlin', boy?"

"No!" Bryce's voice was angry.

"You been screwin' around all over town, from what I've heard. And seen."

Bryce opened his mouth to say something, then shut it, then started, "That's not quite—" then stopped.

Rob pursed his lips and sighed. "Think you better get off my ranch, boy."

Bryce hesitated, then spun on his heel and walked stiffly back to the pickup, climbed in, slammed the door, and drove away slowly.

Rob sat back down and picked up the bridle, his big face impassive, his lips turned down at the corners. He started stitching the bridle again, jabbed himself with the thick needle, swore, and went into the kitchen to wash off the blood. At the sink, he cleaned off his thumb, then put a hand on either side of the sink and hung his head.

MICHAEL SAT in the bar that Saturday night, his pose casual but his eyes narrowed as he watched Bryce Philipson getting slowly more and more inebriated. Bryce fended off several advances from women and even one surreptitious advance by a local truck driver, which raised Michael's eyebrows.

Michael's concern was for more than Bryce's state of inebriation, though. Over in a dark corner near the end of the bar, three pairs of hostile eyes watched Bryce—the three men who had been trying to beat up Bryce the week before. Michael knew the men, having been to school with two of them. Michael had had a long conversation with his father about what had happened between Rob and Bryce, and had pieced together the whole story. What Rob had not told him, Michael could surmise. Bryce was a man in a downward spiral, and Michael glanced from him to the silent group in the corner, his mind racing. He was waiting for an opportune moment to talk to Bryce, to try to set things straight between Bryce and his father. Trouble was, Bryce was surrounded by people and Michael wanted to speak to him in private. He waited impatiently for his chance.

When Bryce staggered out of the bar an hour later, three silent figures followed him, but Michael, head and shoulders taller than any of them, followed the group at a discreet distance.

After the short scuffle that ensued, Michael pulled the near-unconscious Bryce into his own car and drove toward Bryce's ranch. He pulled up at the front, and a young woman emerged from the house.

"Who's there?" she called. "I don't want to see you three on my property again, or I'm calling the sheriff."

Michael was taken aback, then realized that the three men that had beaten Bryce had driven off in this direction. He called back, "It's Michael Johnson, from next door. I've brought your brother home."

She came a little closer to the car and stared at him. "Michael Johnson?"

He looked at her face, which seemed pale, and nodded. "Sure, Rob's son. You know, Rob Johnson from next door?"

Her voice was hard and suspicious. "Nice try, stranger, but I happen to know for a fact that Rob Johnson doesn't have a son. Bryce told me."

Michael said, "I have Bryce with me. You can ask him."

He switched on the light, and she peered into the car, looking first at Michael, then at Bryce. Her voice softened and sounded less tense as she said, "What the hell?"

Ten minutes later, Michael pulled back out of the Philipson's drive and sped toward the Johnson ranch. Beside him, Bryce Philipson groaned in protest at the swaying of the car.

THE NEXT morning, Rob shuffled out into the kitchen, yawning broadly. He flicked the coffee maker on and swore as he reached into the cupboard under it and snagged the hair on his forearm on a loose piece of veneer.

"You're grumpy," said Michael, through a mouth full of toast.

"Up late," grumbled Rob.

"Dad, did you seriously wait up until I got home last night?" Michael asked.

Rob shrugged and lied, "No." He turned around, holding the coffee jar, then stopped dead.

At the kitchen table, holding his head in his hands, was an apparently very hungover Bryce Philipson. Rob was awake instantly and growled, "What's he doing here?"

"He got a little under the weather, and those bastards who beat him up were dogging him at the end of the night, so I drove him home and put him in the spare bed."

Rob leaned over to Michael and whispered, "You brought him home? You'll be the talk of the town for sure. He's gay—you do remember that, don't you?"

Michael chuckled. "Well, he's your boyfriend, so yeah, I kinda figured that."

Rob protested, "He's not my boyfriend!"

Michael retorted, "Oh yes he is."

"I'm not!" Bryce was looking up at both of them, haggard and red-eyed.

Rob glared at Michael.

Michael protested, "Look, *he's* in there at the bar every night drinking himself into a blind stupor. *You're* here sitting at home every night like a bear with a sore tooth. I figure you both may as well sit here and be miserable together." He glared sternly at them both. "I'm going to check on the weaner calves over in the south paddock, and then I might go for a swim in the creek. I won't be back until at least noon. Sort this out. I've had a bellyful of putting up with you, Dad, and I'm not going to keep dragging him out of bars." He tossed back the last of his coffee, glared once more at them both, grabbed his hat, strode out, and slammed the door behind him.

Rob stared at Bryce, who watched until Michael shut the door.

There was a long, awkward silence as Rob and Bryce listened to Michael's footsteps fade in the direction of the stables.

Then Bryce looked up at Rob and asked, "Has he always been like that?"

"Pretty much."

"So."

"So."

Rob couldn't help a half smile. "What are we gonna do with you?"

Bryce's hazy eyes met his. There was hope in them, mingled with misery. He said wistfully, "I guess that's up to you."

Rob put his coffee down on the table and smiled. "Come 'ere."

Bryce rose to his feet and stepped hesitantly up to Rob. Rob saw the exhaustion and misery in the bags under Bryce's eyes and the downward turn of his mouth.

Rob reached a hesitant hand out to take Bryce's, but before Rob could so much as blink he was almost winded as Bryce threw himself into his arms and clung tightly to him.

Rob stroked his hair and murmured, "You know, for a man with the mother of all hangovers, you move pretty quick." He found that it took a surprising amount of strength to peel Bryce off his chest enough to kiss him.

JACK BYRNE is an Australian who lives and works in the Australian outback training horses, doing farm work, and trying to stay out of trouble. He writes from experience (sometimes unfortunate experience!) and has been shot at ("a case of mistaken identity") and bitten by a snake before. He writes on a laptop with a satellite connection and likes to ride or drive out to locations he is writing about to get a real feel for the surroundings.

He is happy to hear from readers; his e-mail is Jackaroo_Byrne @hotmail.com and his website is http://fugitive1701.yolasite.com. He can't promise an instant reply as he goes out working sometimes for a week or so, but he will get back to readers as soon as he can.

The Bear Fetish
John Amory

ROBERT'S PLANE slowly descended over the New Mexican desert, already pitch black at eight in the evening. Through his little oval window, he could make out the grid of lights comprising the city of Albuquerque ahead. Robert closed the portfolio he'd been working on all through the flight from New York City and stowed it in his messenger bag. He tried to divert his thoughts from the legal case he was flying cross-country to investigate by leaning back and eavesdropping on his neighbors' conversation about the season finale of *Game of Thrones*, but he'd never watched an episode and quickly lost interest. An electronic bell dinged overhead, and the pilot's voice drifted through the cabin, informing the passengers of the local weather and final arrival time (about thirty degrees warmer than their point of departure and fifteen minutes ahead of schedule). Robert closed his eyes as the plane dipped and turned, thinking only of the work he had ahead of him in the next two days, despite how much he'd rather think of almost anything else.

A TAXI dropped Robert off in front of the Hyatt in downtown Albuquerque. After marveling at how inexpensive the fare was compared to back home, he checked into his room, a modest one since his firm was footing the bill. Robert heaved his carry-on bag, containing just enough toiletries and clothing for his three-day stay, onto the small table by the window and dug through his messenger for the file he'd placed there earlier. Flopping down on the bed, he cracked the manila folder open and stared blankly at its contents.

The corporate merger had been the bane of Robert's existence for the past several months, as a major bank his East Coast employer represented was acquiring a smaller, regional branch in the Southwest.

Robert was assigned to hand deliver the forms to the bank's owner, an attempt to make the acquisition feel less impersonal, and begin the process of transitioning Sun West Bank into the new regional hub for First Federal. He'd studied the contents of the file, forward and back, to the point that he knew the branch manager's social security number by heart. To really impress these people, Robert was determined to know everything there was to know about Sun West before his meeting the next morning. But after a five-hour flight, his brain felt like mush and refused to concentrate on the words and charts before him.

"This just isn't going to happen," Robert admitted to himself. He reached into the bedside table drawer and withdrew the visitor's guide, looking for an open restaurant. A meal would do him good, and it would wake up his mind enough to retain the last bits of information his file held. Not much immediately jumped out at Robert as appetizing, and those places that did had already closed for the evening. Apparently things weren't open as late in Albuquerque as they were in The City That Never Sleeps.

Fearing his search would be fruitless, Robert called down to the main desk. "Hello, this is room 1017. Is there anywhere within walking distance you could recommend for dinner or a drink?" he asked the voice on the other end of the line.

"Not much is open on Thursday nights past nine," the female receptionist answered. "Even the 7-Eleven next door is closed by now. If you walk two blocks north to Central Avenue you should be able to find something, though. There are a few bars there that may still be serving food. You can find more information on the last page of the guide in your room. Just be cautious. It can be a little sketchy at this time of night."

"I'm from New York, so I should be okay. Thank you." Robert hung up the phone and flipped to the page in the guide that the concierge had mentioned. There were listings for four local bars, all of which were open. The brief descriptions didn't inspire him much, though: two pool halls, an alternative-music spot, and a nightclub. Without many options, Robert plugged the address of one of the pool halls into his cell phone's GPS, hoping that once he got there he could at least gorge on some greasy appetizers.

THE NIGHT air felt good as Robert exited the Hyatt's lobby. A cool but dry breeze floated over him, ruffling his hair. The bitter winter weather of February in Manhattan hadn't transferred to New Mexico, thankfully. His phone's weather app told him the temperature was a delightful fifty-five degrees and clear. He left his jacket in the hotel room and embraced the refreshing wind. In less than five minutes, he arrived at his nameless destination, a windowless building with just a neon sign reading "Pool Hall." A group of thirtysomethings stood outside smoking in leather jackets and ripped jeans, stopping to laugh as Robert attempted to open the hall's door.

"It's members only, my man," one of them quipped. The guy took a long drag of his cigarette, which smelled suspiciously of weed, and added, "Probably wouldn't be your scene anyway."

Slightly offended, Robert asked why. "You just don't look like a local, man."

Robert looked down at his navy Tom Ford suit, his striped satin tie suddenly making him feel absurdly out of place. Blushing, he mumbled a thanks to the group of smokers, all of whom sniggered as he turned right and headed farther down Central Avenue. After a block or so, Robert finally looked up from his perfectly polished shoes and noticed the nightclub from the visitor's guide was just across the street. Now needing a drink more than food, he crossed the street and made his way into Effex.

A well-dressed bouncer checked Robert's identification, clearly a formality since his thirty-one years put him more than a decade over the entrance age, and ushered him through to the main room. The connecting hallway was trippy, a tunnel painted black and white with neon lights changing the white to vibrant purple, yellow, red and blue. Robert was initially disoriented, the enclosed feeling of the tunnel and the flashing lights making him feel like he'd been flipped upside down. He kept his head down and briskly walked to the main dance floor. House music pumped through the club's stereo system, though it was almost quiet compared to the blare that typically accompanied New York's nightspots. Scanning the room, Robert estimated about eighty people to be present, all of them men and all of them overweight.

"What can I get for you?" the shirtless bartender asked when Robert flagged him down. He ordered a vodka on the rocks and asked the burly Latino what tonight's theme was. "It's bear night, sweetie. You a chaser?"

Robert's face got hot with the realization that Effex was a gay club. When he didn't answer, the bartender just shrugged and went about making his drink. "That'll be five bucks, babe."

Once again making a mental note that this same drink would have been at least double back home, Robert handed over a ten and told him to keep the change. "Thanks! And no hard feelings about the chaser comment, okay? I didn't mean to make you uncomfortable or anything. My name's Scrappy if you need anything." Robert acknowledged him with a slight raise of his glass and a suppressed laugh at the ridiculous nickname and turned around toward the dance floor. He nearly smacked right into a tall, paunchy, caramel-colored man.

"Whoa, careful, snazzy!" the man said with a smile. Robert apologized and faced the opposite direction, sipping his drink and taking in the atmosphere. The dance floor was nearly empty, only a few men wildly dancing to the thumping music. Two mustachioed bald guys were sloppily making out in the center of the throng. Robert immediately felt a pang of discomfort and averted his eyes into his vodka.

"I like your suit," someone said, tapping Robert on the shoulder. Robert glanced over his shoulder at the man he'd nearly bumped into and nodded his thanks. The man grinned and moved closer. A smoky, woody scent emanated from him, Robert noticed. "Where'd you get it?"

"It's Tom Ford," Robert replied, still looking off in the opposite direction.

"Oh, okay," the man shouted, trying to be heard over the music and over Robert's indifference. "You must not be from around here, then."

"What makes you say that?" Robert asked, finally facing the unwanted conversationalist. "Guys in Albuquerque don't wear designer suits?"

There was a hint of annoyance in Robert's voice, but the man took it in stride. "No, they really don't. I don't even know where you would *get* a designer suit around here."

"A store, maybe?" Robert said, blank-faced, hoping to get rid of the guy.

"Well, now I *know* you're from out of town. Nobody in New Mexico is that rude. Is there a conference here or something?" The amused smile never left the man's face. Before answering, Robert looked him up and down. The guy was taller than him by a couple inches, so that put him around six foot. His upper lip was unshorn, but the rest of his face was smooth as could be, and the black hair atop his head was just a little longer than buzzed. The man's belly hung over his belt just slightly, straining the final button on his short-sleeved, green-and-yellow plaid shirt. If this were New York, Robert would have assumed the guy was a cop. He just had that beefy look about him.

Snapping himself back into the moment, Robert told the man, curtly, that he was not in town for a conference. "Aha! So you are from out of town!" the man exclaimed. "Whereabouts?"

"Look, I just really want to finish my drink and get back to my hotel. I'm here on business, and I have a long few days ahead of me."

"Okay, not a problem. Just trying to make conversation." The man raised his glass, something golden over ice, and clinked it against Robert's. "I'm Louis, by the way."

"Good to know," Robert said, draining his glass.

"What's wrong, man? I'm just trying to be nice here. Did I do something to offend you?" Despite his tone and questions, Louis's smile never faded.

Robert took a heavy breath. "No, you didn't. I'm sorry. Work has me here for a really big corporate merger, and I just got off a plane like an hour ago, so I'm just not in the best mood."

Louis signaled for the bartender and pointed to Robert's empty glass. "Let me get you another drink. You sound like you could use it. A little more libation, a little more music, and you'll be having fun in no time."

He clapped a meaty hand on Robert's shoulder, and Robert instinctively recoiled. "Whoa, sorry, buddy. Did I scare you?"

Straightening himself out and shaking off the tension that suddenly sprung up in his neck, Robert said, "No, you didn't scare me. I'm just not all that comfortable here yet."

Louis gave him a sideways look. Robert all but wilted under the gaze of his intense chocolate eyes. Then Louis's smile returned. "You're not out, are you?"

The color instantly drained from Robert's face, and he did not answer. "It's okay, no judgment here," Louis continued.

Feeling indignant, Robert took a step closer to Louis. "What makes you think I'm even gay? I'm here on business and don't know anything about the area. Maybe I just wanted a fucking drink."

Louis didn't seem intimidated or taken aback in the slightest. "Maybe." He raised an eyebrow and closed the gap between himself and Robert so that their faces were nearly touching. "But if you weren't gay,

I think you probably would've walked out when the bartender called you 'sweetie' and those two over on the dance floor started going at it."

Robert's eyes flitted over Louis's face, his resolve fading.

"Fine," he said, blinking to break the stare they were holding. "Yes, I'm gay. But I don't like to wear my sexuality on my sleeve, thank you very much."

With a laugh, Louis said, "Really? Because you're wearing a designer suit in the only gay bar on this side of town. No offense, but that's about as close to flamboyant as you can get around here, especially on Bear Night."

Noticing Robert's offended look, Louis tried to correct himself. "There's nothing wrong with that! I'm just saying, what might pass for straight wherever you're from isn't the same here. We're all a little more low-key out here in the desert."

Scrappy dropped off his second drink, and Robert took a quick sip. An uncomfortable moment of silence passed between them, Louis's gaze never leaving Robert.

"I'm not ashamed of it or anything," Robert admitted, feeling a bit looser with the booze hitting his bloodstream. "It's just difficult to be open about who I am in my profession."

"And what profession is that?"

"I'm a lawyer. A corporate lawyer. My department handles acquisitions."

"Sounds interesting enough," Louis said, taking a drink. "And where is this firm located?"

"New York City."

Louis seemed surprised. "Doesn't seem like there should be much problem with you being gay in New York. You all just legalized gay marriage and everything."

Robert took a deep breath, gathering his thoughts. "Yes and no." He took a large swallow of vodka, bending over the bar and trying to form the words he wanted to convey in the correct way. Louis leaned forward and rested his chin on his fist, listening closely. "It's not that it's a problem to be gay in New York. It's not. And of course there are gay lawyers." He took another drink. "But in my field, in corporate law, it's just different. We're supposed to be sharks. Corporate lawyers are mean and hard. If I were out at work, my colleagues and clients wouldn't see me that way. Does that make sense?"

"Sure, I get it. You think that being gay makes you soft."

"No, that's not it. *I* don't think anything like that. But others might, and that could hurt my career." Robert finished his drink with one last gulp and finally looked Louis in the eye. His tone was even and calm, as if he'd rehearsed and performed this same speech a dozen times before. "I'm just used to having to hide that part of myself, for my own good. I knew that choosing this career path also meant choosing to live in the closet, and I'm okay with that. I'm used to being aware of where I am and who I'm with at all times, just in case."

Louis's face fell a bit. "That sounds awfully tiring."

"It can be," Robert went on, fully embracing the lucidity brought on by the two vodkas. "But it's something you learn to live with. That's why I jumped when you touched me earlier. Just a knee-jerk reaction to being in public with another man. Literally."

They shared a melancholy-tinged laugh. "I really am sorry. I hope I didn't offend you," Robert said.

"It's okay. You can make it up to me."

"Oh? How?"

With a smirk, Louis said, "Tell me your name."

Robert smiled and laughed, a genuine one this time. "My name's Robert. Nice to meet you, Louis."

"Likewise," Louis said, raising his glass. Another vodka rocks found its way into Robert's hand. He matched Louis's gesture and tapped his glass with his own.

"Didn't mean to bring your night down, Louis. I had no idea what this place was when I passed it on the street. It wasn't in my visitor's guide at the hotel." Robert was feeling more relaxed, infinitely more comfortable. "Let's bring it back up. Tell me something interesting about yourself."

"Well, for starters, Louis isn't my real name. It's just a nickname I've gotten used to."

"Doesn't really sound like a nickname. How'd you end up with it? Middle name?" Robert asked, the liquor now flowing freely through him and filling his body with a warm rush.

"My real name is Lusio. It's Zuni for 'light.' I just tell people my name is Louis because it's easier to say." He shrugged.

"Zuni, huh? You're Native American?"

"Yeah. I didn't grow up on a reservation or anything. My parents were activists and got really into the politics of the time, so they kind of turned their backs on a lot of Zuni tradition while they were out traveling around the country. They left their families and most of the cultural practices behind, but I guess they still hung onto a little bit of it when they named me. They're proud but modern."

Robert squinted at Louis, or Lusio, seeing him through new eyes. His heritage explained the burnt caramel color of his roughened skin and the near blackness of his irises. He suddenly found the name "light" incredibly accurate as they inched closer together. Perhaps it was just the vodka or the close quarters, but a gentle heat emanated from Lusio. It comforted Robert, bringing him further out of his self-imposed shell.

They talked for hours, ignoring the increasing crowd around them and the music growing ever louder. Robert checked his watch every so often, remembering his meeting in the morning but not caring enough to leave. The conversation was easy, meandering, natural. Louis eventually led Robert to a high-top table in a back corner where it was a little quieter, a little less busy.

"How do you do it?" Robert blurted out at one point. "Isn't it hard to be a double minority?" He paused, realizing how the question must have sounded. "I'm so sorry. That sounded really racist."

Louis laughed. "It wasn't. And honestly, it's not really an issue. Like I said, my parents didn't really raise me traditionally Zuni. They taught me a lot about my heritage, obviously, but we didn't live as strictly as you might think. It helped that my parents were flower children, I'm sure. They were very open."

Robert nodded, signaling him to continue. "Even still, though, being gay probably wouldn't have been too big a deal if I'd been raised with the Zuni. When I was in high school and just starting to realize I was gay, I did a lot of research. The Zuni actually have a third gender, the *lhamana*." Louis's breath caught in his throat as he pronounced the word so foreign to Robert's ears. "We believe that one person can possess both male and female spirits, and those who do are highly respected by other tribe members. The male *lhamana* do things that women usually do, mostly creative things like pottery. That's how I became an artist. I figured I could embrace my Zuni heritage and still do something I liked and was good at."

"What kind of art do you do?" Robert leaned over his drink, his fourth vodka nearly forgotten in the pleasant haze of Louis's company.

"Sculpture and carving, mostly. I'd be happy to show you sometime," Louis teased, waggling his eyebrows at Robert.

"That would be great," Robert said, returning Louis's playful, sideways smile. "How about now?"

IT WAS after four in the morning when Robert and Louis finally made their way to Louis's car. After leaving Effex, Louis suggested they walk around for a bit. Despite his better judgment and the constant reminder in the back of his mind that he was in town for business, not play, Robert agreed. He took in the cool, dry air of Albuquerque at night, allowing the breeze to sober him slightly. Louis pointed out new condominiums being built, important business buildings, famous movie theaters, the stores that sold authentic native crafts as opposed to those that catered solely to tourists. Robert mentioned how nice and quiet the area was for being downtown, and Louis assured him this indeed was the bad area of the city.

"Have you been to the Village at night?" Robert asked incredulously. "This is practically a sleepy farm town in comparison." Louis admitted that he'd never been to New York, and Robert offered to show him around if and when he made the trip out.

By the time Louis turned his beat-up 1990s Chevy onto the highway, the effects of the alcohol in Robert's system had faded and were replaced by a similar, gentle warmth thanks to Louis's company. Robert sighed and rested his head against the window, watching the shapes of the desert emerge and disappear in the car's headlights. The silence was welcome.

Robert was suddenly being tapped lightly on the shoulder once again. He had fallen asleep, but Louis was waking him and pointing out the window at the landscape around them. Robert followed Louis's gaze and gasped.

The sun was rising above the desert, painting the beige sand and sepia rocks in gorgeous new colors. Streams of burnt reds, deep oranges, and cool violets stretched across the vast expanse. As far as Robert could see, the swirling colors melted into each other. The sun itself was neon, crimson melding into hot orange and magenta before reaching out its long yellow fingers across the scene. The scene was boundless, a kind of beauty Robert had never experienced before. It was like a painting come to life, steamy and shimmering in the break of a new day, a new beginning. Breaths refused to come, and tears welled behind his eyes.

"It's like the end of the earth," he whispered. Louis kept his gaze forward, nodding as if they'd just shared one of life's great secrets.

LOUIS'S APARTMENT was in the touristy part of Santa Fe, a little over an hour north of Albuquerque. He lived above a craft store where he sold his creations.

"It's the world's easiest commute," he joked. Louis unlocked the door and led Robert into his small, four-room apartment. The living room was decorated with colorful rugs and throw blankets, filled with geometric patterns and blocky humanoid shapes. The coffee table and cabinets were crowded with miniature animals carved out of smooth stone.

"These are what I make," Louis explained, picking up a carving of a frog. "They're called fetishes. They can be spiritual representations or ritual pieces. The frog was once used by the Zuni during droughts, when they would pray for rain."

Robert took the fetish from Louis and ran his fingers over it, admiring its careful craftsmanship. He returned it to its place and bent down to admire the others. Every imaginable color was represented by precious stones, and he was immediately reminded of the painted desert sunrise he'd just witnessed. He'd never seen such natural beauty before.

Suddenly, Robert seemed to snap out of his reverie. "What time is it?"

"About six," Louis said. "Why? Everything okay?"

"I have that meeting at one. I really should get back," Robert said, making a move toward the door.

"Relax," Louis encouraged, taking his arm. "You have plenty of time."

"No, really. You have a business to run, and I have a really important merger to make happen. I need to get back to my hotel and get some sleep."

"Stay here. The store doesn't open until ten." Robert gave him a nervous look, realizing he was sabotaging himself. His night with Louis had been one to remember, sweet and easygoing. He was inadvertently building his walls back up, the ones Louis had spent the entire night breaking down. Robert took a deep breath and moved away from the door, back into the living room.

"If you want to go to sleep, the bedroom's through there. I can stay out here," Louis said, gesturing to a leather couch. But Robert shook his head, resolved, and walked toward the bedroom. He sat on the bed, facing the open door to the living room, and patted the empty space next to him. Louis got the hint.

"We don't have to do anything, if you're not comfortable," Louis told Robert, his tone understanding. But Robert was tired—of work, of overthinking, of himself. Without another word, Robert placed his lips upon Louis's. The bristles of his mustache were soft, not at all what Robert had been expecting. He let himself sink into the bed, their lips moving in unison. Quietly, Robert removed his own shirt, exposing his thin, if not exactly toned, torso. Louis broke the kiss and ran his thick hands over Robert's bare stomach.

Robert began unbuttoning Louis's shirt, exposing a patch of curly black hair that stretched in a triangle from nipple to nipple and all the way down to his navel. Robert dug his fingers into the forest of matted fur as Louis finished the job of removing his shirt. He caressed Robert's face and urged him forward. Robert buried his nose in the hair and skin of Louis's chest and inhaled deeply the smell of wood, musk, and sweat. It was intoxicatingly masculine.

"What's that you're wearing? The woody scent. It's fucking amazing."

"Piñon. It's actually incense. I burn it while I meditate after my shower every day."

Robert sniffed and licked his way down to Louis's protruding belly. It was just big enough to fit in his palms, soft and heavy and tantalizingly fleshy. He pushed Louis back onto the bed so that he was lying on his back, his khakis tenting.

"Robert, really. We don't have to do this. I want you to be comfortable," Louis said. Robert smiled and looked directly into his eyes, cutting Louis off by placing a finger on his lips.

"No, I want to. Time to get out of my own head and live a little bit."

A FEW hours later, Robert watched Louis pad out of the shower toward the bureau covered in fetishes. The fleshy muscle of his ass swayed and shifted with each step, making Robert smile at the memory of how it had felt in his palms. Louis opened a drawer and removed a cone of incense. Placing it in an ashtray, he lit the cone, and the room was almost instantly filled with the smoky smell of burning wood and clay. Louis sat on the couch across from the bureau, still nude, and closed his eyes. His arms rested lazily on his legs, his wrists limp and hanging in front of his knees, his back ramrod straight, and his chest rising and falling evenly. Robert just watched the look of total peace on Louis's face, admiring the calmness and comfort that colored him. How easy he makes it look, Robert thought, to just *be*.

Slowly, Louis opened his eyes and looked at Robert. He smiled. "Good morning, Starshine."

"Is that my Zuni name?" Robert joked, rolling onto his back and stretching, exposing his naked body to Louis's gaze.

"No," Louis laughed. "It's from a musical. I thought you were gay. You should know that."

Robert laughed and sat up, taking inventory of the damage done hours before. Their clothes were mixed in different piles around the side of the bed, and the down comforter was kicked to the floor at its foot. One corner of the sheets had tugged loose and left the mattress exposed beneath. He reached for his boxer briefs and slid into them.

When he was fully dressed, he looked back up at Louis, who was hovering over the bureau, his head intently looking for something among the tchotchkes. Robert suddenly noticed what time it was. "Hey, it's twenty of! You have to open the store!"

Louis found what he was looking for, palmed it, and gave Robert a steady gaze and radiant smile. "No worries. I can drop you off at the depot, and you can take the Rail Runner back to downtown. Assuming you don't mind, of course." He crossed to another cabinet and pulled out a fresh pair of boxers and pants. Louis slipped the item in his hand discreetly into the pocket of the pants before stepping into them.

"That sounds fine. Will I be back in time for my meeting?"

"Absolutely. The ride's only an hour or so long, so you'll be back with enough time to grab some breakfast and a quick nap too."

When Robert returned a few moments later from the bathroom, Louis was standing by the door with his keys in hand. "Ready? The next train leaves in seven minutes, so we have to hurry."

They made the short drive to the depot, and Louis gave Robert instructions on where to buy his ticket and how to get back to his hotel once he got to Albuquerque. The car came to a stop, and Robert looked expectantly over at Louis.

"I know I'm only here for a few more days and that I'll be working a lot, but…." Robert trailed off, the words suddenly caught in his throat and his face flushing.

"I put my number in your phone while you were in the bathroom. And you know how to find me now." That vibrant smile shone brighter than the sun through the windshield, smothering Robert in its warmth.

"Thanks. I had a great time with you, Lusio." Louis barked out a short laugh at Robert's use of his tribal name.

"Speaking of," Louis began, "I want to give you something." He dug his hand into his pocket and produced the item he'd hidden there back at the apartment. It was a small blue figurine flecked with black, about the size of his thumb. "This is for you."

Robert reached out to take the totem from Louis. He turned it over in his hand, rubbing its smooth surfaces. He gave Louis a knowing glance and a shy smile when he realized what it was.

"It's a fetish," Louis explained. "A bear fetish. In my culture, the bear represents strength and courage. Many Zuni have them for protection. I wanted you to have this to remind yourself that you are strong and courageous and that you don't always need to guard yourself. Sometimes, there are other forces and other people that can protect you."

Robert could feel the hint of tears forming behind his left eye, but he fought it back. He leaned across the passenger seat and hugged Louis, breathing the smell of him and making a memory out of it. He muttered a thank-you into Louis's ear, knowing it wasn't nearly enough to truly thank him.

Louis broke the hug when he heard the bell dinging for the train to begin boarding. "Your train's about to leave. And it just brought a bunch of tourists in who will want some native crafts to bring home to their posh, New York apartment living rooms."

Robert laughed as he opened the car door. He ran around to the driver's side and kissed Louis through the open window. "Thank you for a lovely evening, Lusio."

"The pleasure was all mine, Starshine." Louis gave a wide grin and a slight bow of his head. "Now get on that train. And good luck with your meeting today."

"I'll call you after. Maybe we can get dinner tonight? Have a real, proper date?" Robert suggested, inching toward the yellow and red train that would carry him back to reality.

"I'd like that," Louis called, shooing Robert the remaining few feet to the platform. He threw his car into gear and turned out of the lot, waving to Robert in the rearview mirror.

Robert waved back with his right hand, his left shielding his eyes from the sun that suddenly shone more brightly than he'd ever known it to before.

JOHN AMORY is from New Jersey, yet is somehow not involved in the mob. He is part Italian, though. He has BA and MA degrees in English, and he (very infrequently) teaches college-level composition. Other jobs have included personal assistant, telemarketer, and dancing mouse (don't ask), but he's happy to now add "writer" to that list. He loves reality TV, drag queens, and Trader Joe's cookie butter.

Twitter: @JohnAmory

GoodReads: http://www.goodreads.com/JohnAmory

The Do-It-Yourself Guide to Getting Over Yourself
Robert B. McDiarmid

"The wound is the place where the light enters you."
—*attributed to Rumi*

I DARTED into the coffee shop to flirt with my coffee otter. It's a required part of gay life in San Francisco—we all have our coffee otter.

He was new to the city and managed to get the perfect twenty-something job. He was a barista at the local lesbian-owned coffee shop right off the trolley line and across from the muscle-bear gym. The look of the coffee otter is important—that perfectly trimmed, unnaturally beautiful, thick red-brown beard, sparkly yet simultaneously caramel-smooth brown eyes, big gold hoop earrings, and of course, zero percent body fat showing off his perfectly muscled-up body. I had never been offered the coffee-otter training program in my twenties. I went from pimply faced teen to middle-aged bitter queen in one swoosh of passing time.

Jason was constantly in flirt mode and probably had four or five husbands he was stringing along. Of course, I hated him for it.

"Hey, handsome! Where you been? I've been lonely without you," he said as I walked in the front door. "You got some sun—you were probably off at some tropical location with your big bear daddy getting some honey action."

"Pardon?"

"Ya know—bears makin' honey," Jason said, gyrating his hips like a porn star fucking. "Look at him, Rachel, he's glowing! Positively glowing."

"Bears… making… honey…," I repeated slowly, to make sure he knew how close to nausea I was.

"That's enough with scaring the customers, Junior," said the woman working the espresso machine, turning and winking at me. "Less honey—more money."

"Just don't get any in my coffee," I quipped.

Jason, looking dejected, handed me my coffee.

"Oh, sweetie—don't look so sad. See what you've done, Rachel? You've hurt the baby gay's feelings. Remember when life was all about romance, and everything was new like a fresh rain shower?"

"Okay—now I'm going to vomit," said Rachel.

"Don't think we haven't noticed your tan—and you haven't said a word about the hot men you met in Palm Springs," teased the coffee otter.

"Have you seen Barnum yet this morning?"

"No—he hasn't had the pleasure yet," replied Rachel, "but I'll keep an eye on Miss Barnum…. Jason is too new to be exposed to her majesty."

"I wouldn't worry. Apparently it's Chinese takeout season," I said, using air quotes.

Jason look confused, and Rachel looked repulsed. I winked at Jason and said to Rachel, "Later, Goddess!"

As I walked out of the coffeehouse on a typical dreary foggy morning in San Francisco, I realized the coffee otter was right. I was happy. Since the breakup, I couldn't remember the last time I'd put those words together. My friends had conspired to help me just get over it, once and for all.

GOING TO Palm Springs off-season in the height of the heat hadn't been my idea. My roommate had sent me off on a forced holiday.

Actually, he'd really outdone himself booking the hotel. Besides the hotel being full of hot men—in every direction—my room had a nice mountain view and felt very private.

The Baskervilles felt upscale and elegant, while also giving off that "expensive bathhouse with a pool" feel. Fortunately, both ideas fit well with my plans for the weekend. Why not have some scandalously hot anonymous sex with some hairy bruiser and then be able to wipe my mouth, go back to my room, and have four-star food delivered?

I was soon down by the pool under an umbrella, attempting to have a good time. I threw the self-help book down on the patio next to my pool chair and cursed.

"I need a cocktail!"

The hot desert sun beat down on my body as I walked to the bar.

"I need the foofiest, fruitiest thing you've got," I told the hairless twinkie boy behind the bar.

He blended the juices and lots of rum, handing me the tall, frothy concoction.

"This is all the self-help I need."

I surveyed the sun-worshipping flesh around the pool as I took the first coconutty sip. As I gazed around the pool, suddenly all of the scorched bathers were looking behind me at the hotel, right through me as if I were invisible.

Turning, I joined everyone getting a full view of the man who stepped out of the hotel and down the steps into the pool. He was in his forties, a little gray at the temple, and muscular. He had a Fu Manchu mustache and a few days' stubble. Emblazoned across the front of his yellow swim shorts, with the subtlety of a freeway billboard, was the word "pisspig" in dark black letters.

I took a short glance back at the men around the pool, quickly discovering who found the words enticing or scary. One queen leapt out of the pool as though its entire Olympic length were going to turn dark yellow at any instant. I let out a low giggle, which the bartender shared with me.

"Happens every time he comes out here, some queen figuring he's looking to start a watersports party or something. I'm just glad he's out here, honey, because we finally have ourselves some beef to look at."

As Mr. Pisspig strolled by the bar heading for the pool, I couldn't say that I disagreed with the bartender's appraisal. He looked like he worked out, but he wasn't a chiseled god. He had some scars, tattoos, and piercings here and there—which made watching his body even more interesting. Enjoying the view, I let out a relaxed sigh.

"Careful, hun, you'll gag on the straw," quipped the bartender, smiling, paying back my karma for dismissing him as a witless twinkie boy.

Watching Mr. Pisspig in the pool was fun. It was like being at an auction with everyone's paddles at the ready. Figuring him way out of my league, I walked past him displaying his backstroke form and right to my waiting lounge chair.

I extended my shade umbrella, as if the heat of the desert meant less if you were in the shade. Reluctantly, I retreated back into my book, punishing myself for having promised my therapist I would finish the book while on my vacation.

The title was *The Do-It-Yourself Guide to Getting Over Yourself.* Self-help books don't usually do it for me. They oversimplify and try to make light of what are truly life-changing dramas.

I mean—duh?—would I be reading a self-help book about getting over a relationship if this shit was easy? I'd been dumped—and dumped hard. I was not going to go down easy. I was going for full-tilt drama victim. How could he do this to me? Easy answer. He's a man.

Being dumped is a total bitch. It makes you feel as if the earth has been removed from underneath your feet. You can't feel anything. You find yourself in a total limbo, lost in space, and the sense of helplessness is the worst—nothing you can do. It hurts even more when you know you did nothing wrong, that you were good, but yet not good enough. He chose to take a path full of uncertainties, versus you.

So here I was on a weekend vacation to Palm Springs, drowning in sunlight and vodka, pretending it all never happened. So far, that recipe was simply a disaster.

The book suggested, "Forgiveness is a beautiful gift to yourself. It lets you imagine a time where the injury to your heart is healed and you can reach out to your ex without thinking destructive thoughts, but with an authentic hug full of love."

Oh really? An authentic hug full of love? Simon and Schuster actually gave someone an advance based on that paragraph? This perky author had obviously never met my ex.

I was having destructive thoughts, all right. I daydreamed of picking up the morning paper and seeing that a runaway Russian space satellite had fallen right on his home on Twin Peaks.

"Gay couple dies in horrible and over-the-top-painful melodramatic death as the Romanov Space Satellite fell from orbit, creating a steaming burned crater on Elliot Street where the two were hosting a mad orgy party...," I pretended the article would read. "Both suffering from fifth-degree burns over their entire bodies, the couple would have lived had not the ambulance carrying them to the hospital been hit by an out-of-control N-line train. The couple will be missed by the makers of Crisco and J-Lube."

Okay, so maybe the book didn't speak entirely to where I was at the time. I wasn't quite at the forgiveness stage.

I was officially in what I call the "find the son-of-a-bitch and run a highly sharpened misshapen tool up his ass" stage. I didn't even know the new Mrs. My-Ex-Boyfriend—but just being the new crown owner put him on the "must die soon" list right alongside His-Assholeness.

On top of it all? The new guy had the outright gall to be spectacularly adorable. This totally sucked. I mean, at least I could have been traded in for an ugly troll. No—they had to look gorgeous together. Fuckers!

Mine was the same old story—naïve country boy meets boy in big city, country boy falls head over heels for city boy, city boy says "Move to the city and build a life with me," country boy moves—and city boy breaks up with him just two months later, finds another life-friggin'-partner, and blahblahblah, dramadramadramadrama, country boy finds himself wondering a big, fat "what-happened?" and trying to figure it all out. That's me.

"City boy" was nowhere near as wonderful as the city, though. I did have to admit that moving to San Francisco was the best thing that had ever happened to me, even if His-Assholeness was one of the worst.

I was in love with San Francisco! I wasn't about to leave just because my heart was broken there. But I was still a bit dizzy living in the big city, which is why I found myself on this retreat to the desert over Fourth of July weekend. Of course, leave it to me to arrive on the warmest Fourth of July on *record* to be by the pool.

So there I was in 112-degree heat, sweating by the pool at ten in the morning, trying to absorb the best of the don't-be-a-codependent-sorrowful-sack-of-shit "advantages of self-love" from my book, when next to me on the patio appeared Mr. Pisspig, inches from my face.

Smiling broadly and dripping water from the pool, he towered over me. His swimsuit, now wet, revealed his religious preference and that he was just as hairy inside his swimsuit as outside of it.

"I love that book—it really helped me get through my last breakup. You're brave to read that sort of thing out here by the pool. Most guys wouldn't bring that kind of reading on vacation. Where are you from? Seattle? Vancouver?"

"My pasty white skin betrays me again," I said, laughing, sitting up and extending a handshake. "I'm Bill, um... uh... from San Francisco."

"I'm Arthur. Nice to meet you. I just love her. She has such insight.... Do you follow any of her advice?" he said, motioning toward the book.

"I guess. I used to meditate every morning," I replied, "and, well, I got distracted for a while and need to get back in touch with it."

"It's important—and I think you heal a lot faster when you don't let the negatives distract you from your focus."

"Now you tell me...," I said with another nervous laugh.

"When it's too hot later to be out here by the pool, what do you think? Perhaps we could have an early dinner? Or a drink? To discuss the book," he said. "Room 21. Ring me up later?"

"Um. Sure. Um," I said, staring at his shorts.

"Don't let the pisspig shorts bother you. It keeps the kids away... and it's just one of my many interests," he said with a big wink.

"Okay, Arthur.... I'll call around four or so?"

"Good. I'll look forward to it, Bill. I think I'm going to go find the gym. But I'll look forward to your handsome company later on."

He flashed me a big smile and walked away into the hotel, while all the other bidders on the poolside shot me that "You bitch!" look. I smiled and went back to my book, internally wondering why the hell he'd want my pasty white butt as a dinner date.

The sun very quickly became too much, and even the most adoring sun worshippers headed inside. I didn't get the mystique of somewhere that was so hot by noon that everyone had to move indoors.

My room was large, complete with a lovely deck and a sitting room. I was lying on the bed looking through the local gay rag when the phone rang.

Half expecting the front desk, I picked up the phone.

"Hello?"

"Have you gotten laid yet, Missy? Don't tell me no. No is not a word in the dictionary for you this weekend. You need to be screaming

'Do me now, Daddy!' from your balcony so the entire place can hear," yelled the voice in the receiver.

"No, Your Majesty," I said, recognizing my roommate, Barnum. I had a roommate named after the circus—I should have known better.

"Oh, honey, we can't have you coming back to the foggy city all mopey. Me and Miss Grace won't be able to handle it! She says 'Get laid or don't come home, I'll live with Aunty Barnum forever.'"

"My dog does not care about my sex life."

"Yes, she does. You are happier when you've had some ass—admit it!"

"You are so foul!" I chuckled at Barnum's accuracy. "But you are so right. Ass does make the day nicer. I just saw some nice ass by the pool, honestly."

"He's been looking at ass!" Barnum announced to someone on his end of the conversation.

"…and getting some of that ass, I hope," Barnum said, returning to our conversation. "Oh, I bet it was furry too. Ugh! How you can do anything with a furry ass I'll never know. The whole bear thing is so… so… woolly!"

"That's why I belong at the grown-up men's bar drinking scotch, and you belong at junior-high school-bus stops handing out Juicy Juice boxes."

"You are an evil bitch! My last boy was twenty-one. That's above the age of consent! But it's not about me today. Today is Friday, and it's about you. You're in Palm Springs on a sexual shopping spree. You've been there, what? Nearly twelve hours? And nothing. I'm ashamed of your gayness. Your mother would be so unhappy."

"You don't know my mother that well."

"I'm sure she knows deep in her heart how much ass makes her little Billy happy."

"Oh dear Lord."

"Okay, I'm going to go. Gracey and I are going shopping! I don't care what your therapist says—put down that awful, whiny book. You just need to dip the stick."

"You are so gross! Dip the stick? Where do you learn these?"

"We're outtie—we'll be checking in again. Did you get Furry Butt's number? I'll post updates to your Facebook."

"No! You will not."

"Don't make me make stuff up! I know your room number, and I'm not afraid to post it for everyone in Palm Fucking Springs to see.... Now get out there and work!"

The phone clicked.

BARNUM WAS a character. A sixty-four-year-old waiter at Neiman Marcus, he lived a fantasy life of moisturizer, starched shirts, and constant flirting. He had the fastest tongue in the West, with a comeback to every conceivable conversation topic. Barnum was old-school gay, and I'd had no idea what I was inviting into my life.

I had decided after moving out after "the breakup" that a roommate would do me some good, so I put up a Craigslist ad and told friends. Barnum came up to me at men's chorus rehearsal. At first I thought he was cruising me. A tall, classic Italian, he walked elegantly, actually floating across the floor. He had that dark kind of face that said he had to shave every ten minutes or he'd pop out the most luxurious, beautiful black beard.

He darted over, as subtle as always, and announced, "Your search for a roommate is over, love!" He finished with a startlingly strong hug, all for me. He had the kind of voice that destroys any romantic fantasy. Out of that big, husky Italian frame came an effeminate, girly, high-pitched voice at full tilt.

He handed me a manila envelope.

"References! Check them. But you'll only hear what a goddess I am and what a fool you'd be not to become BRFs." I learned later that meant "Best Roommates Forever."

From that point on, The Barnum Circus and I were roommates. We shared a lovely high-rise apartment we'd stumbled upon at a steal in the rent. I could sit in my boxers and share morning coffee with Miss Gracey while watching the fog mingle with the Golden Gate.

Once I learned not to put my bed on the same wall as Barnum's, everything had worked out great. Barnum had a constant stream of beautiful boys he'd "see" for a few weeks at a time.

"I've never been in a relationship that was open enough for me," he'd said.

Looking up from the newspaper, I said, "I don't think that's possible."

"You're just jealous!"

"Of you and the Cub Scout troop? I don't think so."

We'd dissolved into a smooth-men-vs.-hairy-men squabble and laughed at each other. He really had become a solid part of my life. This in itself was my first stroke of luck, as you always hear the horror stories of people with roommates. The Barnum Circus kept me company those first few months after Steve.

Okay, there you have it. His name was Steve. Barnum called the whole affair "The Steve-isode." It ranked up there with the horrible "Juan-tastrophe," or "The boy that Barnum let get too close."

"Those Spanish boys—you simply can't trust them. They'll have their tongue down your throat while stealing your wallet with their grubby little hands."

Barnum was currently convinced that the men of Asia were for him.

"I could eat Thai every night!"

At least living with Barnum, life was never boring. Besides, he came with a giant, 72-inch plasma television. So I could watch my sci-fi shows in the living room with the volume up a little as he "had Chinese takeout" in his bedroom.

Barnum had been in the bar the night the police raided the Stonewall Inn in New York in 1969—no kidding. He'd lived through Stonewall and the worst of the AIDS epidemic, which claimed many of his friends. He declared himself a dinosaur who had somehow lived past the comet's impact. He was making the most of life in the twenty-first century, no matter what.

After satisfying his lust for the evening, he'd grab the sorbet from the freezer and come finish whatever show I was watching with me on the couch. He found sci-fi confusing, mostly because he found it odd that nobody had sex in space.

"I mean, there's kissing and all that romantic garbage, but where is the look that lets you know that the couple really enjoys fucking? Okay—so bad-guy robots, plagues from outer space—I get it. But doesn't stress make people want to fuck even more? That these people aren't having all sorts of animal sex just isn't realistic. Poor creatures… it's a tragedy!"

Barnum had been very patient with my moods about my ex, but he put his foot down when it came to Celine Dion. The worst thing one can do when brokenhearted is listen to the radio. Every city has that station that plays "music to make you feel great," or basically, "the least offensive hits of the eighties, nineties, and today." These are the kinds of stations that you shouldn't be listening to *at all*, but are incapable of not listening to.

I know these folks mean well. Love songs are supposed to make us feel good. I think it has underpinnings of passive-aggressiveness, though, like Toni Braxton's "Breathe Again." Apparently not having her boyfriend causes her to question whether she'll ever breathe again, but not apparently enough that she can't reach the next Barry Manilow-style upward key change.

It's like pouring salt on the wound every time you turn the radio on, but you find yourself inexplicably drawn to it. I have nobody to blame for this but myself. I left the station programmed in my alarm clock like a ticking time bomb of punishment.

I was lying there asleep one moment—then came the almost silent *click* of the alarm clock, and the room was invaded with unexpectedly full-throttle Mariah Carey at 900 decibels above the pain level. "I can't liiiiiiiiiiiiiiiiiiiive, if living is without you...." To which Barnum banged hard on the wall and screamed, "Die already...."

I came home to a handwritten note on the kitchen table:

Roomy Rule-ette #949832—Mariah Carey isn't allowed before noon. That is the fourth morning in a row of helpless divas blasting low-self-esteem, feel-sorry-for-yourself pop music. It's like you have the tragic diva channel set on your alarm clock. Not good, sweetie.

I'd rather hear your alarm do the garbage-truck backing-up noise than hear this stuff so early in the morning. As for Celine Dion, she's on the permanent ban list. Don't make me hurt you! Thanks, Auntie B.

THE INN described itself as "The upscale gentleman's retreat in the desert."

"What that means is lots of rich horny studs who'll buy a real good breakfast after banging you silly all night long!" Barnum had screeched. "It looks real nice. You can get away and relax. And stop thinking about Steve and just have some fun for a change."

He was, of course, absolutely right. The Baskervilles was a beautiful spot. All arranged around an azure blue pool, with lots of privacy if you wanted it—and wide-open, clothing-optional cruising if you wanted that too. In the evenings they had a DJ poolside, and it was the social place to be in the strip of resorts. Beautiful men were everywhere in small swimsuits or nothing but the telltale armband of a party-only guest who wasn't staying at the hotel. I was simply trying to smile and not look like Eeyore from *Winnie-The-Pooh*.

With a surrendering sigh, I spent the rest of my afternoon back in my self-help book, trying to imagine a world where I could forgive someone for setting off an atom bomb in my heart. It was tough going.

I looked up at the clock around four and decided to call Arthur.

The phone rang and he answered.

"So the pisspig shorts didn't ruin the first impression. I'm glad."

"Not at all, Arthur. How about we go out for some Mexican?"

"El Mirasol?"

"Yeah—the front desk recommended it to me. Have you been there?"

"I'd give up sex for a month for their mole sauce."

"Wow. That good, huh?"

"How's about I come by your room about five thirty, and we'll head out?"

"Perfect. I know it'll be my great pleasure."

We hung up, and I lingered over the phone before setting down the receiver. Laughing, I went in and took a shower.

"Okay, Bill," I thought to myself. "There you have it. A real date. A dinner date. With a pisspig."

The knock came promptly at five thirty, and I opened it to find Arthur in a green Hawaiian shirt and beige unlabeled shorts. His eyes were an intense hazel green with an olive undertone and black specks. Mesmerizing behind his glasses, which were slightly tinted as if to mask those eyes' effects. I had put on a pink polo and beige shorts.

"Well, so much for us going subtle this evening—we're a gay pair from a hundred yards," I said as we headed for the elevator.

"Bill, this is Palm Springs. We're going to be a gay pair at any distance. And at our age, we'll be the young boys out on the town! Chicken, even!"

We laughed our way to the restaurant, and the maître d' knew Arthur on sight.

"Señor!"

"Gomez! *Cóm'está?*" replied Arthur.

Arthur and Gomez talked vibrantly in Spanish until Gomez suddenly stopped midsentence and turned to me.

Scanning me head to toe, he said, "Arturo always brings a book and hides at a corner table." He motioned to Arthur. "So you must be much more interesting than any book!"

Gomez ushered us in to a table on a patio. The restaurant was built square around a lovely patio in the center filled with palm trees and other desert plants.

At one end a small woman sang with her guitar. Arthur ordered a tequila on the rocks, and I ordered a strawberry margarita.

"I have to say, this is the first time one of those bleeding-heart, woe-is-me relationship books got me a dinner date."

"Bill, I don't see it that way at all," Arthur said, smiling and dipping a chip. "You were the only one at the pool who looked interesting. It's true! I've been at the hotel now for three days, and everyone is so intent on getting laid that they leer at me like I'm at the beef counter at Lucky's.

"Then I saw you reading her book and, well, that's all it took. You might watch out for Mitch, the bear in the spandex. He's been after me like a cat in heat, and once he knows we've been to dinner, you'll be 'the other woman.' Those girls hate competition."

"I didn't realize it was that cutthroat around the pool."

"Oh, it really isn't—but like anything else queer, there are guys who simply take it too goddamn seriously.... So—how far are you out of the relationship that went bad?"

Talk about getting to the point!

"About seven months. On what was supposed to be our first anniversary, he announced he'd met someone else. But, whatever," I said, looking down into the chips.

"Men can be real sucky sometimes, huh?"

"Most of the time, actually...."

"Listen," he said, reaching across the table and taking my hand. "I didn't mean to start on a downer. I'm sorry. I'm not much for small talk. I'm being nosy."

"No.... I mean, yes. Well, shit. No. What I mean is that I'm really working at letting go, because I really don't have a choice. I realized that I'd just lost myself in wanting him so much. I mean, to the point where I couldn't imagine myself without him, and I guess I should have," I said, trying to smile.

"Everything is a learning experience, Bill. From that kind of hurt to flirting with a guy in pisspig shorts at the pool, I can tell looking at your face that you've learned a lot from this."

"The only thing I want to figure out is why it was so much fun to love him before he became an asshole—or rather, was he always an asshole and I just didn't want to admit it? It's all a fucking mess…."

Arthur laughed.

"See? Already learning…."

"So Arthur, besides cruising sad sacks from The Recently Dumped Club in your pisspig shorts, what's your story?"

"Well, I was here in Palm Springs to attend a desert conference with an organization I belong to, and I decided to work my tan with some actual rays of the sun instead of the damned booth. So I stayed an extra week.

"I run a small life-coach business out of my home in Taos, that's New Mexico, and I run a website for life coaches and shamans to share information and journeys."

"Oh," I replied. "I've been to Taos, when I was in high school. What an amazing place!"

"Ah, another Boy Scout, eh?" he quickly replied. "I visited there in high school with the Scouts, dare I say a few years before you, and moved there shortly afterward. It is a very spiritual place."

"Sorta like Palm Springs, without Mitch the Bear stalking you twenty-four seven?"

"You could say that, yes," Arthur said, chuckling. "I have a retreat center there for gay men, and I have found a very spiritual place for myself. I'm learning to live a life where I no longer run around frantically reacting to things. Things are pretty peaceful."

"Frantically reacting to things is my world! I'm in marketing," I said, and we both laughed. "Arts marketing. Which in San Francisco is several full-time jobs. I specialize in finding grant money for arts organizations and training people how to get state and federal money for their arts groups. My big work right now is arts in schools, since the government seems to be losing interest."

"That's very lovely, Bill. Work you can be real proud of, I bet."

"You too! I mean—that's big stuff, helping people learn to chill out. That's a big job, although I can't imagine having an entirely gay clientele. So much drama...," I said, growing silent again and staring into the chips.

Arthur waved his hands over the chips.

"Looking for a sign in the tortillas?"

"Sometimes I just want to wish away all the drama," I said, allowing him to catch me wandering away from the conversation into my own head. "It weighs on me, this horseshit. I used to be a happy person, dammit. I owned a home, my dog had a yard, I smiled, I got involved. Now I live vicariously through a roommate, watch lots of sci-fi, and feel sorry for myself. Okay, I need to quit being Mr. Poutypants and turning this into a therapy session."

"It's okay if you want to talk...," said Arthur.

"The thing is, Arthur, I don't want to talk anymore about it. I've been living it full-time for half a year now. I even dream about this shit. How fucked up is that? No, I'd rather not talk about him or the whole fucked-up thing. Gosh, I say 'fuck' too much. How embarrassing!"

Gomez stepped back to the table, and we hadn't even opened the menus. He set down our drinks and silently disappeared again. Here we were, in a giant restaurant, and it felt like we had our own private space.

"Okay," I said, flipping through the menu. "You said the mole sauce was worth giving up sex for. So I should be careful ordering."

Arthur replied, "Well, sometimes food heals much better than a simple blow job. But if one of us has the mole today...."

He leaned in and whispered warmly against my ear, "We can always wake up next to each other in the morning and have sex tomorrow."

He remained nuzzled in against my ear, and I giggled like a schoolgirl. I lifted my margarita glass in a toast, with a big flirtatious smile on my face. It looked like both Barnum and I would get what we wanted after all. "To tomorrow, then?"

Our glasses clinked together.

"To tomorrow...."

Robert B. McDiarmid, a self-described disciple of Henry David Thoreau, is both a writer and an activist. He works very hard to live an uncomplicated life in complicated times.

Robert resides in Palo Alto, California, with his husband, David, and their terrier companion, Miss Kate. An avid cyclist, he has participated several years in AIDS Lifecycle, a 550-mile bicycle ride from San Francisco to Los Angeles, and the Friends for Life Bike Rally from Toronto to Montreal, Canada. In the spirit of giving back to the community, the entirety of his royalties are donated back to HIV/AIDS charities.

Robert is proud to be the author of both *The House of Wolves* from Lethe Press and the much anticipated *Brief Moments*, a collection of short stories soon to be released by Amazon.com. He can be found at http://www.robertmcdiarmid.com, on Facebook at https://www.facebook.com/thoreauinsf and on Twitter @thoreauinsf.

He further authors a healthy cooking blog with recipes and instructional videos at http://www.bobscooking.com. Robert won a San Francisco Bay Area television cooking competition, *The Big Dish*, in December 2013.

Hunting Bear:
A Fairy Tale with a very Hairy ending
Edmond Manning

Chapter 1: Pitter Patter

GATHER ROUND to hear the tale of a twink who dared enter the urban forest, a young buck named Tyler who trusted his best pal Derrick to be his bear guide, leading Tyler to his one and only hairy love. Tyler and Derrick themselves had tussled once, their own night in the forest, sweating and fucking and grinding together, whimpering and grunting, and together they rained upon the forest and each other a splattering of goopy mess, and then reveled in happy exhaustion.

But it was only one night in the forest.

Who knows why?

Who ever knows?

Their chance for love turned into friendship, and it is a hard magic that can transform a friendship back into love. With Derrick's assistance, Tyler the Twink (though he disliked that name) crossed the forest, light of step, hunting for bears, looking for love. But he did not seek out all bears.

One bear specifically.

The Great White Bear, though the man was not technically white, but that's what they called him throughout this Midwestern kingdom, a flavor named Chicago.

And in this kingdom the gays were plentiful, supple and succulent, beefy-strong men who had grown winter hair on their chests, then burned dark in the summer sun. In this kingdom, oft called the city of broad shoulders, its residents also enjoyed the comes-with-the-broad-shoulders features. In other words, it was also a city of fat muscles, engorged biceps, and thick waists. Some of them enjoyed a black treasure trail leading from navel to below, wispy black smoke promising fire destined for ignition. The tree-trunk thighs, chunky butts wrapped in ass-grabbing jeans or maybe wrapped in lazy sweats on a Saturday morning in Boystown. These were the blond farm boys come from Illinois' hamlets. The dark-haired jocks, sweating on their way home from the gym. Balding muscle daddies with a beer belly. Bronze-skinned men standing tall, pumping gas, guzzling beer, holding hands. Men of many colors, thicknesses, and laughs, this kingdom was ripe with these men, strong and big-jawed, a city of bears, otters, and many more forest creatures besides.

Tyler the Twink (who honestly quite resented that name) discussed his quest while dropping off his dogs.

"It's Bear Coffee," Tyler said. "Every Thursday night the bears take over a coffee shop on Broadway. I'm hoping he comes tonight. He has to. I don't have any other leads. I don't even know his name."

Looking down at the dogs, Derrick said, "I don't remember if they're supposed to get a half cup or a cup. Why didn't you feed them at home?"

"I was out of puppy chow. I picked some up on the way over. Don't worry, I wrote it down. Everything. The emergency vet and stuff like that."

"Wouldn't I just call you?"

"Sure, but *after* you call the emergency vet. If it's an emergency. Just don't let them eat plastic off your floor and there won't be an emergency. No chocolate."

Derrick said, "Duh."

Derrick and Tyler had recently crossed a threshold in their friendship, the will-you-watch-my-dogs level, which, as you well know, is something. It is not airport-pickup-at-2:00-a.m. friendship, but Tyler trusted his beloved pups to no other human being, even for a few hours. Derrick and Tyler's fling had been eight months earlier, from which had sprung a tentative friendship, then a more solid friendship, evolving to the point where either could call to announce "I'm not having a great day."

On those days where the kingdom had worn them down, they listened to each other and counseled as best they could. Tyler's advice was often "You're smart. You can handle this and anything they throw at you." Derrick's advice ran along the lines of "You're strong, Tyler. Drink some water. Eat an orange. Maybe a good night's sleep." In fairness to this tale, sleep was Derrick's answer to everything, to stress, to credit card bills, to unrequited desire and occasionally even being tired.

The dog threshold-crossing had literally occurred three minutes earlier when Pitter and Patter, Tyler's miniature pugs who had tentatively crossed over Derrick's kitchen doorway, sniffed their way cautiously into Derrick's second floor apartment. And when Derrick saw their confused hesitation, how long it took for them to actually get inside, and then their accidental skittering across the kitchen linoleum, Derrick's last bit of dog-sitting resistance melted. In fact, he found himself surprisingly anxious for Tyler to leave because he wanted to watch pug antics as they explored his home.

Truly this was a surprise, because Derrick rarely wanted Tyler to leave.

"Luck and cranberries," Tyler said.

The phrase is not worth explaining, gentle reader, just an affectionate good-bye based on a four-month-old joke. You have those intimacies with friends. You know how it goes.

"Good luck," Derrick said vaguely, his eyes following Pitter and Patter's pitter-and-patter pawing around the kitchen, unsure in their steps, occasionally bumping into cupboards. It was adorable.

"Wait," Derrick said, looking up. "Where are you going? Meet who?"

"The guy. The guy I told you about on the phone."

Derrick searched his memory and remembered he had heard a description earlier in the week, a raven-haired man of solid jaw with a tight buzz cut. A shock of black hair pointing straight up. Some slight gray on the sides, suggesting a man in his late thirties or early forties.

Derrick said, "I remember. You saw him near the new Starbucks downtown somewhere."

"Yeah, the construction site in the Loop," Tyler said, already lost in numerous fantasies. "I don't know his name. But he was saying good-bye to his work buddies on the site as I approached, and then I walked behind him for a block and a half until he stopped into that piano bar, the Zebra Lounge."

"Your puppies are gnawing a kitchen table chair," Derrick said, falling in love. "Do they really think they can eat a chair?"

Tyler was used to men falling in love with his puppies, so he ignored his pal. He said, "I had intended to shop for new work shoes, but instead I ducked into the bar because I desperately wanted to see the construction guy kiss another man. Or maybe he didn't know it was a gay piano bar? He drank two beers and left. He tipped the piano player. The whole place even got campy once or twice and he sat there grinning. So, he *knew*. He's definitely gay."

"Could be a straight guy who likes piano music."

"But he talked to someone," Tyler said. "Made two minutes of chitchat with this older guy, a bear with a bushy red beard. After the construction guy left I waited five minutes and then approached Red Beard and asked if I had seen him and his buddy together somewhere, leaving it vague and open, and he said that he barely knew the construction guy who just left. Someone—"

Derrick picked up the thread. "Someone he occasionally saw at Bear Coffee. Right. I remember this now."

"Yes, which is tonight." Tyler checked his watch. "Bear Coffee starts in thirty minutes. I've decided he's going to show up. He has to. I think I'm in love."

Derrick said, "Good. It'll only take you twenty minutes to get there from here. Come in here and talk to me about your dogs so I don't fuck this up. Tell me how to get them to stop fighting or chewing and stuff like that."

Tyler stepped beyond the entryway and smelled his way through the kitchen. Derrick liked to bake things. Tyler liked to sample things. But there was no baking smell tonight, just the reassuring stack of pans and open cookbooks with scribbles in them, doodles, and phone numbers. The whole house felt like you could scribble a phone number anywhere, on a wall, in a magazine cover, which is not to say that Derrick's home was grubby, but it had this comfortable and worn feeling to it, items in wrong rooms but not messy, just really, really comfy. Open paperback books facedown on the dining room table and Derrick's reading glasses on top of a stereo speaker for no apparent reason. Tyler had once visited and found fresh tulips in the bathtub. When asked,

Derrick insisted he was using the bathtub as a "big vase" and invented a ridiculous statistic instead of admitting he forgot why he put them there.

Derrick's living room furniture was plush, two overstuffed navy couches specifically engineered for maximum nap-taking comfort, fat pillows, and a wolf-fur throw rug so realistic you could imagine a naked wolf at the door demanding its return. But the wolf would be shit out of luck; the pelt was synthetic. Mechanical line drawings of bridges hung in sturdy brown frames on the patterned-wallpapered walls, boring illustrations only an engineer could love.

The pups eyed the navy couch and each other, growing their resolve to scale the front, to reach that naptastic summit they intuitively knew peaked far above them. This couch was their Mount Everest.

Tyler said, "Don't let them on your furniture. You'll never get them off."

He snapped his fingers at Pitter, then Patter, and they ceased their scheming, though anyone could tell they resented the master's interference. In defeat, they padded the Berber carpet, a masculine tweed that looked like a browned cookie warm from the oven but—as the pups discovered—did not taste like one.

Derrick collapsed on the couch, lying on his stomach, and asked questions about the dogs, dragging his hand along the floor so the pups could race up, smell him, lick his salty skin, and run away. Tyler never tired of chatting about them so he stayed longer than intended, trapped by the comfort, the ease of Derrick's home, until he checked his phone and realized he would be late.

He hopped up and said, "Oh."

Derrick did not move from the couch. "You're fine. You don't want to be the first to show up anyway."

Tyler said, "How do I look?"

Derrick said, "You look good."

"Duh. I always look good. But do I look *great*?"

Derrick raised himself on one arm and studied Tyler head to toe. He liked Tyler's short copper-colored hair, more brown than red, the natural curl that followed the shape of his ear. He liked Tyler's eager blue eyes, their surprise at so many things and how often they expressed natural curiosity. He liked the big Adam's apple, a flaw in Tyler's beauty but Derrick liked it anyway, along with his lithe body and his faded salmon T-shirt tucked into jeans, jeans that were probably named by someone famous.

Derrick spoke with an inflection that did not register with Tyler. "You look great."

Tyler nodded, satisfied. Derrick would tell him if a hair was out of place. They were buddies.

Derrick said, "Thirty-seven percent of all kitchen accidents happen in coffee houses. Be careful."

"That one didn't even make sense."

"They can't all be winners."

"Thanks for watching the boys. C'mere, you hooligans, and give Dad a kiss good-bye."

They trotted to Tyler.

Derrick said, "Bring me back a cookie or a blond brownie or something."

Tyler said, "Not doing that. Why don't you bake something?"

Tyler stood and touched his pockets to make sure he had his phone, keys, and money clip. A wallet could make your ass look chunky, and tonight was too important for Tyler to look less than his best. He dropped and kissed his pugs good-bye. Again. He thanked Derrick and started to promise he would return at a decent hour, but if his fantasy man wanted to grab a beer after Bear Coffee, wouldn't he go?

As Tyler crossed the apartment toward the front door, Derrick spoke from the couch. "Seriously, bring me a cookie. The desserts cookbook I like has small print and I can't find my reading glasses."

Over his shoulder, Tyler said, "Your glasses are on the stereo speaker. The one behind the big plant."

"Thank you," Derrick yelled lazily, but Tyler had already exited the back door. Derrick didn't bother to retrieve his glasses. He could feel the dogs licking the palm of his hand as they plotted how to use his dangling arm as a ladder to the pleasures of napping above.

Derrick said, "Okay boys, eighty-one percent of all cute pugs are trained to walk toward the door when they have to take a dump. Yes? Please tell me the stats are that high or higher."

Pitter and Patter licked their lips.

TYLER CRUISED Derrick's Andersonville neighborhood in the traditional sense of cruising, walking briskly, admiring the brownstones, noting the green trees showing off their newly minted June leaves. He loved Derrick's neighborhood for its classic Chicago charms and working-class beauty, including a grubby pastry shop with choco-raspberry cupcakes to die for, four nearby Thai restaurants, and two Indian places that delivered when Tyler and Derrick watched bad movies and felt lazy. An assortment of essential businesses made leaving the neighborhood almost unnecessary. Tyler walked to the nearest El stop at a fast clip, but not so fast that he'd arrive sweaty. He knew how to pace himself. He didn't mind if the construction worker arrived sweaty, though. He would not mind that at all.

Tyler worried about some other bear or twink, otter, *any* forest creature sighting his find, his piano-loving construction worker, because when you are stunned by masculine beauty, you worry others will see the beauty too, even though this beautiful person may have been exploring the kingdom for many years before you came along. But everything changed because you're on the hunt now. This is *your* find. Irrational as it was, Tyler felt he must reach the construction man before any other lurker at Bear Coffee noticed him. He knew that was silly. He hurried anyway.

Tyler allowed matrimonial fantasies to knit themselves together, mostly imagined scenes of an unbridled wedding night, getting pounded hard by the large-dicked construction worker who still, as of the wedding night, did not have a name. The large dick was invented by Tyler. Dick size also remained unknown.

Bear Coffee drew forest creatures twice a week in the kingdom of Chicago, a beverage-based gathering of hairy beasts and those who admired hairy beasts. The in-bears knew Thursday coffee was the place to be seen and see. After all, the lame alternative Monday night coffee was defiantly scheduled following some name-calling, man-stealing drama from which no creatures in the forest are immune. Monday night Bear Coffee was not well attended.

The Thursday night crowd could not be contained at a national chain coffee house, for while the chain's greedy accountants would have enjoyed the revenue, the sheer forest of stocky men who showed up caused an occupancy problem. The bears stood still, blinking vacantly on caffeine highs, expecting the coffeehouse patrons to navigate around them. Which they did, but with protruding bellies and flirting, jostling men, it was not easy. So the bears congregated at an independent coffee house, dominated its Thursday evenings, and congratulated themselves for patronizing "the little guy" while simultaneously complaining about the available dessert options.

Tyler arrived in plenty of time.

The beach-house-themed coffeehouse was wide enough for a roving pack of bears to spread out, and they did, thirty or forty of them, many wearing flannel hoping it would award them marks of distinction and originality. They wore boots not necessary for warm weather, jeans cutoffs, and tight shirts, and some wore suspenders. And yes, some men dressed to impress but plenty did not. On the other end of the spectrum, some men dressed exactly as they pleased, which was obvious, because a man trying to get laid would not wear a shirt that ugly unless it was perfect and comfortable.

After ordering his chai tea, Tyler surveyed the room and thought about why he liked bears. He liked the thickness. The thickness of arms and a bit of a gut, the snoring, the unencumbered sex, the willingness to lie around and do nothing. He knew why he was here.

Most men seemed to enjoy themselves just fine, chatting affably and making new friends.

Tyler was noticed, as he knew he would be, a twink in his midtwenties, fresh faced and dressed just this side of preppy. Despite the slightly oversized Adam's apple, Tyler was handsome with sharp features but soft in the face, too, the face of a man you would like to stroke after great sex and say, "I like you. I really do."

Tyler knew this. He nodded bashfully and kept his eyes downcast like a dewy maiden whose father owned a large tract of land, possibly with a magic beanstalk. Dewy as he might like to project, Tyler was no stranger to the beanstalk, having loved on it in a variety of positions, his favorite of which was doggie style. He didn't want to encourage conversation as he waited for his future husband to show. But he didn't want to be rude either, and he found several of these men attractive, or they would be attractive, if not for the construction worker whom, Tyler assumed, would ride up on horseback any moment.

All creatures in the forest know that moment when eyes meet and mutual attraction is revealed. It can be quickly masked, dismissed, or never acted upon. But the fierce honesty in that mutual attraction cannot be hidden, not for the first second when a sharp intake of breath reveals the brain's excited realization, "You might be the one." All creatures know that recognition. Conversely, all creatures of the forest also know when it is not returned. All creatures of the forest know how much that hurts.

So Tyler was scanned and dismissed by several bears who wanted him but did not sense his interest. He was dismissed by other bears who did *not* want him and frowned at him, irritated by his presence at Bear Coffee. A few bears tried to socialize with him, neither caring about his twink-ttractiveness nor wondering why he had come, because these bears liked to make friends and talk to people different from themselves. Tyler engaged in conversation, little more than polite banter, and took the time to learn a few names.

But he never let his conversation distract him from his true purpose that night, finding and winning Mr. Construction, his future husband. His future *husbear*, a term he had heard moments earlier in meeting someone new. He hoped he would not have to use the word *husbear* at any point in his life. He did not feel he could say it without cringing.

While trying to remain discreet, Tyler scanned the crowd relentlessly.

"He's not here," said a voice suddenly at his side.

"He may not show tonight," said another voice, deeper than the first.

"I don't think this is a soy latte," said a third voice.

Tyler had just broken free from a cluster of antiquing bears and now found himself surrounded by three new men. Their approach was stealthy, like woodland fawns.

"I'm Dougee," said the youngest, a cub in his late twenties, thick around the waist with strawberry red hair.

"I'm Roger," said the Latino muscle bear, thick around the biceps with a jet black hairline, slowly retreating.

"I really don't think this is a soy latte," said the third man, who turned and walked back toward the counter.

He would eventually be introduced as Larry, though many referred to him affectionately as "Daddy." He was thick around the neck, affable and honest, though not happy with his alleged soy latte at the moment.

Tyler professed ignorance. "Who's not here?"

"Someone you had hoped to meet," said Roger, scanning the crowd. "A man you lust for."

"But he didn't come," said Dougee, tipping his covered cup toward Tyler. "At least not yet. But you'll stick around for the next two hours in case he does. Because you don't know his name."

Tyler frowned. "How do you know that?"

"We're psychic," Dougee said with an unabashed grin, meaning he lied and didn't mind Tyler knew it.

"You have the look," Roger said, shaking hands. "And you're obviously a chaser. It was Larry who spotted you a second ago while getting our drinks. He knew your story."

At that moment, Larry returned triumphantly. "I was right. It wasn't soy. They're remaking it. Hi. I'm Larry."

"I'm Tyler."

Roger said, "I was just telling Tyler that you knew his story."

"Yes," said Larry. "Here's my guess. You saw this hot guy, hairy, muscular, maybe chunky. You wanted him. You lusted for him. You figured out he was gay and recognizing he was a bear, you hoped he'd show up for Bear Coffee."

Tyler bit his lower lip.

"It's okay," Dougee said. "We're not psychic. But you're new to Bear Coffee and you're obviously looking for someone so it's not that much of a stretch, really. You're hoping he shows up."

"Busted," Tyler said. "Am I blushing? I bet I am. Wow, you guys are good."

"We are psychic," Roger said and nodded seriously.

It was Larry who said, "Don't scare the kid, Roger. Jesus. Is this your first bear crush?"

"No," Tyler said, "not at all. I always liked bears. It's who I'm attracted to."

Tyler thought about the night he met Derrick, heard Derrick's hearty laugh across the bar, and the very moment when he locked eyes with Derrick, the instant fire of their mutual attraction revealed. Derrick's laughter with friends, the crinkle around his eyes, the square, chunky face and his hot, stocky body. Tyler admired the bell curve of Derrick's stomach, and within hours he found himself kissing it, loving it while Derrick groaned and massaged Tyler's skull.

"So why haven't we seen you at Bear Coffee prior to tonight?"

"I dunno," Tyler said. "I don't date much. I mean, I will strike up a conversation with a guy I find hot. I've had some really fun one-night stands with sexy bears. But I guess coming to something like this intimidated me because I figured I would stand out. I thought maybe I'd get dirty looks or something for not being a bear myself. And to be honest, I *have* gotten some dirty looks. A few nice guys said hello, but some guys turn away from me. I'm hairless. I'm not bear material."

"Plenty here who like that," Larry said, his gaze roving up and down Tyler's body.

"You'd be surprised who's into twinks," Roger said, smiling generously and making hard eye contact.

"He must be someone special," Dougee said, "to get you to Bear Coffee. Who is he? Maybe we know him."

This struck Tyler as odd, as the kingdom of Chicago contained thousands of gay men, but then again, perhaps the bear subculture was not as broad as Tyler supposed. He hesitated because if these three men did know the object of his affection, they might try to dissuade him from his quest. Tyler wasn't sure how much to reveal.

Tyler said, "I don't know his name. We've never spoken. I'm not even sure he comes to Bear Coffee."

"We're here every week," said Roger, who had not broken eye contact. "If he comes, we'd know who he is."

"Thank you," Larry said, to the coffee delivery employee. "It's definitely soy? Okay, thank you."

"What does he look like, this mystery man?" Dougee said. "Give us the story. Hung?"

Although he was not particularly attracted to Tyler, Dougee liked meeting new people and flirting with them.

Tyler decided to risk everything and did his best to describe the wall of muscle he had encountered, describing his jaw, the black stubble, the olive-skin complexion. When the vague description did not reveal an immediate match, Tyler said, "He works construction."

"Him," Dougee said knowingly. "It's him."

"Yes," Roger agreed. "He roped in another young stud."

"The Great White Bear," Larry explained. "We know who you're talking about now."

Tyler chuckled and said, "That's his nickname, huh?"

"Yes, obviously," Dougee said. "He's hung. Like, huge."

"Hung," Roger said, making sure to study Tyler's eyes when saying the word aloud. "The rumor is ten inches. Maybe more."

Tyler nodded sagely but didn't want to reveal that this mattered to him.

"But that's not why they call him the Great White," Dougee said. "Not at all. That's not why."

"It's because he's like the whale in *Moby Dick*," Larry said. "Unattainable. He doesn't sleep with anyone. Nobody knows how to reach him. He comes to Bear Coffee once in a while and he's nice, even to the ones who throw themselves at him. But he never goes home with anyone, and he doesn't seem interested in exchanging phone numbers. Not even for casual friends. He's never unkind and he remembers our names from week to week. But he doesn't really make friendships outside of the events. Nobody gets him."

Dougee said, "His name is Mike. Or Big Mike. But we call him the Great White Bear. The longshot. The whale no one can bring down."

"You might be his type," Larry said. "Because I don't think he's into other bears. Have we seen the Great White with twinks?"

"I would imagine you're many men's type," Roger said.

Even Tyler was finding it difficult to not acknowledge Roger's sexual come-on, so blatant it could no longer be called innuendo, so it had best be labeled exuendo.

"I know nothing about him," Tyler said, determined to ignore Roger's exuendo as much as possible. "Only the bit about him working construction."

"He's not here," Dougee said, scanning the crowd. "But Big Mike only comes sometimes."

"Yes, sometimes," Larry said. "Maybe tonight."

"Do you guys know anything about him?" Tyler said with raised hopes.

"Many things," Larry said.

"A few things," said Roger the muscle bear.

"One or two things," Dougee said, "one or two. But how do we know you're sincere about bears? I've seen plenty of guys like you at Roscoe's and in Boystown, flitting around. Why should we tell you? Prove your bear allegiance."

Tyler blushed. "I like bears."

"Really?" Dougee said, rolling the word over his tongue to express incredulity. "Do tell. What do you like?"

Tyler blushed, assuming Dougee was flirting, which he was, but Dougee was also sincere in his question, and Tyler found himself the subject of the steady gaze of these three odd creatures from the enchanted forest.

"Seriously?" Tyler said.

"Tell us," Larry said.

"Tell us," Roger said.

Dougee just nodded.

Blushing furiously, Tyler stumbled for a moment and said, "I like hair. I like hair on a man's chest."

"Go on," Dougee said.

"I like facial hair," Tyler said, stumbling a little less. "Although it's not a make-or-break requirement. Clean cut is hot."

"Why don't you grow a goatee?" Roger asked.

"A beard, perhaps," Larry said.

"Not on me," Tyler said. "I've tried. It looks weird. I like a man with a seven o'clock shadow, two hours later than a five o'clock shadow, meaning it's a little grizzled and unkempt. I like guys who don't tuck in their shirts."

"You tuck in your shirt," Roger said and nodded at Tyler's waist. "And it looks good."

"Yes, but I like it when other guys don't," Tyler said. "It's just what I'm attracted to. I like guys who eat big meals and maybe a few too many cookies. I like guys who aren't afraid to go for a second piece of pie and if they spill a glob of blueberry on their yellow shirt, they don't rush home to change clothes. They shrug it off."

Now that he was on a roll, Tyler could not stop.

"I like guys who don't brush their hair before they leave the house because they simply forgot—"

He caught himself and realized he meant Derrick. But he banished the thought from his head.

"I like men who care less about what others think of them. I like men who don't always shower in the morning. I mean, I like men who shower. But I like the scent of a man, that natural scent from men who would not touch cologne."

Tyler paused. "It's more than that. I like men who have this natural masculinity, like they don't care if they're masculine or not, which makes them all the more masculine to me. I sometimes worry I'm not man enough or maybe I am. I don't know. But I like being around men who don't care whether they are or not because they're too busy being themselves. And damn it, I am man enough."

He searched his new friends' eyes for signs of recognition. "Does any of this make sense?"

"He likes bears," Roger said, and rubbed his muscled pec.

"He likes bears." Dougee nodded in agreement.

Larry did not respond because during Tyler's speech, he had glanced toward the cashier station and noticed only one giant cookie—heavily burdened with colorful M&Ms—remained in the glass case, and he felt an obligation to rescue it immediately.

"What did I miss?" Larry said, returning with his prize.

Dougee said, "We just decided to help Tyler find the Great White Bear."

Roger said, "Well, we didn't *decide*—"

"Oh," Larry said. "Well, then you have to come to the Gay Pride Bear pool party. It's a week from Saturday. Out in Oak Park. Very wealthy bear couple, well, one of them is wealthy and the other married into it. The Great White Bear always goes. He's friends with this couple. You should go."

Tyler's hopes rose but he didn't want to seem overly eager. He said, "I'm not much for swimming."

"You should go," Dougee said. "It's a lot of fun."

"I am also friends with the hosts," Larry said. "You're officially invited."

Roger said, "Wear Speedos."

Tyler thanked Larry, thanked Roger, and thanked Dougee (just before Dougee moved on to greet someone else who looked beddable). He lingered for another half hour, chatting with Larry and ignoring Roger's escalating advances, and then chatting with some new bears who teased him for being a twink and demanded to know if he knew where he was. Tyler took their ribbing as best he could, smiling demurely and assuring them he was right where he wanted to be.

"Tyler the Twink," one friendly bear said proudly, as if he had been the first to come up with this nickname. He was so pleased with himself, he repeated it. "Tyler the Twink."

Tyler tried to ignore it and enjoy the view. And he did, in fact, enjoy the view. He saw thick tufts of hair rising from someone's buttoned shirt and he inhaled deeply, though there was no chance he could smell that chest from across the room. He witnessed hot men with a fringe of hair, and he wanted to touch their smooth heads. He admired a middle-aged man with a gut as he laughed so hard water shot out his nose. Tyler wanted to laugh like that, so hard that he did not care how he looked in public. Derrick had laughed that hard once when Tyler split his pants at the seam, having bent over the sidewalk to pick up some Patter poop. His faded jeans ripped with a comic elongation, a ridiculous sound usually reserved for second-rate sitcoms.

Derrick laughed so hard he had to sit on a stranger's wooden front steps to catch his breath. Tyler's anger at his friend's reaction gradually softened and turned to amusement. Tyler even laughed. Tyler hated public humiliation, *hated* it, though who does love it? And though he could do nothing to undo the horror of his pants splitting, now when he remembered that scene, the memory was mostly dominated by laughter and Tyler smiled. Derrick had accidentally helped Tyler not only live with that humiliation but reframe it. No small trick.

Tyler wondered how Derrick fared with his beloved pooches, and saw that it was 9:45. The Great White Bear was unlikely to show.

Tyler said his good-byes, though Roger encouraged him to stay a bit longer, placing a lingering hand on his shoulder. Tyler assured him the pumpkin hour was closer than it seemed and he had to get beauty rest so he could work his Cinderella day job, the one that paid his bills and kept the pugs' kibble flowing.

When he arrived at Derrick's building, a three-story brownstone, summer vines already snaking hungrily up the tricolored brick, Tyler let himself through the chain link fence and walked alongside the building to the backyard's security gate. He was in luck—it remained slightly ajar from a tenant who hadn't closed it properly. Once inside the yard, he crossed the green grass and then climbed the thick wooden staircase to the second level. As he passed a neighbor's grill, he smelled the remnants of grilled steak. He walked the length of the wooden-planked back porch to reach Derrick's kitchen door. He thought about knocking but found the door unlocked and let himself in.

He stood still and waited to hear noise, surely the jingle and jangle of Pitter and Patter as they raced toward the intrusion. If he were honest with himself, Tyler was the tiniest bit hurt they weren't sitting at the back door waiting for him. He walked through the kitchen, inhaling but smelling nothing baking, and found the trio asleep together, dogs mashed into Derrick's nooks and crannies on the living room couch. Pitter had nestled into an armpit and Patter slept safely between Derrick's thick thighs.

Tyler took out his phone and snapped a photo.

The tiniest click woke the dogs, who were elated to see The One Who Feeds Us, so they stood up and wiggled their behinds, mistaking themselves for bees with wild stingers. They hopped down silently—well, not too silently, but with only a slight jingling—which apparently did not rouse Derrick. Tyler did not wish to wake his friend, so he crept toward the kitchen where he would attach leashes to the dogs' collars. He took the blond brownie from his pocket and put it in the middle of Derrick's kitchen counter.

The dogs growled softly to express their disappointment. The blond brownie was not for them. But Tyler had anticipated this moment before he left home and had brought treats for his beloveds.

Once Pitter and Patter were leashed and smacking their lips, a muffled but loud rumbly voice from the living room said, "That photo better not end up on Facebook."

Tyler smiled but did not answer.

He left with his puppies.

The photo was uploaded to Facebook the next day with the caption Tyler added: *How adorzable!*

Chapter 2: Shallow End of the Pool

A TRUISM of forests, enchanted or otherwise, urban or rural, is that the creatures of said forests do love their watering holes. They gather, look around nervously at the other creatures drawn as well, and tentatively take a few sips. They grow bolder, splashing and teasing, sometimes keeping a cautious eye for predators but many times allowing the pleasure of water (or other relaxing beverages) to ease away their cares. They play.

So it was, this Gay Pride Saturday in June, for the bears who gathered at Chuck and Tim's Oak Park dwelling to pounce and prance and play around their Olympic-sized pool filled with green-blue water, seductively warm and yet still blissfully cool.

Proud rainbow flags flapped noisily in the wind.

Chuck and Tim were known in the bear community as the "pool party guys" and it wasn't until late spring that casual acquaintances made it a point to chat them up, hoping to gain favor in time for an invite to the summer swim bashes. Chuck and Tim didn't mind. They enjoyed the seasonal attention and the autumn anonymity, and very much enjoyed the feast of nudity (and partial nudity) strolling their carefully landscaped backyard.

Oak Park is one of Chicago's first-tier suburbs, and those first-tier suburbs believe in their own beauty as a thing to be cherished and maintained with some dignity. Chuck and Tim's backyard reflected this sensibility, a fenced-in quarter acre featuring a modest grove of elms and a Buddhist meditation bench surrounded by purple-striped lilies and other elegant flowers. The expansive lawn suggested regular custodial care and possibly heavy use of chemicals, but nobody argued the results—thick, plush grass, bright kelly green, interrupted with groupings of tasteful crimson Adirondack chairs. The pool, of course, dominated the backyard, blue undulating water cresting and falling as bears slipped in and out.

Unfortunately, the dignified backyard could not compete with the onslaught of Gay Pride's beer cups, cheap pretzels, and general sprawl of man and towel across the entire expanse. Several Adirondack chairs boasted half-empty beer cups with a few spilled right at their wooden feet. Even the Buddhist bench was desecrated by a discarded plastic plate with leftover soggy vegetables drenched in ranch dressing, curdling under the hot June sun. A miniature rainbow flag had been stuck in the grass near the bench, possibly used as a lawn jart.

The bears from the forest wreaked havoc.

Chuck and Tim did not mind. They were drunk on cosmos and flirting with an early thirty-something panda bear who had moved to Chicago to begin graduate school the coming autumn. The three men would enjoy a raunchy three-way long before the sun set.

And the bears, oh the bears! They wore swimsuits of red and yellow, pink with red strips, purples and greens, Speedos and full-length trunks, everything from laced-up-the-side shorts to sexy thong underwear masquerading as swimwear. And what the bears wore was not even the main attraction—it was what the bears revealed they hoped would snag them notice. Hairy chest after hairy chest in a dozen unique follicle patterns could be spotted on many, *many* men, from sparsely haired to thick black carpet, each attracting their own type of admirer. Men who felt they had something worth seeing below the waist stripped off their trunks in the enclosed backyard so others might admire their virtues, hairy or otherwise.

Tyler absorbed the noise, the clamor, the men pounding potato chips scooped in french onion dip, and smiled at the loud chaos, the quiet conversations in the shallow end of the pool, the congenial air of happiness with the steamy weather, the setting, and with themselves. Although conscious of how his body did not belong to this tribe, Tyler felt in spirit he belonged here. He wore Speedos, orange ones that made his dark copper hair seem redder than it was. His pouch in front was noticeable, not huge, but Speedos worked their magic. Tyler liked it better when men noticed the tight, round curve of his ass, and a few bears had already commented favorably.

He was too nervous to attend on his own, even with the expected familiar faces of his two and a half new bear friends, Larry, Dougee, and Roger (who seemed like half friend and half overly aggressive pursuer), so Tyler dragged along Derrick with the promise of a free Indian dinner after the afternoon's poolside escapades.

Tyler glanced with envy at Derrick's apparent ease with the surroundings. Derrick was all bear, some gut hanging over his navy blue swim trunks but not much, enough stomach to pass as a bear. His dark blond hair was natural, confirmed by the golden-brown swirls across his chest and spreading out across the stomach. Tyler remembered the thrill of running his fingers across that hair, admiring its texture and unique scent. Derrick hadn't shaved in several days, so his facial scruff was the perfect accent, and he held a Sam Adams beer to his lips with the poise of a man who enjoys a cold beer on a hot day, for he licked his lips with pre-satisfaction before he guzzled down a few hearty swigs.

Tyler also held a Sam Adams. But he hated beer.

Although he could not see Derrick's eyes behind sunglasses, Tyler felt he knew them well enough to guess what the man was thinking. Probably something about work. Something engineering related.

"The munchies here suck," Derrick said, returning his gaze to Tyler. "Cut-up broccoli and baby carrots? These are rookie snacks. This is *Pride* weekend. They should do carved-out grapefruit and handcrafted cheese things."

Tyler said, "Oh yeah?"

Derrick said, "*Us Weekly* says thirty-four percent of all parties fail because of lame snacks. They should at least have some Cheetos."

Tyler said absently, "Can't argue with *Us Weekly*."

"Same research showed that twenty-two percent of people who eat broccoli florets do so only because every other snack sucks."

Tyler wasn't paying attention. Not really. He was busy feeling terrified.

He considered himself a reluctant man of action. He took risks regularly because he feared having to live with himself if he did not. Nevertheless, this reluctant risk taking didn't make him feel brave. He felt like a coward every time he risked a brave act. He longed to be one of those who didn't feel fear when risking. The ones who had life all figured out.

He wanted to feel brave.

Tyler knew he would not, *could not*, leave the pool party without asking the Great White Bear out for coffee. He had to do it. Even so, the idea of it terrified him. Once he discovered his dream mate only showed up for Bear Coffee sporadically, Tyler knew he would have to make the most of the next crossing of paths.

Derrick and Tyler navigated the crowd, nodding, chatting with those who expressed interest in friendly banter. Tyler was a little surprised to discover how popular Derrick was, the grunts of approval and occasional "woofs" greeting them as they strolled the concrete deck toward a less densely populated corner where they could mark out some space. Tyler remembered to see his friend as an attractive man. Derrick took the attention with good cheer, occasionally saying "woof" back as if it were a password to keep wandering, go further into the bear forest.

Tyler felt more grateful than ever to have Derrick at his side.

"I hate the word *woof*," Derrick said. "Woof. What the fuck is that? Is he here? Do you see him?"

Tyler said, "No, not yet. We haven't been inside the house, so he could be in there. Give me a minute to drink up some courage. Although I'd love a white wine and not a shitty beer."

"It's a good beer," Derrick said. "Don't be nervous."

Tyler's nerves were frayed in anticipation. He couldn't help but feel snappish.

He said, "In the history of people who were ever nervous in life, how many do you think were helped to calm down by the phrase 'don't be nervous.' What's the percentage on that?"

Derrick looked at him and blinked. "In 1928, a Jewish art history professor was giving his first conference presentation ever in Berlin, Germany, and a colleague said, 'Don't be nervous.' And it worked. He wasn't nervous.'"

Tyler found his patience and elasticity restored. Derrick's ridiculous fact-inventions almost always changed his sour mood.

Tyler smiled. "*Really*. An art history professor?"

Derrick shrugged. "You wanted an example."

"And why'd you make him Jewish?"

"Texture. Got to make the fact sound believable."

"And Germany?"

"Drama. Dark foreshadowing."

Tyler laughed. "I don't know how you make up stuff like that."

With his mouth full of wilting broccoli, Derrick said, "I teach engineering classes at a community college. I have to be ready to make shit up all the time. They ask a lot of questions."

They chatted until Tyler could no longer stand merely standing. He told Derrick to hold the remainder of his beer, not to finish it, and he would return after he jumped into the pool. Tyler felt he might present himself to best advantage wet and dripping. At least then his hair would form wet ringlets behind his ears, which was adorable, he had been told by various twink admirers.

He tried to slip in the pool unnoticed, but as he was different, markedly different, and wearing an orange Speedo with a cute, round booty, he stood out. He glided to the side, four feet deep, and took a few minutes to clear his mind. He thought about why he felt so strongly about Mr. Construction. After all, he had only seen him once. He considered that he did not know the man, know his personality at all, and wasn't that what mattered for something long-term?

He swam to the shallow end, ready to take action. As he climbed the stairs, diamond water drops dripping down his hairless chest, he noticed several heads turn, not toward Tyler, but to the far end of the pool patio. Tyler turned to see him, the Great White Bear, arrive. Perhaps he had only arrived outside from having been inside. But now Tyler understood that others appreciated his beauty as well. When a god such as the Great White Bear showed up, you noticed and thought, "He has arrived."

Tyler stared at him, the dazzling almost nudity of him, the perfectly patterned black fur covering him, not thick but thickish, not everywhere, but covering the best parts. His arms were thick muscle, frosted in black hairs, and apparently *his* were the wide shoulders which made Chicago famous. He seemed to gaze around the patio with the air of friendly nobility, a king who forgot his pen and came back into the main chamber to find everyone in swim trunks and chatting, and as he casually grabbed his pen, everyone noticed him. Because who doesn't notice when the king walks in the room?

He walked to an over-iced cooler and pulled out a cold beer, and only when he stood straight up with the beer to his lips did men notice he wore only a white jockstrap whose bulge strutted forward in such a way as to cause a temporary suspension of disbelief. Yes, gentle readers, it was all cock. Tyler's hopeful stirrings were correct: this bear was hung.

The Great White guzzled his long pull and turned toward the double glass doors leading inside Chuck and Tim's home. The man, all man, one could see from his grizzled jaw, paused for a second and seemed to smile at Tyler, nod at him, maybe with a sheepish grin.

As heads flipped his way, Tyler's head flipped down, and he saw his erection pointing straight at the Great White Bear as if pointing north. For men like Tyler who lived in terror of public humiliation, this moment was a "biggie" on worst possible fears, a full-on erection while a gaggle of men stared and ogled. Some in the kingdom of Chicago would find that very moment a lifelong fantasy fulfilled. Tyler did not.

The Great White Bear disappeared inside.

Tyler's humiliation was completed by the realization that the Great White Bear wasn't subtly communicating "Dude, you're hot," so much as "Dude, you're completely boned up."

Although his first instinct was to submerge and never return to the surface, Tyler couldn't dive into the water. True, the pool water might shrivel his dick instantly. But being watched by eighty-five men as he swam around in a Speedo, the rumor quickly spreading, *the twink is hard*, was not really his thing. He did the only thing he could, which was to climb the pool steps and walk off the shame as best as possible.

"Well," said Roger, approaching from the throng wearing a thong. "That's quite a basket."

"Wow," Dougee said, "you've got a hard-on. Can I touch it?"

Larry stared at Tyler's crotch and said, "Glad you could make it."

"May I see you," Derrick said, grabbing Tyler by the arm and forcibly leading him away. "Just a minute, guys."

Tyler felt himself commandeered away and never felt more gratitude for Derrick in his life. Derrick dragged him four feet away, then another four feet to the left, past a second grouping of bears who wanted to chat with the twink in Speedos. Derrick growled his apology to them in a nonapologetic way, and once they were a comfortable distance from the gathered groupings, Derrick spun him.

In an angry voice, he said, "Do you think feeding Pitter and Patter black jelly beans would give them diarrhea?"

Tyler looked incredulously at his friend, trying to understand the anger and the absurd question.

"What?"

"Black jelly beans. Would it give them the squirts?"

Tyler was too confused by the recent pool humiliation, the exhilaration of spotting the Great White Bear, and his surprise at being found by Larry, Dougee, and Roger at his most embarrassing moment to fully ponder the question.

Derrick repeated the question.

"How could this possibly matter?" Tyler said. "Did you feed them black jelly beans before we left my place?"

"No," Derrick said. "But your erection is gone."

Tyler looked down and saw it was true.

"So you know he's in the house," Derrick said. "And you know he saw you because he nodded right at you. I know you're still reeling but the longer you wait, the harder it's going to be. This is it. If you're going to ask him, go for it. Now or never."

Tyler looked at his friend and felt the familiar rush of deep gratitude for knowing this man. Gratitude for accompanying Tyler to a party he did not wish to attend. Gratitude for the jelly bean question and the quick escape from the three bears who constantly seemed to catch him in embarrassing moments. Gratitude for the shot of courage and confidence.

Tyler nodded.

Derrick was right. It was now or never. If he remained outside and reflected on the erection humiliation, he would analyze the moment, the reactions, and let it undermine his barely registering confidence. It was the right time, but he was scared.

"I can't," he said. "If I start walking across the pool area, everyone's going to notice."

"Okay," Derrick said. "No problem. I got this."

Derrick strode away, closer to the pool, and near a cluster of men watching naked swimmers, he picked up a full bottle of some stranger's beer.

He turned back to Tyler and said, "Go."

A white-haired daddy said, "Hey buddy, that's my beer."

Derrick said, "I'll get you another one in a second."

Derrick poured the beer over his own head.

Tyler wanted to laugh, wanted to hug Derrick for this lunacy. As the golden foam dripped over Derrick's head and chest, Tyler slipped behind the tables and the front row crowds as he made his way to the home of Chuck and Tim. He heard random applause for Derrick's stunt, but it was less spectacular than perhaps he thought it would be, for after noticing his brief distraction, the party continued without further incident.

Tyler had prepared a dozen speeches to give Mr. Construction, *Mike*, as had been revealed at Bear Coffee. But he didn't know which speech he would give, what impression he would make. This was about using what little confidence he had in approaching this dazzling man and winging it.

When he entered the house through the glass doors, he stumbled upon Mike almost immediately, hovering over the square table, a second location for the paltry afternoon snacks.

"These snacks are pathetic," Big Mike said, nodding at Tyler. "I'm going to have to scold Tim and Chuck."

"I think you should date me," Tyler said, aware his voice was going to start shaking if he didn't talk faster, make the whole speech. "Just once. Just give me a chance. I know you're way hotter than me, I get it, but I've got some good qualities too. I may be a twink but I'm more than a twink. I'm smart and goofy and I own two pugs, which I adopted from a shelter where I do volunteer work. There are some good parts of me worth knowing."

Tyler did not like to brag and felt shitty about using the volunteer work as such a blatant and persistent come-on, but he had decided to go full bore after what he truly wanted, a date, one date with the Great White Bear.

Tyler refocused. "I bet a lot of guys ask you out, so I'm just going to say I'm asking you out because I think I'm worth it. Give me a chance to prove it. My treat. Sushi or Thai or Indian is good too. But if you say no, I won't ask again and I won't bug you or make you feel weird around me. If anyone asks, I'll tell them you were very polite about it. I won't be a dick."

Mike did not seem too fazed by the big speech.

"Those were a lot of words," Tyler said. "Sorry."

Mike smiled. "Don't sweat it."

Tyler said, "In my head they didn't sound as much like a speech as that did. That really sounded like a speech, didn't it?"

"Yeah, kinda. Rehearsed. But honest. Sincere."

"Thank you," Tyler said, eager for the compliment, but in truth he was more grateful for Mike sparing him the humiliation of calling him a freak.

Holding a plate of limp broccoli, the Great White Bear said, "Thank you for the invite, but I'm going to pass."

Tyler couldn't believe the words he heard. He thought they had just had a moment together. A moment.

But the answer was clear.

Mike didn't explain any further and after a moment of awkward silence, Tyler said, "Hey, thanks for hearing me out. I do appreciate your responding in a cool way."

Although he would be hard-pressed to admit it, Tyler offered the compliment as a last chance for Mike to say, "You misunderstood me. I meant to say I *do* want to go out with you."

Mike said, "No problem. Enjoy the pool party."

Tyler grinned and said, "Cheers."

He crossed through the glass patio doors and swore under his breath. He couldn't look back. Like Lot's wife from the Old Testament, he was sure he would turn to salt or stone or maybe Jell-O, because his legs felt wobbly. He ordered himself not to turn around and look at Big Mike in his jockstrap holding a plate of shitty vegetables.

Before he allowed the crushing despair to sink in, Tyler considered a more pressing issue: how long was he required to stay before ditching the party? He felt every pair of eyes on him as he walked along the pool area, nodding and smiling to those in his direct path. The erection humiliation was less than fifteen minutes ago. Then Tyler went inside where the Great White Bear was. Then Tyler emerged only a half-minute later. Alone.

Everyone knew. Everyone knew he had asked out the Great White Bear and had failed.

He was wrong, of course. Not every pair of eyes was on him. Some had not seen the erection incident, nor did they care when told about it. In fact, only a few pairs of eyes noticed, those who were jealous and those filled with lust. Tyler couldn't see them or see the difference. He could only see his humiliation. For men who fear humiliation, the whole world is watching.

"What did he say?" Dougee said, appearing at his side as if by magic.

"Are you two now lovebirds?" Larry said.

"Better luck next time," Roger said, shirtless and muscular, shining in the sun.

Roger had finally found an environment where he really did shine, and it turned out his ninja weapon of choice was a cherry red thong. He was muscular, Tyler had noticed—that was apparent at Bear Coffee. But standing in sunlight, Tyler noticed the muscles revealed in natural glory. Roger's junk bulged forward, eagerly, almost, a thick trunk clearly positioned for maximum visibility. He had a big dick. And big muscles to boot. As Roger stood in front of him, blocking his path, Tyler looked down and realized even the shadow cast by Roger was muscular.

Tyler found he could not speak. But it was not Roger's sudden masculinity which sewed his lips shut.

The Great White Bear said no.

Larry said, "Uh-oh. Did he say *no*?"

Tyler's voice shook as he said, "Guys, I need a minute."

He walked toward Derrick, who was shaking hands with a very blond man, younger than Derrick, chunky but nicely curved. Some nice shoulder muscle and a thick chest.

As Tyler made his way closer, he could hear the two men laughing.

"Hey," Tyler said. "What's so funny?"

"Nothing," Derrick said, damping down a smile. "We were just being goofy."

The man nodded at Tyler and said, "I should go back to my friends. Good to meet you."

They parted affably and Tyler forced a terse smile at the intruder.

"Who was that?" Tyler asked sharply.

"Some guy."

"What did he want?"

Derrick smirked. "Is it possible that he might have wanted to talk to me?"

"No, seriously, what did he want?"

Derrick said, "I was serious. He was hitting on me. For some reason, he was amused by my pouring the beer on my head and he wanted to say hello."

Tyler was embarrassed. "Sorry. I thought you were kidding."

"No problem," Derrick said.

Derrick didn't seem to be offended, and Tyler admired that quality again. Derrick chose not to be offended without unassailable proof that insult was intended. Tyler realized he felt irritated that someone would hit on Derrick in his absence.

"He said *no*," Tyler said.

"Yeah," Derrick said. "I figured."

Tyler shot him a dark expression.

"The way you walked back here. You didn't skip. You didn't bounce on the tips of your feet like you do when you're happy."

Tyler felt himself shrink even more into himself. "Could everyone tell? Was it obvious?"

"No," Derrick said. "Only to me. C'mon. Let's go. Let's get our shit and go get some decent food."

"I can't," Tyler said. "I'm humiliated."

"No you're not. You asked a guy out and he shot you down. This is how it works in life. Let's go get naan. We'll steer far clear of Boystown and Pride insanity. Best we can."

"I'm humiliated," Tyler said, letting the words echo through him. "I can't."

Derrick paused. "Okay, you're like broken or something. What happened? Why can't you say anything more than those two sentences?"

"I can't leave feeling this way," Tyler said. "I can't walk out of here feeling stupid and embarrassed. I'll never have confidence about anything ever again. I'll cringe every time I see a bear, wondering if he saw me scurry away from the pool party like a chastised imp. I'm not leaving. Not for another hour at least. When nobody cares anymore, I'll leave."

"That's ridiculous," Derrick said. "How is this sensible? You came here to ask out this douche bag and he said no. Game over. These snacks are not worth snacking for another hour, but I will keep eating them because they're right here. Don't make me eat wilted vegetables. It's not right."

"I'm staying," Tyler said. "Until I can leave with my head held high."

Derrick shook his head. "I poured a beer over my head. Nobody cared. One guy complained about me 'wasting good beer' and it wasn't even that guy's beer. It was someone else's. *Nobody fucking cares,* Tyler. Let's just go."

"This isn't just about the Great White Bear. I humiliated myself with the erection incident," Tyler said. "I have to stay until I'm not feeling humiliated."

"Don't stand here and hang out in their pool while everyone looks at you and makes you uncomfortable."

"It's okay," said Tyler. "You go. I'm staying."

"It's *not* okay."

Tyler crossed his arms and said, "Fifty percent of all friendships end because one friend doesn't respect what the other friend is saying right at the moment the friend is saying it. I'm going to stay. What do you think of those stats?"

Derrick paused and let the passion die a little in his eyes. "Okay. I'm out. Have a good time shaking this off. Don't do anything stupid like go home with someone sketchy. If you want, call me later and tell me how it turns out."

Tyler felt bad now, immediately regretting how he took their statistics game to a dark place, potentially soiling their friendship with the implied threat of its end. He didn't mean—

"Call me," Derrick said. "I'm going to the gym to work out but that probably won't happen. Maybe. I'm gonna get some baking supplies on the way home, so I'll probably just make a pound cake and pretend I went to the gym. Order in Indian food."

"Okay," Tyler said, regretting this ending already. "Hey, wait."

Derrick turned back.

Tyler burned with shame. "Thanks. I know you're looking out for me. I need to end this better for me, not for anyone here."

Derrick nodded. "Okay. That, I understand. But next time don't threaten to end our friendship because I'm trying to stop your shitty mind games you use to be cruel to yourself. I'm on your side."

Tyler felt his eyes well with tears to have this abrupt forgiveness thrust upon him. "Yes. That was shitty. I know. It's been a hard day, and I don't mean that to be an excuse. But it is. My excuse. I really hoped he'd say *yes*, at least to coffee."

"Good luck here. If you want some pound cake, we should hang out before next Wednesday. It'll all be gone by then, and I have to prep for summer classes all day Thursday and Friday. I'll be busy."

"I work late on Tuesdays," Tyler said, glad they were making plans. "Let's do Monday. And I'll buy you the Indian dinner I owe you."

And that was how they parted.

(For those who were interested, Derrick did, in fact, blow off the gym.)

Tyler walked to the shallow end of the pool and sat his orange ass on the steps, off to the side. The water felt colder, damper, more clammy. The rainbow bunting on tables and flags around him sang of fake cheer. Maybe the sun had gone behind the clouds a few minutes earlier, but Tyler only noticed it at that moment.

He watched Derrick's departure and felt himself stirring, warming to him. He sensed their friendship would grow as a result of this fight, this almost catastrophic blow, and the idea pleased him. Derrick was worth knowing. And Derrick loved the pugs, which was cute. Tyler had looked at that photograph several times, his heart softening with each return.

He stood in the water, cooler than he would have liked, and pondered his fate.

Two bears a little deeper in the pool invited Tyler to join them for a beer at the side, and he accepted the libation in a blue plastic cup, sipping through gritted teeth. He chatted about anything other than what had happened. They were cool to him, this couple who thought Tyler could use a friend. The two mens' friendliness reminded others to be cool, and the vibe spread again.

Within twenty minutes, Tyler's plan was working. Crushed as he felt about his lack of future with Big Mike, Tyler felt himself softening inside and had done enough work on himself that he could hear his own weak congratulations for having the guts to take a chance. Hollow as the words sounded sometimes from himself, he tried to believe them the way a child tries to believe in magic.

The bears were cool.

Tyler found himself with another new friend or two and then an admirer who asked if he could rub Tyler's stomach. Tyler laughed and agreed, enjoying the touch. He smiled. Tyler now knew he would eventually leave with his head held high. Roger came into view a moment later, his naked, bouncing cock leading the way. The cherry red thong had been ditched. Roger drew his own crowd of admirers who enjoyed watching him parade around his fat elongated dick. Tyler felt himself waver in his resolve to decline Roger's advances, which were surely to become more pronounced.

Roger, in fact, sat on the wet concrete to drop himself into the pool without a big splash, his fat cock bouncing on top of a cock ring. He slid in next to Tyler.

"Hello, Tyler," Roger said in an even, assured voice, standing naked, his legs spread. "How's it going? You want another beer?"

"It's going okay," Tyler said. "I switched to water. I'm trying to sober up."

"Cool," Roger said. "Wanna leave?"

Tyler was surprised by the question and then suddenly was not surprised. Of course it had been leading to this, his eventual fall at the feet of the Great White Bear. Roger had been biding his time, wanting to be present to win the rebound sympathy fuck. Tyler understood now that Roger had been waiting.

"I'm gonna pass," Tyler said. "Thank you. I appreciate your interest in me that way, but I'm gonna pass."

He cringed to hear himself using the same magic words so recently used on him, moments ago. Well, forty-five minutes ago, perhaps. But there it was. The magic worked. The rejection was honest but did not reveal the psychology of *why*, a conversation far too intimate for chat with a stranger. Best summarized as, *I'm gonna pass.*

Tyler felt empathy for Mike and wondered how often he had to initiate the *I'm gonna pass* conversation.

Roger leaned in and said, "Look, I wasn't trying to be completely forward. I wasn't suggesting we go fuck."

He scratched his balls unconsciously, which made his dick bounce in agreement with his words.

"I just thought," he continued, "since a bunch of guys seem to be gossiping like silly girls about your boner and then your going into the house, you'd want to be gone."

"Thank you, Roger," Tyler said, feeling his resolve grow firmer, "I see you looking out for me. But I'm good. I'm meeting some new people and it's nice. The sun's coming out again."

And it did, for the sun was only behind a cloud long enough to be symbolically important. As Tyler waded away from Roger, he thought about how Derrick would never shame him that way. He would not belittle Tyler into feeling worse. He would not use Tyler's humiliation to take advantage. In fact, Derrick had just proved himself, looking out for Tyler's best interest and stopping when Tyler communicated, "Fifty percent of friendships end...."

Remembering the words made him cringe, but he reflected on how it had ended well between the two of them. The sun shone its happy gay pride on everyone, and Tyler thought about his life lessons from this humiliating adventure. He took a big risk. Became better friends with Derrick. Spotted a creep prior to sleeping with him. All of these were good things.

Tyler sipped his bottle of water on the shallow-end steps and soaked up the sun, almost ready to leave the party. He was in a good place now. He wondered about the pound cake. (For those who were interested, Derrick *did* make the pound cake.)

Like a vision, Tyler could almost see the Great White Bear approach, all six foot three of him, striding into the pool area wearing one of those smallish cowboy hats and the pulsing white jockstrap. It was definitely a vision, a hallucination that Tyler was required to endure before he could flee the pool party, but if it was a hallucination, then why was it carrying two cold beers, ice sliding off the bottles onto the concrete pool deck? That would not be part of Tyler's fantasy.

In his manly fantasies, he preferred white wine.

The beers confirmed the mirage was real, as Mike, or Big Mike, the Great White Bear, strode casually along the length of the pool. Tyler tried to pretend not to notice. Everyone pretended not to notice, while secretly staring. The twin awareness of grace and irritation sprang up in men's hearts as Big Mike came into view. To admire the power of masculine beauty is to admit to grace. The irritation comes with the realization you will never be Big Mike, or someone whose stunning good looks makes heads turn.

And from each end of the pool, heads turned. Some stared openly, some more discreet. His thick legs thundered down the concrete, and those bears hugging the pool's side were suddenly very glad to be standing under that fat, bouncing dick-pouch's trajectory.

Tyler burned with shame and hoped Mike would pass quickly. He almost wished he had made out with Roger, taken him up on his offer to leave. But no. In fairy tales such as these, a hero doesn't fall down, he falls dooooooooooooooown into a pit, or his redemption would not matter to us at all.

Tyler sweated out his humiliation. This time he was glad to be sitting in the pool because *this* time, nobody could point to his emotional state.

As Mike drew nearer, just a few steps away, Tyler decided to nod in a friendly way and then look out over the pool, pretending it was a desert oasis, the Paris skyline, a burning pile of shoes. Anything. But. Here.

Mike stopped two feet away. Tyler found he could no longer ignore that enormous cock pressing against the jock's thin fabric, almost at mouth level. Mike bent and extended a cold one to Tyler.

"Beer?"

Tyler realized he was once again center stage in an impossible drama about to be played out. This could not end well, and Derrick was gone.

Tyler reached out and took one, waiting for whatever smackdown was coming his way.

"I was rude," Mike said. "I turned you down when you asked me out."

Tyler blushed and was glad for the cold beer in his hand, ice water dribbling over his fingers. The coldness balanced the raging heat of shame he felt. At least it was over. Everyone, *every* single person within a five-foot radius, now knew he had been rejected. The minute Mike walked away from this scene, everyone in a twenty, then thirty, then fifty-foot radius would know.

Tyler glanced at the deep end, longing to drown immediately.

Mike said, "If it's okay, I'd like to change my mind. I'd like to go out on a date with you."

Tyler looked up at the bronzed muscle-god staring down at him.

"Not a lot of guys have the balls to ask me out on a date. I appreciate guys with some balls. Let's go out for coffee or something. Are you still game?"

A voice answered aloud, and Tyler realized it was his own. "Yeah, I'm game."

Mike smiled. "Great. I wrote down my cell number. Since you're in the pool, I'll put it over here on this table. Guys, could one of you put your beer on the corner so it doesn't blow away? Thanks, guys."

The two bears who leapt to grab a can of beer sheepishly said, "Sure, no big deal."

Mike turned back to Tyler and said, "I'm gonna take off. But call me. We'll set it up."

Tyler felt like the entire contents of the pool rushed through his soul at once, so much elation and adrenaline, such a deep awareness of how many people were gawking at him for something other than humiliation. Tyler felt he was drunk again.

Mike walked away and all eyes followed, staring at the twin mounds of hairy ass muscle striding with ease into the cave. The dark shadow of hair accentuated the perfect curve of his butt and promised warm, tangy body smells where the two ass globes came together.

It was as if Bigfoot himself had emerged from the house, brought his buddy a beer, and then retreated into the dark recesses of the most secretive parts of the forest. After this latest chapter, all pool creatures from the woods, bears, otters, wolves, and their ilk, collectively sighed with exquisite relief, eager to gossip. Describe their reaction to seeing the Great White Bulge.

Tyler held the beer as proof.

He wanted to leap from the pool. He wanted to race to the paper left behind and stare at the numbers until they seared into his eternal memory and then eat the scrap of paper so no one could share in the joy he felt to witness those numbers.

A date.

With the Great White Bear.

Instead, Tyler played it cool. He twisted the top off his beer with surprising ease, a tiny life victory savored after a major life victory, and he guzzled the best fucking beer he had ever tasted in his life. And Tyler didn't care much for beer.

He left a half hour later.

As soon as he was out of earshot from the house on his way toward the El, he called Derrick to share the good news.

Chapter 3: The Great White Bear

ON FRIDAYS in the kingdom, the flavor of Chicago, those creatures exotic and sweating sensuality emerge from their workday hibernations to explore the big city. Well, not explore exactly, but to visit favorite haunts and feel delight in old friends and new experiences. The food gays tried new restaurants after waiting extravagant times for seating. An orgy for "versatiles only" began in a third-floor apartment in Logan Square, but never quite took off as the host had expected, for roughly seven of the "definite yeses" turned out to be "definite nos." The drag queens applied makeup, and the jocks tweezed their eyebrows and practiced their too-cute smiles in bathroom mirrors before strolling through Boystown for a couple of brews.

The bears came out, frolicking at their specially marked bars and spilling over into others, not really caring too much which territories were theirs. If they liked the chicken wings at Jimmy's on Roscoe, there they went. If they wanted to see the best drag, they sat in the front row at Senior Wiggs and giggled when the faux Donna Summer would point them out and say, "Well, the fat boys took the front rows. Can all you good people see around these dumbass bears?"

On Friday nights, the city played. Especially in June.

The forest loves lovers in June, it really does, and Chicago, broad-shouldered stud that it is, said, *Fuck it*, and broke the heat wave that had made the pool party such a success. The weather cooled to the right temperature, where a kiss in this weather felt warm and inviting, not hot and slobbery against the summer sun. A kiss in June weather was like mint leaves rubbing together, a cool breeze, the smell of earth and flowers. A kiss in June weather—Tyler stopped imagining, told himself not to build up his expectations.

But he was having coffee with Big Mike. Or, Mr. Construction. Or, Big Dick Mike. That name would work for a while too. They had navigated a short phone call to set up the coffee date at a spot they both knew, not the bear coffeehouse, but another one in Boystown, one near the comic book shop on North Clark.

Tyler changed clothes four times before selecting the outfit for the first date, and Derrick was no help at all, refusing to come over because he was working on a project and couldn't be interrupted. He texted: *Wear something yellow. You look good in yellow.* And then promised he would refuse to be more helpful than that because he was working on a deadline. *Good luck. Don't be nervous. Art history professors never get nervous.*

Tyler texted back: *I'm not an art history professor.*

Derrick did not reply.

Tyler wore his faded yellow T-shirt because he did look awesome in yellow, that was true, and sailed to his date with destiny. Big-dicked Mike. The Great White Bear.

After arriving at the coffeehouse a full four minutes early, he memorized the moment when Mike stood as Tyler entered. The moment demanded memorization.

He was suddenly grateful to Derrick and his shirt color advice.

The date went as expected for the first six minutes at least, getting coffee, settling in, sharing a story about something odd that happened on the way here, or something everyday unremarkable, before the awkward realization settled in that this was truly "date chatter."

Tyler considered himself to be an excellent first date because he was always genuinely interested in the other person's story and would not steal the conversation away to make it about him. He knew how to listen as well as share. Tyler asked a question or two and Mike politely answered, not revealing much and then leaning forward.

"I gotta ask you something," Mike said. "What's the deal with the guy who's in love with you?"

Visions of Roger flashed before his eyes. Had someone told Mike they had gone home together? Had some malicious gossip spread?

Tyler said, "Look, I barely know that guy Roger. I've met him twice, and the second time was the pool party. He's handsome but not my type."

"No, not him, the other one. The bear guy wearing blue trunks that were too small for him."

Tyler blanked out but could not remember anyone of that description at the pool party.

Mike frowned. "Your friend. The one who poured a beer over his head."

"Derrick?" Tyler was surprised Mike noticed or remembered. "He's not in love with me. He's just a friend."

"Right," Mike said. "A *friend*. Trust me. I'm psychic. I mean, not for a living, but I get a psychic vibe. He's way into you."

Tyler did not like this conversation, didn't want to discuss this. He wanted to discuss the Mike-Tyler attraction, not another connection that he preferred not to think about.

"We're friends," Tyler said. "Nothing more."

Tyler speedily inventoried interactions with Derrick. Watching the dogs. Derrick fixing his bike. Hand delivering sub sandwiches after a shitty workday two months ago. Derrick did him a lot of favors.

"Okay," Mike said. "I get it. You don't return it. And that's cool. Attraction is there or it's not. You can't force it. Which is too bad, because too often the guy you're into is into another guy, who is into another guy who is into another guy."

"Yeah," Tyler said, not enjoying this conversation in the slightest.

His first instinct was to not press the issue, but Mike seemed to dare him. And in the end, didn't Tyler have to know for himself if the spark was present on Mike's side? After the beer-gifting spectacle poolside, he had assumed so. But now it wasn't so clear.

Gathering his courage, Tyler said, "So, Mike, who are *you* into?"

"Asian tops," Mike said. "Yeah, I know. But Asian top guys drive me wild."

"Huh," Tyler said, wondering if his verbal response conveyed the full measure of his disappointment.

"Yeah, sorry," Mike said. "I wish I could tell you differently, Tyler. When you know what you want, it's hard to accept anything else."

"But you're so hung," Tyler protested.

Mike laughed. "Yeah, it does kinda seem like a waste, doesn't it? But it's surprising how many guys get turned on by fucking a dude with a big dick. I mean, I don't mind. It helps me get laid. And I like to get sucked off and jacked off, so c'mon, it's not a total waste."

Tyler said, "Sorry. I didn't mean to be so rude about it. I was just fantasizing."

Mike laughed. "Fantasize away."

"So why did you change your mind and come out to the pool?"

"I had a psychic vision of you," he said, "and this guy who is in love with you."

Tyler felt the blood drain from his face. "You're kidding. Please tell me you're kidding."

Mike paused and stared into Tyler's eyes.

Mike said, "Well, shit. I'm not going to be able to pull this off."

Tyler was not having a good time.

"I'm not psychic," Mike said. "I can't do this and pretend I am, because I'm gonna trip myself up in a second. And honestly, I've got to be somewhere very soon. I don't really have time for this."

Tyler bristled. "We could have rescheduled."

"Sorry," Mike said. "I'm gonna come clean and tell you the truth. But my sister's kids are staying with me while she and her husband do some intense marriage counseling. Things aren't looking great for the marriage. I've got to either make or pick up dinner. I only did this because I kinda wanted to meet you."

Tyler blushed again. This was very confusing.

"Your friend, the one who's in love with you, stopped inside on his way out of the pool party. He gave me $190 in wet bills to take you out on a twenty-minute coffee date and let you down gently. The money was soaked in beer. I guess his wallet was in the side pocket of his swim trunks when he dumped that beer. I saw it from the house."

Tyler felt his stomach sink.

"One of the conditions was that I wasn't supposed to tell you he paid me. But I can't keep this money. It's too weird. I only said yes because I was so shocked at the moment. Your friend pressed every bit of cash in his wallet into my hand. He also ragged on me and said I humiliated you in front of all those men. He said maybe I'd like to not be a total knob and do the right thing by going out there and asking you out."

Tyler didn't know what to say.

Mike said, "I really did feel bad. I didn't mean to embarrass you in any way."

"It's alright," Tyler said, blushing.

He could only see Derrick's face.

Mike continued speaking. "I've had guys make all sorts of propositions to me over the years. They offer me money to just lie naked while they jack off. A guy once offered me $300 to suck my dick. He was my boss at the time. But your buddy took everything out of his wallet, all this soggy, beer-soaked cash, and shoved it into my hand. He didn't count it and didn't try to haggle me on price, like I'm some kind of whore."

Tyler nodded, not in agreement but to indicate he listened. He heard. Because that was in no way true. Derrick was definitely not in love with him.

"I thought your pal was going to punch me in the face if I didn't agree to go make you feel less humiliated. I thought he was going to punch me, man. I've seen the look. People pick on me in gay bars. If I'm not interested in a guy and he's drunk, suddenly it's a thing. I get attacked just as much as I get people shoving their phone numbers at me."

Mike looked at Tyler. "That's how I knew your buddy was in love with you. He was *that* pissed at me."

Tyler sat in silence.

"You like bears?" Mike said.

Tyler nodded.

Mike said, "So what's wrong with him? Handsome enough guy. Kinda muscular. Not ripped, but he's okay. Kinda chunky. Why can't you be into him?"

"We're friends," Tyler said.

"So?"

"Friends don't fall in love like that. We already fooled around once and it didn't work out."

Mike said, "Well, you should try again. He's carrying a torch for you. He never confirmed it with me, but I could tell. He's in love with you."

Things shifted in Tyler, unidentifiable things, feeling-type things. And he did not know if he wanted this shift.

"Am I being a dick?" Mike asked, and his face expressed that he truly wanted to know.

"No," Tyler said. "No, I'm just thinking about this. He paid you?"

"I don't want it," Mike said. "Here. Take it. He gave me $190 and a dry-cleaning ticket. I think the dry-cleaning ticket was between two bills. But after he left, I realized I wanted to meet you. Just for a few minutes. I wanted to see who was worth this kind of sacrifice."

Tyler looked down, no longer enjoying the scrutiny of his Great White Bear.

Tyler wanted to explain, explain that he was quite ordinary and he knew it. He never pretended to be anything other than ordinary. It was Derrick who invented goofy statistics, Derrick who told Tyler he was unique. It was Derrick who thought Tyler was strong and funny, and he liked Tyler's dorky laugh, and it was Derrick.

It was Derrick.

The words kept getting caught in his throat. He wanted to explain things to Mike, but all the sentences began, "Derrick thinks…," and that would only prove Mike's point even further.

"I don't know what to say," Tyler said with a surprising touch of sadness. "I guess I'm nothing special."

"Not to me," Mike said. "And I don't say that to be rude. I'm saying, I don't *know* you or what makes you tick. But this guy does, your friend. He thinks you're the shit—and if someone thinks you're amazing even after you slept together and what he wanted never happened, well, then there must be something pretty great about you."

Tyler felt a ping inside him, a lightness, and he suddenly wanted to leave. He had achieved the date of his dream and now he wanted it to be over, almost immediately.

Mike laughed and said, "He didn't pay me to say any of that."

This made Tyler laugh and the date was over, the spell was broken. Tyler wanted to leave but couldn't resist asking one more question.

"So why Asian guys? What attracts you to them?"

"They're so beautiful," Mike said. "Strong. Sleek. Usually hairless. I like jet black hair and the slope of their eyes. I like Japanese guys best and then probably Vietnamese. I mean, I hope that's not racist of me, but I dunno. Attraction is like that. I like Chinese guys too. But more than the physical features is the spirit, somehow. Asian guys deal with so much crap and expectations, and some of them that emerge from that are so strong, like they don't give a fuck about how the world thinks of them. But I'm also turned on by the guys who are closeted, so I dunno. It's just attraction."

Tyler thought about how he was attracted to bears.

Tyler said, "Get laid much in Chicago?"

"No. I try. I go to the bar Aqua every Friday because there's these gay Asian guys who play mahjong every week around the corner. They go to Aqua for drinks after they're done with their games. But none of them ever hit on me."

Tyler nodded and thought Mike's voice sounded sad.

"Mike, let's talk," Tyler said. "You need better advertising you're a bottom. I have a few tips."

Mike laughed. "Okay, five minutes. Then I have to pick up dinner for the kids."

Chapter 4: Magical Creatures

ON THE way home from the Friday coffee date, Tyler thought back to the night Derrick came home with him from the bar and allowed himself to remember details. How excited he was in Derrick's presence, how he had all the qualities Tyler admired in a man, the hairiness, the cockiness, the goofiness, the seeming to not care about the world while actually still caring about the world. He was a bear man, through and through. Tyler's knees had felt weak when they kissed for the first time at the bar, and he liked when Derrick's hands squeezed his shoulders and Derrick kissed him harder.

Tyler got back to his apartment, his shabby one bedroom with simple furniture, and tried to remember where Derrick had stood and what they talked about, but it was hard to remember the exact details. Since that night, Derrick had visited over a dozen times, and while he could picture Derrick standing and talking in every room, Tyler couldn't isolate the first visit. He felt bad about that, not remembering the little details. What happened to shut down his heart toward Derrick? But he hadn't shut it down all the way, had he? He and Derrick had grown to be friends and learn nonsexual details about each other and their lives.

The pugs repeatedly nudged his shins, reminding him that he was home now and had responsibilities in the present tense, namely rewarding them with treats for being here upon his return. Pitter and Patter distracted him in the best possible way, and as he had already fed them early dinner before the coffee date, he could offer them nothing but a small scrap of imitation bacon.

They accepted this offering but were disappointed.

Tyler recalled how the sex had been explosive and constant. They spent half the night in positions around Tyler's bed, fucking and sucking and making each other groan. It was damn good sex. But Tyler grew fearful of the intimacy the next morning. Derrick's assuredness in the morning felt too bold, too raw. Derrick pissed with the bathroom door open, and already Tyler found himself resenting Derrick's influence. Derrick suggested breakfast, something with pancakes, and said, "*New York Magazine* reports that only thirty-two percent of all bar-related sleepovers result in breakfast the next morning. Why do you suppose that is?"

Tyler did not know about the made-up statistics. But his heart twisted now as he recalled Derrick's easy manner.

While the pugs explored the apartment for more bacon, something they had been doing for the past two hours, Tyler texted Derrick. He needed to see Derrick immediately.

Derrick texted back: *How was the date?*

This made Tyler tear up. He replied: *I need to see you.*

Derrick typed: *Busy on class stuff tonight. Tomorrow thrift stores?*

Tyler wanted to type *No, now*.

But he did not.

Maybe he needed to think about this first.

Tyler texted: *Tomorrow. Yes.*

Derrick typed back: *Cool. Bring P&P. 10 Amish.*

(Another inside joke, gentle readers, was that Derrick had once misinterpreted Tyler's suggestion of a rough morning time "9:30 a.m.-ish" as the word *Amish*. With great confusion he had asked why Tyler wanted to bring nine hundred and thirty Amish people to breakfast.)

Tyler sat in a kitchen chair, staring at the back door. Perhaps because of the odd humiliations in his life lately—the rejection at the pool party, the public erection, finding out the Great White Bear was only into Asian tops—it occurred to Tyler that as much as he hated public humiliation, he hated private humiliation even more.

A realization formed inside of him.

If the two men dated and Derrick ended up dumping him, Tyler would feel a humiliation unparalleled by splitting his pants seam in public. What if he tried—really tried—with Derrick, and failed? What if Derrick found him boring? Too prissy? What if Derrick got to know him, *really* know him, and decided that Tyler was nothing more than Tyler the Twink? Worse yet, what if Tyler wasn't a good boyfriend, or cheated, or didn't share the same likes as Derrick? He couldn't stand it. He couldn't fail in front of Derrick, a man he had come to admire so much.

The humiliation from strangers could be unbearable. But to fail before a loved one, a man who *loved* you, would be even worse. Looking around his tidy, glum kitchen, Tyler immediately sensed the pattern, how he had pushed men away. Men who had tried to get closer. It had worked. They left. None stuck around and loved him anyway, the way Derrick had. No one but Derrick had believed he was worth the effort.

After Derrick attended a pool party he did not wish to attend, and after Tyler had threatened to end the friendship because Derrick spoke his unvarnished truth, Derrick paid the Great White Bear every beer-soaked dollar in his wallet to ease Tyler's humiliation. And Tyler called Derrick to gloat, not realizing his best friend had acted unselfishly though it must have crushed his own heart.

It would be a long evening for Tyler alone in the forest, much of it spent sitting at the kitchen table.

THE NEXT morning, Tyler felt impatient with the pups as they pooped their morning poop. He wanted to hurry to Derrick's apartment. Everything was different now. He did not express this impatience, because the dogs would sense his hurry and whimper while squatting, unable to perform as commanded by The One Who Feeds Us.

Tyler didn't eat breakfast or dinner the night before, so he didn't need to poop.

Instead, he tried on four different shirts, none of them right, but he could not text Derrick for advice because he had to impress Derrick on his own. Then he got impatient with himself, because all this deliberation was wasting valuable time.

He needed to see Derrick right away.

The problem was, Tyler worried about some other bear or twink, otter, *any* forest creature sighting his find, his baking, pouring-beer-over-his-head man, because when you are stunned by masculine beauty, you worry others will see the beauty too, even though this beautiful person may have been exploring the kingdom for many years before you came along. But everything has changed because you're on the hunt now. This is *your* find. Irrational as it was, Tyler felt he must reach Derrick before anyone else noticed him.

He knew that was silly. He hurried anyway.

And yes, this feeling was similar to what Tyler had felt about the Great White Bear. He knew that. But he knew something else—that this arrow shooting through his heart toward its romantic destination now soared true. This love was different from the infatuation he felt for the Great White Bear.

Tyler took a cab, a ridiculous luxury, but he could not stand the idea of waiting for the El. He and the pups sat quietly in the back seat, imagining all the ways this could play out. (Well, not entirely true; Pitter and Patter gave the matter very little thought.)

Derrick's brownstone looked the same as it had last time Tyler had visited. Everything looked the same, the tree-lined street, the parade of parked cars on both sides, the crisp blue June sky waiting to blossom into July. All of it made Tyler want to throw up. He was that nervous.

Derrick responded to the buzz, and when he met Tyler at the door, he said, "You're early," before turning away and padding down the long hallway into the living room. "I have to find my glasses. They're around here somewhere. Do you want some banana bread? I baked some this morning."

"Yes," Tyler said, "I really do."

But he realized he was answering a question that was not asked, and banana bread would not go down well at this moment.

"I mean, no. No on the banana bread. I love your banana bread. But not today."

Derrick, who had dropped to his knees to better welcome a pug assault, looked up at Tyler. "You're weird. What's up with you?"

"Nothing," Tyler said, and his voice cracked.

"Don't lie," Derrick said, returning his attention to the dogs. "Hey Patter, hey baby. Yes, Pitter, I see you too, sweetie. I got a recipe for baking doggie treats. If you're good, I'll make you something later."

The dogs licked their lips, which was neither a promise to be good nor acknowledgement they intended to be bad.

Tyler never felt more sick with fear in his life. But he knew how he operated. He knew he had to take this risk or always regret the missed opportunity. He tried to comfort himself that he had reached a new place with his fear of humiliation, a willingness to walk through it rather than miss out on life. But this was a cold comfort on a Saturday morning. He just needed Derrick to say yes. That was the only comfort he wanted.

Tyler had imagined many ways of bringing about this conversation, so it surprised him to hear the words come out of his mouth. "I want to go out with you. I want us to date."

Derrick looked up at him quizzically and then stood. Pitter and Patter did not enjoy the end to his affections and protested by propping their front legs against his shins.

Derrick chuckled. "Okay, where is this coming from?"

Tyler said, "I've been thinking it over. I want us to try dating. You and me."

Derrick shifted his weight and considered. He turned and walked toward the kitchen.

"I'm going to cut myself some banana bread. Are you sure you don't want some?"

Tyler followed. "What about us dating? What do you think?"

With his back still to Tyler, he said, "No."

Tyler did not want to hear this reply so he questioned it. "Did you say no?"

Derrick turned, and Tyler could see the anger in his friend's eyes. "Yeah, *no*. You got dumped by that guy yesterday, Mike, and now you're asking me out as the consolation prize. Because you're feeling lonely and horny and rejected."

"I didn't get dumped," Tyler said, pulling the wad of money and tossing it on the kitchen table. "So much as he 'fessed up. He told me about your bribe to ask me out. He couldn't keep your money. Your dry cleaning ticket is there too."

Both men stared at the money for a moment.

"I knew he was an asshole," Derrick said.

"No, he wasn't. He was pretty great. Kind, even."

Derrick shifted his eyes away. "I have things I wanna do today. I have to get a new lampshade for the living room, so let's hit thrift shops first. Cheap Thai for lunch."

"I'm serious. I want us to date."

"No," Derrick said, a little more vehemently. "No way. I'm not the consolation prize because the guy with the twelve-inch cock wouldn't go home with you."

"It's ten inches. He told me."

"Well, fantastic. Whatever. Someone's going to come along and pick me first. I'm going to be somebody's *first* choice."

"You're my first choice," Tyler said, but the words sounded hollow and he knew it.

"No," Derrick said. "I'm not."

The problem is, gentle readers, when you realize truths about your life, you often realize them at the most inconvenient moments—the middle of a fight, right after a humiliation, an unkindness done. Your lightbulb moment conveys truth, like you're actually in love with a good friend, but it's coupled with such shitty circumstances nobody believes you. You want out of the relationship? Discounted because you were angry. You're ready to leave this city? You only said that because your car was stolen. Truth hides in shitty moments, and nobody wants to acknowledge a diamond born of shit.

Tyler knew he should make a big speech regarding all the things he loved about Derrick that would melt Derrick's heart… but Tyler couldn't think of anything. He was too nervous. This moment was suddenly the only risk that had ever mattered, and he was bungling it.

"We should go out," Tyler said. "I'm serious. I want us to date."

That's all he could think to say.

"No," Derrick said. "I don't want to talk about this anymore. You're not going to convince me. Next week you'll see someone else while you're out walking the pugs and you'll be in love with *him*. I get how this works with you, Tyler. I've seen it. The Great White Bear wasn't the first guy you had an instant, intense crush on."

"But it's you," Tyler said. "This is real."

Tyler stopped speaking. He was out of words.

Derrick was out of words as well, so they stood across from each other, standing in Derrick's kitchen glaring at each other in frustration, while Pitter and Patter nosed around Derrick's feet, glad to revisit familiar smells. They liked Derrick's apartment.

In fairy tales such as these, one might encounter a wise wizard, a helpful witch, some mystical creature who understood your predicament and offered helpful prophecy or a glimpse of one future where things work out. But Derrick and Tyler did not know any wizards or helpful witches, though they had met several charlatans claiming to be psychic.

Roger was not psychic. Dougee was not psychic. Even Big Mike was not psychic.

No, the only two magical creatures with psychic powers in this enchanted urban forest were Tyler's pugs, Pitter and Patter.

They did their best to communicate their clairvoyant insights to their master, The One Who Feeds Us, whom they had come to admire greatly for his many sterling qualities. Their favorite of his qualities was that he often sang softly to them while he scratched their tummies.

During the awkward silence between the two men, Pitter and Patter tried to explain that within a year, Tyler and Derrick would spend Saturdays on the couch napping together. Within two years, they would find an Andersonville apartment they both loved and move in together.

They would buy new plates together, have sex on the balcony once or twice late at night, laugh at terrible movie sequels, and generally be quite happy with each other.

Patter wanted to explain how one night after badly burned steak kabobs on the grill and a day of frustrated half-communication, the two men would fight, fight hard, but they would make up beautifully with tender kisses, realizing despite the sharp, painful feelings, neither one was remotely tempted to end the relationship. A formal ceremony including friends and family would eventually be planned but the night of the burned steak kabobs was their true wedding. Pitter and Patter looked forward to the formal ceremony because they would wear miniature top hats and carry the gold rings.

All of these urban forest events were destined for Derrick and Tyler, and the pugs knew it. They tried to express this future with barks, but Tyler did not understand, so he absently fed them both small treats to quiet them. Believing they had successfully communicated their psychic vision, Pitter and Patter licked their lips and trotted away, eager to see if there was anything interesting to eat off the floor in other rooms. On their last visit they had found two Cheetos by the toilet, so they trotted off toward the bathroom.

Tyler said, "You *are* my first choice. I figured out the man I want to date is you. Nobody else. I had to figure this out. I'm sorry it took so long, but it's not about the Great White Bear. It's you."

Derrick pondered this and considered responding in a snarky way to hide his bruised heart. His inner snarkiness surprised him. After wanting to hear these words from Tyler for eight months, he did not trust them, refused to let himself believe Tyler's change of heart. But he bit his lip and said nothing, on the off chance Tyler was sincere. If Tyler could remember his affection for more than a week, Derrick wanted to take the chance. But he wasn't quite ready to engage true hope.

Derrick crossed his arms. "Fine. Ask me out again in four months. In the meantime, don't bring up the idea of dating, even the *possibility* of dating. Let's just keep being friends. And if you ask me out four months from now, I'll know you're serious."

Tyler smiled and said, "Fine. Four months. Mark your calendar."

Derrick's heart fluttered, and he tried hard not to show his hope. "Fine. But don't bring it up in two months or three months or any time sooner. Otherwise our friendship will be weird."

Tyler nodded and said, "Four months. And for the record, there's a one hundred percent probability this friendship is already weird."

Derrick turned his back and picked up a butter knife. "I'm having some banana bread before we go. I added cranberries to the recipe. It's good. You should try a piece."

Tyler smiled and said, "Small piece. Thank you."

What Derrick did not realize, gentle readers, was that although Tyler had failed in his quest to master and tame the Great White Bear, in the meantime he had acquired a skill that would serve him well in the coming months.

Tyler could hunt bear.

And Tyler knew—already knew—that he and Derrick would be together. He sensed, as many magic creatures do within the enchanted urban forest, his very own fairy tale beginning.

EDMOND MANNING has always been fascinated by fiction: how ordinary words could be sculpted into heartfelt emotions, how heartfelt emotions could leave an imprint inside you stronger than the real world. Mr. Manning never felt worthy to seek publication until recently, when he accidentally stumbled into his own writer's voice that fit perfectly, like his favorite skull-print, fuzzy jammies. He finally realized that he didn't have to write like Charles Dickens or Armistead Maupin, two author heroes, and that perhaps his own fiction was juuuuuuust right, because it was his true voice, so he looked around the scrappy word kingdom that he created for himself and shouted, "I'M HOME!" He is now a writer.

In addition to fiction, Edmond enjoys writing nonfiction on his blog, www.edmondmanning.com. When not writing, he can be found either picking raspberries in the back yard or eating panang curry in an overstuffed chair upstairs, reading comic books.

Feel free to contact him at remembertheking@comcast.net.

FOR **MORE** OF THE **BEST GAY ROMANCE**

Dreamspinner Press
DREAMSPINNERPRESS.COM

CPSIA information can be obtained at www.ICGtesting.com
Printed in the USA
LVOW09s1048241014

410351LV00004B/365/P